AUG - - 2021

IN THE FIELD

IN THE FIELD

A NOVEL

RACHEL PASTAN

DELPHINIUM BOOKS

IN THE FIELD

Copyright © 2021 by Rachel Pastan

No part of this book may be used or reproduced in any manner whatsoever without written permission of the publisher except in the case of brief quotations embodied in critical articles and reviews.
For information, address DELPHINIUM BOOKS, INC.,
16350 Ventura Boulevard, Suite D
PO Box 803
Encino, CA 91436

Library of Congress Cataloging-in-Publication Data is available on request.
ISBN: 978-195300203-7

21 22 LSC 10 9 8 7 6 5 4 3 2 1
First Edition

Cover Design by Colin Dockrill, AIGA

For my brothers, sisters-in-law, and brother-in-law:
Stephen, Peter, Elizabeth, Amy, Lisa, and Hershel

AUTHOR'S NOTE

Anyone who knows about genetics will immediately recognize that the protagonist of this novel, Kate Croft, is based on Barbara McClintock, who won the Nobel Prize in 1983.

But this is essentially a work of a fiction. I use some of the facts of McClintock's life and science, but I have no way of knowing what she thought or felt, and the details of her personal life are murky. I have been moved and fascinated by the story of her life and science ever since I read her obituary in the New York Times in 1992. But in writing this book, I intentionally talked to very few people who actually knew McClintock. I wanted to have the freedom to make Kate Croft the person I needed her to be.

I have taken even more liberties with some of the great scientists McClintock was close to. Some readers may recognize some of their science here, but I have no reason to think any of McClintock's scientific friends and colleagues were anything but entirely upright.

As for the science itself, I have done my best to convey it as accurately as possible. Doubtless there are errors, for which I take complete responsibility.

PROLOGUE
1982

In summer at that hour she would have been out in the cornfield already. Hot green smell of rising stalks, sharp blades of dew-damp leaves, wasps buzzing. But it was October now, and dark. Kate had always been a light sleeper, an early riser, eager for what the day might bring. Often, wakeful and restless, she wandered down to the lab in the heavy stillness of three a.m. She kept a cot there, among the shelves of microscope slides and back issues of *Genetics*, in case she got sleepy and didn't want to bother coming back upstairs. After an hour's doze she'd wake with her mind clear as through scrubbed, the work waiting.

This morning though—5:20 by the stove clock—she was upstairs in the apartment kitchen when the phone rang. Drinking coffee in her old seersucker robe, her round steel glasses polished with a carefully pressed handkerchief, she was absorbed in an article about yeast. Some days lately her mind felt sticky, a swollen door she had to tug open, but today it was working fine. When the phone rang—a loud bright trill intruding on the humming silence—she glanced at it darkly. What kind of person called at the crack of dawn?

Two parallel answers, like two parallel streams of bubbles in an aquarium, bloomed in her gut and rose.

But if someone had died, who could it be? Nearly everyone she'd ever loved was dead already.

As for the other . . . Well, it was October.

She lifted the heavy cold receiver to her ear. "Hello?" she barked.

"Is this Dr. Kathleen Croft?" a male voice said. Melodic, affable, vaguely foreign. "I have some very good news."

The words clogged and confused her brain, they were like lights stuttering in the darkness and then going out.

Then he told her what he'd called to tell her: her work, an award, recognition long overdue ... Afterwards she couldn't remember what he'd said exactly. The old ghostly voices swirled around her as if trying to drown him out. Her mother's: *It's a waste of money to send a girl to college.* Dr. Krause's: *Young women don't take this work seriously.* Hiram Cole's: *Science is not something to pass the time with until you get married!*

The committee had recognized her discovery, nearly half a century earlier, that genes could move from place to place on the chromosome, something that had come as quite a surprise.

Well, that was true enough.

But nowhere in the citation was the significance of her discovery mentioned, the true significance that she, leaping from sight to insight, had understood long ago, that genes did not absolutely determine what an organism would be.

It was as though you celebrated Thomas Edison for making a filament of carbon incandescent without explaining what the thing did: light up a dark room.

PART ONE

1923

CHAPTER 1

Outside it had grown colder, but at least the wind had dropped. The white November moon lit up the empty street as, clutching her suitcase, Kate plunged into the night. The moon swam in and out of the trees, and the curtained windows of the houses seemed to watch her as she passed, like the blank black eyes of whales. As long as she was walking she could almost manage not to think. Instead, in the darkness of her mind, she recited the phyla and classes of plants— *Thallophyta, Bryophyta, Pteridophyta*—moving steadily in the direction of the campus as though pulled by a current. It was the way her feet knew to go.

It was quiet. No leaves scudded along the pavement, no cars rumbled, no chattering voices relieved the vacant silence that closed over her like water. In an hour or two, the first buses would start running and the sparrows with their feathers puffed for winter would twitter in the bushes, but right now it seemed not a soul in Ithaca was awake besides herself.

And Thea, of course, shut up somewhere inside the house behind her, her face pink with shock. Kate thrust that face away, deep in the darkness of her mind.

By the time she reached the library, her arm ached and her feet throbbed in their heavy shoes. The great stone building was dark. In a daze, Kate went up to the door and tugged on it anyway. It gave a quarter of an inch, jolting hope up through her, before the bolt caught and held. She turned away and resumed walking (*Gymnospermae, Angiospermae*), and the next time she looked up she was in front of Roberts Hall, the biology building. She set the suitcase down and looked up at the steps with their litter of brown oak leaves. She looked at the heavy double doors above which the great windows, each one as tall as a person, faintly reflected the moonlight. Perhaps because they were bare, they seemed less unfriendly than the ones she had passed in the town with their linen or flowered damask curtains closed against her. She walked up to the wall and laid her hand against the cold grit of the stone. The deep slate sill of the first-floor window pressed into her waist. When the weather was fine, students lounged there, dangling their legs. Kate hoisted herself up, leaning back against the cold glass. Images from the night— pale hard faces and pairs of girls waltzing in sherbet-colored dresses—crowded into her mind. She pulled her legs under her and got carefully to her feet. Grabbing onto the upper ledge with her hands, she peered up. Just above was the window of the biology lab, which Dr. Krause kept open half an inch to combat the gas and formaldehyde smells, and because, he said, he liked fresh air. "When I was a boy in München, we always slept with the windows open. Even in winter!" he had told his Introduction to Biology students. "It was thought to be *good for our health*."

Was the window open now? Clinging to the stone, Kate squinted. The ribbon of darkness along the bottom seemed differently black than the darkness above it. Her fingers scrabbled, searching for holds. Next to her, the decorative brickwork formed a kind of frieze, a band protruding slightly from the rows above and below. Perhaps if she could get her foot onto it, she could hoist herself up. Then again she might slip, tumbling down the façade to land in a heap on the forecourt.

Well. There was only one way to find out.

She felt better now that she had a plan. Besides, she had always liked climbing: the backyard elm tree, beeches in the woods on summer afternoons. As she reached her foot over to the frieze, her body felt light. Her scuffed shoe did not slide. She reached up with one hand, then with the other, pushing with her leg. Yes, it was open! Barely, but it was. She slid her hands under the sash, forcing the glass up until she could duck into the room.

Inside, everything was quiet and dark. The room smelled of fixatives and stains, of dead snakes coiled in jars and living mice in the walls, of ammonia and bleach. It radiated order and rationality. In this room, if you used your mind and the right equipment, you could answer all the questions at the end of the lesson.

How many carpels are involved in the formation of the peach?

Where are the resin canals located in a pine leaf, and what is their function?

How many seeds can you see in a longitudinal section of a grain of corn?

Still, she couldn't stay here. She needed to find somewhere she could hunker down out of sight.

In the hallway, it was darker still. There were no windows, no gleam of moonlight to guide her. She felt her way along the wall, trying all the doors she came to.

The first door: locked.

The second door: locked.

As in a fairy tale, the third door opened. In the dimness, Kate made out the shadowy shapes of a desk, a chair, stacks of books and papers.

Someone's office. No good. No good.

She kept going, trying one door after another until finally, at the far end, by the stairwell, another knob turned. Heart pounding, she peered into a small, windowless storage room. Crates were stacked against one wall behind a thicket of chairs, a lopsided table, and a tower of rusty metal cages that might once have held mice or guinea pigs. Kate pushed a few of the chairs out of the way as quietly as she could. The scraping sound set her heart racing, though there couldn't possibly be anyone to hear. She eased the crates forward until there was a space between them and the wall just wide enough to lie down in. She took off her coat, spread it out, and lowered herself onto it. This was where she belonged— in the dark, on the floor, in a room meant for broken things.

Kate had signed up for Introduction to Biology back in September because her housemate, Thea, was taking it, and she wanted Kate to take it too. "Otherwise I'll be the only one," she said. Thea was taller than Kate, pale and gray-eyed in her plaid, pleated jumpers. A long braid hung down her back, bouncing and swaying when she walked, the strands almost blond where the light caught them.

"The only what?" Kate asked.

"Girl," Thea said.

"Those classes have a hundred people in them," Kate scoffed. But she signed up anyway, and it turned out Thea was right: they were the only two. They were freshmen, and it was 1923. Three times a week they sat next to each other in the front of the big musty auditorium. Thea insisted they sit in the first row. She was from Manhattan—her father was a classics professor—and, unlike Kate's, her family had encouraged her to go to college. "My father said it was a good idea, as long as I didn't think I could learn Greek," Thea said.

Kate's father, a physician, had died in France, in the war, at the age of forty, when Kate was twelve. Before that, at home in Brooklyn, he'd liked to walk out into the countryside with his field glasses, looking at trees and birds and butterflies, once in a while taking Kate with him. She liked to think he would have been happy to see her go off to Cornell, whereas her mother, when the train to Ithaca was called, had pressed her lips together in a thin line like a bobby pin and said, "Try not to embarrass yourself."

Kate loved the house on Myrtle Street, which she shared with Thea and another girl, Lena. She loved its wooden floors, which were mostly bare, and its plain white walls, so different from her mother's fussy wallpapers. She loved the acorn-shaped finial at the bottom of the bannister, the wood worn to satin by anonymous hands. She even liked the cupboard-sized room Thea showed her when she answered the ad, into which a bed and a chest of drawers had somehow been crammed. From the doorway, a single high window looked out onto the neighbor's brick wall.

"It's not a beautiful view," Thea conceded as they stood together, looking up.

But Kate was determined to find everything about her new life lovely. She threw herself down on the coverlet, which exhaled a cloud of golden dust, and tucked her arms behind her head. From here, the window was a rectangle of pure blue. Her mind drifted up, steeping itself in color. "It is from here," she said.

Thea came over and sat on the edge of the bed to see what Kate was seeing. "Blue is my favorite color," she said, looking up at the rectangle of sky. "What's yours?"

"Blue." Kate shut her eyes. Sometimes her body felt too small to contain everything roiling inside it, and she had to shut things out so she wouldn't burst.

In the Myrtle Street house, the girls cooked omelets for all meals, or heated up soup. Sometimes, if she had the money, Thea brought home bagels and salty orange fish from Rosenbaum's delicatessen. Kate had never eaten a bagel before, and she subjected it to a scrutiny that made Thea and Lena laugh. "How do you get a texture like this, chewy yet melting? It doesn't taste anything like a doughnut, like you'd think it would. Doughnuts are cakey and sweet—you fry them in oil—" But of course the other girls knew what doughnuts were, even though Kate was unfamiliar with their foods, and their confusing rules about what you could and could not eat, and their singsong prayers on Friday evenings, which they claimed they only bothered with because they had promised their mothers. Kate liked to watch the candle flames and listen to the minor melodies as they sang the Hebrew words. She liked the way Thea's face looked in the candlelight, tranced and medieval, her freshly washed hair shining. It was the one time of the week she left it loose.

Thea knew about all kinds of things: Freud, Galileo, Yiddish theater. She liked poetry, especially Keats and someone German Kate had never heard of, Heinrich Heine. When Thea was thinking something through, she went so still she almost ceased to breathe, and when she was excited by an idea, her shoulders flared backward and her face flushed and she tugged violently at her braid. For example, when Kate mentioned that she planned never to have children, Thea pulled on her braid and cried, "Don't be silly! Of course you are."

"Why *of course*?" Kate retorted. "If I don't want to."

"Why wouldn't you want to? It's the one thing in the world that's better about being a girl!"

Kate, who had been lining up her arguments, began to laugh. It was so much the sort of thing she might have said herself.

"Women without children always look so mournful, like hungry wolves," Thea said. "Even the fat ones."

"I wouldn't mind being a wolf." Kate was afraid of lightning, and of suffocation—being buried alive—but she wasn't afraid of being hungry. "Babies are sticky, and children are always whining about something."

"You'll change your mind," Thea said.

Kate glared. This sudden primness—the open flower of Thea's face gone chilly, as though made of silk—did not suit her. "I won't," she said. "Why should I?"

"You sound like my sister Hannah," Thea said. "Eat your carrots. *I won't!* Wash your hands before you set the table. *Why should I?*"

"That's a stupid comparison," Kate said. "There's a good reason to wash your hands before you set the table." But she saw that Thea's eyes were full of tears. Kate touched her friend's wrist. It was sharp and soft at the same time: the stem of a leaf, a milkweed pod. "What is it?" she said.

"I miss them," Thea said, sniffing noisily. "I've shared a room with Hannah all my life. Here sometimes I wake up, because Lena breathes so differently." Lena and Thea shared the big bedroom down the hall from Kate's.

Kate didn't miss her family. Even before her father died, she had felt stifled and out of place in that dark Brooklyn house. "I guess everyone breathes in his own particular way," she said. "Like fingerprints."

Thea smiled, even though she was still crying. "Or snow-flakes," she said.

"Pinecones," Kate said. There was a flutter in her chest, as though a moth were caught in there, trying to get out. She'd never had a friend like this before, someone she didn't get bored with and make excuses to get away from, preferring, in the end, to be alone.

CHAPTER 2

In the weekly lab section for Intro Bio, Kate and Thea were relieved to be assigned as partners, even if it was because no boy would have wanted to be paired with them. On the first day, they lugged their microscope over to their bench. The black metal instrument was cool to the touch, solid, with interesting levers and lenses. There was a little platform called a stage that went up and down when you turned a knob. Another knob adjusted the ocular lens—a portal to another world! "Ocular lens," Kate said aloud, testing the words. Perhaps the world she saw through it would be more comprehensible than this one with its hidden costs and unspoken rules and unbearable expectations. Only yesterday her mother had written complaining about the expense of her room and board. Kate tried to shut out thoughts of being forced to go home, but she could feel them in the dark corners of her mind, buzzing like flies.

Dr. Krause came around with a beaker of water and an eyedropper. He squeezed one drop onto each group's slide. "I collected this yesterday in a pond not so far from my house," he said in his lilting accent. "I don't know what's in it. No one knows! Each of you will be the first person in the world to look at this particular drop of water and see what miracles it holds."

A snicker or two rose up toward the stained and flaking ceiling. Dr. Krause frowned, his tangled eyebrows furrowing. "Biology is the study of life," he said sternly. "Life is a miracle! If you doubt that, there's no reason for you to be here."

"Medical school," someone whispered. Kate turned to give

a dirty stare to a square-jawed boy wearing a diamond-patterned sweater. Thea clipped the slide onto the platform and bent over the eyepiece. Her braid was secured today in a pink-checked ribbon. Her fingers worked the focus knob back and forth the way Kate's sister Laura fiddled with her engagement ring.

"What do you see?" Kate said, close to her shoulder.

"I don't know. A shimmering."

"Let me look."

"Wait." Thea's fingers worked the focus knob. "Something's moving," she said. "Lots of things."

"What do they look like?" They had been given a list of organisms their drops might contain, and they were supposed to sketch what they saw.

"A blob," Thea said. "A shimmering blob."

"Let me look," Kate repeated, putting her hand on Thea's arm.

"Patience," Thea said. But she let Kate look.

"Hey, Gold," someone said. "You need help?" Gold was Thea's surname.

"From you?" Thea said haughtily.

"I got a microscope for my twelfth birthday," the boy said. "This pond water stuff is interesting, I guess, if you've never done it before."

"We'll manage," Thea said.

The conversation buzzed in the background as the world inside the microscope rushed into focus. With a flick of Kate's fingers on the ridged knob, the faint shimmering Thea had described resolved into a tumult of individual things. No, not *things*: living beings! There were roundish ones and long spindly ones, greenish ones and transparent ones, swimming and squirming across the field of view. Small creatures like fingernail parings wriggled and flittered. One large monster, shaped like a club with spikes, wobbled around in a slow rotation, while a lithe clear swimmer with a poppy seed eye darted past it. Warmth gathered in Kate's belly and spread outward. This must be how the Earth looked to—to whom? To God? To a star? In this small galaxy, Kate was the Sun, burning.

"My turn." Thea's voice startled Kate back into the room. Straightening up, she blinked at the strange human shapes: their jerky movements and clumsy limbs, heavy heads swiveling on their skinny, stalk-like necks.

At the second lab meeting, Dr. Krause talked to them about corn, only he called it by its Latin binomial name, *Zea mays*. He explained how scientists used *Zea mays*, and before that peas (*Pisum sativum*), to learn how the traits of ancestor plants got passed down to offspring plants. "Gregor Mendel," he crowed sternly. "Now there was a scientist! A humble friar from Brno, in Moravia, unlocking the secrets of life."

Kate, who hadn't heard of Gregor Mendel, nor of Moravia, listened carefully, trying to follow the train of his thoughts.

"What is more important," Dr. Krause demanded, "than understanding how we come to be the way we are? How each of us is connected to our ancestors, yet is also an individual? Explaining these mysteries—possibly, in the future, breeding better human beings! Those are the promises of genetics." The room shifted restlessly as Dr. Krause ticked off Mendel's laws of heredity on his long, hairy, age-spotted fingers. But Kate was hypnotized. Beside her, she could feel Thea breathing faster, both of them taking it all in. Dr. Krause gazed around the room with his soft brown damp eyes, his thick wiry eyebrows rising with emotion. "I only wish I were younger, so I could live to see how it all comes out. I confess I would have liked to be the first to understand something basic about Nature's design. Instead, most of my life has been given over to teaching you ungrateful cabbage heads." But he said it fondly. The long toll of the bell clock interrupted his digression, and he took out his watch and examined it as though needing to establish for himself that the bell was right.

Kate and Thea lay squashed together on Kate's bed on top of the dusty coverlet, waiting for the moon to rise. The night before, Kate had seen it glowing right in the middle of the window, bright as a pearl, and she wanted to show it to Thea. They had turned out the light so they would be more dazzled when it came. In the meantime they quizzed each other for their upcoming test, taking turns in the dark. Kate's side fitted into the curve of the taller girl's. Was this what it was supposed to be like, having a sister? At the foot of the bed, their four shoes wagged back and forth.

"What are the principal parts of a flower?" Kate asked. The hue of the sky seemed to shift as she looked: crow black to charcoal to iron gray. There was always so much more to everything if you looked closely. That was the main thing college was teaching her: a thousand shades and subtleties to what had seemed the simplest truth.

"Pistil," Thea said. "Stamen. Those are the female and the male parts. Also you've got—let's see—petal and sepal." Now it was her turn to ask something. "About the pistil," she said. "Name the part that is sticky and sweet, and the part that ripens into a fruit."

"Stigma," Kate said. "Ovule." Beside her she could feel Thea breathing. If she were a plant, she would be fed by Thea's CO_2.

"Right," Thea said. "Your turn."

"Name one common vector for cross-fertilization."

"Bees," Thea said dreamily. "Aren't bees amazing? I mean, they make honey *with their own bodies!* They communicate by dancing!"

"Yes," Kate agreed. "Bees are wonderful. Much to be wondered at." Was that the edge of the moon drifting into the darkness of the window frame? Or was it just her own wanting that made her think she saw the pale curve.

"God was inspired when he thought of bees," Thea said.

"Do you really believe there's a God?" Kate said.

"Of course!" In the dark, Thea sounded shocked. "I mean, it's not a question: the existence of God. It's a given. *The* given. Even you gentiles know that."

It was warm in the small room. Late September, but the weather was still fine. People said Ithaca would soon be buried under drifts of snow, but Kate and Thea had agreed they'd believe it when they saw it. Now Kate said earnestly, "Everything is a question." Surely they agreed about that.

Thea squirmed. "Not everything. Some things are answers to the questions."

Kate grasped Thea's elbow as though her friend might slip away if she didn't hold on to her. "Listen," she said. "God is too easy an answer. *Why is the sky blue? Why are there mountains here and gorges there? Why is your hair curly and mine straight?* A person could spend a lifetime trying to answer those questions! But if you just say, *It's like that because of God*, you haven't said anything at all."

Thea's springy hair tumbled as she shook her head, loose strands tickling Kate's face. "But I wouldn't say that," she said. "Why would God care if my hair were straight or curly? Or even about the color of the sky! You're talking about one kind of question, but I'm talking about something else. Something deeper."

"What do you mean, deeper?" Kate's stomach fizzed. She felt excited, and agitated, as though something were on the verge of being revealed. She could feel Thea's pulse beating under her skin beside her.

"I mean *behind* all that. Under it. Underneath everything!"

"You mean like the floor?" Kate asked.

"No. Underneath *everything*."

"Like the cellar? Like the foundation of the house? Like the ground?" Her mind began to rattle away down its own track. She thought about the Earth's thin rocky crust, which she was learning about in geology, and the great slice of silicate mantle below. And under that, the dense and smoldering core, so hot that metals turned to liquid and seethed in the darkness. She was not prepared to reopen the question of God; but there was *something*. Something hidden. It had to do with the way disparate parts were connected, maybe. The color of the sky and the location of the mountains and the texture of Thea's hair. Sometimes, if she stood very still—if she kept her mind very still, like a grain of sand—she could feel it thrumming, like overtones on the piano, or like blood in the veins, or like the sound a falling star made in the vacuum of space.

Now the silver disk of the moon moved upward, floating for a long moment in the exact center of the window. But the girls, preoccupied with their argument, didn't notice.

CHAPTER 3

In early October, Kate borrowed a tennis racket and went down to the courts to see if she could pick up a game. It was a cool bright autumn day. The soft yellow leaves of a chestnut tree blew and swooped through the scrubbed air, and spiny green chestnuts lay scattered across the grass. Down at the far courts, two boys dashed around, laughing and shouting. At the near end, a lean blond girl in a long pleated skirt slammed a ball against the backboard, hitting the same spot twenty times in a row. When she stopped to fix her hair, Kate said, "That's quite a backhand."

"Is there something wrong with my forehand?" the girl said.

Kate laughed. "Do you mind if I take a look at your racket?"

The girl held it out. "Slazenger Demon. Brand new model. Want to give it a try?"

Kate ran her hand around the beveled frame. "All right."

She hit five forehands against the wooden slats, then switched to backhands, picking up the pace. It felt good to be moving, her body opening up and settling down like a sailboat finding its angle to the wind. The girl watched her, looking down her long pink nose.

"Thanks," Kate said at last, stopping and handing the racket back.

"You're good," the blond girl said.

Kate blotted her face with her sleeve. "Want to play a set? An education for the mind is all very well and good, but one should not neglect the body."

The girl laughed, showing big white teeth. "You're funny," she said and spun for serve. "Up or down?"

They were quite evenly matched. The girl, whose name was Marian, blasted hard shots to all corners, her height helping her slam the ball off the court, but Kate found she could use spin and misdirection to hold her own. She tapped the ball short when Marian expected her to blast it past her, or lured her in with a drop shot then lifted a lob skyward. They ended up splitting sets, 6-4, 5-7. Kate wanted to play a third—or at least a tie-breaker—but Marian tossed her racket into the grass and lay down under the chestnut tree.

Kate sat beside her and wrapped her arms around her knees.

"If only someone would come along and serve us lemonade," Marian said, and she began to reminisce about the club back in Buffalo with its chipped ice and swimming pool and Saturday night dances. Two years older than Kate, she had come out at a cotillion at the Lenox Hotel when she was seventeen. She was studying French, which her mother deemed an acceptable subject for a girl. "But if she knew what's in some of the books we read, she'd be very surprised." Marian rolled onto her side and looked up at Kate. "Houses of ill virtue. Adulterous women! Young girls brought up not for marriage, but for the other thing."

"What other thing?" Kate pictured secretaries at typewriters, their hair in tight chignons.

"Lounging around all day in silk negligees," Marian whispered, giggling.

"Negligees?"

"And sometimes—" Marian moved closer. "Sometimes two men . . ." Her breath tickled Kate's ear.

Kate was sure she had misunderstood. Nonetheless, her cheeks burned, and she could not summon the words necessary to ask for clarification.

"The Greeks did it, too, Professor Mallory says! Can you believe the scandalous things you learn at college? Of course, I'm really here to get my MRS degree." She stood up and brushed the leaves from the back of her skirt. "You meet so many nice boys up here. Delta Gamma, my sorority, has a lot of mixers. You should rush."

"Do you have a dress I could borrow for a semi-formal?" Kate asked her housemates in the kitchen that evening. "It's a rush party," she added, trying out her new vocabulary. "At the Delta Gamma house."

A little shock ruffled the air.

"It's a lark!" Kate said. "And if they don't want me, I don't care. I don't have to live there," she added, thinking maybe that was what was upsetting them. "I wouldn't leave you in the lurch."

Standing over the stove, Lena stirred a pot of canned mushroom soup, clattering the ladle. "Don't you know about those people?" she said.

"I guess I know you don't want to rush," Kate said. "But why do you care if I do?" She looked over at Thea, who was plonking spoons onto the table.

"I don't care!" Lena said. "Why should it matter to me if you want to spend your time with people who are only interested in status and money?"

Kate turned away. She found the remains of a hard, dark loaf in the cupboard and began hunting around for the bread knife, wishing Lena didn't always buy pumpernickel. "The girl who invited me is perfectly nice."

"They walk around with their noses in the air," Thea said darkly. "It's like they teach them that in debutante school."

"I never said this girl was a debutante," Kate said.

"Well, is she?" Lena said.

"What does it matter?"

"So she is?" Thea said.

Kate felt ganged up on. "Marian's not a snob. Maybe some of them are. I don't know. But then," she added, sawing at the pumpernickel, "there are different ways of being a snob."

"I don't know why they even bother going to college!" Thea said. "All they care about are clothes, and diamond bracelets, and getting married." She banged a plate of pickles onto the table. "And they don't allow Jews."

Kate looked up from the bread board. Thea was standing by the messily set table, glaring at Kate, and Lena was frowning out the window. On the stove, the forgotten soup bubbled furiously. "That's ridiculous!" Kate said. "What makes you say that?"

"The fact that it's true," Thea said.

The smell of scorched mushroom swirled through the kitchen.

Kate had told Marian she would go to the dance, and she meant to go. Besides, what Thea and Lena said piqued her curiosity. Surely they were wrong, but she would see for herself. She wore her own dress, brown with a white collar, the best she had brought with her.

The Delta Gamma house was a large gabled building with a porticoed entrance. Inside, a cornucopia of sofas and low cushioned chairs and little tables with frilly legs sat on a blue carpet. Chandeliers glittered and shivered, and small anchors (the DG symbol) rose in columns up the papered walls. She found Marian in the dining room with a few of the other DGs—Cindy and Lindy and Deb—all with pearls around their white necks. A gaggle of other rushees with shiny hair and dresses in mint green and daffodil yellow crowded around a table of canapés.

"Punch?" Marian offered, ladling out crystal teacups of something pink.

"Thanks," Kate said.

"It's so much tastier than the punch at KKG," said a strawberry blond with sharp little teeth. "What do you put in it?"

"Rose water," Cindy or Lindy said. "Oranges of course. Extract of almonds. And"—she lowered her voice—"don't let the house mother know, but—"

"Hush," Marian interrupted. "It's a secret. If you pledge, of course, you can find out."

Kate sipped the punch, which really was very good.

"That's some dress," Lindy or Cindy said, looking Kate up and down. "It's the exact color of a baked potato!" The gaggle laughed, and Kate laughed along good naturedly, and held out her glass for more punch.

"Careful," Marian said, handing her the refilled glass cup etched with flowers of a variety not found in nature. "Don't go too fast." But the warning went right past Kate, who never dreamed they would serve alcohol to girls.

The conversation turned to football. Everyone except Kate had gone to the game that afternoon, which the Big Red had lost by a humiliating margin. The word was that the quarterback, a senior with a devoted following among the DGs, would be benched the following Saturday in favor of a sophomore whose eyes, it was agreed, were not half so blue as the starter's, which were the exact color of robins' eggs.

"Though of course robins' eggs are not all the exact same color," Kate remarked. "They vary."

"That interception really was not his fault," Deb said.

"What kind of offense did they run?" Kate wanted to know. She had played football with the boys on the street until she was thirteen. "Because a single-wing offense can leave a quarterback vulnerable. But if, on the other hand, they ran the Notre Dame box . . ."

After a minute she noticed that the other girls had drifted away. She helped herself to another glass and wandered into the next room, where several of the Delta Gammas were preparing to perform a skit. There was a stage, covered with a velvet cloth, against one wall. Aphrodite, draped in white, and Athena, draped in silver, recited rhymed couplets and bestowed symbolic gifts on a trio of girls in blue. It was all very grave and allegorical. After the skit, a gramophone was cranked up, and girls waltzed around the room in twos, draped in ribbons and garlanded with flowers. Watching them spin made Kate dizzy. She sat down on one of the little sofas and shut her eyes, opening them sometime later when she felt a tap on her shoulder.

"Are you all right?" It was Marian, her face flushed and rosy.

"Fine," Kate said. "I'm just—" But she couldn't think how to describe it.

"Did you like the skit?"

"It wasn't bad. Who made it up?"

"I don't know," Marian said. "It's handed down."

Kate thought this sounded funny. "Handed down!" she repeated. "Handed! Right or left?" Suddenly she felt much better. In fact, she felt wonderful. "Shall we dance?" she said.

"All right. I'm taller, so I'll lead."

They joined the other pairs of girls revolving around the room. "Dancing is so much nicer without boys," Kate sighed, which made Marian laugh.

After the dancing there was cake with white frosting and tiny edible silver balls, and more punch, golden-colored this time and fizzy. Kate found herself in the middle of a group of rushees speculating about their chances.

"It's hard when you're rushing four different houses," said a girl with a big silk rose pinned to her bosom. "Because you have to memorize the history of all of them."

"But you get to go to four times as many parties," said a girl in lavender ruffles.

"But then you need four dresses," the first girl said.

"But surely you don't get a bid or not based on what you wear," Kate said. The other girls glanced at her dress and then looked away. Kate looked down, scrutinizing the baked potato–colored garment as though it were message in code. Then, spying Marian across the room, she strode over. "Is there a problem with my dress?" she demanded.

"What kind of problem?"

Kate was beginning to feel light-headed. "I may have made a mistake," she said. She put her hand out to steady herself on something, but there was nothing there to hold on to.

Marian grabbed her arm and caught her before she fell. "Careful," she said.

"I might just need to lie down for a minute," Kate said, and began to sink to the floor.

"Not here." Marian tugged her back up and guided her through the room and up a staircase, then up another staircase. They were at the top of the house now, in a dark hall. Marian had to duck to get through the doorway into a room halfway down the corridor. It wasn't much bigger than Kate's room, though it was better furnished. The eiderdown, for example, was like a pink satin cloud. Kate sank onto it and shut her eyes as the walls revolved. "I must have caught a touch of something," she said.

"Silly," Marian said. "You're just tipsy. All that punch."

Kate opened her eyes, incredulous, then quickly shut them again. Marian sat down and put her arm around Kate and patted her shoulder. "It's all right," she said, and Kate leaned her spinning head against Marian's breast. Marian was as soft as the eiderdown. Softer. "There, there," she said in a motherly way. How odd, Kate thought, that she was comforted by this, whereas, when her actual mother did the same thing, it made her shriek. Was it being tipsy that made the difference? Or maybe that Marian smelled so much better than her mother, who exuded an odor of cold cream and silver polish. "You smell like oranges," Kate noted, inhaling. "Or maybe almonds." She sniffed at Marian's collarbone, trying to decide.

"That tickles," Marian said, giggling.

Kate, who as a rule did not like giggling, found she might be changing her mind. She sniffed and snorted, pretending to be a pig, and Marian let out a gratifying little screech and fell backwards, pulling Kate with her while pretending to push her away. Then they were wrestling, almost like the boys in the neighborhood used to do. Kate pinned the bigger girl with a scissors move. Marian pressed and wriggled. Kate pressed back against Marian, who lay under her breathing hard, and, feeling deliciously fuzzy, she wrapped her legs around one of Marian's. Marian shimmied and sighed. A minnow seemed to be swimming inside Kate. Marian's face swam in the gloom, slack and golden against the white pillows. Kate had no idea what the rules were here, so she shut her eyes and let Marian take the lead, like when they were dancing. Marian's hands darted here and there, stroking and probing, apparently in accordance with some well-understood system, one even more unfamiliar and mysterious than the one decreeing that milk could not be drunk with a chicken sandwich and that candles must be put in the sink rather than blown out. Which reminded her.

"Marian?" she ventured when they were lying quietly, squeezed close on the snug bed.

"Mmm?"

"Would the Delta Gammas ever give a bid to a Jewish girl?"

Marian giggled. "You're not telling me . . . Your nose is so nice and small, like a rosebud."

Kate touched her nose, finding it oddly warm and spongy. "But if?"

Marian's bright hair was spread across the pillow and her pearls glowed like little moons. "Oh, Kate, you're so funny," she said. "A kike in DG!" Then she turned over, curled up like a kitten, and went to sleep.

Feeling suddenly much worse, Kate scrambled over her and ran out into the hallway, where luckily she found a lavatory in which to be sick. Then she groped her way back downstairs, leaving Marian snoring gently in her pink satin nest. The gramophone was blaring in the half-empty main room, and shrieks of laughter and strange tuneless chants—or were they songs?—swirled along the corridors as though a coven of witches had taken over the party, mixing potions in the punch bowl.

Out on the cold street, the moon sailed high. The air was full of the rustle and moldering smell of dry leaves, which tumbled and swirled through the night air and swept in hushed conspiracies along the streets. Somewhere someone had lit a bonfire, and the scent of burning stung Kate's nose and eyes, which must have been why they were spilling over. She felt weak, and still slightly dizzy, but if she concentrated on putting one foot in front of another, she was all right. Luckily the way home was mostly downhill. Occasionally a picture from the evening rose up shimmering out of the confusion of her brain: the anchors marching in columns up the wallpaper like white ants, the bright pink flush of the punch in the crystal bowl, which was also the color of Marian's face when—

But here was the familiar mailbox on the corner where she needed to turn. She stopped and leaned against it, pressing her burning head to the cold metal, wondering if she was going to be sick again. She could tell there was more foul noxious matter churning in the depths. One hand gripping the mailbox, she bent over, willing it up. Nothing. Whatever was inside her wouldn't be rooted out that easily.

How could she have been so stupid? She remembered Thea's face in the kitchen, damp with the steam rising from the pot of soup, her eyes stony. *Don't you know about those people?*

At last Kate reached the house and stumbled up the steps onto the porch, where the jack-o-lantern they had carved last week leered up at her with its dark face. By some miracle, her key was still in her pocket. It took perhaps a minute to fit it in the lock.

Inside, no lights had been left burning for her. She felt her way past the coatrack, past the high stern back of the one good armchair and the table that held the bulky telephone set. Her throat burned with shame—her whole wretched body burned—as she flung open the door to her tiny room.

A ridge under the coverlet made her jump back. Someone was in the bed. A slender shape bisected the puddle of moonlight that streamed in through the high window. "Kate?" Thea said sleepily.

Kate sank down on the edge of the bed, her heart galloping.

"I was waiting up for you, but I must have fallen asleep. I wanted to tell you I was sorry. I shouldn't have told you what to do. It was none of my business." She yawned, her breath warm with sleep.

Kate flung off her coat and kicked off her shoes. "No." Her voice came out low and full of phlegm. "No. I was the one who was wrong. They're horrible! And they don't— That thing you said. It's true!"

"You're not telling me you asked!" Thea sat up.

"How else was I going to find out?"

Thea laid a hand on Kate's arm and began to laugh. "Did you go around asking everybody? 'Excuse me, are you Jewish?

And you, are you a Jew?' Was it like that? I can see you with a notebook and a little pencil, recording responses in columns." She clutched the sleeve of Kate's hateful dress. "'Excuse me,'" she said. "'I just need to gather some data before I decide whether to rush the DGs!'" Loosed from its braid, her hair fell in gleaming waves down the flowered cotton of her nightgown. Kate touched it. It felt like corn silk, faintly electric. Thea was still laughing. From above, moonlight fell in a rippling stream, making the mother-of-pearl buttons of her nightgown glow silver and green. Kate lifted a lock of Thea's hair. She thought of the way seaweed wrapped itself around your legs when you were swimming. There was a warm heaviness in her arms and behind her breastbone. She was floating, breathless, through the greenish shimmer toward Thea.

"Hey," Thea said, as Kate's fingers grazed her face.

Kate stroked her jaw, traced a line to the ear. "I'm sorry I didn't listen to you," she said. "I will from now on." She moved closer, burrowing into the slender shoulder. Her cheek found the softness of Thea's breast under the cheerful daisies of the thin gown.

"Kate," Thea said.

"Hmm," Kate murmured. Her body rocked gently, as though tugged by little waves.

"Kate—" But Kate covered Thea's mouth with her own. A long moment passed, then another. Their mouths pressed together, exploring. Thea's skin smelled like the ocean, salty and clean.

Then, abruptly, Thea tensed. Kate opened her eyes as Thea pulled away, scrambling across the bed onto the floor, her tangled hair flaring behind her.

Kate felt wide awake now. Gooseflesh stood up along her arms.

Thea stood in the doorway, her face white, her eyes glittering in the moonlight. If she'd had a lightning bolt, she would doubtless have flung it at Kate's heart. "I wish you had never come to live here!" she cried. Then she ran.

Kate leapt up from the terrible bed. Boiling with shame and confusion, she found her suitcase and flung it open. The only thought in her head was that she must leave. She had to get away from here at all costs. She began to grab things—clothes, shoes, books, hairbrush—throwing them into the suitcase, her mind feverish and blank.

It was foolish to run off in the middle of the night. She knew that! It was farcical. She forced herself to sit back down on the edge of the bed, her hands gripping the mattress, her wrinkled dress spreading like a stain across the rumpled sheets. She loved this room, this house. She didn't want to leave. She wanted—

What did she want? She tried to focus the ragged beam of her attention.

In her mind's eye she could see Thea: her shocked face, her electric hair. The scorching horror of Thea's horror. She had to stand up to push it away, sweat springing out all over her body. Her thoughts raced. There at her feet, the empty suitcase waited to be filled, inviting her to flee. At least she would be in motion. She piled in skirts and underwear. She had no idea where she might go.

Slow down, she told herself. *Slow down!* But she could not. Her palms closed the lid, her fingers snapped the latches. Her eyes took a last look at her room, at the blank dark rectangle of the high window.

In the hall, faint smells of bread and oily fish, and the lavender scent that clung to the bathroom, where the girls washed their hair. She dropped the key on the telephone table and pulled the door shut behind her.

CHAPTER 4

The day after the first night Kate spent in the storage room was sunny. The trees around the quad blazed yellow and orange, scores of leaves breaking free every minute, plunging through the bright morning. Kate's suitcase, now colorfully festooned, was where she had left it to climb into the building, which seemed like a good sign. She carried it up the stairs, keeping her eyes down, trying to be invisible. In the afternoon she walked into town and bought a blanket at a thrift store, then concealed it, along with her suitcase, behind some of the storage room's crates. At night she shut herself in and made a nest of the blanket and her coat, feeling a kinship with the mice scrabbling in the walls. Once she got used to it, it wasn't so bad. She could take her meals at the cafeteria nearby, study in the library, wash in the gym. The trick was to think expansively—to consider the whole campus to be home.

In biology class she sat in the back to avoid Thea, among the boys who dozed or poked at each other, whispering loudly behind their hands. Why were they here if they didn't care to learn? At another time it would have made Kate furious, but her emotions didn't seem to be working properly. She didn't feel anger or pleasure or sadness. A great muffling blankness saturated her, keeping her foggy and dull, even when she caught a glimpse of Thea at the front of the room. Her slim figure, her long braid swaying back and forth like the chain of a hypnotist's watch. In Kate's chest, where her heart should have been, there was a frog desiccating in formalin.

"Your partner has transferred to a different section, I'm

sorry to say," Dr. Krause told her when she went numbly to lab. "Perhaps you could join up with one of the other pairs?" His eyebrows waggled as he scanned the room for likely candidates. "Peterson and Jones," he called.

The boys' eyes slid away.

"I'd prefer to work by myself, actually," Kate said.

Dr. Krause looked doubtful. "I think it will be difficult alone," he said. "Science is a collaborative enterprise."

"I'll be fine." Hadn't Gregor Mendel worked alone? She'd looked him up at the library, learned that he had labored without assistance on his vast project for decades, and that his work had not been recognized till he was dead. Genius, hard work, solitude: was that a tragic life, or a glorious one?

Anyway, the microscope was a reliable partner. She liked how, looking through the eyepiece, she gazed down over the field of view like a hawk hovering over a field of grass and wildflowers.

The freckled boy at the next bench, whose name was Jimmy McFadden, leaned over. "What happened to your girlfriend?" he asked. "She figure out that science isn't for dames?"

Kate straightened up and stared at him. "She was invited to join the honors lab. It covers extra material."

Jimmy blinked. "Thatch," he called to his partner, who was fixing a bean section to a slide. "Did you know there's an honors lab?"

The tall, gawky boy looked up. "Is there?" They had bragged about the As they got on their write-ups. Or rather, Jimmy had bragged, though Kate suspected it was his partner who did most of the work.

"Don't feel too bad," she said. "After all, I'm not in it, either."

On her other side, the square-jawed pre-med student, again wearing his diamond-patterned sweater, was struggling. "Hey, McFadden," he said. "Mind if I take a look?" He nodded toward the freckled boy's paper. Jimmy looked around, saw that Dr. Krause was busy on the other side of the room, and pushed the paper over. Diamond sweater began to copy down the answers.

"Stop that," Kate said.

"Why don't you mind your own business."

By instinct, Kate looked around for Thea, who would have tossed her braid and said something barbed and brainy. But there was nobody there but Jimmy McFadden with his freckles and his ugly orange hair.

"That's cheating," she said. "You're as much of a cheater as he is."

Jimmy leaned toward her, smelling of gluey cafeteria oatmeal. "And you're an ugly witch."

"If I were a witch," Kate said, "I'd make you disappear."

That night, too restless in her makeshift nest to sleep, Kate wandered down the hall and borrowed a microscope from Krause's cabinet. She lugged it to the storage room, set it up on a rickety table, pulled a hair from her head, and fixed it to a slide. She took out her notebook and sketched the forking veins. She looked at a fingernail paring, a thread from her scarf, a whorl of dust, diagramming each one, pretending she was the first person ever to record these shapes and structures. The next day, as she walked around campus, she collected things to look at through the lens later: a leaf, a feather, a shred of orange rind. She imagined a book full of her diagrams, people taking it down and admiring it, their eyes opened for the first time to what had been hidden. In her mind's eye, she saw her father taking it down, turning the pages. Smiling at her, his mouth half hidden under his soft moustache.

Her father hadn't had to go to France. He'd been nearly

forty when the war started. But he was a physician, and they needed doctors there.

She remembered how, when she was young, her legs would ache as she tried to keep up with his tall figure in its tweed jacket and boots, when he would occasionally take her with him on his long weekend walks. Every now and then he would stop and wait for her to catch up so he could point out an interesting weed or flower: Queen Anne's lace, feathery goldenrod, pokeweed with its heavy dangling tendrils of dark berries that people once made into ink. Overhead, finches and nuthatches plunged from tree to tree; underfoot, rigorous ants drew lines with their bodies across the skin of the ground. Butterflies probed the openings of flowers: mourning cloaks and painted ladies, monarchs and their less famous doppelgängers, the viceroys.

Her father taught her to distinguish between the two species. The viceroy flew quickly and erratically, while the monarch elegantly glided. "Look closely," he used to say, even when she thought she already was.

She'd look harder, opening her eyes wide to take everything in.

"Are you looking, Kate?"

"Yes."

"What do you see?"

Black lacy outlines surrounding shards of orange on the flat wings. A hundred shades of green in the woods and meadows all around them. The sun throwing moving shadows across the ground.

Her father explained mimicry, how the monarch was poisonous to birds, which learned to avoid it, and how the viceroy borrowed the monarch's colors for protection. "Just because things look alike, it doesn't mean they are alike."

Was he talking about Kate and her mother with their limp brown hair and pale blue eyes? Seer's eyes, her father said, teasing, which made her mother blush and scoff.

When Kate asked what seer's eyes were, he laughed. "Hocus pocus," he said. "Never you mind."

A better question: how did the viceroy know to mimic the monarch? And what exactly happened inside a chrysalis? Several times as a child Kate had carefully cut open one of the lucent jade green packages, hoping for a glimpse of the secret chimera—half caterpillar, half butterfly—inside. But there was never anything in there but goo.

CHAPTER 5

One morning, pushing through the door at the back of the lecture hall at the end of Intro Bio, Kate found herself face to face with Thea.

"Hello," Thea said. She looked tired, her eyes narrow and fish-gray in her thin wan face.

Kate stared at her, unable to speak.

"I didn't know where you were living." Thea's words drifted through the static filling Kate's head.

"What does it matter?" Kate said.

Thea reached into her pocket and pulled out an envelope. For an instant, Kate thought Thea had written her a letter, and she began to tremble. But of course it wasn't that. Her name, and the address of the house on Myrtle Street, were written in the flawless copperplate of her sister Laura.

"I thought it might be important," Thea said.

Kate reached out and took the envelope. For a moment, their hands held on to opposite ends. Then Thea let go.

"Thanks for taking the trouble," Kate said angrily.

"I had to be here anyway."

Thea stood stiffly with her thin shoulders back, her braid swinging slightly. It was cold, and she was wearing a fitchskin coat Kate had never seen before. She remembered how they had agreed not to believe it would snow until they saw it with their own eyes. She wondered if Thea had thought of that when the first flakes began to fall, as she had. "I hope you didn't have trouble finding a new place," Thea said.

"No."

Silence roiled between them. Somewhere in the building, footsteps rang out and faded away. *Thump thump thump* went Kate's heart, like a mallet on mud.

"You left your navy skirt," Thea said. "And a pair of stockings. And a tin of that tea you like."

"I don't care. Throw it away!"

The front door of the building banged open, and they both jumped back. A boy and a girl in letter jackets with snow on their shoulders came in, chattering. "You *say* that," the girl was saying. "But you don't *know* that."

"I do," the boy said. He was yellow-haired and as bright-eyed as a canary, his gaze fixed on the girl's pink face. "I do know it! I've known it for a long time."

"Prove it." Smiling, the girl moved away from him.

The boy seized the girl's hand and began to run, pulling her behind him up the stairs. Their laughter echoed down over the railings, circling slowly, then died away. Its brief bright presence had altered the temperature in the hall, leaving behind a chill.

After a moment, Thea said, "You didn't have to leave the way you did, you know."

"I couldn't stay!" Kate said.

Thea's head jerked around, but except for the dusty display cases of ragged butterflies and faded sand dollars, they were alone.

"You said—" Kate began. But she couldn't repeat what Thea had said.

"I had to make up something to tell Lena," Thea said.

"Why not just tell her the truth?" Kate said coldly.

"I cared about you!" Thea cried. "I never had a friend like you before! And you had to go and ruin it." They glared at each other.

Kate tried to speak, but her brain felt slow and stupid. What if she said, *I didn't mean anything*? Could things go back to the way they had been?

But she had meant something. Even if she didn't completely understand what it was.

"I cared about you, too," she said.

Words were no good. Kate knew it, and Thea—narrowing her eyes, turning to go—seemed to know it, too. Her taut braid swung like a lash as she stalked toward the door.

All day the letter in Kate's pocket weighed her down. She worried the edge of the envelope with her thumb until her skin was raw, replaying in her mind the moment when she and Thea had both held it, when she had felt the heat coming off Thea's skin in brutal waves. *I cared about you!* Kate imagined rewinding time, climbing down out of Krause's window to the ground, picking up her suitcase and walking backward down the sidewalks and into the house on Myrtle Street. Backing into the little room that would again be hers. Falling onto the narrow bed beside Thea.

This time, she would just lie there. Lie still. Wouldn't she? If she were given another chance?

That night, alone in her nest, she opened Laura's letter.

Dear Kate,

I'm sure you're having a marvelous time at college, but it would be nice if you could manage to write even one letter to let us know that you're still alive. Even if you have forgotten about us, we have not, it may surprise you to hear, forgotten about you. And whatever you might think, we do care what happens to you. Mother is very worried. She'd never say so, but she goes around pulling furniture away from the walls and mopping baseboards, screaming if you get in her way. You might give a thought to those of us who are still here.

Thomas and I have found a beautiful house in Brooklyn Heights. Mother refuses even to discuss a wedding. She says it's because I'm too young, but really it's because of Papa. She can't picture a wedding with him not there for her to lean on. Charlie is no help—you know how he is. He keeps threatening to run away to sea or some nonsense. You are lucky to be far away, but I hope you haven't forgotten that you wouldn't be there at all if I hadn't persuaded Mother to let you go. So, take a few minutes from your exciting new life and write to her.

Your sister,
Laura

An unbearable pressure built up in Kate's head and chest as she read the letter. The room, which she knew to be chilly, seemed far too hot. The stacks of crates and the towers of cages hemmed her in as though she herself were a mouse or a guinea pig shut up in one of the dusty, rusty enclosures. In the weeks since she had arrived in Ithaca, she had hardly thought about her family. Now they came flooding back to her: her tall, aggrieved, selfish sister with her two-carat diamond ring. Her watchful, sensitive brother who was nowhere as cocky as he pretended. Her beak-nosed screech owl of a mother with her flat hard chest and her big moist eyes, operatic and insomniac. These qualities had been kept in check, somewhat, by their gentle, polymath, physician father. Their mother would never forgive him getting himself killed.

Mrs. Croft had always been prone to hysteria. One of Kate's earliest memories was of her mother's bony arms and camphor smell as she caught Kate up and squeezed her close, weeping and shrieking about something. Who knew what? Kate learned early to stay out of the way when her mother got that wild-eyed look.

Kate flung open the storage room door and stumbled into the hall. Up and back she walked, up and back, over the hard tiles that were nearly invisible in the dimness.

The feeling of suffocation in her mother's embrace, like being buried alive.

Was that why her father had volunteered to go to war?

Was that why, even before that, he was seldom home, always at the hospital, or his medical office, or out making house calls? Sometimes he let Kate go with him, and she would sit in the front seat of the parked Ford as the sky emptied of light, daydreaming until he came back out, whistling tunelessly, his black bag swinging from his hand.

"You bored, pumpkin?"

She would shake her head.

"You're a patient little thing. Ready to go home?"

"Can we get an egg cream?"

He would pull out his watch and frown at it, making some sort of calculation. Then—sometimes—they would go to the neighborhood drugstore and sit at the counter. Sometimes he would tell her about his patients: rich women and waitresses, sailors and shopkeepers. He might tell her about a tricky diagnosis, talking to himself, she knew, using language she didn't understand, but she didn't mind. She liked the sound of his voice talking. Liked the syllables of the big words loosed into the air like balloons. She could feel the pleasure he took in laying out the logic that had led him, step by step, to the right conclusion.

"You have to think things through," he liked to say.

She thought she knew what that meant. Certainly she knew the meanings of each of the words. But in his mouth, with his warm, tired eyes gazing down at her, the sentence seemed to have for him a kind of particular luster. A grand significance she couldn't quite grasp.

At last he'd reach into his pocket, jingle his change. "Your mother will be missing us," he'd say.

It was impossible to know whether that was true or not. All her life, it seemed, Kate's mother had wanted something from Kate that she could not give. First, she had wanted Kate to be a boy—it was bad enough that she had one girl already—but there was nothing Kate could do about that. Later, when Kate behaved, in some ways, like a boy after all—playing baseball, bringing snakes home from the woods, sprawling in an unladylike way on the sofa—her mother liked it even less.

Mostly, though, what her mother hated was that Kate liked to be left alone. Even when she was very small—two years old, or maybe three—she could sit contently by herself for an hour or more. Not playing, not babbling, just . . . what? Thinking. Looking. Existing in time.

"Stop sitting like a lump!" her mother would cry. "Go do something."

Why did her mother care? What was she bothered by, exactly?

Then, when the tall figure stalked toward her, Kate would run away shrieking from the fierce, grabbing hands.

But she always let her father swing her up onto his shoulders. She liked being taller than everyone else, being a kind of extension of her father, like the flower at the top of a stalk. She liked the view from up there, the tops of people's heads and the sky almost close enough to touch.

In front of her now, a door swung open. A craggy figure loomed up, haloed in yellow lamplight, its eyes black knots in its face. Kate swallowed a cry of fear.

"Miss Croft?" the astonished figure said.

Dr. Krause! It was his gaping office she stood in front of, gasping. As if, by thinking about him, she had summoned him!

"What are you doing here?" he demanded. "Did you get accidentally locked in?"

Kate seized the suggestion. "Yes!" she said. "I stayed late and then . . ." But she stopped, looking up into his shadowy face. She did not want to lie to him. "Actually," she said. "I'm living here."

"*Living?*" he repeated, as though it were an English word he didn't know. He looked her up and down: her wrinkled clothes, her bird's-nest hair. "Young lady, you can *nicht* be *leben* here! It's impossible."

Kate held his gaze. "I am, though," she said. "It is *possible.*" Together they looked toward the open door of the storage room halfway up the hall.

Dr. Krause coughed. He shuffled in bedroom slippers along the corridor toward the parallelogram of tea-colored light. He peered around the door of the storage room, then looked back at Kate. "How long?" he demanded. "How long have you been *living* here? Like a *stow-a-way!*"

"I'm not hurting anyone."

"That's not the point. There are rules, you know, Fräulein Croft." Then he saw the microscope, perched on the old, scarred, lamed wooden desk. Next to it, her notebook lay open to a diagram of a magnified shred of a hardboiled egg she'd brought from the cafeteria. She waited for him to accuse her of theft to compound her offense of breaking and entering; to call the dean; to send her back home to her mother. But he said nothing. He shuffled forward in his backless leather slippers, picked up the notebook, and held her sketch to his eyes. He tapped the pockets of his cardigan till he located his glasses. Pushing them onto his nose, he peered closer, frowning behind his beard. In her mind, she saw what he was seeing: the carefully shaded globules linked together in irregular peninsulas, the secret geography of egg. Licking the pad of his big index finger, he flipped slowly backward through the pages, peering at her drawings of the fingernail, of the hair. Of the variegated, irregular islands of dust.

At last the old man set the book down and blinked at her over the tops of his glasses. "These are good," he said.

"Thank you," Kate said.

"Come," he said. "We will talk."

Dr. Krause's office smelled of coffee dregs and tobacco and dried-up oranges. Stacks of books teetered on shelves or lay splayed open on water-ringed tables, bristling with scraps of paper. More paper was pinned to the walls with long rusty pins: charts labeled in odd, slanted handwriting; graphs; lists of binominal names; typed letters; old brownish photographs of bearded men in antiquated hats. Towers of blue books, some faded nearly beige by time, slumped on the windowsill amid the green and purple foliage of potted plants. How could anyone think clearly in here?

Dr. Krause put a coffee pot on a hot plate, lifted an armful of books from a chair, and indicated that Kate should sit. "So!" he said. "You have been living in that storage room? I work here late, many nights, and I have never seen a sign of you."

The thought of him here, when she'd believed herself to be alone, horrified her. "But the building is locked," she said.

"I have a key."

He shuffled over to the hot plate, took the lid off the coffee pot, peered in, and poured them each a cup. The coffee was thin yet sludgy, barely lukewarm. Krause took a sip and rattled the cup back into its saucer. "Your drawings are very clear and precise," he said.

Kate blinked at him, unsure what to say.

"You have a good eye." He drew the final word out so that it seemed to contain a multitude of syllables. "Not that you had any business taking a microscope," he added.

"I was careful!" Kate said. "No one was using it."

"And if I should come into your room and take your diamond ring when you weren't wearing it, and put it on my hand, and you found out!" he said. "How would you feel then?"

"I don't have a diamond ring," Kate said.

Dr. Krause waved her remark away. "I am thinking to offer you a position," he said.

Kate stared at his wrinkled face and thin, crooked smile.

"I am making a small study of the coloration of the coleus plant. *Plectranthus scutellarioides*."

"I thought—" Kate began. What had she thought? That he was merely a laboratory instructor?

"I have a little space in the greenhouses where I grow my plants. I always have a student or two helping me. A lot of the work is just basic care and maintenance. Routine, you know. But crucial. There is also the taking of measurements. And making charts and drawings. The assistant I have now is not so good at this. He scribbles."

"I see," Kate said, trying to keep up.

"I couldn't pay you," Dr. Krause said. "But you might find it interesting." From under his tangled eyebrows he looked at her curiously. Patiently. The way, she supposed, he might look at one of his coleus plants.

Kate swallowed another sip of the terrible coffee. The cup was fine white china, gold-rimmed, with a delicate handle shaped like an ear. It made her think he must have had a wife once, though his presence here late at night in his bedroom slippers suggested he didn't now. "All right," she said.

Krause beamed. "Very good! *But:* you must move out of the storage room into a real place of living. A decent place. Do you understand? That is my condition."

Kate looked around at Dr. Krause's water-ringed desk and his stacks of books, the faded journals piled on the dusty rug. There didn't seem to be much difference between his office and the storage room. But she said, "I understand."

CHAPTER 6

Krause delivered Kate to the greenhouse the following afternoon. "Thatch will show you the ropes," he said.

Kate recognized the lab partner of Jimmy McFadden: tall, gawky, sandy-haired John Thatcher, whose trousers were always too short. "You're the girl who promised to make Jimmy McFadden disappear," he said, holding out his hand. "Yet I still see him all over the place."

Kate gave him her hand, which he crushed in his. There was probably twice as much of him as there was of her, even though he was so skinny. "I thought you were friends," she said.

"*Friends* is a strong word."

Outside, where the back of Krause's overcoat was disappearing up the path, the afternoon was cold and damp. Soon snow would smother the hills and settle heavily along the roofs, but here in the greenhouse the air was warm and smelled of earth. Bright lights dangled on adjustable cords from a web of metal struts crisscrossing the glass ceiling, and rubber hoses lay coiled on the sloping concrete floor. Long piers, also concrete, lined the room like pews in a church, supporting rows of plants, each with its own cryptic label: 47-GA-6031, 72-BL-2267. Kate recognized canary grass, African violets, Indian corn.

"Professor Whitaker is doing interesting work with corn," Thatch said, running his big hand along the sword-like leaf of the nearest maize plant.

Kate didn't know who Professor Whitaker was. "Dr. Krause said corn is good for genetics experiments," she said, showing off. Beginning to perspire in the tropical warmth, she unzipped her coat. Her long limp hair clung to her neck and straggled over her shoulders. "Because you get clues from the seeds a year before the plant comes up."

"Krause is okay," Thatch said. "But everybody wants to work with Professor Whitaker."

"Just okay?" A few days before, she had never even dreamed of being a research assistant, yet here she was feeling disappointed.

"You have to start somewhere," Thatch said cheerfully, stopping in front of a row of richly colored coleus plants: red and amaranth, flamingo-pink and moss-green. "It's always summer in here, which is going to be nice in January. And February. And March! And there's lots to learn. Something unexpected is always happening. Of course, sometimes that's because someone made a mistake. Got the plants mixed up, or didn't do the protocol properly. On the other hand," he went on, his eyes glinting, "it might be because you have stumbled onto something."

Kate tossed her coat in a corner. The warm moist air filled her lungs, and she felt the oxygen energizing her cells as though the plants were making it just for her.

Krause's experiments, Thatch explained, had to do with the patterns on hybrid coleus leaves. "He crosses certain plants with certain other plants, then tests them to see how sunlight affects the color."

He showed her the back room that served both for storage and as an office, and he demonstrated how to cut paper shapes to affix to the leaves to prevent light exposure. It was finicky work. Kate was surprised by how deft Thatch was. The excess paper scraps fluttered away, leaving perfect ellipses or precisely irregular fringed ovals. "You should have been a girl," she said, tossing her hair out of her face and trying to concentrate.

"I grew up with my hands inside farm machinery," Thatch explained. "On my family's dairy farm. Inside cows, too," he added, then turned red.

Kate kept her eyes politely on her cutting, but what did she care if he stuck his hands into cows? Her father had delivered human babies. She worked the scissors around a tricky curve, using one of his cutouts as a pattern.

"I'm here to study dairy science, really," Thatch said. "Other than Bio 1, I'm taking Milk Composition and Intermediate Cheese."

"How about ice cream?" she asked, laughing. "I'd take a class in that."

"That's next semester," he said.

Kate saw he wasn't joking. "So you'll go back and run the farm when you graduate?"

"My father wants to modernize. I wish I could study botany, though. Plants are so interesting." He looked at her appealingly. His nose was a bit too long and his forehead was a bit too broad, but with his regular features and nicely shaped mouth, he wasn't bad looking.

"Are they?" Her hair had fallen into her face again, and as she tossed it back, she saw that she had cut her shape too small, mangling Thatch's prototype in the process.

"Cows are big and stupid," Thatch said with sudden passion. "Plants are subtle. Canny. They can't run from their predators, so they grow thorns and secrete poisons. They can't hunt down a mate, so they make beautiful scented blossoms to lure bees."

Kate pulled her hair back, twisted it into a knot, and slid a pencil through it. "I think it's amazing that they live on sunlight," she said.

"Think how wonderful that must be," Thatch agreed.

"Except on cloudy days." The knot of hair was already loosening. Greasy-feeling strands slid onto her temples and slithered down her cheeks. Again the scissors slipped.

"You'll get the hang of it," he said.

Kate flushed. "It's my hair. It makes it hard to see." She turned her chair around and thrust the scissors at him. "Can you cut it? Here." She touched her neck just below her ear to show the length she wanted.

"Cut it *off*?"

"It'll only take a minute."

"No. I won't."

"It's not a whim," Kate said. "If that's what you're worried about."

He tucked his hands into his armpits. "It's not right."

Kate didn't like the embarrassed look on his face, as though what she had asked were somehow shameful. "What's not right?" she demanded. "A girl with short hair? A girl deciding how she wants to wear her own hair? A girl asking you to help her do what she wants to do with her own hair?"

Thatch just shook his head.

"And how," she wondered aloud, "does that *not right* compare with, say, the *not right* of cheating? On a lab report, for example." She hadn't known she was going to say it—hadn't even known she was thinking about it. But now that the words had surfaced, she was glad. She'd been angry about it all this time without even realizing.

Thatch's face tightened. "I didn't cheat."

"You let that boy copy."

"That was Jimmy."

"It was your work, though, wasn't it? So what's the difference?" She tossed her head. Her hair clung to her sweaty neck.

"There's a difference," Thatch said.

They were both sweating now, in the humid greenhouse, both of them flushed and hot and irritated. "You knew he was doing it," Kate said. "You knew, and you didn't say anything."

"I didn't snitch," Thatch said. "If that's what you mean."

"So if Jimmy committed murder, you would just keep

quiet?"

"That's not fair," Thatch said.

"Okay, forget it," Kate said. "Will you cut my hair or not? After all, you're the one with the *experienced hands*." She waited for him to blush.

But he didn't blush. "You can do what you like with your hair," Thatch said. "But count me out."

Kate seized the hair and positioned the scissors.

"I can recommend a good barber," Thatch said when she hesitated. "If you're worried."

Snip snip snip. A moment later, the hair lay on the floor between them like the dead thing it was. Kate ran her hand along the ragged ends.

Thatch looked at her curiously. "How does it feel?"

A shimmering bubble seemed to be inflating inside Kate's chest: buoyant, odd. She ducked her head, feeling how easily it moved. "It feels light," she said.

Kate found a room in a boardinghouse full of graduate students who spent their time elsewhere: in the submarine depths of the library churning through the murky pages of old books, or in the far-flung experimental barns raising better chickens and sheep. She sent a note to Myrtle Street asking that her mail be forwarded, but she didn't go back for her things. They could keep them, throw them out. Stick pins in them and burn them. She didn't care.

Dr. Krause gave her a fat book to study: W. E. Castle's *Genetics*. When she wasn't in class or in the greenhouse, she liked to stretch out on the sitting room chesterfield with a mug of tea and read it. "The human mind is characterized above all by curiosity, the source of all our wisdom as well as of our woes," Castle wrote. "We demand a reason for everything, and if none is forthcoming from an outside source, we straightway construct one for ourselves out of our own imaginings."

Was that true? Lots of people didn't seem curious about anything much. With its confident, direct, slightly pompous style, the book seemed to speak to her directly, the ideas soaking into her brain. Sitting on the hard, slick horsehair, she flipped through plates illustrating the coloration of hybrid guinea pigs.

There was a chapter on Mendelian terms: *homozygote, gametes, unit-character*.

There was a method for calculating the probabilities of unit-characters being passed from parent to offspring, with capital letters representing *dominant* unit-characters, and lowercase letters representing *recessive* ones:

	C	C
C	CC	CC
C	CC	CC

	c	c
c	cc	cc
c	cc	cc

	C	c
C	CC	Cc
c	Cc	cc

She learned that a recessive unit-character could be passed along unexpressed for generations until the right circumstance caused it to show itself again.

Kate had always been interested in where things came from and how they worked. In hidden connections, like the one between the caterpillar and the butterfly. In what was going on under the rubbery skin of the visible world. These connections might be revealed at the most unexpected times and places. Once, when she was four or five, she had wandered into the kitchen to find her mother standing over the stove, her face shiny, stirring something in a great black kettle. As Kate stood watching, her mother lifted the ladle to her lips. A dark red viscous liquid, runny and goopy, trickled down her flushed, pointy chin. Blood! Kate stood in the doorway, frozen with horror, until her eyes fell upon on the great heap of strawberry hulls lying on the kitchen table. She felt an electric jolt as two ideas connected. Blood, that most mysterious of substances—usually glimpsed only when you fell and scraped your knee, or cut your forehead on the edge of the coffee table—came from strawberries! It was years before she worked out that her mother had been making jam.

A few days later, Kate told this story to Thatch. "I was so pleased with myself," she said. "I had discovered a piece of the mystery of the universe!"

Thatch laughed. "You actually thought your mother was cooking blood on the stove?"

"That's not the point," Kate said. She ran a hand along the blunt ends of her hair, which she'd had evened out at a beauty parlor in town. The hairdresser had scolded her for cutting it so short.

"You must have been a strange child." Thatch looked at her with an expression she couldn't read, not quite admiring, not quite critical. "A queer little duckling."

Kate picked up a new piece of paper. "You're not listening," she said.

"I'm listening all right," Thatch said.

"I've been reading a book Dr. Krause gave me about genetics," she said. As Thatch had predicted, she was getting better at cutting the shapes. She liked the feeling of the excess paper being sliced away.

"Castle? Isn't it fascinating?"

"It's a whole *system* for understanding how things are connected under the surface!"

"And the pictures. Those photographs of guinea pigs!" Thatch leaned toward her. "The ones where they're upright and fluffy are okay. But then there are those plates where they're dead on their backs."

"Stretched out like popsicles," Kate said, laughing. "And the rats with their poor naked tails." She was a little jealous Krause had given Thatch the book, too, but on the other hand, it was nice to talk about it with someone.

"Ratsicles!" Thatch said. They were both laughing, tossing out the colors of the ratsicles that could also be flavors—cream, chestnut, chocolate, cinnamon. Then, when it was almost time to go, Thatch said, "May I buy you a soda? Seeing as it's pay day."

The steadiness of his gaze made her turn away. "Where do you work?" she asked, fiddling with one of her paper fronds.

Thatch sounded puzzled. "Here."

Kate stared back up at him: his big square face and the wing of sandy hair flopping over the forehead. His powerful innocent farmer's jaw. "Dr. Krause *pays* you?"

This time it was Thatch who turned away. Busily, he began to straighten up the mess on the table.

Kate stood up so abruptly her chair clattered backwards. She dropped her scissors on the table and went to get her coat.

"Don't be mad," Thatch said. "Let me treat you. After all, I can afford it." He tried to make it into a joke.

Kate walked out into the cold November afternoon. It had begun to snow. *I couldn't pay you,* Krause had said. Not: *I never pay my assistants.*

Maybe he only had enough money for one student. Or maybe Thatch had started out working for free too, only earning a wage over time.

Large wet flakes swooped through the cold on wild gusts of wind, freezing the back of her neck. She felt wild too, something blowing through her that might have been rage.

But what did it matter? She tried to reason with herself. It was a privilege to work for Dr. Krause! It was an opportunity to be part of something amazing, pulling back the curtain to peek at the secret gears and pulleys. The snow tumbled and plummeted. At the bell tower by the library, three crows stood, glossy against a blinding white sea. Snow filigreed the telephone lines and filled up the trees. When she was a girl, her father had taught her to see each tree as its own universe: a web of birds, bugs, squirrels, moss, bats. Had explained how—impossible though it seemed—the whole system was powered by sunlight. That weightless yellow brilliance emanating from an object ninety-three million miles away, yet pouring itself into every corner, every crevice. How proud he would have been that she was working for someone—a professor!—who was trying to learn how it worked. He wouldn't care whether she was paid or not.

But it bothered her.

When she came into the hall of the boardinghouse, with its smells of damp upholstery and stewed tea, a figure with a disheveled braid, huddled in a fitchskin coat, was perched on the edge of the sitting room chesterfield. Kate's heart began to thump as her body recognized Thea before her brain did.

Thea jumped up, urgent yet hesitating. "There was a telephone call," she said. "Long distance."

"What?" Kate said. "What?" Long distance was for illnesses, for death. The confused thought slid through her mind: *Thank God her father was already dead!*

"Your mother," Thea said, trying to explain. But she was nearly as flustered as Kate. "Your mother called. She says there's an emergency. She says you need to come home at once, but that no one has— No one is . . ."

"Everyone's alive?"

"Yes."

"But—what happened?" Kate's mind started to tick through possibilities.

"I don't know," Thea said. "She wouldn't say. Just that you should come home."

"Isn't that just like her!" Kate cried.

Thea looked around the cramped hall. "Do you want to telephone them?" she asked. "Is there a telephone here?"

"No." That was the answer to either question.

Thea paused. "Do you want to come back to Myrtle Street with me and call from there?"

Kate's mind fizzed and sputtered. She could not speak.

"Sit down," Thea said. "I'm going to make you a cup of tea." She took Kate by the sleeve and led her carefully over to the chesterfield.

As Thea began to move away, Kate reached up and pulled her down. "Don't go," she said. For a moment they sat close together on the hard horsehair seat. Under the fitchskins, inside the birdcage of bone, Thea's heart thumped steadily—Kate could hear it, or feel it. Or maybe she just knew it. "What should I do?" she asked.

"You have to pack a suitcase," Thea said. "You have to find a taxi to take you to the train."

"I can't!" Kate swung her head wildly. She would die if she had to go home!

"You can," Thea said. "I'll help you."

"But if no one's dead, why do I have to go?" Kate raised her face and looked up imploringly into Thea's.

Thea reached out and touched the back of Kate's neck. She smelled of candle wax and of the sugared violets she liked to eat. "What happened to your hair?" she said.

Thea packed Kate's suitcase and wrote a note to the landlady. She nudged Kate to her feet and herded her out the door. The snow was coming down hard now, billowing in gusts that stung their faces and made it hard to see. They walked arm in arm because the sidewalks were so slippery.

"It'll be all right," Thea said. "You'll see. It will be fine. Didn't you say your mother tended to be dramatic?"

Kate nodded, full of dread: the solemn chilly house with its dark, polished woodwork. The hall table with its burden of hothouse flowers in a Chinese vase. The long velvet drapes behind which, as a child, Kate used to hide, certain that no one would ever find her there. The sounds that came from behind her mother's door after Kate's father died, which no one ever spoke of.

They turned at the corner, leaning into the wind. There were no taxis, few cars on the street at all.

"We can walk to the station if we have to," Thea said. "It's not so far. Here—let me take the suitcase."

Kate's mind felt dull and stupid. Her face was numb and her toes tingled in her wet shoes, but she felt she could walk like this forever, the two of them alone together in a world filling up with snow.

Far too quickly, they reached the station, a great cold empty space under a high, grimy roof. The smells of coal and damp and something singed. "Come with me," she said.

Thea let go, pretending not to hear. "What luck!" she said. "There's a train boarding now."

CHAPTER 7

What had been snow in Ithaca was cold rain in Brooklyn. Rain fell in fine, needle-like diagonals, penetrating Kate's coat and her tightly wrapped scarf, stinging her ankles, gurgling all around her in gutters and in drains. It was after midnight when she arrived at the door of her parents' house—her mother's house—her cold clothes clinging to her, heavy as mud.

Laura answered the bell and let out a cry, clutching her dressing gown to her throat. "My God—your hair!" she said. "For a moment I thought you were Charlie."

"What's happened?" Kate stood dripping onto the foyer floor.

Laura pushed her toward the kitchen. "Mother's finally sleeping," she said. "So keep your voice down. Couldn't you have let us know when you were arriving?"

It was warm enough in the house, but Kate began to shiver. She sank into a chair at the round pedestal table where she had written hundreds of school essays, drunk thousands of glasses of milk, bickered with her siblings tens of thousands of times. "Is she sick?" she asked.

"Well, of course the whole thing has made her ill!"

"*What* has? What's happened? Tell me!" Kate swiped at her tears angrily. "I got a message saying to come home, and I came home! I got the first train! I'm here!" She looked around. "Where's Charlie?"

Laura sat down too, across the table. Her hair gleamed in its bright artificial waves like corrugated metal. "He's run away." She laid her hands flat on the tabletop: perfect nails, delicate lacework of blue-green veins, the big ring sticking up.

"Who has?" Kate asked.

"Charlie," Laura said.

Kate's heart began to pound. *Thwap, thwap, thwap*, as though someone were striking a tetherball with a bat. "Where has he gone?" she asked cautiously, as though the way she asked the question might have some influence on the answer.

Laura fiddled with her ring. She turned it this way and that, making the berry-sized diamond cast sprays of light across the walls. "He left a letter saying he was joining the Merchant Marine. Mother fainted when she read it. I mean, she actually fainted! Luckily Thomas was here. Otherwise I don't know what I would have done." Thomas was the fiancé.

"What could Thomas do?" Kate cried. "He's not a doctor."

"Keep his head," Laura said. "Telephone Dr. Lawrence."

"Surely you could have done that. You have fingers."

"Stop," Laura said.

Kate stopped. Whatever had happened, it wasn't her sister's fault. She put her head down on the cold table. "I'm just—" But what was she, exactly?

"I'll make tea," Laura said.

"I'd rather have coffee." Kate's head ached and her thoughts oozed inside her skull.

"We'll never sleep if we have coffee."

"We're not going to sleep no matter what." The Merchant Marine!

Laura took down the percolator and began to scoop out the coffee grounds. It was calming, watching her move around the room with her familiar, gliding, water-bird movements. Kate unbuttoned her overcoat and threw it over a chair. She unlaced her sopping shoes and peeled off her stockings. "Well," she said, "at least everyone is all right." Not dead, she meant.

Laura wheeled around, the aluminum percolator glittering in her hand like a medieval weapon. "All right?" she repeated, alight with fury. "Who's all right? Mother is beside herself. God knows what Charlie is enduring, and with his asthma! He couldn't possibly know what he was letting himself in for. And I'm supposed to get married at Christmas! I will, too, don't think I won't. If anyone thinks a stupid stunt like this could stop me."

Oh, you had to admire Laura. At eight she had spit at a boy on the street who'd called Charlie a sissy. At twelve, ice skating alone on the pond, she had sprained her ankle and hobbled all the way home, her face gray with pain. At fifteen, when their father went to France, she learned how to drive because their mother couldn't. How Kate had loved speeding along beside the bay with her sister, their hair blowing, sea gulls keeping pace high in the blue sky. "What will happen to Mother?" Kate asked. "Will she agree to move in with you and Thomas?"

"With me and Thomas?" Laura stared at her, her eyes glittering like her ring.

"She can't live alone, can she?" Kate said. "The way she is?"

"No, of course she can't!"

"Then I don't see—"

But suddenly she did see.

"No," she said. "I won't. I absolutely won't."

"You have to," Laura said.

"Anyway," Kate said, "you can't get married without Charlie."

Laura banged the percolator onto the stove. "He knows when the wedding is," she said.

There's something wrong with me, Kate thought. Amiss,

askew. She had the wrong thoughts, wanted the wrong things. A cuckoo in the nest, an ugly duckling. What had made her like this? Every time she tried to think about it, a fog rose up. It was like at the end of a movie when darkness closes in from the edges of the screen until the kiss of the reunited lovers, or the iron bars of the jail cell where the criminal is imprisoned, or the endless field of long grass waving is blacked out.

Marriage, of course, had always been their mother's ambition for her girls. For Charlie, too, but not in the same way. But anyone could see what happened when you married: life became a thicket of china patterns and babies. Kate wanted—desperately—to go to college.

Her mother, ladling soup into bowls at this very table, had said: "It's a waste of money."

"Waste?" Kate had repeated. "A waste?" All those years of learning: to just stop, *that* would be the waste! It was as though you brought a child up to the age of five and then, just when it had learned to dress itself, you smothered it.

"People go to school until they finish," her mother said. "Then they're done."

"I'm not done," Kate said. "I'm not finished."

"Bring these bowls to the table, please."

Kate flounced to the stove.

"Use a cloth," her mother warned. "They're hot."

But Kate carried the bowls in her naked hands.

The clock chimed six, and Laura and Charlie appeared. "What's going on?" Laura asked, looking back and forth between her mother and sister.

"If you don't let me go, I'll die!" Kate said. Her heart would seize up like a poorly maintained engine and give out.

"College is not for women!" Her mother was shouting now, although before their father died, she had prided herself on never shouting. "Women who go to college end up as marginal people! What would you be fit for then?"

Kate stared at her mother, who would rather her daughter die than become a marginal person. A person people like herself wouldn't want to know.

"Honestly, Mother," Laura said. "I don't see how Kate can get any odder than she already is. Thomas says he doesn't know how the two of us can have come from the same womb."

"Sit down!" their mother said. "Eat your soup. Charlie, take some butter for your bread." But Charlie, though physically sitting on his chair, his curls untidy and his old shirt frayed at the cuffs though there were perfectly good shirts neatly folded in his bureau drawer, had absented himself in every way that mattered. Mrs. Croft turned back to Kate. "I don't know why you want to torture me!" she said.

"I don't!" Kate cried. "I just—"

"Spoiled!" her mother interrupted. "We spoiled you, your father and I! All of you children. Telling ourselves spanking was barbaric. Telling ourselves a child's individuality ought to be cultivated." It was true; they had done that.

"No," Laura soothed. "No, Mama. You were wonderful parents."

"Please let me go," Kate begged.

"Why not let her?" Laura said. "Otherwise she'll be living here forever!"

"Nonsense," their mother said. "Kate has many talents. And she's not unattractive. There are plenty of men who might . . ."

Kate could not speak. She felt flayed, boiled. Her flesh clung to her like a cloak of maggots. She wished she could burn away to nothing—blow away to nowhere. Better still, to *be* the fire, to *be* the wind! Sunlight, hurricane, earthquake. Pure thought. "Father would have let me go!"

"If your father were here right now, you wouldn't dare speak to me that way!" her mother shouted.

"I wouldn't have to, because he would take my side!"

But in fact, she didn't know if he would have or not. She might have the gift of patience; she might see clearly. But she was still a girl.

"Ungrateful!" their mother raged. "Even when you were a baby, you were like that. Screaming when anyone picked you up! Turning your head when I tried to feed you! Refusing to sleep!"

"I was a *baby*!" Kate cried. "You can't hold that against me!"

Her mother picked Kate's spoon out of her bowl and flung it across the kitchen. Soup sprayed onto the floor and up the clean white walls. "When your husband is killed in a war he had no business in, you can talk to me about what's fair," she said.

That summer, with high school behind her and the empty future stretching out to the horizon, Kate began to have trouble sleeping. At night she lay like a stone listening to the old house creak and sigh, feeling the air settling over her like a shroud. One morning, the air in her bedroom was so thick it was impossible to get up. Outside the door, footsteps pattered, doors banged, people called up and down the stairs. A while later, someone began playing a Chopin mazurka on the piano. Every note jangled her brain, and she pulled herself under the covers like a turtle. She hugged her knees and rocked, a hard bundle of darkness in the darkness.

Sometime later, the door banged open and her mother, coming in with a duster and seeing a body in the bed, shrieked, then recovered herself and threw the covers back. "What's wrong with you, Kathleen? Are you sick?"

"I'm tired," Kate said scratchily, tugging the sheet back

up. "I didn't sleep well."

Her mother's cold hand clapped down on her clammy brow. "You're pale as a ghost." No need to say out loud what she was thinking: *If only your father were here.*

"I'm fine. I just need to sleep."

But she could not sleep. For a day and a night she lay staring at the inside of her eyelids, wide awake.

On the third day, her mother called Dr. Lawrence, who had been a friend and colleague of Kate's father. He came to the house and examined her, taking her pulse and listening to her heart, frowning thoughtfully. "She's all right, Abby," he said to Mrs. Croft, standing just outside the door where Kate could hear every word. He prescribed licorice powder and a boiled diet. "It sometimes happens to girls at this age. Perhaps there's a young man involved."

"A young man!" Mrs. Croft scoffed. "This one won't give the time of day to young men. *She* wants to go to college, *she* says!"

"College?" The doctor and her mother were moving away down the hall, their voices growing fainter.

Kate could hear the stairs groan, the high, distraught timbre of her mother's voice, but she could not make out the words. Then nothing: just the frantic whirring of the cicadas in the trees outside her window, and a car passing by on the avenue, and the distant rhythmic chanting of a jump-rope song.

Sometime later, her mother banged back into the room. "I've written to Cornell University," she said. "You can enroll in the agricultural school for nothing. But don't go blaming me if it doesn't work out!"

Kate stared up at her mother. Her hair was streaked with white like a badger's fur, and her skin was gray. A button on her black dress hung by a thread. "When do I leave?" Kate said.

*   *   *

The morning after Kate's late-night arrival, there was a family conference: Kate, Laura, their mother, and Thomas. The stated purpose was to decide what to do, though this apparently meant different things to different people. Mrs. Croft wanted to discuss how to "rescue" Charlie—how to get him home. Laura and Thomas, who understood that this was impossible, wanted to discuss logistics moving forward. Kate, who agreed with them, wanted to discuss logistics, too, but her idea of what should happen next was not at all like theirs. Kate liked Thomas well enough, but it felt wrong to have him taking part in an intimate family conversation: wrong to have him sitting on the gold brocade sofa, where Charlie should have been. Not to mention their father.

Mrs. Croft was wearing black, as she had in the early days of her widowhood. Her hair, already whiter than it had been when Kate had left last summer, was pulled severely back from her gaunt face. The bruised circles under her eyes were the size of silver dollars. She clutched Charlie's letter in her hand, smoothed it on her black bombazine lap, peered at it through her smeared pince-nez on its silver chain. "If we could find out what ship he was on, maybe I could write to the captain and tell him to send him home." She looked around at her remaining children with an eager, baffled, bruised-looking face. "Why would he do a thing like this?" she cried. "He was happy. He had friends. Everyone always loved Charlie! He was such a sweet, affectionate boy. Ladies would stop me on the street when I had him out in his carriage to tell me what a beautiful baby he was."

"You never know what people are really thinking," Thomas said soothingly. He was a tallish, nice-enough-looking young man in a well-cut suit. Sharp-eyed, with flat, slicked, brilliantined hair. Not as handsome as most of Laura's boyfriends had been, but richer. "People aren't rational, you know, never mind what Adam Smith said. In my experience, it's always an expensive mistake to think they are. The question is, what do we do now?"

In the silence that followed this statement of the obvious, the ticking of the gilded mantel clock was audible for a long time.

"You couldn't expect Charlie to stay at home forever," Laura said. "Decisions would have to have been made sooner or later."

"Decisions?" said Mrs. Croft. "What decisions?"

"The house is awfully big," Thomas said.

"Not to mention expensive to maintain," Laura said.

"The house?" their mother echoed, blinking. "This is the house where you were born."

"The best thing," Thomas said, "is to take professional advice. For example, we might consult Mr. Ewing." Mr. Ewing was the family lawyer. "I'm sure if we called him, he would come see you tomorrow."

"I need to go back to Ithaca tomorrow," Kate said. She spoke loudly in case anyone planned to try to ignore her. "I can't miss school."

"Don't be ridiculous," their mother said.

"This is important," Laura said. "Don't think you can avoid—"

"I can't fall behind," Kate interrupted. "Exams are coming up."

"But," their mother said. "Now that Charlie . . . Surely you see that everything has changed."

"No!" Kate said. "I don't see that at all!"

The bones of her mother's face seemed to burn under the putty-colored skin. "I won't pay," she said. "I won't pay for it anymore."

"You don't need to pay for it!" Kate cried. "It's free!"

"Not your housing. Not your board!"

Kate stood up from the sofa where her father used to lie on Sunday afternoons, the newspaper over his face. "You promised me," she said.

"Unnatural!" her mother cried. "Unnatural child!" In her black dress, the gauntness of her face sharpening her nose and chin, she looked more like a witch than ever. Kate could see her standing over her cauldron in the kitchen so many years ago, stirring and stirring the dark red brew.

She was halfway up the stairs when Laura caught up to her, caught her by the arm. "Mother is just upset," she said. "You know she doesn't mean it. If you'll just stay, a little while. A couple of days—a week at most! We can work something out. Maybe you can transfer to a college in the city. Thomas and I could help with the tuition."

Her sister's hand was a rubbery vise, a tentacle sucking her down. Kate yanked herself free, almost tumbling backward down the steps.

"Careful!" Laura cried. "Why do you always have to act like a wild animal!" She loomed over Kate in her good wool dress and heavy dark hair, her smell thick and yeasty under her lilac perfume.

Kate pressed herself against the balusters. The air seemed as devoid of oxygen as though all the plants on the shivering planet had withered away. She thought of the greenhouse, of the leafy coleus plants in their tranquil rows, vigorously alchemizing CO_2. "Keep your money," she said.

CHAPTER 8

At the station, Kate discovered barely enough money in her purse to buy a ticket. Her mother's monthly bank deposit, due next week, couldn't be expected now. The heat on the train was out of order. The passengers huddled in their seats as they lurched north, stamping their feet like horses, their breath hanging in clouds.

At the boardinghouse, there was a note from Thatch. It had been printed in pencil on graph paper in small letters:

Dear Kate,

Where did you go? Dr. Krause was angry that you missed lab yesterday. I can't believe you'd be foolish enough to run away just because you were mad about something that doesn't mean anything. Dr. Krause asked me what happened to you, and I said you must be sick. He said would I make sure you know that he wants to see you in his office.

You owe me for lying, because I don't think you really are sick, any more than he does.

Yours truly,

John Thatcher (Thatch)

Could Thatch really think she had skipped lab because she found out he was getting paid? The idea made her sad, and then it made her angry. She crumpled up the note and tossed it away.

In the morning, she was waiting in the hallway outside Dr. Krause's office when he arrived in his heavy overcoat and

RACHEL PASTAN

Russian fur hat, his beard dripping as the frozen conden-
sation of his breath began to thaw. "You missed lab, Miss
Croft," he said, rattling his keys. "Which, as you know, meets
only once a week."

"I'm sorry," Kate said. "There was a family emergency."

Dr. Krause unlocked the door and went stiffly in. She
followed, standing to the side while he removed his coat,
unwound his scarf, and pulled off his leather gloves, huffing
and coughing. When at last he sat down behind his desk,
she sat, too, on the edge of a well-worn Cornell insignia
chair piled with scientific journals. Dr. Krause picked up
his pipe and banged it out into a green glass ashtray. "I gave
you a position as a research assistant, Miss Croft. I did not
report you to anybody for moving into a storage room in
Roberts Hall. Do you understand that these things were
not nothing?"

"Yes," she said.

"You want me to believe you are serious, yet you do
not come to my lab, which you know is an essential part of
class. The *most* essential part!" The ends of his spittle-fleck-
ed lips sagged. "A family emergency, you say. Somebody
died?"

"No."

He waited for her to say more. When she didn't, he began again in the same monotonous, haranguing tone. "I overlooked a lot when I gave you that position," he said. "Most
people, you know, would not even have considered giving
a job like that to a girl. Do you know the reason? Because
young women don't take this work seriously! That's why." He
shook the empty pipe at her.

"I do take it seriously," Kate said. "I do." There was a liv-
erish stain on the lapel of his jacket, and his beard looked
more disheveled than she remembered.

"I could change my mind about that job," he said "There

76

are lots of other students I could give it to. Reliable students. Serious students!"

Job, he said. But you got paid for a job.

Out the window, the white campus sparkled under the snow: light, fine snow that lay like a great puffy cloud over the lawns and roofs. Narrow paths crisscrossed the campus in an intricate pattern, connecting buildings. The sky was so blue it hurt to look at it, and trees held their white-clad branches high. The world on this hill overlooking the Cayuga Valley felt clean and new and bracing. She could not bear to leave it. "It won't happen again," she said.

"John Thatcher said you were sick. Well: people do get sick. But they could send a message."

"Thatch was mistaken," she said. "I wasn't sick. I had to go home. To Brooklyn. Suddenly." *My brother*, she thought. But Charlie was none of Krause's business.

Slowly, with stiff knuckles, he began to stuff tobacco into the bowl. Kate watched him: the long fingers, the hairy backs of his hands through which age spots were visible, matching the stain on the lapel. Once the pipe was going, he seemed to relax. His eyes under his tangled eyebrows looked brighter. "He also said—John Thatcher—that you have been spending a lot of time in the greenhouse."

"Yes." She tried to say more—that she liked it there, that she cared about the work—but no words came.

"He said you are a quick study," Dr. Krause said.

"Thank you."

He looked up sharply. "*He* said! Not me. I will have to see the evidence."

"Thatch has explained to me about the experiments you're doing," Kate said with effort as puffs of brownish smoke began to straggle from the bowl. "How wonderful if you can figure out what makes the coleus leaves change color."

"If!" he echoed indignantly.

Again Kate was thrown into confusion. "I just meant if you had time, before you retire. I heard you were retiring next year."

"Retiring from teaching, yes. I've had a lifetime of students already. Two lifetimes! But research—that's a different story. Once you get the research bug, you do not recover from it so easily. The experiment taking shape in the mind. The excitement of waiting for the plants to reveal themselves. Reveal their secrets, just to you! Do you understand?"

"I think so," Kate said.

The pipe was going nicely now, the smoke feathering diagonally up toward the flaking ceiling. "Well," he said, "I will give you another chance."

"Thank you, Dr. Krause," Kate said stiffly.

"Thank John Thatcher."

"But there's one thing."

The chair creaked as he leaned back, puffing hard on his pipe, his cheeks bulging and deflating like the rubber bulb of a pipette. "Hmm?"

"I need to get paid."

"What?" Smoke rolled from his long nose in twin dragon streams.

"Thatch gets paid," she said. "John Thatcher. For the same work."

Dr. Krause banged the pipe against the desk. "Mr. Thatcher is more experienced than you, young lady."

"By a month! But I've caught up. I can do everything he can."

Dr. Krause squinted at her as though he was really looking at her for the first time. She felt cold and exposed, like a salamander when its log is lifted. She raised her chin. He wasn't the only stubborn one.

"In another month, I'll be doing it faster," she said.

Slowly, he brought his pipe back to his mouth. His lids

drooped, revealing the red-veined skin. Out the window, a crow flapped slowly across the sky, a black shape bisecting the white world.

"*You* wouldn't work for no money, would you?" Kate said.

"It's a privilege to do this work!"

Kate agreed with him—she did! But she couldn't take the words back. She needed money. If he wouldn't pay her, she'd have to get a job as a waitress, or washing dishes in the cafeteria, and she wouldn't have time for both classes and the greenhouse. She blinked furiously to stop the tears. The last thing she wanted was his pity.

Dr. Krause fumbled in his pocket for his handkerchief, and for one terrible moment Kate thought he was going to offer it to her. But he didn't. With his gaze fixed on the empty space out the window where the crow had been, he nodded, and wiped his own watery, rheumy eyes. "All right," he said.

Thatch was in the greenhouse measuring the plants with a tape measure. "Need help?" Kate said.

Thatch let the metal tape slither back into the casing. She watched his face open with pleasure, then immediately close up again. He fingered a leaf on the nearest coleus plant. "Where did you go?"

"Something suddenly came up."

"I hope it was important."

"You might hope it wasn't important!" Kate retorted.

He sighed and let go of the leaf. "You're right. I hope it wasn't important."

She walked over to the binder and picked it up. "You measure, I'll record."

"Is everything okay?" Thatch asked at last.

She looked around at the coleus in their tranquil rows,

vigorously alchemizing CO_2, and sighed. They stood together awkwardly under the bright lights, among the black coiled hoses, among the silent plants lined up as though in pews. "Shall we get started?" She turned the pages with their neat columns of carefully penciled notations. "I'd hate to waste Dr. Krause's money."

Thatch's face went scarlet. "What if I split my pay with you," he said.

Kate looked up.

"It's not fair that I get paid and you don't. We both know it's not because I got here first. I wouldn't have blamed you if you didn't come back." He was so thin in his slightly too short khaki pants and white shirt, all ribs and scrawny limbs—almost like a scarecrow except for his warm, serious eyes rimmed with dark lashes.

"Oh," she said. "That's—"

"I'd hate it if you left," he said. "I'd feel awful."

Kate felt awful. Though she didn't know why she should.

"And maybe, after a while, Dr. Krause would change his mind."

"He already did," Kate said. But Thatch wasn't listening.

"You wouldn't have to feel you owed me anything. I mean, there wouldn't be any strings or . . ." His face, which had returned to almost its normal color, flushed again. "I couldn't give you half," he said, and looked down at a small spider creeping across the concrete floor. "Because I have to—I mean, I could give you forty percent. For now, anyway. Would that . . . ?" He looked up shyly.

"He already did," Kate repeated, louder. "Krause. He changed his mind. He is going to pay me."

Thatch blinked. His eyes were hazel, a hue not addressed in the section on eye color in Castle's *Genetics*, which covered only blue and brown. "You talked to him?"

"This morning. In his office." She paused, waiting for

him to catch up. "So, you see, I don't need your money."

The spider, black and thick with short strong legs, detoured to get around a drain in the floor.

"Good!" Thatch said. "I mean, it's good he changed his mind."

Kate thought he sounded disappointed. Perhaps he had hoped there might be strings after all. But then he smiled—such a warm and generous smile that it almost made him handsome.

Kate smiled back and ducked her head. The plants around them glowed green as jade. Thatch stepped toward her. Animal heat blazed off him as he stood over her, shading out the light.

She pushed the binder toward him and moved to the nearest row. "On second thought," she said, "I'll measure."

PART TWO

1928

CHAPTER 9

"I have an idea." Kate stood in the doorway of Thatch's tiny office watching him brew coffee on the hot plate. His back in its white shirt hunched as he measured the grounds.

"What kind of idea?"

"How to see maize chromosomes clearly enough to describe them!"

Thatch lifted his head. No one had been able to see maize chromosomes that clearly. When you managed to capture them under the microscope at all, they were tangled and indistinct, like a litter of kittens in a darkened room. If you could find a way to switch on the lights and really *see* them, that would change everything. His spoon tapped against the side of the coffee pot in quick triplets, but he only asked calmly, "What does Cole say?"

Cole was Kate's graduate adviser, a youngish, literal-minded, nearsighted assistant professor working on trisomics in corn. At least, he was her adviser until she figured out how to get a better one. "I haven't told him yet." Kate waited for Thatch's frown. Thatch believed in running everything by one's adviser. But then, his was a perfectly reasonable Minnesotan named Lund who liked Thatch's ideas, when he paid attention to them. Thatch sometimes lamented Lund's lack of attention—"I wish he would actually advise me"—but Kate envied Thatch's freedom. Cole wanted to know everything she planned to do, and mostly, when she told him, he shot down her ideas. "I wanted to see what you thought first," Kate said. "Why should Cole ever even have to know about it, if I've overlooked something?"

But she knew she hadn't overlooked anything.

In one of their last meetings before his stroke, Dr. Krause had said, "You have a good brain, Miss Croft. That is a piece of luck. Make good use of it." As though her brain were separate from her: an instrument, like a violin, that she might play well or badly. In the years she worked for Krause, Kate had come to see that he was not a terribly good scientist. He had ideas—possibly even good ideas—but he got so excited about them that he raced ahead instead of proceeding by considered steps. When designing his experiments, he forgot to keep in mind the one simple thing he wanted to prove. She remembered her father's words: *You have to think things through.*

But Krause had helped her in important ways. He had opened the door.

After college, Kate and Thatch had moved more or less seamlessly into Cornell's PhD program in botany. Now they were both subjects in the maize kingdom ruled by Evelyn Whitaker, though neither of them worked for the Great Man directly. Still, they attended the lab meetings he presided over on Tuesday afternoons, and he nodded to them when he passed them in the halls, not knowing their names, probably, but recognizing them as stewards of his realm as surely as if they had worn his coat of arms on their lab coats—Thatch's always shabby-looking, Kate's laundered and neatly pressed. On first meeting them, people tended to take Kate and Thatch for a couple, but their relationship, whatever it was, wasn't that. Still, there was no one better than Thatch to toss an idea around with, or to share a pot of coffee or a bottle of whiskey. Kate had learned to appreciate Canadian Club, which Thatch got from a friend (he always had a lot of friends), and which burned down through her all the way to the pit of her stomach, clearing away the static. She had learned a lot over the past five years: how to slice a maize root cell into sections and fix each section to a slide with paraffin; how to tease a glimmer of an idea into a testable hypothesis; how to walk through a field or a greenhouse and see what had changed from the day before—to notice what was worth noticing. How to make it clear to a boy that she wasn't interested in him that way without having to come out and say it. Not that boys were falling all over her. But there was a certain kind of boy—generally a scientist or a musician—who admired her: her sharp eyes and her deft hands and her quick mind. Her blend of reticence and bluntness. It was nice to be admired. It was even nice, from time to time, after a couple of drinks, to neck in the dark on someone's sofa or on a park bench, as long as you knew you could call a halt when your body froze up. Which, so far, hers always did.

"Fine," Thatch said now. "What's your idea?"

Kate came into the cubbyhole and cleared off a space for herself on the desk which was wedged between a wobbly bookshelf and a filing cabinet that didn't close properly. But at least Thatch had an office. Kate had only a desk in Cole's lab, the scarred surface of which she cleaned every few days with a solution of sodium bicarbonate and warm water. Her papers were always filed, her books alphabetized, her microscope sheathed when not in use to keep off dust. Cole, whose papers—and, worse, his slides—were scattered everywhere, had complimented her on her "housekeeping skills" with the desultory approval of a man whose wife picks up his socks. "You might bring a little of that elbow grease over here," he had said once, watching her move the cleaning rag in careful circles. But Kate had replied, "I'd be afraid I'd make a mess of your things," and that, thankfully, had been that.

Cole's research program was struggling, and he had a wife and three small Coles at home, the youngest still in diapers. But he wasn't an ogre. He tacked his children's crayoned pictures on the wall over his desk. When he was in a good mood on Mondays, he asked Kate what she had done over the weekend. Though he had to know that mostly what she did with her weekends was work. "All work and no play," he liked to scold, possibly meaning well.

Kate had met Mrs. Cole once, when she came into the lab to bring the bagged lunch her husband had forgotten (a neighbor was watching the children, she explained), on which occasion she had looked Kate up and down with curiosity and promised to invite her for dinner. So far, thankfully, she hadn't gotten around to it. Kate dared to hope she never would.

Kate accepted a cup of Thatch's hot-plate coffee and waited until he was seated and looking up at her. With his lanky body and his big square face and his floppy hair, Thatch still looked like a farm boy. But he had won the ag school prize the year they graduated and was gaining a reputation in the botany department for the clarity of his thinking. Last year, he'd had his name on a paper of Lund's that had been published in *Genetics*, after which he had gathered his courage and traveled upstate to break it to his father that he would not be coming back to manage the cows.

"I learned about a new method in my cytogenetics course," Kate said. She explained, carefully and clearly, about Belling's technique. There were two things you had to do to make this technique work. First, you prepared a new stain, called acetocarmine, which made the chromosomes stand out vividly under the microscope, like birds against the sky. Second, you squashed the cell under a slip cover, flattening it whole rather than slicing it up like a ham. This was called the squash technique. Belling had done it with *Datura* cells— jimsonweed, with its pretty, poisonous flowers—but Kate thought it would work with corn, too. "I don't see why it wouldn't," she said.

"Are you telling me no one has tried?"

"Well, people have *tried*," Kate said. "It just needs a few adjustments. I'm fairly sure I can do it."

"Even though nobody else has been able to." Thatch laughed. But he was listening.

"So you see why I can't tell Cole yet." Again she did her best to control her voice. Even with Thatch she wanted to be careful not to seem overconfident or naïve. But her excitement bubbled up, and she could feel her face glowing. She bent her head and sipped the coffee, which was muddy and strong. Her heart was skipping impatiently. If you could count and characterize the chromosomes of corn—as had been done for fruit flies—the whole field would be busted open!

Thatch said nothing. He was thinking it over. He knew her track record for doing what she said she would do.

"If I don't do something soon," she burst out, "I'll never do anything! Cole's project is going nowhere. You know it. Everybody knows it. Even he must know it! If he would admit it, at least it might be possible to get him to do something else. It's dishonest, really, if you think about it, the way he keeps plugging pointlessly away. Not to mention a waste of resources."

What was especially galling was that Cole's project was actually promising. It involved trisomics, plants whose cells had an extra copy of one of their chromosomes, an abnormality that made them useful to study. Often, as it turned out, it was the mutants and anomalies—the organisms that flouted the usual rules—that were worthy of attention, shedding light on normal processes. But Cole's grinding, unimaginative methods weren't yielding any insights so far, nor did they seem likely ever to.

"Maybe he's just in a slow patch," Thatch said. "Maybe you can help him get through whatever the roadblock is."

"Then he'd really hate me."

"He doesn't hate you."

"He doesn't like me," Kate said.

"You mean you don't like him. Anyway, he doesn't have to like you. He just has to supervise you."

"He's supervising me, all right," Kate said. "Right out of the field." She knew Thatch didn't like it when she talked like that, but she couldn't help it. She needed to do some work that stood out. "Maybe I should take the idea to Whitaker," she said. "He'd see its value." She looked at Thatch. "Wouldn't he?"

"You can't go over Cole's head," Thatch said. "Talk to him. He's not an idiot."

"What makes you so sure?"

Thatch looked annoyed. Then, as though that wasn't enough, Jax Harrison stuck his head around the doorway. "So sure of what?" he said.

Kate glared up into Jax's pale, mobile, snub-nosed face. "We were just gossiping."

"Would you like some coffee?" Thatch asked. "There's still a bit left in the pot."

"No, thanks. I prefer mine less sludgy."

Jax was a year ahead of Kate and Thatch, already working on his dissertation project. It was said he had defied his father by refusing to take over the family empire of tree farms, paper mills, and pencil factories. He was working on male sterility—nonviable pollen—which seemed to be carried on a single gene. It was an intriguing problem, and possibly an important one, though not one on which he had yet made much progress. Still, if the maize chromosomes could be characterized, even Jackson Henry Harrison III might be able to solve it. He cracked the knuckles of his long white hands. "I have some gossip, though," he said. "I'll tell you mine if you tell me yours."

Kate and Thatch glanced at each other. Her look said

Make him go away, and Thatch's said *Be nice*.

"We weren't really gossiping," Thatch said. "Kate was just running an idea past me."

"And Thatch was telling me it was a bad one," Kate said quickly.

"I didn't say that."

"What's your gossip, Jax?" Kate said. "You're dying to tell us."

"What do you have to trade?"

"Don't be an ass," Thatch said.

Jax peered back down the hall as if someone might be listening. Then he stepped into the tiny room and shut the door. Kate inched farther back on the desk. The three of them were crowded together, close enough to touch. The room smelled of coffee and of dry rot, and of Thatch's plain soap, and of Jax's awful Gauloises cigarettes, which he claimed to have developed a taste for while wandering around France. "It's about the new student," Jax said. "The one from Kansas."

"What about him?" Kate hadn't met Paul Novak, who was transferring to Cornell to work directly with Whitaker. According to Whitaker's secretary, Miss Floris, he was reputed to be charming as well as brilliant, a rising star offered up by a friend of the Great Man's to grace the maize kingdom.

"Have you wondered why he gets to work with Whitaker while the rest of us are farmed out to junior faculty?" Jax said.

"Presumably because he's some kind of genius," Kate said.

"It turns out he's related to Whitaker somehow. His mother is Whitaker's second cousin!"

"I can't believe that's the reason," Thatch said.

"That's not even the good part," Jax said. "The good part is that he was asked to leave the University of Kansas, after which Whitaker invited him here." His foxlike face gleamed with pleasure.

"Asked to leave?" Kate said. "What for?"

Jax shrugged. "Burglarizing the petty cash? Getting a girl pregnant? Your guess is as good as mine."

"Maybe he ran over the dean's flower garden with his car," Kate suggested. "Or killed someone."

"Where did you get this so-called information?" Thatch said.

"Don't believe me if you don't want to," Jax said.

"We'll believe you if you have some proof," Kate said.

Jax pulled a rumpled packet from his pocket and tapped out a cigarette. "What kind of proof would you be looking for? A tear-stained letter from a girl pleading with him to marry her?"

"That would do," Kate said.

"Please don't smoke in here," Thatch said.

"You'll just have to believe me or not," Jax said, lighting the Gauloise.

"Open the door at least."

Jax opened the door.

Kate waited for him to leave, but he just leaned against the jamb, blowing smoke back over his shoulder. "How's your project coming along?" she asked him.

Jax's predatory face pushed forward, making him look more foxlike than ever. "I have some new data, actually," he said. "The slides are very suggestive."

Kate let her heels bang against the desk drawers. "What do you mean, *suggestive*?" she demanded. "Give me one of those."

He passed her the packet and she tapped one out, ignoring the shiny silver lighter he proffered and taking a matchbook from her trousers pocket.

"What do they suggest?" Thatch asked.

"I'm working it out," Jax said.

Kate inhaled the foul smoke. She was sure the slides

were just as uninteresting and unrevealing as Jax's slides always were. But then, you never knew. Maybe he was actually onto something, while she languished in the wasteland of Cole's dubious ideas. "Let me know if you want me to look at them," she said. She was getting a reputation not just for focusing the microscope but for seeing what was of interest on the slide.

"I can analyze my own data, thank you," Jax said.

"If you say so," Kate said. "But, anyway, let me know."

CHAPTER 10

In the early morning, as every early morning in the growing season, Kate walked out to the field to see the plants. This was the best part of the day: the body moving, the mind fresh and sharp as a wave, taking everything in. She noted daily growth as well as any changes or irregularities, checking for damage from insects or animals or the wind, grateful when there wasn't any. The crows rasped shrilly in the oaks, calling back and forth across the treetops. They would alert one another when the ears were ripe. People tried foiling them with scarecrows, with tin cans, with ten-year-old boys armed with stones. The men even unbuttoned their flies to water the plants when they thought she couldn't see. What sometimes worked was to get a dead crow, shot by some farmer, and leave it lying bloody on the ground. The birds got the message. She wouldn't have minded sitting out in the field with a shotgun. Corn plants were living things just as much as birds were.

It had thunderstormed in the night, but the rain (three-quarters of an inch according to the gauge on her windowsill) had stopped before dawn. The warm damp air buzzed with gnats and damselflies and a few black wasps. The ground was a lacework of puddles and mud, and the sun, trying to burn through the banked clouds, was a coin of brightness in a vast pale sky. Kate moved slowly down the rows. Drops of water clung to the plants, which were as tall as she was. Water gleamed on the long swords of the leaves, and on the thick strong stalks, and the tight sheaths of the ear shoots, inside which the cobs were developing. A wooden stake at the base of each plant identified its series and parentage, but Kate didn't need the labels to know which plant was which. Each one was a little different from any other—thicker leaves or thinner, the color deeper or paler, more or fewer side tillers branching off the main stalk.

Now, pausing partway down the row, she examined a tall plant that held its broad leaves high. She grasped the shoot, trying to judge the state of the ear inside, then ran her hand up along the shaft of the highest furled leaf, testing the tip where the tassel would soon burst through. Then it would be time to fertilize, and the whole department would be out in the fields, working frantically—even Victor, the janitor, a widower with a teenaged son in and out of trouble, as Kate knew from talking to him late at night when everyone else had gone home.

The plant's stem was tall and stiff and damp, a deep piney green in the pearly light. Kate had her knife with her to take root cuttings on which to try the new stain. On a sudden impulse, she made a neat slit high up on the stem where the pollen was developing. As she sliced out a sliver of tissue, a few drops of liquid welled up. Under the green, inside each bright grain, a universe hummed. Overhead, the pollen-yellow sun burned a patch of blue in the watery sky. Who said the root tip was the best place to look? Just because they'd been taught to do it that way.

A few years back, before she got to his lab, Hiram Cole had tried to solve the problem of characterizing maize chromosomes. He hadn't made much progress, though. Eventually he'd shelved the idea and moved on to trisomics, the problem he was struggling with now. It wasn't impossible he'd be open to picking the old work back up. Kate was at her lab bench, and Cole was bent over his microscope on the other side of the room, when she blurted out, "This would all be so much easier if we could tell which chromosome was which."

Cole grunted. He stood up and stretched, rubbed his hands over his face, then hunched back over and reaffixed his eye to the eyepiece, fiddling with the focus knob.

"Really!" Kate said. "We should sort out the chromosomes first. It's an interesting problem. Then we could come back to trisomics afterward."

"It's a hopeless tangle," Cole said. "Like trying to identify leeches in mud."

Now was when she should tell him her new idea. Or would it be better to wait until he was in a better mood? The way things had been going lately, that might be never.

It was true that chromosomes were famously elusive. Most of the time they were invisible, and you couldn't see them at all. Sometimes, though, they materialized out of the depths of a cell's nucleus, wriggling like snakes. What was the secret of their appearances and disappearances? No one knew. Twenty years earlier, working with sea urchins, Theodor Boveri had shown that the chromosomes carried the genetic material, and by now the general choreography of cell division was well understood. Still, much remained unexplained. No matter how many sections she made, or how carefully she prepared them—no matter how precisely she focused the microscope— the maize chromosomes she studied remained indistinct and confused. Leeches in mud, as Cole said—though with real leeches you could wade into the mud and pull them out, pin them to a board, and dissect them.

She stared at her supervisor's hunched back and his thick head of hair. More hair curled at the collar of the lab coat, which had been overstarched by Mrs. Cole. "Dr. Cole?" she said.

"What?" He had abandoned the microscope now and was pawing through a pile of reprints like an angry bear in a garbage heap. "What?" he repeated, turning toward her, his eyes dark under his blunt black brows. "Go ahead."

"It's nothing." Kate turned away so she didn't have to see his face. There had been a teacher in her primary school, Mrs. Donnelly, whom Kate hadn't been able to bear looking at either. A horrible ugly woman: ugly in her soul. Every morning Kate had cried and kicked and refused to get off the floor and go to school. After going to talk to the teacher, Kate's mother had let her stay home for the entire winter. "As long as you keep out of my hair," she'd warned. Kate never knew what had happened between the two women. She never asked, and her mother certainly hadn't told her. What had she picked up, at eight, that she'd had no name for? Stupidity, callousness, cruelty? Some teachers rapped children's knuckles back then, but it wasn't that. All that winter, when she should have been in school, she had walked three miles to the frozen pond by herself to skate. She knew the way through the woods and fields from walking with her father. She could still remember the texture of the bark of certain trees and the friendly creaking of the branches around her.

Kate knew she should be grateful to her mother for intervening for her that way. She *was* grateful. Her mother hadn't been as terrible a mother as Kate sometimes let herself believe. She was a smart woman, a stubborn woman. It wasn't her fault Kate had been difficult, had loved her father more. Not her fault her husband had died too young.

And what about Charlie running away? Had their mother made life at home unbearable for him, once his sisters were grown? Kate tried not to ask herself that.

Charlie was different when he came back from the Merchant Marine. Quieter, moodier. His long curls were gone, his hairline ebbing. He found work as a longshoreman on the wharves in Brooklyn, hardly the career their mother had imagined for him. Like Kate, he was unmarried. Only Laura had turned out anything like what their mother wanted.

Laura wrote to Kate sometimes: neat, bossy letters on creamy stationery. She harangued Kate about writing back, about coming to visit. She boasted about her boys, who seemed always to be losing teeth, getting As on geography tests, and performing in piano recitals. She wrote, "Mother's getting old, you know. How hard would it be to come and see her?"

Kate always read Laura's letters, often more than once. But she could seldom bring herself to answer them. She would roll a piece of paper into the typewriter and stare at the blankness, exhausted by the effort of thinking of something to say.

Kate lived by herself in a small upstairs flat on a quiet street. Just a room, really, with a sort of kitchen in one corner. Good enough for heating soup, as she was doing tonight: crumbling crackers on top, eating with one hand and scribbling notes with the other.

A hopeless tangle.

Leeches in mud.

Cole would be home now, snug in his little white house with its neat peaked roof and window boxes (so she imagined, never having seen it), eating creamed chicken and canned peas. Little Cole Number One would be spilling a glass of milk and blaming Little Cole Number Two, and Mrs. Cole would be wiping Baby Cole's chin, and the dog would have gotten into the garbage again. Now *that* was a tangle! Snarled, intractable, and dull.

The maize chromosomes, on the other hand, were an intriguing puzzle. She pictured them in her mind's eye, dark elongated blobs on the slide in her neat paraffin sections, the nuclei frozen at the metaphase stage of meiosis. Tracing the intricacies of cell division on microscope slides was like trying to re-create *Swan Lake* from a few scattered photographs. You missed most of it.

Still, Kate had looked at so many slides over the years—hundreds, maybe thousands! Each time she bent to the eyepiece, she took in a new instant of the ballet. Now the dancer's arms were level with her chin; now her head tilted upward toward her partner; now her hand opened like a flower. Each image, each instant, lodged in Kate's mind, precise and fixed. Each one found its place in the sequence. Sitting at her small table on one of her two mismatched chairs, the soup finished, cracker crumbs scattered across the pressed tablecloth, Kate could almost see the corps of dancers swaying, moving together and then pulling apart: the thick, stubby leeches stirring sluggishly in the mud.

Made from cells taken from the root tips of a growing plant, paraffin sections were the standard in the field. But—precisely because they *were* sections—each image was only partial: not a snapshot of the whole but just a piece of it. You couldn't even really know which piece you were looking at: the dancers' torsos? Their feet? How much better if you could see the entire stage at once! That wholeness was what the squash technique promised.

The next morning, Cole got into the lab late. Anyone could see the mood he was in from the way he nearly knocked over the coatrack when he hung his jacket up. Kate knew better than to ask what the matter was. Anyway, she didn't care. When she had the lab to herself, she could sink into the work undisturbed, and she could keep the window open, which made Cole sneeze. He had a pollen allergy: unfortunate in a maize man. When he worked in the field, he had to wrap a handkerchief around his face. Of course, this morning, by the time he blustered in, she had forgotten about the window, which he slammed shut, making the distillate in her beaker jump. "How many times have I asked you?" he said.

Well, he'd never asked her, actually. He'd only said, the

first time she'd gone to open it, *That stays closed*.

"Sorry," she said. "It seemed like you weren't coming in."

Cole grabbed a lab coat and jammed his arms into it.

Kate waited until he'd had a chance to settle down, but not so long that he'd got too involved in what he was doing. Then she said, "I had an idea about a new way to try and see the chromosomes more clearly. I've been reading up on Belling's technique. What he does is—"

"I told you we're not going to do that." His eyes were inflamed—she really shouldn't have opened the window—and he had an ink stain on his right lab coat pocket.

"What you actually said was that it was a hopeless tangle, so we should leave it for later. But it seems to me that with one or two modifications—"

"It's not a question of modifications. It's a question of priorities! Our priority is the trisomics problem, which is more than enough to keep us busy. I'm hoping we can get a paper by the end of the year, but at this rate it's hardly a sure thing." Then he took a breath and said in a calmer tone, "I'm not saying characterizing the chromosomes isn't important. But I worked on it for two years without much to show for the time. However, I don't consider the project abandoned. Once we get this paper submitted, we can discuss moving forward, if you like."

Discuss. The word hissed in her ears with its wary qualification. *Hoping, once, if*. The obfuscating double negative of *not saying it isn't*. She tried to look up at her supervisor, but her eyes could only see as far as the forefinger he was holding up, the black hair sprouting from the knobby knuckle.

It was true that Cole badly needed this paper: it had been two years since he had published anything. If he didn't want to be a junior person forever, he'd have to do better than that. Still, she said, "I don't see it taking a lot of time. And if we *could* solve it, the trisomics would really go very quickly. Very possibly it could end up saving time."

Cole pressed a hand to his red-veined eyes and did not reply.

"I'm going out for a cigarette," Kate said.

She stalked down the empty hall. There was nothing much wrong with Cole's plan, except that it was slow and unimaginative. He had been trained to do things a certain way, and that was the way he would do them until he died. He was like those middle-aged matrons you saw still wearing the fashions of 1900. Her mother, for instance.

She didn't really feel like smoking. Thatch wasn't in his office, and he wasn't in the big airy lab he shared with Lund and Lund's other students. Kate wandered back the other way, peering into doorways, watching her fellow maize subjects making slides or looking at slides or recording data gleaned from slides, or else compiling and reviewing that data. Everyone was busy, moving purposefully, some with their heads held at a slight angle as though to catch their data from a new vantage point, unawares. Men, every last one of them. Adam's apples, brash voices, shadows of beards by the end of the day. It was all right, it didn't matter. But sometimes it exhausted her.

Jax was in his lab, humming as he peered into his microscope. His hair was slick, carefully parted, and combed back into shiny perfect spines, making him look like a complacent porcupine. If he put as much care into his science as he did into his hair, things would be better all around. "Jax," she said.

Jax looked up as though he had been hoping for a distraction. "Hello, Kate."

"How's that suggestive data coming?"

"Good," he said. "Not too bad." He rolled one shoulder, then the other, then the first again.

She came into the room and nodded toward the microscope. "Let me see."

"This isn't the best preparation," he said. "The ones I was looking at yesterday were better."

"Let me see anyway." Kate bent over the scope, her fingers reaching for the knobs. The barest pressure of her thumb and suddenly the slide opened into clarity. Kate let out her breath slowly. Yes, there they were, the chromosomes: fat and stubby at this stage like garden slugs. There, too—just emerged from the murk—were the filaments of the spindle that would guide them toward the opposite ends of the cell, after which the cell would divide.

But something was wrong. The snapshot of cell division laid out under the microscope, busy as a train station, didn't look right. "They're not paired up," Kate cried, suddenly making sense of what she saw. "Lots of the chromosomes. They're just, single!"

"Of course they're paired up. Let me look."

Kate peered harder, taking it all in. Some of the chromosomes were partnered, the way they were supposed to be. Others, though, while they might be more or less in the vicinity of another chromosome, were too far off, so that the duos were more like strangers sharing a park bench than like couples promenading. "They're univalent," she said. She raised her head and stared at Jax, whose nostrils were twitching. "Univalent! How can they possibly make viable gametes if they don't pair up?"

Jax stepped forward and put his eye to the scope.

"See?" Kate said. "Those ones at the top are fine. But the ones toward the bottom are all floating free. Unattached!" Suddenly she was furious. How lucky Jax was to have a slide like that! And he didn't even know it. He didn't even know what it was. If she hadn't come along . . . She stared into his oily dark hair, so shiny she could see herself reflected in it: a distorted shimmer. "Do you see?" she demanded.

"I knew it was interesting," he said. His hand reached

absently toward the focus knob.

"Don't touch that!" she said.

He dropped his arm; he knew she was right.

"If I hadn't come along," she said, "you'd have tossed this slide, I bet!"

"Of course I wouldn't have!"

"You didn't even see what you were seeing."

"If they're univalent, they can't possibly make viable gametes," Jax said slowly to himself. She could see him beginning to forget, as much as he could manage to, that she was even there.

CHAPTER 11

That evening, Kate stayed in the lab long after Cole had gone home. She finished up the table she was making and filed it away. Then, safely alone in the quiet room with the door shut, she took out her notes on Belling's squash technique and the carmine stain. Whatever she did after hours was her own business, just as it was Cole's business whatever he was doing now: carving a roast, or dozing in an armchair, or making more little Coles. She fired up the Bunsen burner and began on the preliminary acetic acid solution. When it was ready, she added the carmine, one drop at a time, watching the color bloom in the beaker as she stirred with the glass rod. While it cooled, she went to work on the ferric oxide. It was a fiddly business. She had to start over twice. But except for the waste of materials, she didn't mind. Time glided past unmarked as breathing, the minute hand sweeping the clock face clean, the spinning earth sailing through space. Kate's mind was on the work: the heat, the flask, the pipette, the solution. The stain, when it was done, would be the rich red of a king's robe. Everything humans were—everything in the universe—was constructed from simple chemicals, which, it was believed, had been forged inside stars. You had to concentrate to hold on to a truth like that. You had to stretch your mind wide open to let it in.

In the morning, once again, Cole was late. Maybe he had another meeting. Maybe he was sick. Maybe the hay fever had laid him low. Sometimes he sent a message when he wasn't coming in, but other times he just failed to appear.

For an hour Kate worked on the trisomics project, speeding through the new slides, each of which told her nothing: Nothing. Nothing. Nothing. Nothing. She noted the details of the nothing in her log. When she finished this, Cole still hadn't shown up. It was nearly eleven.

She had intended to wait till evening, after he went home, to try the new stain, but she couldn't see the point of that now. She got out the right notebook and settled in. The sun streamed through the windows, making shafts in the air like bars of gold, through which she walked back and forth fetching things from the shelves and cabinets. At her bench, steady-handed, she tapped the cover slip gently with the needle end of a probe.

Suddenly, loud footsteps and the door was flung open. Cole barreled in, his head thrust forward and his shoulders hunched. He didn't say a word to her, didn't even glance her way. He jammed his arms into his lab coat, went to his bench, and began looking through his slides, picking them up and screwing them to the microscope stage so violently she was sure he would break something.

Kate tried her best to be invisible, moving silently, keeping her head bowed. If he asked her what she was doing . . .

But maybe he wouldn't ask. Sometimes they didn't speak for entire afternoons! As long as their silence lasted, it was as though they did not exist for each other: as though each of them was alone, which was, she was sure, how they both wanted it. Her heart was beating fast as she screwed the first slide to the stage, but it wasn't because she was afraid of being caught. It was the excitement of what she might see.

She lowered her face to the eyepiece.

And there they were. Long dark threads—the chromosomes! So clear. Her body seemed to melt away. It was as though she disappeared inside the microscope and stood among them as they unspooled like a nest of caterpillars someone had spilled out onto the grass. She looked and looked, as hard as she could.

Each chromosome was squeezed in at the middle, as though it was wearing a belt. But the indentation was not exactly in the same place on the different chromosomes, any more than a belt was worn in exactly the same place by different people.

One chromosome had a dark knob toward the top: a bulge like a mouse makes in the snake that has swallowed it.

Like snakes, too—or like people—the chromosomes were all slightly different lengths. If only you could stretch them out, line them up like children waiting at the classroom door to be dismissed! Kate traced each one with her eye, memorizing it, so that later she could line them all up in her mind. If she could see just a little more clearly . . .

Cole cleared his throat. He slammed shut a drawer. He sighed loudly and rattled his glassware. Kate was counting: one, two, three, four, five . . .

"Miss Croft!" Cole barked.

Kate's head jerked up. "What?" It was always hard, moving from one world to another. A rending of something.

"I said, we're nearly out of acetic acid."

"Oh! I can order some more. In the meantime we can borrow—"

"Haven't I asked you to be frugal with the reagents? Do you have any idea how much it costs to run a lab like this?"

She did know, actually. She had seen the budget when he'd left it lying around. She knew, too, that her labor came cheaper than Thatch's or Jax's—or than that of any of the male graduate students. "I'm sorry," she said, and bowed her head to conceal her blazing joy.

The sun had moved around the building and the overhead lights were on by the time Thatch loped into the lab with the cheerful air of a dog with its ears pricked up. He had another young man with him, tall and serious-looking with a square, solid face and square, solid farmer's hands. Well, they were all farmers here, even Whitaker. Even Jax, who had grown up on Beacon Hill and gone to Dartmouth.

"This is Paul Novak," Thatch said. "Paul, this is Dr. Hiram Cole. He's trying to nail down some tricky maize trisomics. This is Kate Croft, a year ahead of you in terms of seniority, probably light-years ahead in terms of raw brain power."

"Pshaw," Kate said.

"I understand you're going to be working directly with Professor Whitaker," Cole said. There was something in his voice as he pronounced the Great Man's name: a chilly bile Kate hadn't heard before.

"Yes," the new student drawled, yawning and looking around the room. "Trisomics, eh?"

Cole, blinking like a rabbit in his overstarched lab coat, began laboriously explaining the project, while the tall young man rocked back and forth on his heels.

After a few minutes, taking advantage of a pause, Thatch broke in, "By the way, Cole, congratulations!"

Cole looked blank. "What for?"

"I hear you and Mrs. Cole are expecting another baby." Thatch grasped the older man's hand and shook it.

"What a surprise!" Kate said. Well, no wonder he'd been out of sorts! "All my best wishes to you and Mrs. Cole."

"Thanks, thanks." Cole looked past Thatch's head in the direction of the door. In another minute, he found an excuse to exit through it.

"My goodness," Kate said when he was gone. "The last one is barely walking."

"I guess he's a quick worker," Paul remarked.

"Not in every way," Kate said.

"Poor Cole," Thatch said. "He's not so bad. Just a little plodding. Whitaker shouldn't have assigned you to him. Just being in the same room with you saps his energy. Anyone can see that."

"Is that right?" Paul asked.

"I told you, Kate's a phenomenon," Thatch said.

"Have you asked Whitaker to reassign you?" Paul was wandering around the room, peering at things.

"Asked *Whitaker*?" Kate said.

"Maybe he would." Paul yawned again. "If you asked him."

"You're in a position of influence," Kate said. "Maybe you'd ask for me." She wondered if it was true that he and the Great Man were related.

Paul was picking up Cole's slides, holding them up to the window and squinting at them. He managed to look both alert and bored, as though he were searching without much hope for something worth his attention. If he really had gotten a girl pregnant, Kate thought, he certainly wouldn't have married her. "How did you know about the baby?" she asked Thatch.

"I was passing by Whitaker's office and Cole came out. Looking not very happy. And Whitaker said, *Congratulations on the new little F1 anyway!*" That was a joke: F1 was the term for the first generation of a genetic cross. "My guess, and this is informed by a conversation with Miss Floris—that's Whitaker's secretary, Novak, she likes chocolates, in case you ever need anything—is that Cole went to see Whitaker to ask about some sort of promotion now that he's going to have another mouth to feed."

"I guess Whitaker couldn't help him out," Kate said.

"Couldn't, or wouldn't."

Now Paul was standing by Kate's microscope which still held the slide with the carmine-stained chromosomes. "Do you mind?" he asked.

"It's not—" Kate began. "I don't . . ." But she wanted him to see! She wanted everyone to see. Besides, she was sure he wouldn't have any idea what he was looking at.

Bending over the scope, Paul's loose-limbed body grew taut. "This is maize?"

"Yes."

He raised his head and looked at her differently: a charged, hard, calculating look. "I've never seen maize chromosomes so clearly. What did you do?"

"It's called the squash technique," she said. "The stain uses carmine and ferric oxide. But really I'd like to get them clearer than this."

"So you got Cole to agree?" Thatch asked.

For a moment Kate had forgotten all about Thatch. But there he was, watching her steadily. She knew he knew she hadn't asked Cole.

Paul began to pepper Kate with questions about her preparation. "Cole must be beside himself," he said.

"Oh," Kate said, feeling her cheeks pinkening. "There's no need to mention this to him. I'm still working out the details."

"So you didn't talk to him," Thatch said.

"I will," Kate said. "Obviously."

Paul's hard eyes glinted. "A little private project on the side?" he said.

"Dr. Cole wants to just concentrate on the trisomics for now," Kate said primly.

"Then he's a fool," Paul said. "I wouldn't be surprised if you could see those well enough to characterize them."

She felt as though it were she who was splayed out under the microscope, his eye boring down. "Let's not get ahead of ourselves," she said.

Thatch walked over and put his eye where Paul's had been. Paul's sudden lazy, self-amused smile made Kate wonder how she could have thought he looked like a farmer. "So your advisor thinks you're working on trisomics, but really you're secretly characterizing chromosomes?"

Kate lifted her chin. "I'm working on trisomics," she said. "Almost all the time."

Paul laughed. Then he said, almost casually, "I'm working on triploids." Triploids were like trisomics, except that, instead of just one extra chromosome, they had a whole extra set. He began to tell her about his project, which was quite interesting, and not so different from Cole's—which, she knew, might be a problem. But she couldn't worry about that. All the time he was talking she was aware of Thatch bent over the microscope, his eyes on her slide. At last she couldn't stand it anymore.

"What do you think, Thatch?" she asked. "They're clear, aren't they?"

"Very clear." Slowly he straightened his long back. His face was clouded. "Cole's not going to be happy that you did this without talking to him."

"He's never happy," Kate said.

"I see I've walked right into a blackmail opportunity," Paul said cheerfully. And then, when Kate's head whirled around, he added, "Kidding. Of course. But, Miss Croft, maybe you'll let me bend your ear about triploids sometime."

"Kate," she said.

"Kate," Paul said.

She could feel Thatch's exhale, like a quiet snort.

"I'd hate to waste my time basically duplicating what Dr. Cole is doing," Paul said.

"I wouldn't worry about that," Kate said. "He's hardly making any progress. He'd do better if he listened to me, but so far he hasn't, much."

"Kate," Thatch said.

"It's only the truth," Kate said.

"For my own sake," Paul said, "I guess I should hope he keeps on not listening."

CHAPTER 12

At the Tuesday lab meeting, people took turns reporting on the progress of their work. Today Jax stood at the foot of the long conference table. The overhead projector beside him sent out waves of heat. It was July, and the thermometer on the lab windowsill had read ninety-six at noon. A big fan on a steel pole rumbled in the corner, the tepid breeze rattling everyone's papers. All around the table, the men in their khaki pants and white or blue shirts with the sleeves rolled up sweated, wiping their foreheads with their handkerchiefs. Thatch appeared to be listening closely, and probably he was. He had the gift of being interested in everything, and he seemed to have room for everything in his clear, capacious mind. Paul, sitting beside him, was frowning over a scratch pad on which he seemed to be doodling. Cole seemed lost in his own thoughts, his head tilted up toward a corner of the ceiling where a cobweb fluttered. Whitaker puffed on his pipe, his eyes half closed. It was not unheard of for Whitaker to fall asleep during presentations, but this did not prevent him from asking sharp, informed questions the moment the lights went up.

From the foot of the table, Jax droned on, reviewing the work that had been done up until now, the approach he and his adviser had at first pursued, and their initial lack of success with that approach. "But finally," he said, "I had a breakthrough."

Kate sat up straighter, staring at Jax, whose haughty face stretched into an expression of nonchalance as he slid a new transparency onto the glass.

"Diakinesis," he said, "turns out be the crucial stage. As

you can see from this sketch, the chromosomes are not pairing up as we would expect." He looked up at the screen, admiring his own drawing.

Sweat stood out on Kate's face, dripping into her stinging eyes. She stared at Jax's sketch, which was like the slide she had seen under his microscope, only exaggerated, the unpaired chromosomes slightly farther apart.

"They are univalent, as you can clearly see," he said. "As such, they are unlikely to pair up and make viable gametes."

Everyone was paying attention now. Paul was frowning thoughtfully and drumming the eraser end of his pencil on his scratch pad. Cole stared furiously at the screen and mopped his brow. Whitaker was nodding, the smoke from his pipe jogging up and down, making a new pattern—a pattern of approval—as Kate waited for Jax to tell the room that *she* had looked at the slide, that *she* had told him what was there. To look at her, to nod in her direction, to say her name.

Carelessly, Jax surveyed the room, savoring his triumph even as his face wore a studied waxy blandness. As his eyes swept past hers, Kate thought she saw a glimmer, like a shard of hate, flare out. He switched to the next transparency.

After the meeting, as the men stood around chatting, Kate took hold of Thatch's sleeve and pulled him out of the conference room. She led him down the hall and into his office and shut the door. The room was stifling. Thatch leaned against the wall and gestured to her to take the chair, but she was too angry to sit. "*I'm* the one who saw that the chromosomes weren't pairing up!" she said. "*I'm* the one who showed Jax. It was right there on the slide, but he didn't see it."

Thatch blinked several times, quickly, as he often did when he heard something he couldn't square with his view of the world. As if clearing his vision would resolve the problem, wash the unpleasantness away. The ends of his lips twitched down and then up again. She knew he wanted to shake his head and tell her she must be mistaken. Instead he said, "Start at the beginning, please."

The short history came out in a series of terse, orderly sentences, which she offered up like sticks of dry firewood, waiting for him to strike the match. Instead, he stood for a long time, his shirt very white against the dark paneling of the walls.

"That's not right," he said at last.

Kate raised her palms in a quick, sharp gesture. "You mean it's wrong," she said.

He nodded slowly. "It's wrong."

"I should have said something," she said. "I should have stood up during the questions and said, *Isn't that sketch based on the slide I looked at and told you that the chromosomes on it were univalent?*" Sweat bloomed under her arms and slid down her sides. She wanted to walk up and down, to burn off some of the rage, but there wasn't any room in here. "I'm going to talk to Whitaker," she said. "I'm going to tell him what Jax did."

"You can't do that," Thatch said.

"I can't *not* do it!" Unable to bear the heat of the room another a moment, she opened the door and stood half in and half out of the room, fanning herself with her hand.

"You just do your work," Thatch said sternly. "Kate, are you listening? The trisomics project. You help Cole finish the trisomics project, and you make sure it's as good as it can be. And then you can talk to Whitaker about working with someone else."

Kate stared at him. "But it's not right!" she said. "You said so yourself."

"You can't win this fight," Thatch said.

"How do I know if I can or not if I don't try?"

"Kate," Thatch said, more gently now. "You're a marvelous scientist. That's what matters. If you go snitching to Whitaker—"

"Snitching!"

"That's not the right word," Thatch said. "That's not what I meant."

"What did you mean, then?"

Thatch took a moment, getting his thoughts in order. She could see him calculating which arguments would have the best chance.

"Do you think Whitaker will believe you?"

She just stared at him.

"Where's your evidence?" Thatch said.

"It's the truth!" Kate said. "You know it is."

Thatch considered her as though she were an experiment that might have a flaw in its design. Then his eyes went up over her head. He said in a different voice, "Hello, Novak."

Kate turned and saw Paul standing behind her, smiling his lazy inscrutable smile. It was impossible to know how much of their conversation he had heard. "Do I smell coffee?" he said.

Kate slipped past him into the hall. She stalked back to her lab, her mind humming with fury—at Thatch now as well as Jax. She had thought he'd understand, but that had been a mistake. He couldn't, any more than a hedgehog could understand a bee. She stood outside the door of her lab for a moment, composing herself, and then she went in.

In the lab, Cole stood over Kate's desk, looking through a stack of papers, his hands all over her neat graphs and tables. "I need you to compile all the data from the last two seasons as quickly as possible." His face was damp and red, and the bags under his eyes were like dark mirrors, reflecting her own dark mood back to her.

"Why?" she asked.

"Didn't you hear Jax Harrison's presentation? Everyone is getting ahead of us! I'm not waiting. I'm writing this paper now."

"You can't." Panic flapped inside her. "The data aren't good enough. We need to wait till the end of the season at least. Or maybe—"

But he wasn't listening. "Did you hear what I said?" His shrill voice ground against her, and the redness seemed to leak out of his sweating face and slide all over the room. "By the end of the week."

Kate nodded.

But he was looking at the mess of papers on her desk and didn't see. "Do you understand?"

"Yes." She pulled the word up from her churning gut and pushed it out with her tongue. The heat seethed around them. If only it were winter: clean white fields of snow. Long frozen ponds, silent except for the wind and the hiss of the blade as the white-laced skate kissed the ice.

She went out into the hall again, shutting the door carefully behind her.

The light from the big windows at the end of the hallway drew her. She pressed her blazing forehead against the cool glass.

Down on the lawn, a couple was picnicking. The boy set his half-eaten sandwich down on the blanket, leaned toward the girl, and said something near her ear that made her laugh. A few yards behind him, a crow eyed the sandwich. The girl, who had two long braids tied at the ends with pink ribbons, rummaged in a paper sack. She pulled out two apples and handed one to the boy. The crow hopped nearer. It made a winged leap and seized the sandwich in its hard, curved beak. "Hey!" the boy shouted as the crow flapped upwards, carrying its prize. The girl covered her mouth with her hand.

The thief settled on a branch about twenty feet up, just opposite Kate's window. She could see the sandwich clearly: thick slices of pink fatty ham. The bird cocked its head and looked straight at her with its bright, black eye as if to say, *What do you think of that?* Then it tossed the sandwich in the

115

air, caught it again, and gulped it down.

All along the hall, the labs and offices stretched away toward the stairwell. Each dark wooden door had its pane of frosted glass, and the walls between the doors were hung with photographs taken every year at the spring picnic. So many people toiling away in the fields of the maize kingdom! So many bright minds, and also of course the dull ones. Some lucky people, and others who never had any luck at all. Why had Whitaker assigned her to work with Cole? Was it because he wanted her to fail?

If Jax had just turned and said, *Kate gave me some valuable help with this project.* Again the anger burned through her chest, lodging in her throat like a chicken bone. Probably Thatch was right that she shouldn't go to Whitaker. But she could talk to Jax about what he had done. Slowly she drifted down the hall toward his lab. She knocked on the door, first softly, then, when no one answered, louder. "Jax?" she said. She turned the knob and went in.

There was nobody in the room: not Jax, not his advisor, not the other graduate student, Bill Muller, who would be leaving at the end of the season for a job in Illinois. The Great Man was known for getting his vassals good jobs.

On Jax's bench, his microscope stood beside several small envelopes of corn kernels, each neatly labeled. She had been standing just here when Jax looked at what she had told him was there; as he had muttered to himself, *If they're univalent, they can't possibly make viable gametes*—repeating, word for word, what she had said.

Kate picked up the nearest envelope, opened the flap, and poured the dried seeds into her hand. They were mostly yellow with sprays of dark brown speckles. She felt their weight, smelled their dry milky smell. One of the great things about working with maize was that you could learn so much from the kernels. There was information in the color of the flesh and in the arrangement of the speckles or streaks or spots. Every summer maize men (as they were called) waited impatiently for harvest: that first peek at the seeds that would give you a hint what your crosses had accomplished. You couldn't do that with drosophila! Carefully, Kate slid the kernels back into their envelope and picked up another one. These seeds were deep maroon with wispy colorless stripes. *You didn't even see what you were seeing*, she had said to him. Her palm holding the dry seeds was clammy.

She knew what Thatch would say if he knew where she was. *You're lucky he wasn't there. What good did you think talking to him would do?* Sometimes she hated Thatch, with his decency and his social ease, his confidence that there was a right way to do everything.

No, that wasn't true. She didn't hate him. But she wished he understood how lucky he was.

She would have to make her own luck. She had known that for a long time.

The seeds in her hand were a lovely rich color, like garnets but warmer, the pale streaks thicker on one side and finer on the other. Every maize kernel in the world was different. She could picture almost every important kernel she had ever worked with, they sorted themselves into cubbyholes in her brain like keys behind the desk in a great hotel.

Perhaps she'd just play a little trick on Jax.

She picked up the envelope with the yellow seeds, poured them out, and slid the maroon ones in. The yellow seeds went to the envelope the maroon seeds had come out of. She imagined Jax's confusion as he looked inside, before he understood that the seeds had been switched. Probably he'd think he had made a mistake—had put the wrong kernels in the wrong envelopes himself. Well, he could stand to feel a little self-doubt. A little humility in the face of the grand enterprise to which they had pledged their lives.

CHAPTER 13

It was getting dark when Thatch stopped by to see if Kate wanted to get some dinner. "I have a lot of work," she said. "Cole is in a frenzy."

"You have to eat," Thatch said.

"I'll eat later."

"Did you have lunch?"

"I think so."

Out in the hall Paul's voice said, "Is she coming or not?"

"Are *you* going?" she asked as Paul's big tawny head appeared in the doorway.

"Thatch says it's possible to get a decent meal in this town. I'm calling his bluff."

Kate's desk was covered with paper. Her hand ached from penciling figures into tables, and the figures themselves were starting to blur. Really it was the pointlessness that was so exhausting. If she'd had some useful work to do, she could have kept it up all night. "Give me five minutes," she said.

Three abreast, they walked through the hot evening down the hill to the Cayuga Grill, where Kate had never eaten before. With its padded booths and autographed photographs of celebrities, it wasn't the sort of place she and Thatch could really afford. "Fancy," she said as the waitress brought over a basket of warm rolls and a dish of cold whorls of butter on ice. Overhead fans stirred the air, making the hems of the tablecloths flutter.

"This is where Whitaker takes visitors," Thatch said. "Miss Floris told me. I thought we could pretend we were big shots."

"Which we will be someday," Paul said, examining the

menu. "At least, I will be." That was his idea of a joke.

Kate hadn't thought she was hungry, but when her bowl of soup was gone, she borrowed a chicken leg from Thatch's plate and gnawed it clean. Paul, who had ordered sirloin steak, ate half then pushed his plate away.

"What's wrong with it?" Thatch asked.

"Nothing," Paul said.

"Isn't it cooked right?"

"It's cooked fine."

Thatch shrugged. "Maybe Kate wants it."

"No, thank you," Kate said. The thought of eating off Paul's plate made her uncomfortable. All through dinner she'd thought she felt his hard green eyes on her, but every time she looked up to meet them, he was looking somewhere else.

For dessert they ordered ice cream. Kate and Thatch had chocolate, and Paul had butter pecan.

"You put away a lot of food for such a skinny girl," Paul noted as Kate tucked into her bowl.

"That's a personal remark," she said, flushing.

"More like a scientific observation."

"Anecdotal," she said. "One data point."

Paul leaned back into the dark red leather of the booth. "I suppose we'll have to take all our meals together for a while, for the sake of the data set."

Again Kate found her cheeks burning. It was not a feeling she liked. "If your triploids aren't taking all your time," she said coldly.

"If you can fit in a side project," Paul said, "I can, too." He meant her carmine stain, and the clear, vivid chromosomes it had revealed. A thrum of longing went through her. This afternoon she'd had another idea, something that might make the slides even clearer. If she tried the stain on the material she'd taken from the pollen cells, rather than the root tips . . .

But that would have to wait. "I can't fit in anything,"

Kate said. "Cole is on a rampage. He's determined to publish this paper without waiting for this season's data." She ran her spoon around the side of her bowl to get the last sweet streaks.

"That's sudden," Paul said. "Why?"

And then they were back to Jax again. Kate looked at Thatch, but he was stirring cream into his coffee and wouldn't meet her gaze. Still, she knew what he was thinking: that she ought to keep her grievances to herself. Paul watched her steadily. The whole force of his attention was fixed on her; it was like a weight pinning her to her seat.

If she told Paul what Jax had done, might he perhaps mention it to Whitaker? She sat up straighter, wishing she didn't have to look up to look him in the eye, and began to describe how she had looked at Jax's cells, and how she had told him what he had failed to see, and how he hadn't bothered to give her any credit. All the time, at the edge of her vision, Thatch stirred his coffee. The loud clink of his spoon against the cup was the sound of his disapproval.

Paul's face, listening, was a mask: sun-brown skin, square jaw, full lips compressed with attention, straight tawny brows. When she was done, he said only, "Next time you'll keep your insights to yourself, I guess."

Her anger blazed up. "Of course I won't!"

"You've seen what happens." Paul shrugged. "People take what they can get their hands on."

"Not everyone is like Jax."

"Of course they're not," Thatch agreed.

"Lots of them are." Paul looked from one of them to the other, confident in his view.

"What Jax did was wrong," Kate said. "It was dishonest."

Paul laughed, but then he saw her face and stopped laughing. "Maybe," he said. "But it's still Jax's work. Sometimes people say things that help you along the way, things that help get you where you were going. But it's still your work."

The high booth with its gleaming leather was making Kate claustrophobic. Everything was sweating, not just her hot flesh but the water glasses, the cream pitcher, the crystal dish of butter whorls sinking into a soup of melted ice. She longed to dip her hand into that cold soup and splash her face with the water. If Paul hadn't been there, she'd have done it just to make Thatch laugh. "It's Jax's work," Kate said, "but my help was hardly trivial. If I hadn't come along and looked at his slide, he wouldn't have had a result at all. It's wrong not to acknowledge that."

"Maybe he would have seen it later that day. Or the next day."

"Maybe he wouldn't have," Thatch said.

Kate glared at him. Did he think she couldn't speak for herself?

"The point is," Paul said, "that right and wrong, the way you mean them, aren't the relevant categories here."

"What do you mean, the way she means them?" Thatch asked. "What other meaning is there?"

Paul's shoulders were broad in his striped shirt. His sleeves were rolled neatly up well past his wrists, and his forearms gleamed with golden hair in the light from the wall sconces. "We all want to solve problems," he said. "We want to get the answers right: *that* kind of right. That's what we're doing here. That's what science is."

Thatch banged his spoon down on the tablecloth. Kate could see that he was shocked. She was shocked, too—part of her was—but at the same time she saw what Paul meant. "Yes," Thatch said. "But not at any cost."

"Would you have done what Jax did?" Kate asked Paul. She really wanted to know.

Paul smiled a thin, scimitar-like smile. It seemed to cut

through the heavy air and the whir of the fans and the fog of assumptions and preconceptions Kate carried around inside her head all the time without even noticing. "I wouldn't have needed to," he said. "I would have seen it myself."

Thatch laughed.

"If I were you," Paul said to Kate, "I'd try and forget it." Which was more or less exactly what Thatch's advice had been.

"I don't want to forget it." Then, though she had meant not to mention it, she went on, "As a matter of fact, I took matters into my own hands." She began to describe the trick she had played on Jax.

As Paul listened, his eyelids drifted slowly down as though he were being hypnotized, until his eyes were just green slits. "Well, well," he said.

"To give him a little jolt!" Kate said. "To give him a surprise when he opens the envelope and finds the wrong seeds!"

"You shouldn't have done that," Thatch said. He pushed his empty cup away and his voice was low and cold.

Kate turned her head on the long stalk of her neck. "It was just a joke," she said.

"He'll write his paper all wrong," Thatch said.

"He'll figure it out in two seconds!" she cried. "He'll just think he made a mistake and put the seeds in the wrong envelopes!"

"He won't," Thatch said.

"Of course he will! He's not that much of an idiot."

"Can you identify all your seeds by looking?" Paul asked. He sounded absolutely serious.

"Of course!" She turned to him incredulously. "Can't you?" But she began to feel a hot wave of dread.

"No," Paul said. "No, I can't do that."

Kate looked from one man to the other. The rich ice cream rumbled in her stomach in uneasy combination with Thatch's chicken.

"I think you should tell him," Thatch said.

"Fine. I'll tell him," Kate said flatly.

"Tomorrow," Thatch said.

"He's going to be pretty mad, I bet," Paul said cheerfully."

Kate dug into the pocket of her trousers and pulled out a couple of dollar bills. "Please excuse me," she said. "It's late. I've got a lot of work to do." She tossed her money on the table and slid out of the booth.

Outside, the night was warm and still and overcast. Kate walked quickly along the street and turned up the hill toward campus. The heavy air pressed down on her head. Her body buzzed unpleasantly as though filled with gnats, her stomach and mind both churning. She needed to think. Tomorrow she would talk to Jax. If he was furious, well, then he was furious! There was nothing she could do about it. Her eyes were adjusting to the darkness now. She could see bats fluttering down between the trees, the big leaves of the elms hanging absolutely still. Did the trees rest at night, freed from the endless business of photosynthesis? What was it like to be rooted to one spot as the birds came and went, as insects burrowed under your bark, as men approached with axes?

Or maybe she wouldn't talk to Jax! Why should she? Her legs ached as the hill grew steeper, but it wasn't a bad feeling.

Back at the lab, she set to work on Cole's endless tables. She worked slowly, careful not to make a mistake. The night ground on: ten o'clock, eleven o'clock, eleven thirty, eleven fifty-two. Her stomach was leaden and her head ached. A nap would help, but the floor was too hard to lie down on. It wasn't even very late, not by her standards. She often worked till one or two in the morning. They all did. She thought about what Paul had said. *We want to get the answers right. That's what science is.* Under that theory, doing this useless work for Cole was wrong—more wrong than what Jax had done to her.

She got up and stretched, took a lap around the room to wake herself up. Past Cole's desk, past the laboratory benches, past the filing cabinet and the equipment shelves. Up on the highest shelf, toward the back, her little bottle of carmine stain seemed to call to her as she went by. *Here I am*, it said in its soundless voice. *Here I am, waiting.* She took another lap, thinking how she would reward herself for finishing the tables by looking at the material from the pollen. Next week maybe, if she worked fast. The clock in the library quad began to toll, one day wheeling into the next. It was the hour of ghosts, of deadlines missed and enchantments broken. The last stroke rang out. She could feel its reverberations in her body for a long time.

On her third lap, as she passed the shelf, she stopped and took the bottle down.

CHAPTER 14

Kate was still at her desk at nine a.m. when Cole came in. "Good morning, Miss Croft," he said, pulling on his lab coat. Dust hung motionless in bright swaths of sunlight. The sky out the window was a clear, liquid blue.

"Good morning, Dr. Cole."

"How are those tables coming along?"

She stared up at her advisor blankly. A great arm, like the arm of a giant, turned over a page in her mind. She pulled a few sheets of the trisomics table over what she had been working on. "Fine! They're coming along fine."

"Don't tell me you've been here all night," he said.

"I'm not tired."

It was true: she was too thrilled to be tired! How could she be tired when she'd spent the last few hours looking at the sharpest, clearest maize chromosomes anyone had ever seen? The squash technique on the new material had worked beautifully. And now, hidden under the half-completed trisomics tables, was the diagram she'd made.

There were ten chromosomes: ten exactly. People had guessed there might be, but she was the first person to know for certain—the first person in the world.

In her diagram, which she'd titled "A Preliminary Sketch of the Ten Chromosomes of *Zea Mays*," Kate had arranged and numbered them from tallest to shortest. Already each of the ten, with its own characteristic shape and markings, was familiar to her. Knobs of various sizes bulged like burls on tree trunks, while the arms on either side of the centromere were distinct, distinguishable, like the shapes of different sorts of leaves. Clear as day! She felt as if she were absorbing light from the air through her skin and turning it into electricity.

"I know I told you to hurry," Cole said. "But there's no need to go to extremes. A person needs his sleep."

She blinked up at him. "Don't worry about me."

"It's my job to worry about you." His face softened, and he sighed, and took a step toward Kate's desk. "Go home and take a nap," he said. And then he added, "I'd hate you to make a mistake because you were tired. Not that I think you will. I know you'll do a good job. You're always so careful and thorough."

The words, meant more or less kindly, choked Kate. Careful and thorough! An epitaph for a shoeshine boy.

Cole went over to his desk by the window and got to work: looking at notecards, scribbling on a pad. His back in his overstarched lab coat was a dull white oblong against the rectangle of sky. Kate slipped the diagram into a folder, slipped the folder under her arm. "I guess I will," she said.

No one answered when she knocked on Thatch's office door. He might be in the lab, of course, but really what she wanted more than anything was a cup of coffee and a quiet place to think. She opened the door, which was never locked, and went in. She turned on the hot plate, measured the water, and scooped out the grounds, using the precise, deliberate movements she'd seen Thatch use a hundred times. She sat in his chair, waiting while the coffee brewed. Behind her eyelids she could see the chromosomes lined up in their perfect order, one through ten. Warmth pulsed through her. The rich smell filled the room.

She must have drifted off, because the next thing she knew the door was opening and a voice that wasn't Thatch's was saying, "You can smell that halfway down the hall." Startling awake, she saw Paul filling the doorway, the ends of his tawny hair brushing the top of the frame. "Well," he said, seeing it was her. "I hope you made it home last night before your coach turned into a pumpkin."

She jumped up, annoyed that he'd caught her sleeping. "You're not mistaking yourself for Prince Charming, I hope." She poured the coffee and passed him a mug.

"You get a lot done on Cole's trisomics?"

"Not really." She tried to keep her voice steady. "Not on the trisomics."

The way he was looking at her—steadily, attentively, the way she looked at her slides—it was as though he already knew. "What?" he asked, stepping forward into the tiny room. She could feel the heat of him, smell the clean cotton of his shirt.

"Shut the door."

He did as she said. She hesitated, then she opened the folder and pushed the diagram toward him.

Paul studied the sheet of paper. Kate watched his face as comprehension broke over him. For a moment, his expression cracked open and she could see the excitement on his naked face before the mask snapped back on. "My God, Kate," he said, his eyes boring into her. "You really did it!"

"Well," she said as casually as she could manage. "Belling's stain worked like a charm." But her heart was pounding. The room didn't seem big enough for the two of them.

Paul looked back down at the diagram. "The slides I saw weren't clear enough for this," he said. "What else did you do?"

She told him about using the material from the pollen instead of the root tips.

"What gave you the idea to do that?"

"The root tips weren't working very well."

He looked up into her glowing face. "That's not an answer."

She cast her mind back, trying to remember how the

idea had come to her. "I just thought of it. That's all."

He studied the diagram some more. "You know," he said after a minute, "you could get Whitaker to write a covering note to the *PNAS*."

PNAS was the *Proceedings of the National Academy of Sciences*. Paul was saying the work was good enough to publish in a place like that. Kate was startled. She hadn't thought that far ahead. "Do you think he would?"

"He'd be an idiot not to."

When the door swung open, they both jumped. "Drinking my coffee in my office and you couldn't even leave me a cup?" Thatch said. But Kate could see he was happy to find them there.

"Take a look at what Kate's done," Paul said.

Thatch took the paper Paul held out. A bright rosy flush came over his face as he examined it. "Oh!" he said, looking up. "Oh, Kate!"

Ripples of pleasure spread through her.

"You said you could do it," Thatch said, so joyfully that she half expected him to embrace her.

"It wasn't hard," she said. "Once you had the idea."

But then, in the pause that followed, something seemed to slip, or shift, like the sun going behind a cloud. "I can't wait to see the slides," Thatch said.

Paul set down his empty cup on the desk. "Let's go look at them now!"

Kate panicked. She thought of Cole in the lab amid a snowstorm of papers, desperately trying to hammer his trisomics data into some kind of shape. "I'll show you later."

And then Kate saw Paul understand what Thatch had already guessed: that Cole still didn't know. It didn't bother Paul—she could see that, too. "The thing now is to publish it," he said. "As soon as possible. If you could do it, maybe somebody else has done it, too."

"Paul thinks Whitaker might send it to *PNAS*," Kate told Thatch, looking just past the side of his face.

"Well," Thatch said coldly. "Paul knows Whitaker best."

"I'd be glad to talk to him about it," Paul offered.

"No," Kate said, flushing. "I'll do it."

"After you talk to Cole," Thatch said. "After all, he worked on this for *two years*."

"Tell Cole what?" From the hallway, Jax's head appeared over Thatch's shoulder. "Worked on what?"

Nobody answered him. Thatch turned slowly around. "I'd invite you in, Jax," he said, "but you can see there's no room."

"I'm just going," Paul said. "Congratulations on your result, Jax. It was brilliant of you to notice those subtle separations." He pushed past Thatch and clapped Jax on the shoulder.

"Hello, Kate," Jax said. "Is there any coffee left?"

She couldn't answer him.

"I thought you liked yours less sludgy," Thatch said.

Jax shrugged. Then he saw the piece of paper lying on the desk. "What's this?" he said, picking it up. "A preliminary sketch of . . .? Oh, wow!" Agog, he stared at Thatch. "Where did you get this?"

Kate found her voice. "It's mine."

"Yours?"

"I made it."

Jax laughed, his snub nose flaring.

If she hadn't labeled it, she thought, speechless with rage and shame, he never would have even known what he was looking at!

"She did make it, you idiot," Thatch said. "What's wrong with you?"

Kate's face burned. All of her was burning: with fury and pride and exhaustion. Thatch's disappointment in her for not telling Cole had ruined her moment of triumph. His anger at Jax, though it moved her, didn't change that. She seized the diagram from Jax's hand and slapped it back into the folder. "It's just a preliminary finding," she said.

"I don't understand," Jax said. "How did you . . .?" His mouth twitched into an abashed smile. "It's amazing, Kate," he said. "It really is."

"If it holds up," she said.

"I mean it! It's incredible, really, what you've— Assigning linkage groups comes next, doesn't it? After that, I bet we can track down sterility without much trouble at all!"

"We?" Kate said. But Jax's head was full of sterility. She could see he was picturing the problem nicely solved and written up. Would he credit her even then? Would he bother to put her in a footnote? "Jax," she said. "I have to tell you something."

"What's that?"

"I hope you won't be upset. It was meant as a joke, but I realize now . . . Well. What happened was, I stopped by your lab to talk to you, but you weren't there. There were some envelopes of seed on the bench. W-618 and W-623. And—I switched them. I'm sure you noticed. But just in case you didn't."

Jax's face went tight. "My seeds?" he said.

"I switched them," Kate repeated, feeling calmer. "It seemed funny at the time. I thought . . . Anyway, I'm sorry. It was stupid. But no harm done, I trust."

"You tampered with my corn?" Jax's ears had turned bright red and he stepped toward her.

"She said she was sorry," Thatch said.

"You twit!" Jax said.

"Don't you yell at me!" Kate cried. "You didn't even mention me when you presented on Tuesday. You didn't say I helped you see what was on that slide!"

"You didn't help me," Jax said.

"You didn't see anything before I showed you!"

"You're a crazy bag," Jax said. "That's what you are."

"Stop it," Thatch said.

Jax wheeled toward Thatch. "As for you," he said, "what you see in that titless know-it-all is anyone's guess!"

"Get out of my office!" Thatch said.

"I bet you're not even getting any." Jax swatted at the empty mug Paul had left, which fell to the floor. Too solid to break, it rolled slowly and heavily under the desk, a few drops of sludge spilling across the boards.

CHAPTER 15

Kate couldn't show the diagram to Cole while he was in such a state about his trisomics, but she was reluctant to go over his head and show it to Whitaker either. Thatch was right about that. Like it or not, Cole was her advisor, and she didn't know how Whitaker would respond if she failed to respect the chain of command.

In the meantime, she worked on Cole's tables. Cole had started coming in early, sitting at his desk all day long with a stubborn, anxious, miserable expression, laboring to draft his paper. Over and over he drew black slashes through whole paragraphs and started them again. He crumpled sheets and threw them away, rubbed his red tired eyes, and groaned. And all the time Kate's diagram lay in its folder in her top left-hand drawer where she could feel it glowing darkly like a hot coal. She avoided Thatch and Paul as much as she could, coming and going when they were unlikely to be around. But even when they were both in their labs and she was working at her desk, she could feel them—the same way she could feel the presence of the diagram, or Cole's anguish, or Jax's malice.

It was Jax—the fact that he knew about the diagram—that made her have to do something soon.

At the Tuesday lab meeting, Kate could hardly listen to the presentation. The weather had grown even hotter and more stifling, and everyone was out of sorts. Thatch looked tired and unhappy. Cole looked even tireder and more unhappy. Jax acted as though she were invisible, which was a relief. Only Paul seemed unaffected, greeting her in his usual ironic, aloof friendly manner. Even Whitaker, sitting at the head of the table with his unlit pipe in his teeth, looked wilted, his eyes falling shut almost immediately after Vargas began his presentation, an audible snore rumbling from his throat toward the end, startling him awake. As soon as the meeting finished, she slipped out of the room, took the stairs to the lobby, and pushed through the big double doors into the blazing afternoon.

The experimental fields were at the far end of campus, a twenty-minute walk. Down and up a hill, past the dairy barns, beyond a little windbreak of trees. It probably wasn't any cooler here, but it seemed cooler. The air moved with a slight breeze, and a yellow finch bounced cheerfully through the shimmering blue.

In Kate's field—which was really Cole's field—the corn hissed and whispered in a friendly, familiar way. The plants were getting tall now, they were almost up to her shoulders. On the scattered surface of puddles from last night's rain, water striders crouched weightlessly, and smoky clouds of gnats drifted by. Kate walked slowly up the first row. Over the tops of the stalks she could see the blue-gray stone of the campus buildings. She crouched down so she was lower than the corn, its sharp sturdy leaves a fortress. Insects whirred. A cloud passed over the sun. She sat on the grass between the rows. To spend time in the field was to be filled with the sense of things beyond sensing—movements too slow to see, scents too faint to smell, sounds too low even for dogs. Inside the shoots, the ears were bulging, the fine silk invisible inside the green sheaths. She lay down. The ground was warm underneath her. It pressed back gently against her chest and stomach and thighs. Sometimes, when she was very tired as she was now, a scrap of memory drifted up: a soft arm, the look in a pair of sharp gray eyes, a long braid swaying. The last time Kate had seen Thea was from far away on the other side of the stage at the teeming graduation ceremony. Thea was camouflaged in her cap and gown, but Kate recognized her instantly. No one else held herself as straight. If you could understand how chromosomes determined what kind of corn plant a seed would become, would it be possible someday to know what made a person want what she wanted?

The next morning, as soon as she walked into the lobby, Paul said, "Everyone's been looking for you!" He seemed to have been lingering by the doors.

It was a few minutes after nine o'clock: later than she usually got in, but hardly late. "Why?"

"Something happened to your lab."

She stared at him. "Happened?"

"Someone tossed it."

Kate rushed to the stairs.

"Maybe it was you," Paul said, easily keeping pace as they climbed to the second floor. "Knowing what a jokester you are."

Kate stopped short in the doorway of the lab. A messy moat of papers encircled her desk, fanning out across the floor. Her slides were scattered, too, the glass glittering in the sun that streamed in. The air felt like soup. On Kate's lab bench, her microscope lay on its side like an overturned monument. Yet Cole's desk—Cole's lab bench—were untouched. Messy, but no messier than usual. At least, she didn't think so. She hurried over to her microscope and righted it. Nothing seemed to be broken. "Jax!" she said. "It must have been Jax."

Turning slowly around to take in the chaos, Paul shrugged. "Possibly."

It was hard to absorb it all, let alone believe anyone could have done it. "Where's Cole?"

"He was here a few minutes ago, shouting like a football coach."

Surely he couldn't have . . . Surely he didn't hate her that much!

Miss Floris poked her head around the door. "I heard you were struck by a tornado," she said, casting her sharp eyes around the room. "My goodness!" Her hand went to the front of her neat silk blouse. Then she nodded to Kate. "Dr. Whitaker wants to see you."

"What does he want?" Kate could hardly breathe.

"He just said he wanted to speak to you as soon as you got in." Miss Floris turned to go, then stopped and turned back. "Dr. Cole is with him," she added kindly.

Whitaker's office was large and full of things. It had big windows on two sides, the blinds drawn nearly to the sills against the summer heat. An enormous wooden desk sat on carved eagle's talons, its surface crowded with neat stacks of folders and journals, brass dishes of strange coins and dusty fossils, and a tiny live tree growing in a shallow bowl. Whitaker sat behind his desk. Cole slumped in a chair nearby, dabbing at his face with a folded handkerchief. When he saw Kate in the doorway, he sat bolt upright as though an electric shock had gone through him.

"Come in, Miss Croft," Whitaker said.

Kate stood on the mustard-yellow rug with bright geometric designs. "I've just come from the lab," she said to Whitaker, who was regarding her, unlit pipe bouncing in the corner of his mouth. "It's terrible! I can't imagine who . . ." But she stopped herself. Because of course she could imagine. She waited anxiously to hear what he would say, but it was Cole who spoke.

"What's this?" he demanded, and shook something at her—a piece of smudged and wrinkled paper.

Her diagram. Kate's heart began to thud so loudly she was sure they both must hear it. "Where did you find that?" she said. But she knew. The paper must have been left lying around when the room was tossed, and Cole must have noticed it. Or else he was snooping in her desk and found it himself, in which case—

"Miss Croft," Whitaker said. "Please sit down." She sat in the chair he indicated, which had been designed for a taller person. He reached his hand toward Cole, who reluctantly handed the diagram over. Whitaker slid it across the desk to Kate. "Did you make this?" he asked.

Kate took the rumpled paper and smoothed it on her lap. "Yes."

"That was my project," Cole said.

Kate could feel her face widen stupidly: mouth, eyes, pores. She looked up at Whitaker. "I know Dr. Cole worked on characterizing the chromosomes in the past. But he hasn't actually been working on it for quite a while. Not since I've been here."

Whitaker took his pipe out of his mouth and spoke sternly. "That's because he's finishing a major trisomics paper, with which you are supposed to be helping him. Not going behind his back and analyzing his data."

"It's not his data," Kate said.

But Whitaker wasn't listening. "Dr. Cole is your supervisor, Miss Croft. That means you do what he tells you to do."

"I *do* do what he tells me!" Kate said. "Even when there isn't any point."

"You see?" Cole said. "You see what I have to deal with?" Sweat dripped from his face, and dark patches spread down his shirt. He seemed to be melting like an ice cream cone as Kate watched in fascination and disgust. "That's what you get when you let women do science," he said. "Negligence and disrespect!"

Whitaker banged the pipe down in the wide clay ashtray, and a cloud of ash leapt up and settled across a recent issue of *Science*. "Miss Croft, you're a first-year graduate student, is that correct?"

"Second-year."

"You must be very bright, I suppose. We don't get very many young women here. But obviously there are some things you haven't understood."

Kate could feel tears rising—tears of fury and of self-pity. She hoped she could keep them back until she got—where? Not to her lab, which was really Cole's lab. "I understood that the problem needed solving," she said. "And I could see a way to solve it." Her voice sounded calm and distant, as though someone else were speaking.

Whitaker lit his pipe. "A way nobody else could see."

She pressed her lips together so as not to speak.

He shook the match violently out. "Dr. Cole is your supervisor, Miss Croft, as I said. As you know without my having to remind you. Among other things, that means you will show him respect. He's been doing this work a long time, and you will learn from him."

Kate bowed her head. She would gladly have learned from Cole, she thought, had there been anything to learn.

The tears streamed down the moment she shut the door to Thatch's room. Thatch got up from his desk and stepped hesitantly toward her. She hunched her shoulders and put her hands over her eyes, but she didn't resist when he touched her back and pulled her close. The top of her head reached only to the middle of his chest. Her tears seeped into his soft shirt, but she sniffled hard to keep back the snot. "Did you hear what happened?" she asked.

"I heard someone messed up your lab. I heard Whitaker called you into his office." His big hands lightly rubbed her shoulder blades. After a minute she pulled away and blew her nose.

"Cole was there. Did you hear that?"

He nodded.

"He had my diagram! They didn't even mention what happened to the lab!"

"*Cole* had it?" Thatch said.

"Whoever messed up the lab must have left it lying out. I could kill Jax! It must have been Jax." She looked at him to see what he thought. She was afraid to tell him her other idea, that it might have been Cole.

"I can't imagine that anybody . . ." he began, but he had to stop. Because, of course, somebody had. "What did Whitaker say about the diagram?"

Kate pulled herself up onto the desk and let her heels bang against the drawers. "What did he say? He said I shouldn't steal my advisor's project!"

"You didn't steal it!"

Kate glared at him. "You thought I was wrong, too."

"I didn't think it was wrong for you to *do* it. And I certainly never thought you stole anything. I just thought—"

"I know what you thought," Kate said.

There was a silence. Then Thatch asked, "But when Whitaker was done yelling, what did he say about the diagram?"

Again the stupid tears began to fall. She swiped them furiously away with her fists. "Nothing! Nothing! All he said was that I shouldn't steal data, and that I should respect my advisor. He said . . ." She wanted to tell Thatch how Whitaker had said she might not understand certain things because of her sex, but her tongue refused to shape the words.

It wasn't possible to stay away from the lab forever. When she went back in, Cole was sitting at his desk with his back to the door, looking busy with something, and didn't acknowledge her entrance. His slouched torso in its pallid lab coat looked monstrous. Kate began straightening up the papers, the slides, the overturned bottles. Waves of hideousness, emanating from Cole's corner, washed over her, chilly and sickening. When everything was in order, she stood looking at him, wondering what she could say to him.

"I never set out to go behind your back, Dr. Cole," she said. "I tried to talk to you about the chromosomes."

Cole's pen scratched across the paper, which she could see was speckled with blots.

"Anyone might have done that work," she said. "Everyone knew it had to be done. I mostly only worked on it late at night."

Cole slapped his desk. He turned and looked at her, his eyes screwed up in his face like a pig's. "I don't know why I was the one to get stuck with you," he said. "If anyone had asked me, I would have said that it was a waste of time, and I would have been right! Science is not a game. It's not something to pass the time with until you get married."

Kate's head buzzed and her feet were freezing. She felt as though she were floating out to sea on an iceberg. "I did in a week what you couldn't manage in two years," she said. But the buzzing was so loud she wasn't sure whether her words were audible or not.

CHAPTER 16

Kate was at home reading *Wildflowers of New York State* after dinner when the doorbell rang. She went to the window and saw Paul slouching on the sidewalk, his hair looking very tawny in the evening light. "What do you want?" she called down.

He looked up, shielding his eyes from the glare. "I thought I'd see how you were doing. I guess you had quite a day." A slow smile spread across his face, though God knew there was nothing to smile about. Nonetheless she went down the stairs and let him in.

"Would you like a cup of tea?" she asked primly.

"All right."

She could feel the heat coming off him as he followed her up the stairs.

Back in her apartment, she filled the kettle, rattled cups and saucers, jangled spoons. From out on the street came the thump of the *Journal* landing on the stoop and the jingle of the paper boy's bicycle bell. "That was me once," Paul said, settling himself on her old flowered sofa. "I delivered papers. Ran errands, shoveled snow. My father died when I was ten, and I helped my mother as much as I could."

Kate made herself stop fidgeting and sit down across from him. She could see the hungry look lurking behind the closed watchful expression he habitually wore. She thought he was waiting for her to offer sympathy, or perhaps to tell him about her own childhood, but she had no desire to do either of those things. Her chest felt heavy as though her blood were slowly curdling. "Are you really Whitaker's second cousin?" she asked.

He smirked, leaning back against her cushions. "You've been listening to gossip."

"There's a hypothesis out there. I'm trying to verify it."

This made him laugh. "Second cousin twice removed. I never met him before I came here. But I'd heard of him, of course. When I got interested in genetics, I decided to focus on corn partly because of him."

"Did you," Kate said.

"You could say I was inspired. And now that I've met him, I think we share certain traits, Evelyn Whitaker and I."

"You both seem to think highly of yourselves," Kate said. "If that's what you mean."

Paul smiled. "Among other things."

Kate got up and found the milk and sugar. She couldn't fathom why she had let him come in, or why he had wanted to.

"If you're trying to insinuate that I got my position through family connections, I don't deny it. But so what? That's how things work."

"Not for everyone," Kate said.

"It's not as though I don't deserve it," Paul said.

Kate wondered about the second half of the rumor, the part about him being kicked out of the University of Kansas, but she didn't see how she could ask. "What did you hear about what happened today?" she said instead. She was standing up and he was sprawled on her sofa, yet somehow he seemed to have more authority.

"I heard that Whitaker saw your diagram. I heard he let you have it and that you stood up for yourself. That has people buzzing nicely. But I wasn't surprised."

"I only said I hadn't stolen Cole's data," Kate said. "As though Cole had any data anyone would want to steal!"

"That's what I mean."

Kate stared at the wisps of steam beginning to slip from

the kettle's spout. "I don't know what's going to happen," she said. "How can I keep working with Cole? He despises me. Whitaker thinks I'm a thief. Probably he's going to ask me to leave."

"Nonsense," Paul said. "He won't do that."

"But he said—"

"He's not stupid," Paul interrupted. "He may not have figured out how good you are yet, but he's beginning to. And he knows what a mediocrity Cole is."

That hadn't occurred to her. "Do you really think so?"

"Of course. Everyone knows that without your help, Cole will never publish anything. Maybe even Cole knows it."

As she let that idea sink in, Paul got up from the sofa. He turned off the stove, took the empty teapot from her hand, put it down on the countertop, and kissed her, bending over awkwardly. The kiss took her so much by surprise that she could do nothing immediately except let his mouth press against hers, first softly and then harder. His tongue probed the contours of her teeth. He seemed to want to lap her up. He clasped her neck, slid his calloused hand down her back, then squeezed her backside, making her shudder with pleasure. She turned her face away from his big wet tongue but allowed herself to be pulled toward him. Her breasts pressed into his chest and his fingers continued to knead her rear end, while her own hands clumsily patted the expanse of his back, not knowing where to settle.

"Good work rises to the top," he murmured in her ear.

It had been a strange day, to say the least. It seemed fitting that the night should bring more surprises. She let him lift her up—which he did easily—and carry her across the room to the sofa with its slipcovers of faded violets, where he deposited her. He undid some number of buttons—her blouse, his trousers—very quickly and dexterously. When he found the tips of her breasts with his thumbs, she gasped, embarrassed at first, but then beyond embarrassment. His hand slid down her belly under her waistband, his fingers testing and investigating almost casually, creating one new sensation after the next as she lay, splayed and helpless, on the sofa cushions.

Then he stopped. She waited alertly to see what came next.

"Give me your hand," he said gravely, and she did. He took it and put it where he wanted it. "Ah," he said. And, "Ah-ah-ah"—a naked sound she didn't like at all. He wrapped her hand tighter and pushed it up and down. His face was a fist. When the milky liquid spurted out, it was impossible not to think of a corn tassel bursting from the stalk.

Paul sighed and lay back drowsily among the flat cushions.

Kate's own perplexing body still buzzed insistently, but she didn't even really know exactly what it wanted, let alone how to ask for it.

The next morning, when she got to the lab, Cole wasn't there. She went about her work as calmly as she could, though part of her mind was busy waiting for him to come in, and another part was waiting for Paul. She was sure he would come and see her. But the morning dragged on and no one came. On an ordinary day she would have relished working alone and uninterrupted, but today was not an ordinary day. Several times she caught herself staring blankly into space, wondering what would happen.

At last, close to eleven, footsteps approached the door. Not Cole's shambling ones but long strides. She turned eagerly to greet Paul, but when the door opened it was Thatch who came in instead. He looked worn out and also excited, and his hair stood up all over his head. "Whitaker wants to see you," he said.

Her heart closed up like a clam. "I'm out, aren't it?" she said. "That's it."

"No!" Thatch shook his head like a dog shaking itself after swimming. "No, it's not that. I spoke to him."

"You—?"

"Spoke to him! I explained what really happened. What you did. Using Belling's stain, and working at night. All of that."

A wave of fury rose from her belly and reddened her neck and face. "Without asking me?"

Thatch paused. "He understands," he said, but more tentatively. "I told him what you did—how it was all your own ideas and your own data. And he understands."

"How could you go behind my back?" Kate cried.

"I was trying to help you." He stared at her as though the force of his gaze would make her understand.

"Did I ask for your help?" This humiliation, at the hands of someone who claimed to be her friend, felt like the most monstrous betrayal of all.

"Kate," Thatch said. He looked stricken. Was that her fault?

Was it his fault he had come in when she was waiting for someone else?

She shut her eyes and pressed her hands down hard on her desk. She knew what he said about wanting to help was true. It might even be true that she'd needed his help, but she didn't want to need it. Not his, or anyone's. She opened her eyes. "You should have asked me first."

They regarded each other in silence.

"This is a good thing, Kate," Thatch said at last.

She pushed herself up. "I guess we'll find out."

In Whitaker's office, her rumpled diagram lay in the middle of his desk in a clear space between the stacks of journals and the dishes of coins and the tree in the dish. Kate sat on the edge of the same uncomfortable chair she'd sat in the previous day, while he puffed on his pipe. "I've heard about Belling's technique," he said. "But I've never used it myself. Is it difficult?"

The tree seemed to be some sort of spruce, with tiny bluish-green needles spiraling along the branches. What did you have to do to it to get it to grow like that? In nature it might reach two hundred feet high. "I had to try it a few times before I got it right."

"Write out a set of instructions." He didn't seem angry, nor was he penitent either. It was as though their conversation of the day before had never happened. "I'd like to see a draft paper within a week. It should be short. Just a note explaining what you did, and the diagram. Then we'll discuss it. Now, let's talk about exactly how you harvested the pollen."

Kate missed the next thing he said because—although she knew what he meant—the words conjured her hands on Paul.

She was in Whitaker's office for the better part of an hour. After a while she began to relax, almost to enjoy their conversation. He asked direct, insightful questions, and he listened to her answers without interrupting. Some of the things he asked, she found she didn't have answers for. She would have to go back to the lab and think them over. But that was fine. It was more than fine: it was joyous. He was spurring her to think harder. He wanted to discuss the work on linkage groups, which would come next. "After Dr. Cole submits his trisomics paper, we can talk about that."

Kate was so thrilled that she didn't even consider explaining to him about Cole's trisomics, what a waste of time that project was. Anyway, when he read Cole's draft, he would see for himself.

"All right then," Whitaker said, and she understood that she was dismissed.

She stood up. "Professor Whitaker?"

He had already picked up a manuscript and begun to read. "Yes?"

"I want you to assign me to work with someone else."

He thrust the manuscript down impatiently. "People have disagreements," he said. "It's part of science. What's more, it's part of life. My advice to you is to talk to Dr. Cole and work it out."

Kate nodded. "I don't think that's possible in this case," she said. "He thinks I'm not serious about science. He told me so."

"That's ridiculous," Whitaker said. "Anyone who talks to you for five minutes can see how serious you are."

Kate couldn't think of anything else to say, so she remained silent, standing there on the mustard-yellow rug with its mysterious geometric shapes, her eyes drawn back to the strange tree, which she supposed Whitaker found beautiful.

"All right," Whitaker said. "You can work with Johannsen."

Thatch was waiting in the hall when she came out. "What did he say?" he asked, though he must have seen from the way she glowed that things had gone well.

"Let's go outside," Kate said. "It's such a lovely day."

They went out to the lawn and sat under a bur oak with its elegant, multilobed leaves. The heat had broken, and the soft grass smelled strong and sweet. A blue jay swooped past them, flaunting its gaudy wings. Everything was conspicuously, ridiculously beautiful. Still, Thatch sat with his long legs sticking glumly out, chewing on a stalk of clover. "What did Whitaker say?" he asked again.

"He said I can work with Johannsen," Kate said. "Look at the gall on that branch." She pointed up to a knob half hidden in the leaves. It reminded her of the deep-staining knobs on the chromosomes. "How does the tree know to make it?"

"It's to contain some parasite," Thatch said absently.

"I know! But there are lots of kinds of parasites, and the trees makes different galls for each one. A specialized response. Isn't that amazing?"

"Listen," Thatch said. "I'm sorry I talked to Whitaker behind your back. I shouldn't have assumed I knew what was best."

"That's all right," Kate said. "It's worked out. He wants me to draft a paper! He had some good questions I have to think about." As she enumerated them for Thatch, some of the answers began to take shape in her mind. "The work on the linkage groups is a big project," she said. "Much more than one person can do. You should take part of it."

Thatch's stalk of clover was all chewed up. He tossed it aside and picked another one. "Maybe we can work together," he said.

"And Paul will want part, I'm sure. When I talk to Whitaker, I'll see how he thinks we should go about it." Already she took for granted that she would be meeting regularly with the Great Man.

"I feel I owe you something by way of apology," Thatch said. "Why don't I make you dinner this weekend?"

"For goodness' sake, Thatch," Kate said. "I've said it's all right."

"A congratulations dinner, then. I'd like to."

"All right. If you really want to. We can invite Paul, too."

There was a silence. Thatch spat the clover stem out. "The more the merrier," he said.

Back inside, Kate found Paul in his lab and told him what had happened. He smiled his slow crooked smile. "Didn't I say good work rises to the top?" He grasped her hand briefly, then let it go. For the rest of the day she could feel the ghost of his touch on her skin.

*   *   *

On Saturday evening, Kate, Thatch, and Paul sat on kitchen chairs in Thatch's backyard, which was raddled through with pink patches of lady's thumb and long tangled networks of creeping Charlie. He had built a fire pit to grill frankfurters over, had set a bucket of water close at hand just in case. "I used to be a Boy Scout," he said, which came as no surprise. Kate had baked a chocolate cake with raspberry jam between the layers. She felt excited in an unfocused, confusing way, as though an old slow horse she'd been riding had suddenly broken into a gallop. The world seemed to be rushing toward her, all green and gold. Paul had brought beer and a bottle of whiskey, obtained God knew where. Also a phonograph and one record, "The Santiago Waltz." He wound the phonograph up and the strains of the music drifted into the trees. He held out his hand to Kate, and they revolved around the yard as Thatch tended the fire, laid out the potato salad, and sliced some tomatoes from his garden. Kate broke away from Paul to examine the tomatoes, which were a surprising dark purple color.

"They're Black Prince," Thatch said. "I got the seeds from my grandmother."

Kate picked up a slice with her fingers and bit into it. "So sweet," she said, licking juice from her chin.

Over dinner they discussed whether the pigment that made maize kernels purple was the same pigment the tomatoes had. They discussed varieties of tomatoes and varieties of sweet corn (different from the Indian corn they studied) and whether it was possible ever to find out what the tomato had been like before selective breeding. "Vegetable history," Kate said dreamily. "That would be very interesting." Everything seemed interesting, suddenly.

It was a clear, warm, moonless night, the great span of the Milky Way glittering. Paul cranked up the phonograph again, and again he and Kate danced, an inch of charged buzzing air between them. Then he put the needle back to the beginning and she danced with Thatch, and then with Paul again. This time he held her very close in the darkness. Her ear was against his chest, and his heart thumped so loudly she couldn't feel her own heartbeat at all. When the record ended, she said she was tired and went to sit down. But Thatch said, "You danced with Paul three times."

"It's not a contest," she said. But she stood up again.

"Life is a contest," Paul said, stretching out his long legs and throwing back his head to gaze up at the stars.

"Don't be glib," Kate told him.

"What do you think it is, then?"

"A web," she answered. "An infinitely large fabric in which everything is intertwined. And lucky people like us get to spend our lives poking and prodding at the seams, trying to understand how it all fits together."

Paul laughed, a single loud hoot like a baboon. "That's a very romantic notion."

"It's not romantic in the least!"

Thatch restarted the record and came over and took her hand, and they moved together in the dark. His hand was firm on her waist, and hers rested lightly on the damp back of his shirt. Paul sat smoking, the tip of his cigarette an orange glow.

"What about you, John Thatcher?" Paul said. "What do you think life is?"

"Shut up, Novak," Thatch said. "I'm busy."

When the record ended, Kate said, "That really is it for me. It's been quite a week. Give me a cigarette, will you, Paul?"

"A triumphant week," Thatch said, as Paul passed her a cigarette and leaned over to light it for her. Thatch found his teacup of whiskey in the grass and raised it. "Here's to you, Kate Croft! And your diagram. And to many more exciting discoveries."

"And not having to work for that idiot Cole anymore," Paul added, lifting his teacup. "He'll have to struggle through his trisomics all by himself, God help him."

"Poor Cole," Kate said. "Showing my diagram to Whitaker didn't work out the way he thought it would at all."

"I never thought I'd hear you say *Poor Cole*," Thatch said.

"Cole didn't show it to him," Paul said.

There was a pause.

"What do you mean?" Kate said at the same time Thatch said, "Who did then?"

"I did," Paul said.

Kate tried to speak, but she was so shocked that no words came out.

"Why?" Thatch said.

"Because I thought he should know about it."

Kate found her voice. "Did you wreck the lab, too?" She knew she should be angry, but she just felt blank and baffled. Life was a contest, he'd said. He was making up the rules as he went along.

"No," Paul said. "That was Jax. He told me he was going to." The glow of his cigarette dimmed and brightened.

"He told you?" Kate was trying to keep up.

"People talk," Paul said. "Even when they know they shouldn't."

"And you didn't stop him?"

"I didn't think he was serious," Paul said. "Besides, I don't think I could have stopped him."

Thatch got out of his chair and strode over to stare into the fire. "Do you know what I think life is?" he said. "It's the struggle of decency against corruption. That's what I was taught when I was a child, and it's what I still believe." He picked up the bucket and heaved the water onto the flames. The wet coals hissed.

Thick curtains of shadow lay all around them. Kate turned toward the place where she knew Paul was and said, "What did you do in Kansas that they kicked you out for?"

Deep in the muffling darkness, cicadas whirred and frogs chirruped over the sounds of the cooling fire. Kate could feel Thatch's alertness, his thousand invisible antennae bristling.

"I wouldn't have thought you were the kind of person to listen to libelous gossip," Paul said.

But she refused to let him sidetrack her another time. "*Is* it libelous?" she demanded.

"I'd say so," Paul drawled.

Gradually her eyes adjusted to the absence of the firelight. She could see Paul's tall shape on the kitchen chair, his legs stretched out across the dark grass, his white shirt glowing faintly, the red tip of his cigarette. "Then why did you leave?" she asked.

"Isn't the opportunity to work with Whitaker reason enough?"

"It is," she said. "But is it the reason?"

Paul laughed unpleasantly. "If I tell you it is, will you believe me?"

"I never pegged you for a liar," Kate said.

Paul tossed the end of his cigarette toward the dead, damp fire. "Well, thank you," he said.

The firefly spark that was Kate's mind seemed to drift like a balloon, up out of her body and away. She was tired. She didn't want to prosecute Paul.

But Thatch said, "So nothing happened? In Kansas?" And then, when a minute went by, he repeated, "Are you saying nothing happened?"

Paul swatted at the darkness as though dispersing a crowd of gnats. "There was a misunderstanding," he said. "That's all. About crosses. You know how things get at fertilization time. Anyone could make a mistake."

Yes, she knew. You started in the fields early, day after day, rushing to finish while the pollen was viable: reaching up high to take the brown bag off the tassels, shaking the pollen into the bottom of the bag, painting it onto the trimmed silks under the crackling glassine shoot bags, stapling them on again to prevent contamination, noting down the crosses with a slippery grease pencil—all as fast as possible, again and again, while the sun burned down and the mosquitos buzzed and the sharp leaves cut your hands. You could never be careful enough. Skin was slashed, sunburned, stung. Pollen was accidentally scattered from the bag, or the bag was insecurely stapled and fell off and blew away, or numbers were transposed so that the wrong plants were fertilized. Data was contaminated, results were called into question. If you had an intriguing result—an interesting anomaly—people would say you had made a mistake at fertilization. That was why, when she had her own project and her own field, Kate was going to fertilize every plant herself! She would have to grow less corn—she knew that—but the trade-off for certainty was easy to make.

Not that people wouldn't still accuse her of errors.

"You made a mistake?" she asked Paul. "You crossed the wrong plants?"

"I might have," Paul said from out of the dark. "It was all just blown up out of proportion."

"Might have?" Thatch said.

Paul turned toward the other man's voice and said—slowly, coolly, as though he were doing Thatch a great favor by answering—"It was exactly the kind of mistake anyone might have made."

Something lodged in Kate's chest, under the breastbone, making it hard to breathe. Every moment she could see Paul more and more clearly: his square jaw and fine long nose, his narrow shoulders and strong grasping hands. The way he sat, leaning back so casually, his face tilted toward the stars. "You crossed the wrong plants on purpose," she said.

"No," he said.

"You didn't?" Against her will she leaned toward him.

"They were the right plants," he said. He spoke slowly, distinctly, his words ringing out in the darkness like a bell.

The thing in her chest bulged. It was as though she had swallowed an egg.

"I don't understand," Thatch said.

But Kate did. He meant that the plants he'd crossed were the right ones for his purposes. He'd fertilized with pollen of his choosing, making crosses that suited his own aims. He had hijacked someone else's experiment to learn what he wanted to learn. "Did you get the result you wanted?" she asked.

Paul tipped the chair back, balancing on its two back legs, his face parallel to the cold plane of the sky. "They destroyed the seeds," he said. "Before I could find out."

Thatch began gathering up the dishes and empty glasses. They rattled and clinked in his arms as he carried them back toward the lighted house.

PART THREE

1933

CHAPTER 17

The wedding was supposed to be in the garden, but when the rain showed no sign of letting up, it had to be moved indoors. Guests sat in neat rows of white chairs in the hotel ballroom with its handsome black-and-gold-striped wallpaper. Thatch didn't mind, but Cynthia cried so much that the ceremony had to be pushed back half an hour. When at last she came down the aisle, very tall, like a young giraffe, in her blowsy tulle—leaning hard on her father's arm, her thin dark face puffy and blotched—Paul, who had come up from Cambridge the night before, leaned over to whisper into Kate's ear, "I thought she was supposed to be pretty." With his dove-gray suit and his deep blue tie and his self-satisfied expression, he wouldn't have looked out of place beside Kate's banker brother-in-law.

Kate shushed him. Then, as the string trio began its crescendo, she leaned over and whispered back, "She is, usually. She's very fetching in a lab coat."

"I bet she majored in botany because she heard it was a good way to catch a husband."

"Oh, I wouldn't think so," Kate said. If there was one thing you could say about Cynthia, it was that she was sincere. Her motives were always decent, and they were always right out in the open.

Cynthia had been a junior last fall when she and Thatch had got to talking at the annual botany department picnic. Four months later, when they announced their engagement, the plan was for her to continue on and get her degree, perhaps even begin work toward a master's. But somewhere amid the preparations for the wedding, and the hunt for a perfect little house to rent, and all the thank-you notes to write for the engagement presents, not to mention the constant assumption by everyone that she would of course be giving up her studies (after all, what use could she have for a degree now?), that intention had been abandoned. People thought Thatch had encouraged her to quit, but Kate knew he was disappointed. Not that he would say so in a million years.

Cynthia had suspected it, though. In her earnest, ardent way, she'd come to Kate's office one afternoon a few weeks before the wedding to ask if Kate thought she was letting Thatch down. "I'd hate to think that John thought less of me," she said, worrying her little diamond on its thin bright band, then looking down at Kate with her doe's eyes. "Do you think he'd be happier married to someone with a degree?"

Kate, who had samples to fix and crosses to plot out, tried not to fidget. "Of course not. Thatch couldn't be happier. He thinks you hung the moon!"

Cynthia's spindly olive-dark hands were pressed together in her lap. The little diamond cast a spray of light across the ceiling. "Thank you for talking about this with me," she said. "John respects you and values your friendship so much. I just want him to be happy." That was how she talked: with complete, straightforward sincerity. Well—if that was what Thatch wanted!

Still, that sentence lingered uncomfortably: *I just want him to be happy.* As though anybody ever just wanted any one thing. Yet Cynthia was not simple-minded.

"I suppose he got tired of waiting for the perfect woman," Paul murmured now. His breath was warm on Kate's neck, from which a cameo dangled on a chain, its weight making her feel constricted and ill at ease. "Twenty-eight is a little old to be a virgin, after all."

Kate pretended not to hear. She leaned forward as though intent on not missing the moment when Cynthia's father transferred his daughter's hand to Thatch's. Her throat felt swollen, and the weather made her head ache.

Thatch smiled down at his bride. It had to be admitted that he looked radiant, with the pink rosebud in the buttonhole, and his face pink, too, under his freshly barbered hair. Behind the wedding party, vases of fresh-cut but artificial-looking arum lilies and freesia stood in for the flooded garden. On the other side of the tall windows, the rain came down in sheets, beating at the wavy panes like an uninvited guest. Somebody should have shut the drapes, Kate thought, wishing that the rain would stop—not merely for Thatch and Cynthia's sakes, but because of the havoc it might be wreaking this very minute in her field.

Paul had been the first of them to leave Ithaca. He had sped through his PhD with a nervy singularity of purpose, then, with Whitaker's help, landed the Harvard job. This despite the fact that it was the Depression, work no easier to come by for young scientists than for anybody else. Luckily Cornell was generous with instructorships, which were basically a way of keeping promising young people in the field for a couple of years post-PhD until something turned up. Kate was finishing out her second year as an instructor, Thatch his first. He was more anxious about the job situation than she was, though. After all, he had Cynthia to think about, and probably, before long, a small Thatcher or two.

After the wedding luncheon, the chairs were pushed to the sides of the room and the string trio played out-of-date waltzes under the swags of ivy and white roses, while the crystal pendants of the chandeliers glowed in the oyster-gray light. Kate felt ridiculous in the violet dress she'd bought for the occasion. She began to move to the corner where Whitaker was holding court, but Paul put a hand on her shoulder and asked her to dance.

"No thank you," Kate said.

"The happy couple expect it," Paul said.

"Don't be ridiculous," Kate said. "Besides, my feet hurt in these shoes."

"I'll tell you about my fascinating Harvard experiments if you dance with me." His hand drifted down to hers and tugged gently.

"What makes you think I care about flies?" Kate said. It offended her that Paul had switched from corn to flies when he got to Harvard, but she let him lead her to the dance floor anyway. He smelled so familiar inside his gray suit, sharp and faintly electric, like the air during a thunderstorm.

"Flies are very interesting," he said, turning her in expert circles. On the other side of the room, the newlyweds were revolving slowly as Cynthia attempted to subdue her billows of tulle.

"I hear fly rooms stink of rotten bananas," Kate said.

"Who cares? You get a new generation every eight days."

"What do you want with more data than you can analyze?" Her purple organza collar chafed, and the heel of her left foot hurt where it rubbed against her shoe. Paul pulled her closer so her ruffles brushed his lapels. The dance floor was filling up, but he stepped unerringly into open space and began to describe the experiments he was doing, cutting the eye buds out of mutant drosophila larvae and transplanting them into other larvae to track down how eye color worked. Despite herself, Kate was interested. "Maize is too slow, Kate," Paul said. "Science is speeding up."

"Corn still has a lot to offer." The rain, which had briefly subsided, began to beat down harder, and Kate thought again of her seedlings as Paul spun her relentlessly along.

"Even drosophila might be too big and slow," he said.

Kate laughed.

"People are beginning to study bacteria, Kate. It's an exciting world outside of Ithaca. New ideas, new techniques. X-rays! No more waiting and hoping nature throws a mutation your way."

"Look," Kate said. "They're cutting the cake." She had heard about the X-ray work being done in places like Missouri, and she thought it was very interesting. But she wasn't about to tell Paul that.

The music stopped. Paul kept hold of Kate's hands. He bent his head toward her, and she could feel the heat coming off of him. "It's time to get out," he said. "Whitaker's getting old."

Kate glanced at the corner by the window where Whitaker was smoking his pipe, surrounded by a group of younger men. It was true that he had very little hair left. The lines in his face had deepened, the tip of his nose grown pendulous. "There aren't any jobs," Kate said.

"There are always jobs."

She had forgotten how clear and hard his eyes were beneath those fierce, tawny brows. All around them, people were making their way toward the table where Thatch and Cynthia stood smiling before the tall, immaculately white cake with its manufactured roses. Thatch put his arms around Cynthia's waist, both of them grasping the cake knife. Then together, solemnly, they sliced down through the white icing and pale yielding layers.

"The symbolic thrust," Paul said, close to Kate's ear, as Cynthia's father, spectacles glittering, began to make a toast about the seasons of life. Kate was finding it hard to breathe inside the organza.

"By the way," Paul murmured, "I was supposed to stay with Lee Wilson, but he says his wife's cousin is in town and could I find another bed. I don't suppose . . . ?"

"You know how small my place is," Kate said.

Tears trickled down Cynthia's smiling cheeks as her father droned on. Thatch pulled her head down onto his shoulder. The father kissed his damp-faced daughter and shook hands with his new son-in-law, beaming and sweating and wiping his brow.

Then Whitaker stepped forward, chiming a spoon against a glass. "Today, Thatch and Cynthia are starting out on life's great journey," he began in his dry, thin, clear voice. He spoke about companionship and solace, about bumps in the road and the pleasures of the quiet life. Cynthia had wiped her tears with a lace handkerchief and was listening intently, her eyes bright. Kate fidgeted. How could such a brilliant man give such a dull toast? She could feel Paul behind her thinking the same thing. The warmth of his breath and the faint electric smell of him dilated something inside her. Thatch looked so happy with his bride nestled like a bird under his arm. She hoped things would work out for him. For him and Cynthia. And why shouldn't they? The back of her dress brushed against the front of Paul's trousers. He leaned forward, letting out a sigh, and she instinctively stepped away. In her distraction, she missed the beginning of the sentence that ended ". . . and I told him I had just the man for the job! So here's a toast to Dr. John Thatcher and his lovely bride, and to their new life in New York City."

Kate turned to Paul. "What did he say?"

"The Rockefeller Institute."

All around the room, the guests broke into exclamations and applause. The color of Thatch's face deepened, and he beamed with embarrassment. Cynthia was smiling as though her face would break open, her eyes teary again, as a flood of well-wishers moved in to congratulate them all over again. Outside the windows, the rain fell steadily. Kate stood stunned.

"I told you there were jobs," Paul said. He took her arm

and pulled her along with him toward the corner where Whitaker was refilling his pipe.

"That was a very nice toast, sir," Paul said. "And quite a wedding present you arranged."

"Look at you, Novak," Whitaker said. "To see you now, no one would ever guess you were raised in Kansas."

"I was just telling Kate about the delights of fruit flies."

"Don't waste your breath," Whitaker said fondly. "Kate is a corn man through and through."

"There was a genetics job at the Rockefeller Institute?" Kate said.

"Not officially." Whitaker bent his head and touched the match to the bowl. Mottled spots the size of quarters stood out on his bronzed head. "They didn't want to advertise. They just called me and asked if I could recommend someone."

"And you recommended Thatch," Kate said. Her voice sounded hoarse and scratchy. She cleared her throat, but she could still feel the indignation making a lump while puffs of smoke floated peaceably across the room as they must have at many a treaty signing between American colonists and Indian chiefs.

"The timing was right," Whitaker said.

"I got my degree a year ahead of him," Kate said.

"You'll be fine, Kate. You've been doing wonderful work. Paul, make sure Kate tells you about her new project. It's a very smart idea."

Across the room, Thatch and Cynthia were feeding each other pieces of cake. The musicians had started playing again, and the mood in the room was gay. Two people had been successfully bound together, their genes promised to each other. Thatch would love being a father, Kate thought. Though, of course, he'd be extremely busy with his new job. "Are there other unofficial openings?" she asked.

"You still have your instructorship," Whitaker said. "When you publish this project, everyone is going to want you."

Kate walked away across the parquet, trying to swallow back her rage, forcing herself to think about her field. She had crossed plants that each had broken chromosomes to each other, and she longed to see if their progeny would look the way she thought they would. If the storm washed her seedlings away, she'd never know.

In the lobby, as she waited for her coat, Paul appeared. "You're not leaving already?" he said.

"I have to check on my plants."

"I'll come with you."

She shook her head. "I have to stop by my place and change."

"I'll give you a lift."

She was tired, it was exhausting to resist him, he had a car. Besides all that, there was comfort in being with someone who knew her. Especially now that Thatch was married.

When they got to her apartment, wet despite their raincoats, Paul followed Kate as she went into the bedroom. When she turned to shoo him out, he came close and stroked her hair, then took hold of her breast through the scratchy purple fabric. Well, she thought, here was Paul getting what he wanted, as usual. Was it what she wanted, too? It was hard to say.

Paul unbuttoned her damp buttons, then stood back and looked at her half-naked body. He was still in his dove-gray suit, heat radiating off him. Her hand reached up to touch the bare skin above his collar, but he intercepted it, cupping it in his large palms, then guiding it to the crotch of his fine wool trousers, his eyes fixed on her. His size and stiffness was so much like an ear of corn that she almost giggled. She wondered how long she would have to leave her hand there before she would feel all right about taking it away.

At last he lifted her palm to his mouth and kissed it, sucked lightly on the tips of her fingers. A faint ringing started up in her ears.

It was dim in the small room. The rain pounded heavily on the roof. "Look at you," Paul said. He began to touch her: her breasts, her belly, between her legs. Her breath came faster.

She shut her eyes and listened to the rain as the damp organza fell to the floor. His hands moved slowly over her. Then he grasped her elbow and together they crossed to the bed. She lay quietly, eyes open now, watching Paul remove his clothes. When he stretched out naked beside her, the springs groaned. They lay facing each other on top of her old coverlet.

"Kate," Paul said.

Her skin prickled with gooseflesh.

The bed creaked as he shifted closer. His damp hair brushed her throat, and she shivered. His tongue explored her breast, his lips closing around her nipple. She concentrated all her attention on that place—that feeling—not to miss any of it. He moved to the other breast, his hands squeezing her backside, and she rubbed herself against him like a cat. It made so much sense that honey was what bees rendered from their bodies after fertilizing flowers. She wanted to laugh—having a thought like that now! She wanted to stop and tell Paul.

But she didn't—couldn't—stop. Her body moved urgently, rubbing itself up and down against his hard pale thigh. It only took a minute or two. Then she lay back, flushed and buzzing. Her throat ached as her breath slowed.

"Kate," Paul said again. His teeth seemed to bite her name carefully out of the air. Naked, there was so much of him. His body was like a wall between her and everything else. He took up almost all the room in the bed. He nudged her over until she was on her back on the coverlet, then lifted himself on top of her.

"Mmm," he said, and sighed with a droning sound like a distant swarm of bees. Then he drove himself in.

Kate took a sharp breath at the pain. She watched his eyes narrow as he eased in deeper. They were fiercely focused, but she couldn't tell what they were focused on. Not on her.

Would Thatch and Cynthia still be smiling tiredly at lingering guests in the hotel ballroom? Or would they be by now in Thatch's old Ford on the way to Niagara Falls? That would be a brutal drive in this weather. Kate's mind jumped ahead—she couldn't help it—picturing Cynthia's olive skin flushing as she sat on the edge of a big white bed . . .

Paul leaned more heavily onto her and began to make strange sounds. A bittersweet smell was leeching out of his skin. The rain was coming down harder now, rattling the window.

She had to get to her plants.

She began to move her body slightly. She lifted her hips, pressing back against Paul's groin, ignoring the pain. Waves of heat seemed to pour out of him, burning through her. He went very still. "Wait," he said, drawing back.

But she was done waiting. She reached out and pulled him closer. His face clenched and he collapsed on top of her. The room stank of salt and musk.

After a moment or two, he rolled off. A sticky wetness trickled down her thigh. She thought of pollen spilled from paper bags at fertilization time, the bright yellow grains that stained your fingers. If she were a plant, she never would have found herself in this ridiculous position, splayed and pinned on her white candlewick coverlet like a moth.

"I want to ask you something," Paul said.

There were short tawny hairs all over the bed, not to mention a stain. She would have to wash the coverlet. It would take ages to dry in this weather. "What?"

"I need a simpler test organism."

Kate stared at him. Then she began to laugh, which made her cough. She seemed to have something stuck in her throat. "Simpler than flies?" she croaked.

He raised himself up on an elbow and looked down at her. His face was glowing, and he was frowning with excitement. "I have an idea about how to trace the action of one single gene. It's a good idea, but it won't work in drosophila."

Kate wriggled down to the foot of the bed so she could get up without climbing over him. It was still raining. She felt weak and disoriented, but she needed to get to the field. She picked up Paul's shirt and pants and threw them at him. "Time to get dressed," she said.

"Think about it, okay?" he said urgently. "Some microbe maybe. Something that lives on one particular nutrient base. Something that's easy to grow."

It was dark outside, though the long summer day was far from over. Gray-black clouds blew across the sky like smoke, and fine needles of the interminable rain flashed silver, then splashed into spreading puddles, gleaming green and purple over the oily pavement. The sound of the driving rain filled the air, which smelled of mud and asphalt and lightning. Overhead, the branches creaked and groaned on trees that shook their leaves fiercely, sending down secondary showers. Kate got into her car and drove out to the field along the black streaming streets. She felt numb, stupid, half-panicked.

The wedding. Whitaker's toast. The thing that had happened in her bed.

When an insect infected a tree, the tree grew a hard, knotty boll to contain it.

The car splashed through puddles and fishtailed around curves. Her windshield wipers clacked, and her headlamps made two foggy yellow tunnels through the dusk.

At the field, she parked in the sodden grass. In the gray light she looked across at her rows of plants, only six or eight inches high, now drooping and limp. Leaving the engine running, she got out of the car, her headlamps illuminating long dashes of rain. Rain beat down on her oilskin hat and on the shoulders of her slicker, found its way under her collar and slithered down the back of her neck. Her boots squelched along the soft ground. She could see that the whole lower part of the field was flooded. Rivers of water swept along the rows, and some of the plants were nearly swimming in it, their leaves all pulling downstream. The mud tugged at her boots and the chilly rain dripped down her face as she made her way toward them, wondering if she could somehow redirect the rushing water. She turned in a slow circle, trying to think. The stream pulled at her ankles. Then, carefully, she lowered herself down. Her knees sank into the cold muck. She knelt by the first plant and ran a hand along its leaves, which were splayed out like a girl's long hair, straining downstream as though longing for freedom. Plunging her bare hands down, she pushed the cold ooze toward the base of the stem. If she could build up the dirt around each plant, she might save some of them.

Slowly, slowly, she worked her way down the row. The rain pelted her, and the mud clung to her stiff fingers, and her soaked trousers were heavy as clay. The water flooded over the tops of her boots and squished in her socks. Four plants, six plants, eleven. Here and there one was gone, swept away in the stream, a missing tooth in a jack-o'-lantern's grin. A data point she'd never get back. All she could do was hope it wasn't a crucial one. Still, she was saving more than she was losing.

Well, maybe not. But she was saving a few.

Her hat blew off in a gust and disappeared into the night, which had somehow fallen. It was very dark now, the glow of the car's headlamps casting the only light. On she worked, her body numb, her mind blank. She didn't notice the rain lightening, letting up, fading into a cold mist. When she was so stiff she could hardly move, she looked up and saw, for one quick moment, the moon—a glowing white disk at the crest of the sky—before the clouds billowed in to hide it again.

When she got home, she stripped off her clothes just inside the front door. The mud had penetrated everywhere. Her belly and thighs were coated with it, and silt clung to her underwear. Her throat burned and her head throbbed. She should run a bath, she should make a cup of tea. Instead, she dragged herself into the bedroom, where the bedcovers lay rucked and stained. What difference if a mud-daubed body lay down in them.

That night her cough got worse and she could not get warm, not even under two quilts. Shadows moved across the ceiling, and outside the window, leaves rustled like ghosts. At last a gray gleam crept in and a few pale fingers of sunlight spilled onto the floor. She dragged herself up out of the ruined sheets. Out the window, the sky was pink and gold. The storm was gone. She should go out and see how her plants were doing, but the very thought seemed to make her dizzy. She sat down hard and shut her eyes. Something twitched inside her and she dragged herself to the bathroom to cough out a tablespoon of yellow gunk. It was as if the storm had made its way inside her, coating her lungs with scum. She ran water into the tub, climbed in. Sometime later, she got out again, leaving a residue of mud. She made coffee, thinking if she behaved as though things were normal, they would be normal. She dragged the sheets off the bed and forced herself to spread new ones, though she could not manage to tuck them in. She got back into bed and lay coughing and dozing as the sun moved across the room.

*   *   *

The next day, she didn't feel any better. She thought of the beef tea and soda crackers her mother used to bring her when she was ill, the awful syrupy medicine in the special long spoon. She could hear the sharp voice in her head: *You can't get better if you don't eat, Kathleen.*

To escape the voice, Kate dragged herself out of bed. She wobbled into the kitchen, supporting herself on the backs of chairs. She ran the tap, filled a glass of water, drank it down. Half a loaf of bread sat on the counter in the center of a pool of crumbs. What was that doing there? It belonged in the bread box. Her eyes snagged on the loaf as though hypnotized: the brown crust, the pale soft flesh, a scrim of something green spreading. Left out on the counter, it had already grown moldy. Had she forgotten cutting herself a slice? A spasm of coughing made her bend over the sink. No, she thought, Paul must have cut into the loaf before he left. He must have left the crumbs on the countertop, left the bread out for the mold to find. *Rhizopus stolonifer.* With its proclivity for asexual reproduction via spores, mold was actually very interesting. If people could do that, it would save a lot of trouble. She wandered over to the window, looking down at the street, which the rain had washed clean. She was shivering again, but she didn't want to go back to bed. She sat at the little table she used as a desk and watched the sun glitter in the puddles. The leaves of the tulip poplar tree glowed such bright green she could barely bear to look at it. The world after the storm was too radiant—blazing—as though the light were interlaced with blades. She wondered about Thatch and Cynthia, if they were standing even now beside the roaring Niagara with their arms around each other. If they were talking about the future: about New York and all that awaited them there. She felt a cough begin to stir inside her and she held her breath. Better not to think about all that.

She picked up a pencil and began doodling on a pad. Certain molds, she had read, had been found to have curative properties. So many wonders, so many unexpected gifts from the natural world if people would only pay attention. She sketched the half-eaten, mold-fuzzed loaf, drew in some oversized spores. Just last spring a botanist named Bernard Dodge had come to Cornell to lecture about Neurospora, which he claimed would be more important to genetics than corn someday!

But how to tell what was ridiculous from what was true? Wasn't that one of the essential questions? Paul had said *flies* were too big. Why not mold, then, she thought idly. *Rhizopus*, or *Neurospora*, or something else. Dodge had extoled *Neurospora's* qualities as a model organism. She squinted down at her pad and found she had written *Paul* in clear dark letters. Talk about ridiculous! She raised her pencil to strike the name out, but then, struck by a thought, she moved her hand an inch to the left and wrote "Dear" before the name.

Dear Paul,

I have been thinking about your organism question. How about Neurospora? Bernard Dodge says it's easy to grow and its haploid life cycle makes analysis straightforward.

If mold isn't simple enough for you, I throw up my hands.

Yours,
Kate

With a last burst of energy she found an envelope and a stamp, scribbled down his address.

*   *   *

Someone seemed to have dug a knife into her side, the kind they used for slitting open the sheaths of corn tassels to extract the pollen. She lay splayed out on the sheets, panting between spasms of coughing. How much time had passed since the field? Two days? Four? There was a ringing inside her head, and a distant knocking like a loose shutter rattling. That couldn't be good. It came and went and came again, and the knocking grew louder and more insistent. The sheets were soaked with sweat, and sweat rolled down her cheeks into her ears. Something rattled—she heard it distinctly—though whether it was inside or outside of herself was hard to know.

"Kate?" a voice said. Then again: "Kate? Kate?" A single up-rising syllable like the call of an osprey.

She opened her eyes. The light hurt. A man's face bent over her, drawn and familiar, which she could not place. Not her father, though, because there wasn't any moustache.

"Lie still," said the moustacheless mouth.

Oh! It was Whitaker!

"I'm going to lift you up now," the Great Man said. And he did: as easily, almost, as if she'd been a child.

CHAPTER 18

She was sitting in a patch of sunlight on a rug woven with flowers, watching dust motes float and spin, blown upward by no breath that she could see.

She was standing on a path between banks of snow higher than her head, more snow spilling ecstatically out of the sky. She could hear her father's voice saying, "The flakes are so large because the air is getting warmer." He was always interested in weather.

She was crawling on hands and knees to the dog's dish to see how the dog food tasted. Her mother slapped her—sharp and sudden as lightning: "We are not animals!"

But why was one slapped for wanting to know?

She was looking up into the white face of a woman dressed in white who said gravely, "There now."

Kate struggled through a veil of mist. Those must have been dreams. Dreams of her childhood, and then another dream, too, of someone in white speaking in a voice like a bell. A great weight, like a gored ox, pinned her down. Then suddenly, like a towering and icy wave, came the realization that she had failed to fertilize her plants; she had overslept—she'd been sleeping forever, it seemed!—while the pollen ripened on tassels which she hadn't even bagged. She blinked hard and pushed herself up, and a knife blade sliced through her chest, and everything went queer and fuzzy. A voice, very clear and loud, spoke from somewhere to her left.

"You really must stop trying to get out of the bed. Where is it you think you're trying to go?"

"The field." Kate's head buzzed, and she let herself sink

back down. "The pollen is only viable for a few hours . . ." She'd just rest a minute, and then she'd get up.

"You'd better forget about that," the voice advised.

Slowly Kate's vision cleared. She was lying in a strange bed in an unfamiliar room with ugly brown curtains and a high white ceiling with a tea-colored stain in one corner. A woman stood in the doorway, dressed all in white: white lab coat, white slacks, white shoes. Not a nurse—no winged cap—and not an angel either (no wings). Her black hair was pulled back in a chignon revealing long white ear lobes.

"What happened?" Kate asked. Her body was beginning to come back to her. Her bones ached, and her flesh felt like jelly. Every time she breathed, the knife in her side leapt and stabbed.

"You've had pneumonia. You were very ill, but you're getting better now." The tall woman leaned over the bed and pressed her fingers to Kate's neck, moved them down, probing gently. She produced a stethoscope from somewhere and listened to her chest, then helped her turn over so she could listen to her back. Kate's breathing loosened. Her woeful body, that old enemy, slowly unruffled its feathers. She slept.

When she opened her eyes again, someone was giving her a bath, right in the bed, with a basin and a sponge and a small rough hand. The water sloshed and splashed. It dribbled down Kate's back and the sponge moved back and forth, efficiently and smoothly. She searched out the face, but it wasn't the one from before. This face was red and round with two small pebble eyes.

"I'm just cleaning you up before the doctor comes," it said.

"The doctor?" Was that her voice, sounding like a rusted gate?

"Dr. Sonnenfeld. She's the one who was here when you were brought in. It ought to have been Dr. Winkler, only he couldn't get to the hospital because of the floods."

The floods! Against the blank scrim of her mind, rivers of water flowed down rows of plants, the long leaves swimming in the current, skimming over the cold heavy mud. It hurt to think about it—or something hurt.

"I need to get up," she croaked urgently, turning her head back and forth. She needed to get to the field.

"Hold your horses! Here's the bedpan, right here."

"No," she said, and tried to explain—but actually it seemed she did need the bedpan. Hot urine soaked into the sheets, immediately turning cold. The round face pursed disapprovingly. Drenched in shame, Kate shut her eyes and let the fog take her.

A rustling, soft footsteps, a clean, astringent smell. A hand touched her cheek, moved to her throat, encircled her wrist. Not the rough touch of the nurse but dispassionate, cool as a leaf. Kate opened her eyes again, cautiously. Above her stood the tall woman from her dream with the dark hair and the white coat.

"Hello, Dr. Croft," the person said. "How are you feeling?"

"All right," Kate said, or tried to say. Her voice was scratchy and phlegmy, air moving unevenly through her throat.

"Would you like some water?"

Kate nodded.

The woman held out a white cup. She was long and lean as a lynx with dark eyes and dark arched brows. Water trickled into Kate's parched mouth. "I'm supposed to be hiking in the Laurentians," the lynx woman said. "But the roads were all flooded, so I came to work. Something always gets in the way of my holidays."

Kate tried to follow this. The pain had ebbed, but her mind seemed to drift just outside of her skull like a swarm of gnats. The cup went away and something smooth slid between her lips, probed its way under her tongue. The doctor frowned at her big wristwatch. She retrieved the thermometer and held it up to the light. "Ninety-nine point five. Excellent."

Kate flushed with pleasure as though it had been a compliment.

Thatch appeared: his worried face, his sandy-colored hair standing up, the way it got when he ran his hands through it when it was wet. "There you are," he said. His voice sounded thin and high as though carried on the wind from far away.

"Where?" she said. Everything was fuzzy, everything was soft-edged, bleeding into everything else: Thatch into the white wall behind him, a pale hand with blue veins (her hand?) into the sheet.

"In the hospital," he answered gravely.

"You're supposed to be on your honeymoon," she said, remembering.

"I was."

So a lot of time must have passed. Then she remembered. "I had pneumonia! Is that right? Someone told me that." The face floated back to her: pale with that knot of dark hair. She noticed that her ribs hurt.

"That's right. Lucky Professor Whitaker went looking for you. He was worried. Because you never miss work."

Whitaker saying, *They asked me to recommend someone.* Saying, *You still have your instructorship.*

"How was Niagara?" she asked hoarsely.

"We couldn't get there. There was so much rain, the roads were washed out. We ended up at a motel in Canandaigua."

Canandaigua! Poor Thatch. Not the wedding night he had anticipated. She began drifting away. Something about what he said made her almost remember something, but she couldn't think what. She couldn't think, really, at all.

"Cynthia sends her love," Thatch said. "She would have liked to come and see you, but she's feeling under the weather."

Then she did remember: the floods. "My field," she said.

"Hush," Thatch said.

"I need you to go check." A whining was starting up in her head like a great mosquito. She remembered the coldness of the mud, the places where the plants were missing like candles that had been blown out.

Thatch's face drew in. He looked tired, his lashes clotted and sticky. "You need to concentrate on getting better," he said.

With a great effort, she reached a hand toward him. It didn't look like her hand, but she supposed it had to be. Hands were so odd, if you thought about it—strange waving appendages, that you used to mediate between yourself and the world. "Please go check," she said. She spoke urgently but slowly, pushing out one word at a time.

Thatch put his other hand over hers and squeezed. "You rest," he said. "I'll come back later."

She made one more effort, raising her head, straining her neck, feeling the blade knifing through her. "Please," she said.

Behind Thatch the door swung open, and a tall broad-shouldered nurse came in with some instruments on a metal tray. "Lie back down, please, Kathleen. Your beau can come back another time."

Kate tried to catch Thatch's eye as the nurse stuck a thermometer in her mouth. She couldn't speak, but she could see he understood.

"Everyone's fields were flooded," he said quietly.

"Sir, the patient needs to rest now."

Kate's eyes widened.

"Yours, mine, Whitaker's. Yours survived the best. But that's not saying much. A few plants in each row."

So it was for nothing—all that effort! All that planning and scheming, weeks and months of preparation, midnights worrying. Plowing the field herself because otherwise the ground wasn't even enough, organizing the seeds in their brown paper packets so she always had the right one to hand, marching back and forth all day in the heat with the hand planter blistering her palms, dragging out the sprinklers every day at dawn. Her final drenching vigil in the rain. Which had landed her here.

"I'm sorry," Thatch said.

"I don't want to have to ask you again," the nurse said.

Gradually Kate's strength began to come back to her. She could stay awake for an hour at a time, she could drink a cup of broth. She could sit up and look out the window, where the sky showed, over the course of long days, every shade of blue. She'd read about a Swiss meteorologist who had invented a device to measure the color of the sky. She wished she had one, but it was a slight wish, transparent and feather-light. Lying in this drab room day after day, nothing seemed to matter very much. Thoughts drifted into her head and out again like clouds. Even the thoughts of her plants—washed away!—hardly stirred her now.

There seemed to be two worlds, the world of before with its pressures and demands—data to be collected, slides to be prepared, images analyzed, papers written—and this new slow crepuscular one, bounded by four white walls. Now the clockless days were marked not by hours or by tasks but by a nurse spooning soup into her mouth and by the taking of her temperature and the administration of various foul medicines, the names and purposes of which she couldn't be bothered to inquire. All of it drifted by, piercing or muffled depending on the state of her head. Everything was a jumble, pain coming and going for no reason she could discern, exhaustion overtaking her like a summer thunderstorm, then wakefulness returning—chaotically, confusingly—so that she opened her eyes to check whether it was day or night. The only thing she anticipated with any kind of feeling was the appearance, once a day, or occasionally twice, of the doctor.

Dr. Sonnenfeld was nothing like Kate's father. He had been jovial with patients, treating them like naughty children who would, nonetheless, be given sweets. Dr. Sonnenfeld was cool, reserved, faintly acerbic. She liked to work in silence, which was fine with Kate. Her hands, careful and sure, probed here, then here, so gently, while the white face, frowning slightly in concentration, stared at nothing. She worked quickly but methodically: throat, tongue, chest, belly, back. The silence washed over Kate like a balm as she gave herself over to that confident, unhesitating touch. You could feel her competence—her intelligence and skill—in the light, listening pressure of her long cool fingers. "You're doing very well," she said one day, when she was done, standing back as though Kate were a piece of work to be proud of. "Heart strong. Breathing clearer. No temp." She took a pair of spectacles from her pocket and made some notations on a paper.

It was restful to be nothing but a collection of data. "Can I see?" Kate asked.

"See what?"

"What you're writing."

A glimmer of amusement crossed the doctor's face as she held out the clipboard.

Kate's eyes skated over the inky marks, which might have been either letters or numbers. It was not unlike looking at markings on an ear of corn: there was a pattern there, if only one could figure out what it meant. Somewhere in that constellation of scribbles, Kate's essence was hidden.

Various visitors came and went: Thatch; her landlady; Miss Floris, bearing chocolates. Whitaker came twice, once bringing hothouse flowers Kate suspected Miss Floris of having both suggested and procured, and congratulating himself for having saved her life. "I expect some extra good work from you after this," he said, waving his unlit pipe in the air, handing the flowers to a nurse to put in water. "The minute you're out of this bed, I expect to see you in the lab."

Well, where else would she be?

Yet, with the whole season lost, it was hard to think about the lab with anything but dread.

As Kate got a little stronger, Dr. Sonnenfeld would stay and talk after her examination. "As a scientist, I thought you'd like to know that you're a bit of an experiment yourself," she said one morning as Kate leaned against the pillows. "We gave you a new kind of drug, a sulfonamide. Prontosil. It's said to be very effective against pneumonia. And so it's proved to be, in your case, anyway."

Kate did like that. "Am I part of an organized trial?" She pictured herself as a plant among many plants in an experimental field, tagged and watched.

"No. But you're one of the first patients we've treated with it at this hospital."

"Prontosil." Kate's mouth wrapped itself around the syllables.

"It was discovered in Germany. It's a kind of dye. In fact, I've been wondering if it would turn your skin red. It does that in some people, but I don't see it." Her gaze traveled along Kate's arms, which rested on top of the white sheets. It moved up her throat and across her face. "They say there's going to be a revolution in treating infections. A whole generation of new miracle drugs." Dr. Sonnenfeld had an interesting smile, genial and skeptical.

"You sound like you don't believe it."

The doctor shrugged. "I haven't seen a lot of miracles."

She was standing by the window. The light, streaming in, hurt Kate's eyes. The sky behind her was very pale, as though the blue had been spread infinitely thinly over something white and glaring.

Kate let her lids droop. "It must have seemed like a miracle the first time van Leeuwenhoek looked into a microscope."

Dr. Sonnenfeld laughed. "That was a long time ago."

"Just think about all the scientists in their laboratories all over the world," Kate said dreamily. "Thousands of them at their benches, busy as bees. Or is it beavers?" Either way she could picture them—buzzing and crawling, gnawing and dragging—but the picture made her tired. She yawned. The light dimmed. The doctor must have pulled the curtains.

"I'll let you rest."

But Kate didn't want to rest. She opened her eyes and looked up into the doctor's face: tiny starbursts of wrinkles around the mouth and eyes, thick dark arched eyebrows. "I'm not tired," she said, yawning again.

The doctor laid her hand on Kate's forehead, feeling for fever. A shiver ran from Kate's skull all the way down. "Are you cold?" Dr. Sonnenfeld asked. She pulled the sheet up higher.

Dr. Sonnenfeld was interested that Kate was a scientist. She asked her informed questions about corn; about the laws of heredity; about the culture of the botany department. She herself had gone to Vassar. "Where that female astronomer taught," she said. "The one who discovered the comet." After medical school she'd returned to Ithaca, where she'd grown up, to be close to her mother after her father died.

So they both had dead fathers.

"I would have stayed far away if I were you," Kate said.

"My mother is a kind of magnet," Dr. Sonnenfeld said.

181

"People are drawn to her. Children, dogs. Guests are always coming to stay temporarily, and then they don't move out for months."

Kate tried to imagine that. "What did she think about you becoming a doctor?" She wondered, too, what Mr. Sonnenfeld thought. If there was a Mr. Sonnenfeld. The doctor didn't wear a ring, but that could have been because she worked so much with her hands.

"She would have liked me to be a musician. I used to play the flute. She was a wonderful pianist, my mother, until the arthritis hit her. I think she could have been a professional. Instead she became a nurse, for a while, before she was married. I like to think of myself as having followed in her footsteps."

It was odd to have a doctor who talked about her mother. It made her seem almost not like a doctor at all.

The stethoscope made its cool circles on her chest. Ripples undulated out from the place where the drum rested—here, then here.

"You're much better," Dr. Sonnenfeld said. "We'll discharge you soon."

"Discharge me." For a moment Kate couldn't remember what that meant. It had to do with electricity, didn't it? With letting energy out, producing a spark.

"Do you have someone who can help look after you for a while, until you're stronger?"

Kate gaped at her: her pale tired face with its dark, steady eyes.

"When you go home, I mean. Perhaps a relative who could come and stay with you."

"Oh, no," Kate said. "That's out of the question."

Dr. Sonnenfeld smiled her interesting smile. "It's what people do, you know. A sister, perhaps."

Kate thought of Laura in her jewel-toned silk dresses,

heating up soup in Kate's tiny apartment. "She has two small children to look after."

"Perhaps you could move back to your parents' home for a few weeks."

Kate turned away and looked out the window where the top of a spindly hemlock swayed under the weight of a crow that had suddenly landed there. She had only been back to the house in Brooklyn a handful of times since she went away to college. The chilly relationship she maintained with her mother was only a step or two away from a breach. "I'm very self-sufficient," she said.

"You're making things difficult, Dr. Croft."

Kate liked that Dr. Sonnenfeld called her Dr. Croft. The horrible nurses all called her Kathleen.

"I can't keep you here much longer. And you're not strong enough to be on your own."

The crow smoothed its glossy wings with its beak.

"If you gave me your family's address, I could write to them. They are your family, after all."

But why was that supposed to matter? In every way that counted, Kate had made herself.

CHAPTER 19

The knock was so quiet, so tentative, it sounded like someone knocking on the door across the hall. But then a face appeared, thin and dark and smiling shyly.

"Cynthia," Kate said.

"Is it all right if I come in?"

"Of course." Kate pushed herself upright, pulled the sheets around her, and smoothed them, while Cynthia stood just inside the doorway. "Are you feeling better?" Kate asked after what felt like a long time.

Cynthia blushed. "I should be asking you that." She held a jam jar with a few stalks of purplish joe-pye weed, which she set down on the little table beside Whitaker's fiery gladiolas. "They can't compete, can they? But I thought they were pretty."

"I like wildflowers," Kate said.

"Weeds," Cynthia said.

"Butterflies like them, too." The air between them felt thin and brittle, like a scrim of ice. Kate wondered if she could pretend to be tired and need to sleep. Perhaps a nurse would barge in with a thermometer or a medicine bottle. Kate didn't think she and Cynthia had ever been alone in a room together before. Mostly she didn't bother trying to make small talk with people, but this was Thatch's wife. "Little glassywings," she offered. "American ladies. *Vanessa virginiensis.*" Perhaps naming butterflies wasn't exactly small talk, but it was the best she could manage.

"I love the Latin binomial names," Cynthia said. "Don't you? *Eutrochium dubium.*" Gently she touched the untidy flower head.

"I always forget you're a botanist."

Cynthia's doe eyes turned to her. "Was."

"You could always change your mind and go back to it."

"No. I like plants, but I'm not disciplined."

Kate knew lots of scientists who weren't disciplined. But she thought it was probably time to change the subject. "I was sorry to hear about the honeymoon," she said. "The flooding, I mean."

"And I was sorry to hear about your plants." Cynthia's big eyes were full of pity, which was unbearable. "John has told me how they're everything to you."

Were, Kate thought. So Thatch talked about her with Cynthia. Well, why wouldn't he? They were married, after all.

"But he said there were a few left. Perhaps you can salvage something."

"When do you leave for New York?" Kate asked. "You must be excited."

Cynthia touched the flower again, very gently, with her thin olive forefinger. "The Indians used *Eutrochium* to treat fevers," she said.

"Plants do have extraordinary properties," Kate said. "Since they can't escape their enemies by running, they have to be crafty."

Cynthia laughed, which made her look suddenly pretty, the way Kate remembered her looking. "That makes a person feel uncomfortable about eating a carrot," she said.

In fact, Kate often felt uncomfortable eating carrots. Fruit was one thing—the plant offered it to you of its own free will—but who could say that a carrot felt less pain than a cow? "How's Thatch?" she asked.

"John's all right. Just a little anxious. So many changes."

"They're going to love him at the Rockefeller."

Cynthia's eyes fell to her lap, where her hands lay neatly

185

folded as if she were in church. "Of course, not all the changes are professional."

Kate didn't know what to say to that.

"Do you mind if I tell you something?"

"Go ahead," Kate said, though she wanted no confidences.

Cynthia raised her large dark soft eyes to Kate's. "We're going to have a child."

"A child!" Kate echoed, trying not to sound horrified. Her mind felt rubbery. How on earth could the girl know already? Or did that mean that before the wedding...?

None of her business.

"He must be thrilled!" she said loudly to blow those thoughts away.

Cynthia leaned closer. "I haven't told him yet."

A well of dread opened in Kate's gut. "Why not?"

"I want to wait till it's more ... I mean, in case anything happens. I'd hate for him to be disappointed."

"I'm sure everything will be fine," Kate said. For the first time in a long time she thought longingly of her apartment: its cramped quiet rooms, its old soft pillows and smells of books and furniture wax. Its door that locked.

Cynthia's gaze seemed to pin Kate in place on the pillows. "I had to tell somebody," she said. "He cares about you more than anybody. So in a way, that makes us almost like sisters."

Kate did her best to smile.

"But what about you," Cynthia said. "How are you feeling, really? When are they going to let you go home?"

"Soon. I'm so much better! Only the doctor insists I can't take care of myself." Kate was still so indignant that she forgot to be cautious. "She suggested— As if I could possibly! But it doesn't bear talking about."

Cynthia's face lit up. "Of course you'll come to us!" she said. "At least until we leave," she added, remembering.

"Oh, no!" Kate tried to sound firm rather than panic-stricken. "I couldn't let you do that."

"But I'd like it," Cynthia said. "It would take my mind off things. Which would be so good for me."

"You just got married!" Kate sat up straighter. Her short hair, grown shaggy now, stuck out every which way as though electrified. "It wouldn't be right."

Cynthia scooted her chair closer and leaned over the bed. She smelled of heavy, oily hair and lily of the valley. "On the contrary. It's the most right thing I can think of. I know John would say so, too." Cynthia leaned down farther still and took Kate's hand. Her hair fell forward like a veil, blocking out the air. There their hands lay on the beige hospital blanket: Cynthia's thin and long, the nails perfect ovals, the skin smooth and dry. Kate's hand looked small and pasty, the blue veins showing. "We have to take care of one another," Cynthia said.

When she was gone, Kate lay back on the sheets. The mauve flower head of the joe-pye weed seemed to watch her as though its hundred tiny florets concealed eyes. If she could show Dr. Sonnenfeld that she was strong enough, surely she would let her go home. Carefully, she pushed herself up and swung her legs over the side of the bed. One bare foot and then the other reached down toward the floor. The tile was cold. Slowly, she pushed herself upright. A distant ringing began inside her head. Out the window, the hemlock tree stood, its needles green and black, very peacefully, wanting nothing of her. She took a step toward the window. The tree—kind or indifferent—disregarded her clumsiness. Another step. Something was happening at the edges of her vision. A flickering darkness encroached from the sides until there was only the tree—its deep, impervious green. Then something struck her head. Oh—the window! She leaned against it for a long moment, the hard glass soothing in its coolness.

*　　*　　*

"Dr. Croft," someone said. "Dr. Croft! For heaven's sake."

Kate looked up. Dark stern eyes under disapproving brows hovered over her as she lay sprawled on the floor. "I thought I'd just . . ." she said, or tried to say. How had she come to be here, sprawled on the cold floor?

"Lie still," the doctor said as Kate struggled to sit. "Do what I say, please. Now: can you move your arms? One at a time. Your legs? Good. All right. Let's get you up." She drew one of Kate's arm around her shoulders, put her own firm arm under Kate's back, and lifted. She was surprisingly strong, or else Kate had grown very light. She smelled of antiseptic and clean cotton and something else. Oranges? Kate's head flopped back against the doctor's chest as she bore Kate in her arms across the room in a few long strides and laid her on the bed—not gently, but adeptly, like a seamstress laying out a bolt of cloth. "If Nurse Johnson had found you, she would have been very cross."

Horrible thought! "Just send me home," Kate said.

"I've said that's out of the question."

"I'm perfectly capable—"

"Of collapsing into a heap on the floor," the doctor said. "Yes, I know."

"I just got a little dizzy."

Dr. Sonnenfeld held up her hand. "Stop arguing for ten seconds and listen, please," she said. "I came to tell you that I've solved your problem."

CHAPTER 20

The trip from the hospital to the long room under the eaves wore Kate out. Dr. Sonnenfeld and her mother practically had to haul her up the two flights of stairs, one on each side. Collapsed at last in the soft bed under a quilt of orderly flowers, her bones ached and her head buzzed with pain. With an effort she drank water from the glass Mrs. Sonnenfeld held out to her. "Thank you," she said. "I'll try not to be a difficult patient."

"And I will try not to be a difficult nurse," Mrs. Sonnenfeld said. She bent over the bed and looked Kate over. "My daughter says you are a stubborn person. I, too, am stubborn. So: we should get along very well."

Kate was amused by this, but faintly, through blurred layers of exhaustion.

The sun streamed in through the open window, and a light breeze carried the scent of roses into the room. Ever since the floods, the weather had been perfect, the most beautiful summer anyone could remember, everyone said. But for Kate, the passage from the hospital to the car and the car to the house had been nearly unbearable, the air so fresh it abraded her skin, the light too sharp, the smell of the mown grass rank and overripe.

"Could you shut the window?" Kate asked. "And the curtains?"

"Fresh air is good for you," Mrs. Sonnenfeld said. "If you shut yourself up in the dark, you will shrivel like a grub."

But Dr. Sonnenfeld went over to the window and shut it. Mrs. Sonnenfeld snorted. The doctor came and stood over the bed. "Mutti will take good care of you," she said. "And I'll come and see you when I get home."

"Pardon?" Kate struggled to keep her eyes open.

"My room is right under yours. But don't worry. I don't snore or play the gramophone, even when I'm here. Which is hardly ever."

It hadn't occurred to Kate that Dr. Sonnenfeld actually *lived* with her mother. Her heart began to beat a little faster: *ga-lump ga-lump ga-lump*, like a rabbit bounding slowly across a field.

Mrs. Sonnenfeld was a stout woman with a soft powdery face and a peremptory, musical Bavarian voice. She wore dark wool coatdresses and sturdy buckled shoes, and trotted up and down the steps of the big three-story house with her white hair floating around her head like a cloud. From her perch at the top of the house, Kate listened to the sounds she made moving from room to room: the rumble of furniture pushed away so she could mop behind it, the hiss of steam as she attacked her ironing, the clatter of cooking pots on the polished range, the rise and fall of her melodious German as she talked to the dogs. There were three dogs, Irish setters with shiny, silky auburn fur and feathery tails waving like flags: Lily, Holly, and Rose. Their long nails clicked on the hardwood floors and scrabbled on the stairs, and sometimes, out in the yard, they goaded one another into howls when the paperboy whizzed by. They knew better than to chase him, but their passionate desire to charge his gleaming bicycle required some kind of outlet.

Ten times a day Mrs. Sonnenfeld clomped up to Kate's room—no hushed nurse in rubber-soled shoes but a solid competent dervish carrying trays and wielding thermometers, giving sponge baths and insisting that Kate change into a clean nightgown every day; that she finish the last table-

spoon of broth; that she walk up and down the third-floor
hall to build her strength but that she *not* under any circumstance try the stairs. And so, even as she lay mostly confined
to bed, her days began to take on a shape: Mrs. Sonnenfeld's
visits with trays of soup and rice pudding; the movement of
the sun across the braided rug; her own repetitive trek up
and down the third floor hallway with its dark green wallpaper scattered with bright shapes that might have been meant
to be leaves.

And then, at the end of the day, Dr. Sonnenfeld's appearance in the doorway of the convalescent room.

Often, despite her best efforts, Kate would have fallen
asleep by the time the doctor got home. She would awaken
to the creak of the door swinging open, to the freshness of
night air and the faint pungency of cigarette smoke the older
woman carried in with her on her clothes and in her hair.
Dr. Sonnenfeld would lean against the wall, lifting her chin
and blowing smoke out through her red pursed lips. Or she
would sit in the sturdy oak-and-leather chair by the bed, still
in her white coat, a glass of whiskey balanced on the chair's
broad arm, peeling an orange in one long spiral with her slow
deft hands.

Kate sat propped up on three pillows against the headboard,
which was carved with flowers and pomegranates. "Did anyone come in today with anything interesting wrong with
them?"

"No one ever has anything interesting wrong with them.
I thought medicine was going to be exciting, but mostly it's
amazingly dull. Cuts, infections, broken legs. Alcoholism."

"I broke my leg once. Jumping out of a tree."

"Why did you do that?"

"I was trying to see if I could fly. I was six."

Dr. Sonnenfeld slid a section of orange into her mouth.

Outside, the crickets were calling loudly in the bushes, and once in a while a firefly (*Lampyridae*) flitted by, its greenish light leaving an afterimage in the dark. "I used to dream about flying. Across the meadow and out over the lake. What lovely dreams!"

"It looked easy when the birds did it. I was shocked when I went down so hard." She had almost forgotten this, but it came back to her now: the chilly, cloudy autumn day. The smell of pine needles and the rough texture of the bark under her hands. The dipping flight of a goldfinch, yellow against the white sky—her father had taught her to identify finches by the way they flew—the moment before she launched herself out of the tree.

How fast the ground had risen up.

"My mother was so angry. She had to stop what she was doing and rush out and see what I was bawling about."

"It must have hurt a lot."

"I don't remember that. Just being furious that it didn't work." Wildly flapping her arms, and still her body plunged like a stone! She had shrieked in frustration when her mother ran toward her calling out, "What in the name of heaven is it now, Kathleen?" How her father's face had floated into her field of vision at last. "I remember my father talking to me as he set the bone. He asked me how it had happened, and I told him, and he didn't laugh or get mad. He told me about giant air balloons that carried baskets you could ride in. He said, if I promised not to try to fly again, he would take me up in one someday." She could picture her father so clearly in his dark suit and hat, his neat sideburns. The grave expression on his kind calm face.

"And did he?" Dr. Sonnenfeld asked.

It had been a promise between them: that was what Kate had always thought. A promise he had died before getting a chance to keep. But maybe it was just what you said to a child to make them behave? To take their mind off their pain? Because it was true that there must have been pain, even if she couldn't remember it now.

"Did he?" the doctor asked again. She leaned forward, her white throat gleaming in the lamplight, the smell of oranges drifting out from her hands. "Kate?"

Her name in the doctor's mouth, like a chime being struck, echoed through all the chambers of her body.

Kate graduated to scrambled eggs and boiled chicken. Mrs. Sonnenfeld said she was doing so well that she could come downstairs and have her lunch in the kitchen. Upstairs, in her room, the sheets and walls were white, the furniture honey brown. Down here, colors glared and shimmered: orange lilies in a vase, a red bowl of purple plums, bright yellow curtains fluttering at the windows. She was confronted with tongue in caper sauce, pink and green on the china platter. The dogs galloped in, tails waving, nudging their narrow skulls under Kate's hands. "*Aus! Aus!*" Mrs. Sonnenfeld cried.

Kate stroked the silken heads. "I don't mind."

But Mrs. Sonnenfeld flapped her apron, shooing them away, and the dogs, sighing, crept back into the hall. Kate put a morsel of meat into her mouth. Mrs. Sonnenfeld sat down across the table and watched her. "You like tongue, I hope?"

Kate nodded, though the fatty stuff felt odd in her mouth. "You're not eating?"

The older woman patted her stout waist. "I can live off my stored belly fat. Sarah says I should do reducing exercises, but it just happens with age, this expanding. She'll see." She pointed her double chin at Kate. "You, too. Such a skinny chicken now, but when you are an old lady, and your children are all grown, it will be a different story."

Kate looked up into the soft-cheeked face with its fierce expression. It seemed nothing you could say would bother

Mrs. Sonnenfeld much, or change her opinion. "I'm not going to have children," she said.

Mrs. Sonnenfeld snorted. She reached for the platter of tongue, pulled off a soft piece, and popped it into her mouth. "I, too, did not meet my husband for a long time," she said, chewing. "These things are hard to imagine before they happen. But then, in a breath, everything changes."

The dogs had crept forward into the doorway. They lay three abreast, their long noses quivering on the threshold, their tails sweeping the hall floor.

"When did Mr. Sonnenfeld die?"

"Oh, many years ago now. Well, he was older. It was natural that it happened that way. It was part of the bargain." Her plump fingers reached for the platter.

"Not everyone gets married," Kate said after a pause. "Your daughter, for instance."

"Sarah!" Mrs. Sonnenfeld scoffed, flapping her hand. "Sarah has always been impossible. Ever since she was a little girl, she has done exactly as she liked. I always told her, men don't like women who act so smart!"

"Some men do," Kate said, thinking of Thatch.

"It was her father's fault, anyhow. He spoiled her."

"Spoiled?"

"He was always for her buying. China dolls, silk frocks— too fancy for a small child. He used to travel a lot for his business, and he always brought her something back. Something *expensive*." Mrs. Sonnenfeld made a face, her lips glistening from the fatty meat. "When she was nine, he got for her a doll's house like you never saw. A doll's mansion! Furniture, miniature plates and cups and bottles of milk. Oh, she loved it, though. She would play with it for hours. She loved her dolls. She loved tea parties and dressing up in my hats. Such a waste!" The older woman's eyes were damp. She pushed her chair back and got up, filling the kettle, pulling her handkerchief from her apron pocket, keeping her back to Kate.

Kate looked at the dogs, still lying with their noses in the doorway. Quietly she slipped her unfinished portion of tongue to the floor. Two of the dogs stayed obediently where they were, their eyes fixed longingly on the meat, but the third—slightly smaller than the others, with the brightest, blackest eyes—leapt forward and gobbled it down. By the time Mrs. Sonnenfeld returned to the table with a plate and a knife and fork of her own, having decided to have a little lunch after all, the dog was back in its place.

"Not that I'm not proud of my Sarah," Mrs. Sonnenfeld said, heaping her plate.

Thatch had to stoop to get his head under the doorjamb. "Look at you up here, like a bird in its aerie," he said. "You're feeling better?" He and Cynthia were leaving for New York in a few days, and he had come to say goodbye.

"Yes."

"You scared me in the hospital. You were barely a wisp." Kate thought he looked wisp-like himself. Thinner, his face drawn. Had his cheekbones always stuck out like that? "You'll be going back to work soon, then," he said.

Kate looked up at the slanted ceiling where the shadows of leaves moved over the surface. A freight of sand seemed to be sluicing back and forth through her skull. When she thought about setting up a microscope, she was sure her fingers would fumble. If she tried reading a paper, her mind would shut down like a lens aperture closing. She could feel it starting to shut down now. "I keep thinking about the field," she said. "The way it looked in all that rain." Darkness, the drowned plants tugged by the current, their roots clinging hopelessly to the dissolving ground.

"There are still a few plants left."

She looked at him furiously. "And what good does that

do me? I can't tend to them! I can't shoot-bag them! They're useless."

"You'll replant," Thatch said. "In the spring. Everyone will be replanting."

"Not you," Kate said, more sharply than she'd intended. "You're moving on."

"I lost a year's data, too," he said.

She took a breath, trying to hold back her anger as she had tried to keep the water back in the doomed field. "How's Cynthia?"

Thatch looked out the window where the leaves of a tulip poplar (*Liriodendron tulipifera*) waved gently in the hot afternoon. "I worry about her," he said. His fingers drummed on his bony knees. "She's so thin. As thin as you." He smiled unhappily, his gaze flitting to Kate's face and then away again. "Just looking at food seems to make her feel ill."

"Well, it's natural," Kate said impatiently. "For someone in her condition."

The room went still. "What do you mean?"

Kate stared at him. It had been weeks since Cynthia had confided in her! "It didn't cross your mind that the signs you just described have an obvious implication?"

Thatch stood up and went to the window. His hands gripped the frame. "How do you know?"

From the back, he still looked like the boy she'd first known, scrawny and tall and loose-limbed, his sandy hair untidy. "Thatch," she said. "She wanted to protect you. That's all. She was worried something bad would happen. She wanted to wait till she was sure everything would be okay."

Thatch's chest expanded and contracted mechanically inside his wrinkled blue shirt.

"It's good news, Thatch," Kate said. "A new little F1."

CHAPTER 21

Kate was awakened by the racket of the dogs rushing down the stairs that meant Dr. Sonnenfeld had come home. The night lay all around her, deep and still, the face of the clock on the bureau bathed in darkness. After a minute, the dogs quieted. Kate strained to hear a footstep, or a cabinet opening, or a door shutting. Maybe it had been nothing, just the dogs hearing a noise out on the street. She turned over.

What was it she had been dreaming of? An ocean? Floating in black water under a starry sky . . . She shivered in the breeze from the open window, turned on her other side, drew her knees together under the covers. Pressed them tight. Her mind felt dreamy, yet stimulated and alert, as though little lights inside it were blinking on and off. Her thoughts jumped restlessly. To calm herself she began reciting the botanical phyla and classes: *Thallophyta, Bryophyta, Pteridophyta* . . .

It was odd to have been away from plants for so long, to think of her lab sitting empty all this time.

Gymnospermae, Angiospermae.

There must have been footsteps in the hall, but Kate hadn't heard them. Now, suddenly, the door sprang open. Dr. Sonnenfeld stood in the doorway, a tall shadow. No tumbler of whiskey, no cigarette, her hands dangling at her sides.

"What's wrong?" Kate said, sitting up.

"I'm sorry. It's horribly late. I didn't mean to wake you."

"I was awake already." As her eyes adjusted, she saw how stricken the other woman looked. "Is your mother all right?" Kate said.

"She's fine! No. It was something at the hospital. I just. . ."
She leaned against the doorway, her eyes glittering.

Kate was on her feet without knowing she was going to
stand. She crossed the room and took Dr. Sonnenfeld by the
arm and led her to the bed and sat her down. "It's all right,"
she said, sitting down beside her. "Can I get you a glass of
water?" Under the surface softness of Dr. Sonnenfeld's arm
she could feel the hardness of muscle and bone.

"These things don't usually. . ." The doctor stopped, then
began again. "Usually I can—"

But whatever it was she could usually do, she couldn't do
it now. Instead, she leaned toward Kate, just the smallest shift
of weight. It was an intensification of heat Kate felt, a prick-
ling of her skin. Dr. Sonnenfeld's white blouse, her swan's
neck, her long pale earlobes looked ghostly, as though Kate
could pass a hand right through her. "What happened?"

"I should get something to eat. I think I never had any
dinner."

"Tell me," Kate said. Anyone could see the words pushing up right there in her mouth behind her closed lips. "Sarah," Kate said.

The dark head lifted.

"Sarah. Tell me."

They were sitting so close together that the white face
was just inches from Kate's own—close enough to feel her
breath, to be startled by the minnow twitch of a muscle
jumping in her cheek.

"Whatever happened," Kate said sternly, "I'm sure it
wasn't your fault." Inside her nightgown, inside her skin,
inside the sturdy cage of her ribs, her heart thumped. Slowly, Kate reached toward her and touched the narrow back.
Dr. Sonnenfeld—Sarah—turned. Her mouth grazed the
side of Kate's mouth. Kate drew back half an inch in case
there had been a mistake. For a moment they were like two

hummingbirds, each beating its wings fifty times a second in order to stay perfectly still. Then, almost imperceptibly, a head inclined, and the other, like a mirror, followed it. Lips touched—the barest brushing, like a moth grazing a leaf— yet the whole room seemed to rise up whirling.

It was still dark, but out the window some bird in the leafy arms of a tree had begun to sing.

"Mutti will be getting up soon," Sarah said.

Kate lay stretched out on the sheets, naked, her skin flushed and warm. "Kiss me," she said.

Obediently, Sarah turned her head. Lips, tongue, teeth. Hands caressing, seeking out the tenderest places, the hollow above the collarbone, the damp crease at the back of a knee. The lowest vertebrae, like the place a stalk met the ground.

The bird sang louder. The sky was perhaps not completely black.

Sarah pulled away. "Listen," she said, sitting up against the headboard with its carved pomegranates.

Kate reached for her silken thigh, burrowed into her lap. Sarah didn't have to warn her. She was good at secrets.

"Listen," Sarah said again.

"Shh."

"I need to tell you about what happened at the hospital."

Kate stopped nuzzling. She rolled over on the rucked sheets and looked up at Sarah. The outlines of her strong face and her sharp clean collarbones, her wide shoulders and her pomegranate-shaped breasts were growing more distinct. Any moment Mrs. Sonnenfeld would get up and lumber down the stairs to let out the dogs.

"The person who came in last night: it was your friend. The one married to that man you work with."

"Cynthia?" Kate said, though she was sure it couldn't be.

"She lost her baby. She lost a lot of blood, too. She waited a long time to come in."

Kate sat up and pulled the sheet up around her.

All the time she and Sarah had been together in this bed, Thatch would have been sitting in a hard chair in the hospital beside another kind of bed entirely, in which his wife lay. A bare field washed with blood. "Will she be all right?"

The sky was visibly changing now, charcoal gray lightening to lead gray, slate gray, oyster, ash. When she spoke, Sarah's voice was clean and hard and precise as a medical instrument. "Miscarriage happens to a lot of women. Usually it means there was something wrong with the fetus. That it wasn't viable, that there was some sort of major defect."

"Will she be all right?" Kate asked again.

Sarah turned her face toward Kate, and her expression, too, was hard, shining. Blazing with something. Fury maybe, or compassion, or failure. "She was so unhappy. Stricken. Deranged by grief!"

"Will she be able to have a child?"

But Sarah was saying something quite different. "And then, somehow—when everyone was out of the room—she cut herself. Her wrists."

The olive skin, the bones jutting as she turned the diamond ring on her finger in Kate's office; as she and Thatch pressed the knife down through the wedding cake. The skin slit, the blood in the bluish veins spurting out. "Is she *dead*?"

"No! No. The nurse found her."

Kate got up and began to look around for her clothes. She had worn nothing but nightgowns and robes and slippers for weeks.

"What are you doing?" Sarah said.

"I need to go and see them." Him, she meant.

"Get back in bed," Sarah said. "You're still weak. It's the middle of the night."

But it wasn't the middle of the night, not any longer. And she wasn't so weak anymore. She tried the drawers of the bureau: linens. She tried the closet: a man's gabardine trousers folded over a hanger. She turned back to Sarah. "I need something to wear," she said.

From down below, now, came the sound of a door opening, the pattering of canine toenails, the phlegmy noise of Mrs. Sonnenfeld clearing her throat as she crossed the landing to the second-floor lavatory. Kate's head began to feel odd. There was a ringing coming from somewhere. She put out her hand and braced it against the wall.

Sarah jumped up and grasped Kate by her bare thin arm.

Kate pulled away. "I've been inside too long, that's all." But her head was spinning, and she had to sit down on the floor.

Sarah fetched Kate's nightgown and slipped it over her head. She lifted Kate's arms and threaded them through the armholes as if Kate were a doll. Kate remembered what Mrs. Sonnenfeld had said about how Sarah had loved dolls, how she had loved the dollhouse her father had given her with its miniature chairs and tables and bottles of milk. So different from what Kate had loved: walks in the fields and baseball games in the street with the neighborhood boys. What made them so different? Had they been born that way? If you could go back in time and switch them, place them in the other's household . . . From downstairs came the sounds of pans clanging, water running, Mrs. Sonnenfeld speaking German to the dogs.

Sarah put her hands on Kate's shoulders. "I thought I might take that holiday I missed. My aunt has a house she lets me use. On Cape Cod. We could go there for a couple of weeks. You could eat. Lie in the sun. The dogs love it! You could get your strength back." Her fingers were making light circles on Kate's collarbones, and Kate felt the touch all the way down her spine. Light streamed into the room from the window. Her breath churned through her body. Twenty-eight years old, and every part of her felt unfinished, translucent. Mutable. She had always wanted to see the mystery creature inside the chrysalis. Now, she was it.

"Sarah!" Mrs. Sonnenfeld's voice sailed up the stairwell. "Are you up? I'm making oatmeal! If you are not eating it, I will be very annoyed."

Kate froze, but Sarah walked casually to the door. "I was just checking on our patient," she called down.

CHAPTER 22

K ate agreed to the trip to Cape Cod. Afterward, assuming she'd regained her strength, she would return to her own apartment and go back to work.

But before they left, she had to go see the Great Man. On her way down the hall to Whitaker's office, she peeked into Thatch's cubbyhole. Someone had already colonized it. She was shocked to see how different the space looked: the bookcase half full of unfamiliar books, the desk jammed into a different corner in a futile attempt to make the room seem bigger, the burnt toast and chemical fixative smell drifting out into the hallway instead of the smell of coffee.

Opening the door to her own lab was almost as strange. Here were her packets of seeds, her dusty lab notebooks dense with penciled tables, her trays of slides, her orderly cabinets. Her microscope in its black sheath as though in mourning. When she took the cover off, its contours were cold under her hands. She touched the ridged knobs, leaned her face toward the eyepiece. Drew back.

In Whitaker's outer office, Miss Floris was typing furiously, a cigarette burning in the ashtray on her desk. That Miss Floris had been Whitaker's secretary forever, and that she had never married, provoked the usual stupid jokes among successive waves of graduate students, but to Kate it suggested that she was better than most people at keeping her private life private. Now she got up and came around the desk to embrace Kate. "We were so worried," she said. "Even *he* was. When I saw you in that hospital bed, you looked like a husk that might blow away. But you look fine now! You look like yourself."

"I'm much better," Kate said.

"I hate to think, if he hadn't gone to your apartment."

Kate waited for Miss Floris to mention Cynthia, but she said nothing. Maybe she didn't know. Or maybe she was just practicing her discretion. "Is he in?"

"Dr. Zimmer is with him. He's here to give a seminar. They were supposed to be finished an hour ago."

Kate knew of Fred Zimmer, a maize geneticist who was doing pioneering work with X-rays: using them to create dozens of mutations to study rather than waiting for nature to toss one up. They'd corresponded, and he'd irradiated some of the stocks she was using, but she'd never met him. "Should I come back?"

"Certainly not. Go right in."

Kate knocked and opened the door. Behind his vast, li-on-clawed desk, Whitaker reclined in his chair with his legs stretched out, the heels of his work boots on the blotter near the miniature tree that looked unchanged since the first time Kate had seen it. The other man—Zimmer—was leaning forward as though he had been talking intently. Both men were smoking pipes, the blue-gray trails rising in converging streams toward the window.

"Good to finally meet you," Zimmer said, shaking her hand. He had an alert mild face and looked not that much older than she was.

Whitaker was beaming. "I saved this girl's life," he said. "She was dying of pneumonia, blue and limp as a beached fish, and I found her and carried her to her salvation."

"He broke into my apartment," Kate said, sitting down. "I'm a beneficiary of the willingness of the modern scientist to prevail by any means necessary."

"The Chinese would say that means you're responsible for her life forever," Zimmer told Whitaker.

"I'm looking out for her all right," Whitaker said. "I'm

making her into a first-class corn man." He smiled. "It's good to have you back, Kate."

"I'm almost back," she said quickly. "My doctor says I just need a couple of more weeks and then I'll be right as rain."

The stem of Whitaker's pipe made a little clicking noise against his teeth. "She's lucky I'm fond of her," he said to Zimmer. "I know half a dozen men who would start tomorrow."

"It's the same at Missouri. I get letters from qualified people every week. But unless they bring their own funding, there's not much we can do."

"How are the fields?" Kate asked. "Thatch said nearly everything was lost."

"The worst flood in a generation," Whitaker said. "But somehow you still have a few plants standing." He said this mock-accusingly, or maybe actually accusingly, his lips either smiling or pretending to smile. "The gods must have a soft spot for you."

She sat up straighter. "Not that it matters," she said. "Since I wasn't able to bag them."

Whitaker took his boots off the desk and fiddled with his pipe. "Thatch did it."

She blinked at him as he tapped the ashes out. "What did Thatch do?"

"He bagged the plants for you before he left."

Kate could not believe it. "He would have told me if he'd done that."

"He meant to go see you, but at the last minute— Well. He asked me to let you know. The point is, you can fertilize them if you do it soon. If the plants that survived give you any crosses worth making."

Kate stared at Whitaker, who was refilling his pipe rather clumsily. "He bagged them?" she repeated.

"There weren't many," Whitaker said. "It couldn't have

taken him long." He turned to Zimmer and began to explain his plan for the university administration to build a protective berm with a channel to funnel water away from the fields to mitigate future flood damage. "We're the most productive department in the division," Whitaker said. "Pick any measure you like. Publications, citations, fellowships. Then something like this happens, and everything is set back a year."

"The drosophila people don't have these problems," Zimmer said.

"It's in the university's interest to protect our work," Whitaker said. "But they behave as though it has nothing to do with them."

"You have to show them something exciting. You have to make them believe you're on the verge of something big." Zimmer turned to Kate. "I'm trying to start up a whole X-ray institute at Missouri."

"That's a wonderful idea," Kate said.

"We're getting some very interesting variegation. Interesting patterns on the kernels."

Kate felt a pang of envy. If there hadn't been a flood . . . If she hadn't gotten sick . . .

But Whitaker said Thatch had shoot-bagged her plants, so maybe the whole year wouldn't be lost.

"What kind of variegation?" Kate asked.

"All kinds. On the leaves. On the stalks. Intriguing patterns on the kernels."

"He's getting ten times more than we've been seeing," Whitaker said. "It's incredible."

Kate, too, was studying variegated plants. The kernels would be colorless when they should be red, or the leaf ribs would be yellow when they should be green. That was simple to explain: a dominant gene was knocked out and a recessive one expressed. But Zimmer's corn sounded as though it was in a different category entirely. "I'd love to hear more about it."

He smiled. "It's the subject of my talk."

She hadn't planned to go to the talk. She'd promised Sarah not to tire herself.

Whitaker looked at his watch. "Speaking of which."

Kate followed the men out of the office and down the hall. She felt unreal, semitransparent, a ghost haunting the place it had once belonged.

In the seminar room, Zimmer strode up and down, waving a piece of chalk, his ideas unfolding like a series of immaculate handkerchiefs. X-rays, mutations, markings, ingenious crosses. Every detail was carefully established, every leap of logic both cunning and plainly laid out. Warmth rippled through her chest as he showed slides of the markings on the kernels he had grown: white kernels with purple streaks, yellow kernels speckled purple and red. "I'd like to say there's a pattern here," he said, "but so far we haven't found one."

There had to be a pattern, Kate thought: a cause to explain the effect. That was how nature worked. It might be— must be—subtle. Complex. But it was there.

After the talk, she drove out to look at her field.

It was a hot dry summer day with only a few puddles spread across the verges. Sparrows and phoebes sang in the branches, and smoky clouds of gnats drifted through the damp air. The reflections of the clouds swimming slowly across the puddles' surfaces made the shallow water look depthless. Water striders crouched on weightless legs, waiting for prey.

In the field itself, twenty-six plants were scattered across the rows. Twenty-six out of the two hundred she had planted. They were chest-high now, green and straight. She walked up to each one, walked around it, touched its long sharp leaves. Glassine envelopes were stapled neatly over the shoots, and the brown paper bags fastened over the tassels rattled faintly in the breeze. Thatch had done a neat job. She couldn't have done a better one herself.

Kate was so tired by the time she came through the kitchen door that she thought she might lie down right on the linoleum.

"Where on earth have you been?" Sarah said. "I expected you hours ago." She was sitting at the kitchen table doing the crossword, her dark hair in its chignon, her glasses on, looking severe and regal as she smoked.

Thinking better of the floor, Kate pulled out a chair. The dogs came skittering in to greet her, nuzzling her with their long noses. "It took longer than I thought."

"You're as pale as a ghost." Sarah got up and nudged the dogs away. She stood over Kate and began to take her pulse.

"I'm fine," Kate said. Sarah's fingers were warm on her wrist. "I'm just tired."

"I'll say whether you're fine or not."

Holly wriggled into the space between them, and Rose followed suit. "Out," Sarah ordered. "They think they can get away with anything when Mutti's at bridge club."

Holly looked at Sarah and wagged her tail. Rose let out a happy bark. Lily sat politely, ears pricked, waiting to be praised.

"*Aus! Aus!*" Sarah cried, letting go of Kate's wrist and clapping her hands.

The dogs retreated behind the threshold of the hall.

"German-speaking Irish setters," Kate said.

"They don't *speak* German," Sarah said. "Now I have to start again." But before she could, Kate seized Sarah's hand and kissed the fingers, the palm, the wrist. Sarah made a sound in her throat and let Kate draw her closer. The skin of her inner arm was cool and silken. In Kate's mind's eye she could see the way the skin would look under the microscope: the whorled cells, the nucleus. The threads of the chromosomes that somehow made Sarah who she was.

CHAPTER 23

Sarah's aunt's cottage hugged the top of the dune. Its porch, supported by long stilts buried in sand, seemed to float over the beach. "It has to be rebuilt after storms," Sarah said as they went out onto the weathered boards to watch the green waves crashing, then unfurling their lace along the sand.

"Are there hurricanes?"

"Nor'easters mostly."

The wind ruffled their hair. The waves heaved and sighed.

"I love storms," Kate said. "Maybe we'll get one."

"I should hope not!"

"I love them as long as they stay far away from my cornfield," she amended.

"No talking about work," Sarah said. "That's rule one."

The cottage was just two rooms. The big one was living room and kitchen combined, with a table where you could eat looking out over the bay. The bedroom had two narrow beds, which they pushed together. The wicker furniture creaked when you sat down, and there were faded cushions smelling faintly of mold, baskets of seashells and baskets of pebbles, a big iron bucket of driftwood to burn in the stove. At the windows, white gauzy curtains shifted with every breath of wind. On the floor, yellow rush mats lay instead of rugs on the blue-gray boards. The books were damp, the drawers in the dressers were warped and sticky, the sheets on the bed worn soft by a thousand washings. The nearest neighbors were half a mile away. They had brought only Rose with them—the smallest dog, niece to the other two, who were sisters and inseparable. Rose was also, Kate thought, the most human of the dogs, the way she looked at you with her dark, good-humored, intelligent eyes. "She knows all about us," Kate said as another wave slid back, exposing the pale slope of the sand.

Sarah took Kate's hand and guided it to the buttons of her dress. Inch by inch her white skin revealed itself in the afternoon light. The breeze sucked the curtains in and out across the sills. Rose, understanding that a walk was not imminent, jumped lightly onto a chair and went to sleep. From the beach came the sound of the slow waves gathering and gathering, so languorously it seemed they would never break.

Sarah liked to sleep late. She liked to drink coffee on the porch in her bathrobe, her dark hair loose, her big feet bare on the splintery boards. The sun would be high in the sky before she was ready to get dressed, to put her hair up, to poke in the icebox for something to eat.

Kate had seen a sign on a bulletin board in town about a place to go berry picking.

"Why would you want to leave this?" Sarah asked, gesturing to the water, the sky.

"It will still be here when we get back," Kate said.

"It's here now." Sarah had found a copy of *Anna Karenina* on the bookshelf, and she was stretched out on a chaise longue on the porch reading, her big sunglasses making her look like Greta Garbo.

Kate walked to the edge of the porch. Down on the beach, sanderlings chased the surf back and forth. A dragonfly flitted above the green tips of the dune grass. "Let's go for a walk," she said.

"Take Rose."

"I want you to come."

"You're very demanding."

"And you're very lazy."

Sarah turned a page.

Kate watched her, frowning slightly in concentration under her hat, her eyes moving steadily back and forth across the page the way the sanderlings moved up and down the beach. "What's happening in that book that's so interesting?"

Sarah shrugged. "Life." She yawned, and the top of her robe fell open. Kate came over and nudged in next to her on the chaise longue and opened the rest of the robe.

"I'm reading," Sarah said.

"You can read anytime," Kate said.

Sarah smiled her genial, ironic smile and put the book down, splayed out on the boards so as not to lose her place.

Sarah let Kate coax her out to the marsh to look at birds; she turned out to know the names of most. She agreed to go blackberry picking and collected twice as many berries as Kate. "My aunt used to pay by the bucket," she explained.

Her aunt, it seemed, had also been the one who'd taught her the names of the sandpipers and the oystercatchers and the various terns. "She had a life list the length of your arm," Sarah said, as they sat on the porch drinking gin-and-tonics and eating blackberries. She had found a pad of drawing paper and some pastels in a drawer and was frowning over something she was sketching. "She used to drag me out of bed before dawn and make me carry the binoculars."

Kate sat with her knees pulled up, her chin resting on them, watching Sarah. "You're a person of many hidden talents."

"I'm a dilettante, basically," Sarah said. "A dabbler."

"You're a Renaissance man," Kate said, smiling.

"Whereas you, Kate Croft, are a visionary."

"Nonsense," Kate said, blushing.

"You are, though." Sarah looked up from her drawing,

tilted her head. "You're always looking at something that's not there."

"I'm looking right at you now," Kate said. It was hard, in fact, to take her eyes off Sarah: her measuring gaze, her long neck, the line of white along the edge of her swimsuit.

Sarah turned the sketchpad around. Kate was startled to see that the drawing was of herself. Here was her ordinary face with its slightly pointy chin and snub nose; here was her mousy, wispy hair, disordered by the wind. But Sarah had done something with the eyes. They were not the plain medium brown Kate knew from the mirror, but nearly amber, wide open, and blazingly clear.

For dinner that night they had broiled fish with local tomatoes and corn.

"We're eating your work," Sarah remarked as she nibbled her way neatly along the cob and back again: the typewriter method. Kate ate one section all the way around, then moved down: the rotary method.

"No. This is sweet corn."

"It's corn."

Kate shrugged. "It's *Zea mays*. But this is the boring kind. All the kernels are the same. My Indian corn is all different colors."

"Ah," Sarah said.

Kate put down the ear she was eating. "What we do is, we look at the characteristics of each kernel, and we try to match each one to the chromosomes we can see under the microscope. We're making maps. I'm making a map of chromosome nine. Chromosome nine is very interesting because—"

Sarah smiled. "My fault. I forgot rule one."

Kate looked away and picked up her corn again. After a while she said, "Don't you miss your work at all?"

"When I'm here? With you? Are you joking?"

"Don't you even wonder how your patients are doing?"

Sarah helped herself to another fat tomato slice and poured them both more wine. "It wouldn't help them if I did."

On their last full day, Kate poked her head into a half-collapsed outbuilding and found a little skiff with oars. Sarah, who had finished *Anna Karenina* and moved on to *The Bostonians*, agreed to go rowing. They dragged the boat up through the sandwort and beach plums to the top of the dune, then pushed it over the edge and let it slide down. The tide was high, and it wasn't long before a wave stretched far enough up the sand to help them get launched. Kate fitted the oars into the oarlocks and began to row: out toward the dark blue line of the horizon and then down along the shore in the direction of the public beach.

"Let's go the other way," Sarah said. "There'll be children screaming in this direction." Her dark hair blew sideways across her face.

"This is against the current. You always row in the hard direction first."

It was pleasant out on the water. The breeze was fresh, and the boat skipped along as Kate leaned into the oars. Pretty soon they came up on the public beach. As predicted, children were screaming, possibly joyfully, jumping into the waves and bursting up again, streaming with water, while their parents lay sprawled out on brightly colored towels, looking stunned.

"You're not fond of children?" Kate asked.

"Not particularly. Are you?"

"I can imagine liking certain ones. I was thinking about your mother saying how much you loved your dolls."

Sarah laughed. "That was a long time ago. And, as you've doubtless noticed, Mutti thinks what she wants to think."

"I like your mother," Kate said.

"Everybody likes her. Everyone thinks she's wonderful. *I* think she's wonderful. I'm just saying that she looks at me and sees what she wants to see."

Kate maneuvered the boat to skirt a drift of seaweed. "My mother thinks, whatever anyone does, they're doing it to punish her." She pulled on through the rippling water. The day was so clear that the curling wrist of Provincetown was just visible in the distance, the Race Lighthouse standing sentry where the land came to an end.

"Are you getting tired?" Sarah asked after a while. "I could row."

"I'm not tired."

"You've gotten your strength back."

"I guess I can move back into my place, then. When we get back." The words came out sounding bitter. Kate pulled even harder on the oars, ungracefully, and an inch of bilge water sloshed back and forth in the bottom of the boat. Sarah, leaning back against the bow, laid one arm over her face to shade her eyes and trailed the other hand in the water. It was infuriating, how languid Sarah looked. Kate dropped the oars and moved toward the middle of the boat, which bucked. "I guess you can row, if you want to," she said.

Sarah eased herself into the stern. The crow's feet around her eyes deepened as she squinted into the sun. Kate settled herself as Sarah worked the left oar, turning them around. She had a long clean stroke. Kate remembered how, when she had first seen her in the hospital, she had thought she looked like a lynx. In a minute, they were flying through the water, the current with them now.

"You don't have to move out," Sarah said flatly.

Kate looked hard at Sarah: her carefully neutral face, her wild, windblown hair.

"It's further from campus, of course. But you've seen how much room we have. And of course, Mutti would adore it."

215

Overhead, a tern let out a harsh trill and dove hard, skimming the water, then soared up again, gulping down a fish. On the surface, the water looked barren, but really it was full of life: stripers and flounder, eel grass and tiny shrimps and dozens of different kinds of algae.

"I suppose I might get a new car," Kate said thoughtfully.

On their final morning, Kate woke with the first shift of the sky from black to gray. Sarah's weight on the old mattress made a shallow burrow, and Kate rolled into it, resting her cheek against Sarah's back as the room emerged from the shadows.

The path to the beach was sharp with dune grass and broken shells. Rose pranced ahead, nosing at clumps of bracken. It was chilly, but Kate liked the scouring wind. There were pretty fluted scallops, bunches of translucent jingle shells the color of amber, a few mottled and shiny purple oysters, stacks of slipper limpets. Kate walked along the water's edge, watching Rose pouncing on the surf as it receded, her feathery tail held high. She galloped back to check on Kate, ran ahead, galloped back. When Kate was a girl, they'd had a dog named Clementine who loved the beach. For a moment she might have been eight years old again, having escaped the summer rental house, a folded-over jelly sandwich in her pocket. Oh, how she used to run on those mornings! She remembered it so vividly, the way her knees would lift so high she practically floated through the air. She could run for what seemed like miles like that: effortlessly, without tiring, the waves hissing and sighing at her feet, her mind drifting, going transparent as a soap bubble, until she was existing from moment to moment with a perfect blank consciouslessness, the way a tree existed, or a blade of grass. Years later she'd read a book that described how monks in the mountains of Tibet ran just that way—steady, high-stepping, unwearying—across the cloud-capped peaks.

Twenty years ago! Yet it seemed to her she hadn't changed much in all that time from that odd, curious, private, stubborn child.

Her feet splashed in the shallow surf; her arms pumped and her legs floated up. She moved like an arrow through the damp gray air. Time receded. The sky was enormous, open, pale and filled with light.

When she got back to the house, Sarah was up and dressed, though it wasn't yet eight. Her bags were packed. The bed was made up with fresh sheets, and all the dishes were washed and put away. "Where in heaven's name have you been?" she said.

CHAPTER 24

Sarah said it was too early in their trip to make a stop. She said it would be difficult to find the place since the university buildings weren't marked on the map. She said Mrs. Sonnenfeld was expecting them and they shouldn't waste time.

"We won't stay long," Kate said. "Maybe he won't even be there."

Sarah honked at a truck piled high with straw bales that bounced and shifted at every bump in the road. "I don't understand why you suddenly want to see this person. You didn't say one word about it till now."

"I couldn't," Kate said. "Because of rule one."

In fact, the idea of visiting Paul had only occurred to her when she saw the Boston-Cambridge road sign. But once she'd been seized by the idea of stopping, she could not bear to just drive by.

They reached Cambridge near eleven and left the car by a big grassy park just north of Harvard Square. Sarah tapped her elegant shoe on the bumpy brick sidewalk while Kate asked passers-by where the biology labs were. It turned out they weren't far. As they walked, Kate looked around at the large buildings with their decorative brickwork and tall windows. The campus wasn't elegant, but it had a seductive air of not caring what you thought of it. "It's this one," she called to Sarah, who was lagging, then herded her inside.

"You're bossy now that you're well," Sarah said.

"You're getting to know the real me."

After the bright August sunshine, the lobby was dim.

They peered up at the directory board, and there he was: *Prof P Novak — 201.*

Nerve had gotten Kate this far. But as she contemplated the door of 201 with its brass embossed name plate, nerve began to fail her. Still, it was too late to turn back. Sarah was watching, her lips pursed. Kate knocked, and turned the knob, and in they went.

The room was empty.

"We tried," Sarah said.

Kate moved farther in and began looking around. It was just an ordinary lab, nicely equipped, with long shelves of notebooks, and tall wooden filing cabinets, and benches with microscopes and racks of petri dishes and Bunsen burners. It was nicer than her own lab, but not tremendously nicer, though it was on the corner with windows on both sides. She walked over to a bench and began peering at a few petri dishes where fuzzy colonies of various sizes and textures bloomed on the agar medium. A notebook lay on the bench nearby, and she opened it, scanning the pages.

"Stop that," Sarah said.

Kate frowned and bent closer, reading more slowly.

Footsteps approached, and Kate clapped the notebook shut. Someone was striding down the hall. Kate knew that stride. The next moment Paul came into the room. He was wearing field khakis, although, having abandoned corn, he no longer worked in a field.

"Hello, Paul!" Kate said. "You weren't here, so we just barged in."

Paul looked surprised, but not for long. He came over and clapped Kate on the shoulder. "Good to see you!"

"This is Dr. Sonnenfeld. We were driving back from Cape Cod, and it turns out you're right on the way. I thought I'd stop in and take a look at your setup."

Paul turned to Sarah, taking in her striped blue dress

with its matching jacket, the scarf she wore to protect her hair from the wind. She looked very haughty and very beautiful. "A pleasure to meet you, Dr. Sonnenberg. Are you a geneticist as well?"

"Sonnenfeld," Kate said.

"I'm not a doctorate kind of doctor, I'm afraid," Sarah said. "I'm a physician."

Paul smiled. "A real doctor. Even better."

Sarah untied her scarf, tucked it away in her purse, and removed a comb.

"We can't stay long," Kate said, trying not to be distracted by the sight of Sarah combing her hair. "I just thought I'd take a look at your flies. But you don't seem to be working with flies. In fact, you seem to be working with *Neurospora*!"

"You've been snooping." He looked delighted. "Yes, as a matter of fact. I got your note back in June. I meant to write and thank you."

"How could you possibly have gotten my note?" Kate demanded. "I never mailed it." Everything that had happened since she got sick had blotted out, more or less, the night of Thatch's wedding. But it came back to her now, in all its confusion of pleasure and displeasure. That was the last time she had spoken with Paul, or communicated with him in any way.

"You must have," Paul said. "Because it certainly arrived."

Kate felt he wasn't listening to what she was saying. "I didn't have a chance to mail it," she repeated. "I wrote it right when I was getting sick."

"I heard about that. It was pretty serious, wasn't it? I'm glad to see you're better now."

Yet he hadn't so much as sent a card.

"She almost died," Sarah said. She had coiled her hair into a knot and was pinning it in place.

"How frightening. What was it?"

"Pneumonia," Kate said.

"Maybe you don't remember mailing the note because you were ill."

"I don't forget things," Kate said.

"Maybe your boss mailed it," Sarah suggested, peering into the mirror of her compact. "When he broke into your apartment."

"Whitaker broke into your apartment?"

"He thought he had to, apparently. To save my life. Anyway, how's it working?" Kate asked as Sarah shut her purse with a snap. "The *Neurospora*."

"Extremely well, actually." He walked over to the petri dishes and began to tell her what he had been doing. First he had produced several mutants of the bread mold that were unable to make a particular amino acid the organism needed to survive. Then he'd linked that inability to the fact that the mutants were missing a specific gene. No gene, no amino acid. As he spoke, his words seemed to enter her brain directly, his ideas leaping from his mind to hers. It was so clear once he began to explain! She forgot about what had happened between them, that he hadn't written, that Sarah was standing impatiently by the door. His idea—missing gene, missing amino acid—was so sharp and bright, like the blade of a knife. He showed her a couple of slides, and she peppered him with questions, and then she looked up from the microscope to see Sarah's face.

"Come look," Kate coaxed. "It's incredible."

"We really have to go," Sarah said.

Paul smiled at her. "Stay for lunch at least. You'll be my guests at the Faculty Club."

"I'm so sorry." Sarah's white neck stretched longer. "Another time."

"Sarah's mother is expecting us," Kate explained, peeking into the microscope for one last look.

"Because I have some things I'd love to discuss with you," Paul said to Kate.

"You're hoping to cash in on some more of my good ideas?" But she was smiling. She couldn't help it.

"I could use your help with the cytology. I can't make the chromosomes out at all." He spoke urgently, as though he were thirsty and she held a jug of water.

"Kate," Sarah said.

"What do you know about the meiotic cycle?" Kate asked, still staring down through the lens. Sometimes, if she stared long enough, it was as though she'd drifted into the cell itself, the structures and organelles all around her as big as life.

"Not much. Well, nothing, actually."

"Kate," Sarah repeated, this time in the tone she reserved for nurses.

Kate looked up. "Let's just stay another hour," she said. "An hour's not going to matter."

Sarah lifted her chin in Paul's direction. "Will you excuse us a moment?" she said, and strolled out into the hall.

"Someone's used to getting her own way," Paul remarked.

"Oh, for godsakes," Kate said, shooting him a look.

She found Sarah standing at the end of the hall by the window overlooking the biology quad. Despite the hot, dry summer, the lawn was lush and green. Across the way, the frieze of another imposing brick building was engraved with animals: a snake, a turtle, something that looked like an aardvark.

"We've come," Sarah said. "We've exchanged greetings. Now it's time to go."

"We need to eat lunch anyway," Kate said. "Why not stay and see what the Harvard Faculty Club is like?" She tried to keep her voice calm and light, but she was too stirred up. Couldn't Sarah see how important this was to her? After a week of not even talking about science!

Sarah opened her purse again and began once more to rummage inside it. "I wouldn't have guessed you were so susceptible to prestige."

"Prestige has nothing to do with it. This idea Paul's had—what he's figuring out about how the genes actually work—it would be good to be part of it."

"So you're not talking about just staying for lunch." Sarah began taking things out of the purse and laying them on the windowsill: the comb, the compact, a lipstick-stained handkerchief.

"What Paul said is true. He can't do the cytology by himself. This is what I'm good at, Sarah." She didn't say she was the best. She didn't say this was what she had made her career on. Her career so far.

A memorandum book. A roll of Life Savers. A glinting silver cigarette case. "I don't see why you even want to help him. It sounds like you gave him the idea that made this whole thing possible in the first place, and he never even thanked you."

"That's not the point," Kate said. "The point is that the problem is interesting."

"Mapping chromosome nine isn't interesting enough?"

So Sarah had been paying attention. "Not as interesting at this!" Missing gene, missing amino acid—how did that work? What did the gene do, exactly? She could feel ideas stirring deep inside her brain, swirling up toward consciousness on rippling currents.

A fountain pen, a monogrammed money clip, a small silk pouch with a knotted drawstring. "Maybe you'd better find your own exciting project to work on," Sarah said.

Kate laughed. "It's not so easy." How to convey that this was no ordinary idea; that it was a once-in-a-lifetime idea. She saw that—maybe more clearly than Paul did himself.

But no, Paul saw it. She could tell by his confidence and by his powerful need, by the determined way he was drawing her in—reeling her in—the hook set, the lure flashing silver in the dark water.

Sarah tossed the little pouch to Kate. "For you," she said.

Kate caught it. The silk was pale green, embroidered with pink rosebuds. It was about the size and weight of a walnut.

A once-in-a-lifetime idea, she thought, if the cytology could be worked out. If someone else didn't get there first. (Were other people working on it? She'd have to find out.) If it wasn't a mistake. A glitch in the data.

But Kate knew it wasn't a mistake. She knew.

"Look inside," Sarah said.

"Listen," Kate said. "This is important."

"I've been listening," Sarah said. "Please just look inside."

Kate loosened the drawstring.

"Careful," Sarah warned. "Don't spill it."

Kate cupped one hand and tilted the pouch with the other. A stream of sand poured out into her palm.

"It's from the beach at the cottage," Sarah said softly. "A memento of our time there."

The coarse grains sparkled, beige and pure white with a few flecks of something greenish. The smell of the beach: dried seaweed and decayed mollusks and chilly water.

"I was going to wait and give it to you when we got back. But at this rate, that might be never." Sarah held herself carefully, her dark hair shining in its pinned knot.

Kate laid her hand on Sarah's sleeve. "Thank you," she said. "It was a very nice holiday. It was the nicest holiday I've ever had."

"Please don't ruin it," Sarah said. "Retroactively." Then she stepped back, frowning down the hall.

Paul stood in the doorway of his lab, watching them. "I

didn't mean to interrupt anything," he said. "I just wanted say, there's a guest house, Kate." He spoke very gravely—very formally—like a suitor in a novel. "If you wanted to stay for a couple of days, I'd be happy to put you up."

CHAPTER 25

Kate told Sarah she'd be back Sunday, but then she pushed through the last bits of work in a great flurry in order to make the Saturday afternoon train. It had taken no little effort to sort out *Neurospora*'s cytology, but she'd gotten it done, and in just a couple of weeks. After the long summer of illness and idleness, her brain felt bright and clear.

Paul was pleased. Early that last morning, she walked him through the meiotic cycle—prophase, fuse, synapse, and then the extraordinary elongation after the synapse where the chromosomes ballooned up to fifty times their usual size. That was the crucial stage, the moment you could make out their markings.

"I knew you'd do it," Paul said, looking up from the microscope, his green eyes glinting with pleasure and triumph. "We'll go out tonight and celebrate. We've earned a good dinner. We'll toast to the meiotic cycle."

But Kate had already checked the train schedule. "Next time," she said.

"Whatever's in Ithaca can wait another day," Paul said.

Something in the way he said it made Kate think he knew what it was she was hurrying back to. Knew and understood it, and at the same time discounted it.

"This is great work, Paul," Kate said. "Whitaker is going to be so proud of you. He's going to take all the credit." She laughed, and he laughed, too, and stopped pressing her to stay.

He drove her to the station in Boston and waited with her on the platform. They talked about what came next—the new experiments he'd have to do, the first paper he would write—until the train thundered in, blasting dust and grit over them. Paul took her hand. "This was quite a time," he said.

For a moment, she felt the thrill of their connection. Women and men, sweating in their summer dresses or in their shirtsleeves with their cuffs turned back, descended from the broiling train, which would pause here for just ten minutes before barreling north. The pleasure of what they'd done was a coolness settling through her. She squeezed Paul's hand, then hopped up onto the train.

Dusk was falling as the train pulled into Ithaca. Kate walked up the hill from the station, the grass softening from green to gray under the massed trees. At the Sonnenfeld house—usually quiet on a Saturday night—lights blazed, and the sound of the gramophone drifted out onto the street. Kate stood at the back door listening, then lifted the latch and went in.

"Hello?" she called as she moved through the kitchen, which smelled of roasting meat and cut flowers. A frantic scramble of footsteps, then the dogs were there, whining and jumping up, their shiny auburn fur silky and clean.

"Holly! Rose! Get down." Sarah appeared in the doorway, tall and lean in a sweater and pleated skirt, her hair as bright and silken in the lamplight as the dogs' long ears. "We didn't expect you until tomorrow."

"I managed to get away early."

Sarah sauntered over, kneed aside the ecstatic dogs, leaned down, and touched her cheek to Kate's. The smell of her—oranges and cigarettes and lipstick—washed over Kate like the first cold ocean wave. "A friend's come for dinner," Sarah said. "Mutti made her famous veal roast."

In the pause that followed, a voice in the other room could be heard saying, "I might go to Canada. There's snow on some of the mountains all summer."

"I don't think you've ever met Justine," Sarah said. "She's been away, training in Switzerland."

Kate followed Sarah into the living room, where Mrs. Sonnenfeld enveloped her in a whirlwind of talcum powder. "Kate!" she pronounced, savoring the consonants.

"Sorry to barge in."

"Please," Mrs. Sonnenfeld scoffed. She directed Kate to the leather armchair.

"Kate, this is Justine Garr, the skier," Sarah said. "Justine, this is Kate Croft, the geneticist."

Justine was tall with a wing of blond hair on either side of her tan, hard face. Her eyes were startlingly blue and light-flecked, the irises rimmed with black like a Siberian husky's. "Pleased to meet you," she said.

"Justine skied at Lake Placid," Sarah said. "She took eighth in the slalom. Now she's training for Garmisch."

It look Kate a moment to realize Sarah was talking about the Olympic Games. "You must be very good," she said stupidly. Justine smiled. She wore a long white jacket that cinched in at the waist and a svelte white knee-length skirt from under which her shins gleamed in their silk stockings.

"Ah, Garmisch!" Mrs. Sonnenfeld said. "We took holidays there sometimes when I was a girl. In spring, the mountain was a sea of wildflowers. All pink, like walking up the side of a cloud when the sun is setting."

"There won't be any wildflowers when I'm there."

"You should see Justine ski," Sarah said to Kate. "She's like a flash of lightning on the slopes."

"You've skied together, then," Kate said.

"I've chugged along in her wake once or twice." Sarah took out her cigarettes and lit one, blew smoke through her red pursed lips.

Mrs. Sonnenfeld turned to Kate. "Sarah says you have

been working very hard, when you should still have been resting. Just look at the pouches under your eyes. Tonight you will go to bed early, and tomorrow you will sit out in the garden and admire my flowerbeds."

Kate smiled. "Tomorrow I have to go look at my field."

Justine laid a finger on Sarah's wrist. "What are those, Players? Let me have one."

Sarah held out the silver case. "Help yourself."

The skier, thrusting her hand in, spilled the contents all over the floor.

After Justine Garr had gone home, and the washing up had been done and the ashtrays emptied and the sofa cushions plumped, Mrs. Sonnenfeld let out a long sigh and announced that she was heading up to bed.

"I'm coming up, too, Mutti," Sarah said. "I'm bushed."

"It's Kate who should be bushed," Mrs. Sonnenfeld said.

"I'll just finish this cigarette first," Kate said.

Kate went out to the back porch to smoke and wait for Sarah to come out. Ten minutes passed, then another ten. Leaves whispered on the branches of the tulip poplars. Bats fluttered and plunged above the black lawn. It was quiet here in Ithaca after two weeks in Cambridge, where the trolley clattered and groups of carousing undergraduates swarmed by at all hours. The first few nights, unable to find a way into the *Neurospora* problem, she'd lain awake in the dark listening to the clamor, doubting herself and missing Sarah and worrying about her plants. But after she'd broken through— after everything began to come clear—she had slept soundly and awakened early in the August heat, impatient to pick the work up again. She had thought about Sarah less, but that didn't mean she didn't miss her. Now, sitting in darkness, looking out into darkness, her longing lodged in her throat like a bone.

Tomorrow she would see her field. She would get the first hint whether her few long-shot crosses had produced anything interesting. She knew it wasn't likely. Still, she had to work with the data she had, which was better than no data. Sarah had been right about one thing: she needed to find a project that was as exciting as Paul's. Half as exciting.

At last Kate went back into the house, moving clumsily among the shadowy furniture. At the second-floor landing, she hesitated. Mrs. Sonnenfeld would be asleep in her room at one end of the corridor, dreaming of mountain slopes covered with wildflowers, perhaps. At the other end was Sarah's room. Kate took off her shoes and slipped along the hall and tapped on Sarah's door.

No answer.

She waited and knocked again, softly, but loud enough.

Still no answer. Was she asleep? Angry?

Had she slipped out to meet Justine Garr?

Tomorrow I'll see my field, she reminded herself, as she marched back down the corridor and up to her own room, shoes in hand. She pushed the door open carelessly so that it banged against the wall.

Out of the darkness, Sarah's voice said, "I thought you'd never come! I've been waiting hours."

Kate stopped dead on the rug. She began to tremble—with relief, or with fury, or maybe just exhaustion. Sarah sat up on the bed. Her hair was loose and tangled, and her thin cotton pajama bottoms rode up her long pale shins. She seemed very far away to Kate, on a different scale, like a figure in a dollhouse. Kate longed to step through into that dollhouse and lie down in Sarah arms, but something prevented her. She kept thinking about the blond Olympian, her obvious intimacy with the family. What would have happened if Kate hadn't shown up? Did Sarah wish she hadn't?

She could turn around and walk down the stairs and

out of the house if she had to, she told herself. She had done something like that before.

She pushed the memory back down into the dark where she kept it hidden. But its horror was not so easily dissipated.

To calm herself, she opened the suitcase she had carried up before dinner and began to unpack. One by one she shook out her white blouses and slipped them onto hangers and hung them on the wardrobe rail.

"What are you doing?" Sarah said.

"Putting away my clothes." Nightgown in the top bureau drawer, underclothes and socks in the next drawer down, cardigan sweaters in the bottom drawer.

Sarah leaned back against the headboard. "Did you figure out that man's cytology for him?" she asked coolly.

"Yes."

"Well, that's good. He must be pleased."

"He is." Her face felt hot and soft, her belly cold and metallic. She knew they were fighting, but what were they fighting about?

"I guess it was worth it, then," Sarah said.

"I don't know what you mean."

"Worth sending me back alone. Worth two weeks apart."

"I didn't want to be apart," Kate said.

"If that were true," Sarah said, "you wouldn't have stayed there."

"I came back as quickly as I could," Kate said. Couldn't Sarah see that only something that mattered deeply could have kept her there? Was it really necessary to spell all that out? At the bottom of her suitcase was the little pouch of sand Sarah had given her. She took it out and stood holding it in the dark.

"I don't like him," Sarah said. "He's arrogant and self-centered."

"I know," Kate said. "I know all about him." She forced

herself to turn away from the dresser and go over to the bed. She sat carefully on the very end, holding the pouch of sand, and looked at Sarah. She looked very fragile and beautiful in her dark blue pajamas.

"He looked ready to eat you up," Sarah said.

"No one's going to eat me up," Kate said. "Besides, what about that skier?"

"Oh, for heaven's sake!" Sarah said. "Why are you being so stupid?"

Was she being stupid?

The mattress shifted as Sarah moved toward her. Kate could feel the warmth of her as she crouched, inches away, her arms wrapped tightly around her knees, the smell of her sharp and thrilling. "I hate being away from you," Sarah hissed. Then she tilted forward and buried her face in Kate's neck.

Something hard and rubbery inside Kate's chest slackened, opened. "I missed you so much," she whispered fiercely into Sarah's ear.

It was such a relief to realize it was true.

In the morning, Kate got up early, slipped an apple into her pocket, and drove to campus. Even though she knew what to expect, it was still a shock to see the decimated field, like visiting an old friend who has been ill.

But the twenty-six plants that had survived the flood looked healthy enough, their stems sturdy, their leaves lifting toward the cool clear sky. Slowly, Kate moved from plant to plant. The carefully fertilized ears swelled in their sheaths, ragged shocks of browning silks drooping from the tips. Most of the leaves were bright green, but a few were mottled or striped. Some of these changes were caused by known mutations on chromosome nine, and these were what she was particularly eager to see.

She was halfway through the field when something caught her eye.

On a whitish leaf covered with small green streaks, two long odd patches lay side by side. The leaf itself—its background pattern—wasn't what was odd. She'd seen that kind of thing before.

But the patches were something else altogether. One thing that was peculiar: they were adjacent, yet they didn't match. She crouched down in the dirt to see better.

Like the rest of the leaf, the patches had pale green streaks. But in one patch, there were very few streaks compared to the background: a sparse flurry. In the other patch, by contrast, there was a blizzard.

Two different oddities, unfurling side by side. Different, yet clearly related.

Reciprocals.

One with fewer streaks, and the other with more: as though some fixed quantity had been divided unequally between them.

As though one had taken some of what belonged to the other.

A loose fist of heat moved through her chest.

Step by step, her mind climbed the ladder—yet so quickly that the idea felt like one full-blown thought. The words bloomed in her mind: *twin sectors*.

Twins, but not identical twins. One had gained something that the other had lost.

Side by side as they were, the cells of the two sectors would have developed from a single ancestor: one cell that had divided and distributed something unevenly. But what?

What was gained? What was lost?

Her heart raced like a bird skimming a wave. Here, in her field, she had stumbled on a door in the wall.

PART FOUR

1935

CHAPTER 26

Dusk was creeping up from the woods by the time Kate finished the harvesting. Her back ached and her clothes were stiff with dust and sweat as she dragged the sacks of corn to the drying shed. But she felt good. This season's crop was all descended from the twin-sector plant of two years before, and she had high hopes for it.

"You look like a pig that's been wallowing in mud," Sarah said as Kate came into the kitchen. "Mutti left a plate in the oven for you. She's off at a concert."

The kitchen, with its checkered floor and yellow gingham curtains, was spotless. It smelled of roast pork, oregano, and flowers. On the table, fringed crimson tulips yawned wide, pollen dusting the linen cloth with dark purple grains. The dogs sniffed at Kate's trousers with interest until Sarah chased them away.

It hurt to bend over and unlace her boots. It hurt to peel her socks off her feet. "I'm going to get everything dirty," Kate said.

"Then you'd better undress right there."

Kate started unbuttoning her filthy shirt. "Sarah," she began. The letter had arrived four days ago, and she still hadn't said anything about it.

"Wait," Sarah interrupted. "I'll do it." She took her time, easing each button through its buttonhole, her fingers as close to Kate as they could get without touching her. Kate's breath fluttered. She swayed forward, but Sarah drew back. "Patience."

At last Sarah finished the buttons. She moved around

behind Kate, easing the blouse off her shoulders, tugging the sleeves down by the cuffs so that Kate's arms were pulled taut behind her. Kate shivered. "Listen," she said.

"Are you cold?" Sarah teased. "Let me put your shirt back on."

"No," Kate begged. "No." She let the thought of the letter fall away.

The khaki trousers had buttons, too, which Sarah undid even more slowly. Kate's legs trembled, waiting for the brush of Sarah's fingers. At last she was naked. Slowly Sarah began to touch her breasts, her sides, her sensitive ass. Kate reached out and pulled Sarah close. She kissed her neck and mouth, tugged at her until they fell together onto the cool clean floor, closed her eyes.

"Look at me," Sarah said.

Kate opened them again and looked. Sarah's face was lovely close up, the clean planes of bone under the skin, the tiny freckles scattered like stars. She was still dressed, but that problem was quickly solved. Grazing Sarah's spun-sugar breasts with her lips was almost too much pleasure to bear. Kate's eyes closed again the way they always did, her mind drifting away to wherever it went, leaving her body behind, that robin's-egg shell of nerve endings like bundles of ribbons.

Later, as they lay entangled on the floor, a pattering of rain started up in the leaves of the poplar outside the window. Sarah was already dozing, but Kate was wide awake. "Sarah."

"Mmm."

Kate looked at her white shoulder and at her dark hair, threaded now with a few silver strands. Maybe she should wait a little longer. Wait till Sarah woke up on her own; till tomorrow; till it was too late to do anything and silence had become its own answer.

"Sarah," she said. "Listen."

Sarah blinked her eyes open. "We should get you into the bath."

Kate blurted out: "I got a letter from Fred Zimmer. His institute has finally gotten some real funding, and he's offered me a job." In the silence that followed, it seemed odd for them to find themselves naked on the cold checkerboard kitchen floor.

Sarah sat slowly up. She tossed her hair back over her shoulders and raked it back from her face. "Isn't that marvelous!" she said. And then, almost casually: "I forget where Fred Zimmer works."

"The University of Missouri," Kate replied, though she knew Sarah hadn't really forgotten. "His X-ray institute is doing amazing things. I wouldn't be surprised if he won a Nobel Prize!" The rain began to come down harder. It tumbled along the gutters and rang in the downspouts.

Sarah nodded slowly. "It's about time. After all those dumbos not giving you your due for so many years."

"It is," Kate said.

"Maybe you can use it as leverage with Whitaker."

Kate had thought of that. Whitaker had been increasingly cranky about the one-year extensions to her instructorship he kept giving her. But ultimately people did not stay at the institution where they did their graduate work. She needed to get out into the world. Get her work better known—herself better known. "Maybe," she said.

Heavy raindrops immolated themselves on the window. Sarah looked up at the kitchen clock and Kate's eyes followed. Mrs. Sonnenfeld would be home in half an hour. She was always prompt returning from concerts or her bridge club or her library volunteer meetings; yet she was never early. "Missouri is very far away," Sarah observed.

"Yes," Kate agreed. "But I'm sure they have sick people there."

Sarah's laugh was bright as a bell. "Of course, I could never leave Mutti," she said. "And she could hardly be expected to pick up and move at her age."

Thunder jangled Kate's skull. The windows blazed white and went out. The dogs galloped in from the living room, tossing their beautiful silken heads like ponies.

It rained all night, and Kate lay awake listening to the rain. Sometimes it fell so softly that she almost couldn't hear it: hissing out of the sky with a sound like a phonograph needle after the record is finished. It was still raining at dawn when she heard Mrs. Sonnenfeld get up and go downstairs. When Kate got to the kitchen, the percolator was on the stove, and Mrs. Sonnenfeld was scolding the dogs, who were standing, shivering and whining, by the open door, refusing to go out. The rain wasn't so much falling now as floating, descending slowly as though lowered on silken threads. A cool mist blew into the house. Clouds billowed and shifted in the sky, shark gray and charcoal gray and pearl. Kate smoothed Holly's long ears. Could there be a gene for the fear of rain? Could such a gene be linked, perhaps (as long as she was speculating), to the genes for fine long bones and glossy coats? She pictured the genes for different traits all riding the same chromosome like strangers sharing a train compartment. "Poor things. They were bred for beauty, not courage."

"Nonsense," Mrs. Sonnenfeld huffed, pouring cream into a pitcher. "They're just spoiled."

The Plant Breeding building was full of people talking, opening and shutting doors, rattling file cabinets, typing letters, fixing slides. It was disconcerting how few people she knew well here anymore. They moved around the labs and halls taking up the space where Thatch and Paul and even Jax ought to have been: the new young crop of students with their rumpled lab coats and their hooting laughs and their confidence. The promising young men. All of them relied on her characterization of maize chromosomes. All of them used her staining technique, whether they knew she had invented it or not. When she passed them on her way to the bathroom or the conference room, she felt they looked through her without seeing her. In her lab, though, she could forget about them. She could close the door and forget about everything but the work.

The season before, Kate had bred her twin-sector plant, like a champion stallion, to a range of other maize plants. Under the microscope, she had seen that the chromosomes of many of the offspring showed a breakage, specifically on chromosome nine. Over and over again she saw it, on the same chromosome, and in the same spot: two-thirds of the way down the short arm.

It wasn't random, then. It was a pattern.

On the table, Zimmer's letter lay in its buff-colored envelope with the Mizzou seal on the back. On the front, her name and address were neatly typed: *Dr. Kate Croft, Instructor, Department of Plant Breeding.*

Breakage in the same spot, two-thirds of the way down the short arm of chromosome nine. A pattern.

Instructor.

So pleased to be able to offer a home for the study of the exciting phenomena you are seeing in your plants . . . Finally shaken funding loose from the Dean for a two-year position . . . Confident that with good results more funding will be forthcoming . . .

Instructor. Whereas Paul and Thatch were assistant professors.

In the hallway, on her way out to the drying shed, she ran into Whitaker.

"There you are," he said, though she had been in her lab all morning.

"Here I am," she agreed.

"I want to talk to you. Come along to my office, please."

Kate had to move quickly to keep up with the old man's long strides. He was still vigorous at seventy, though his face, brown from working in the sun, was beginning to be stained with liver spots, and his temper had become more erratic. She reminded herself that there was no reason to think she was in trouble. He probably just wanted to talk over a result. But the timing worried her.

Yet even if he had found out she was considering leaving, why would that anger him? He wanted her to leave. That was clear every time she had to ask him for another year. Maybe he was irked that she had been offered a job he had had no role in arranging. Even though he kept on not arranging one.

"How does your harvest look?" he asked as they strode through the outer office, where Miss Floris, half hidden behind a vase of dahlias, sat typing.

"Good, I think. I was just going out to see what's what."

"Didn't lose many plants?" The question, asked jocosely, was a way of ribbing her for the way she managed—or micromanaged—her field. Everybody else planted many plants, as many as a thousand, knowing they'd lose a lot to pests and to chance. With so many plants, you needed help at fertilization time, which meant you gave up some level of control, and mistakes were often made. In order that there would be no mistakes—in order that she would know, absolutely, the genetic makeup of each plant—Kate fertilized every ear herself; checked them all for damage daily; watered carefully. She was able to grow only about two hundred plants a season, but each one was an intimate.

"Not too many," she said. In fact, she had lost two.

Seated at his claw-footed desk, Whitaker took his time lighting his pipe. Kate sat in the chair by the window wondering if she should beat him to the punch, come out and tell him about Zimmer's letter. Ask his advice, maybe.

Well, she knew what his advice would be. *Go. Go.*

"Have you heard from Thatch, lately?" Whitaker asked when he had got his pipe going.

"Thatch? Not very lately, no."

Whitaker was looking out the window, where the clouds were finally breaking up. "I've invited him to come give a seminar," he said. "Next week."

Kate wasn't aware of any particularly seminar-worthy work Thatch was doing, but then, as she'd said, they hadn't been in close touch lately. "I'll be glad to see him," she said.

"Weren't you writing a paper together?" Whitaker asked. "On the bronze locus?"

"He dropped off. Busy with other things, I guess."

"But his name will still be on it?"

She shook her head. "We talked about the idea at the beginning. And I used some of his stocks. But in the end, he didn't do any work."

Whitaker frowned and pulled on his pipe. After a minute he turned his hawkish stare on her. "I'd like you to put him back on."

Kate laughed. "I'd be happy to have his help. But you'd better talk to him about it."

Whitaker's face was stern. "I want his name on the author list."

Kate stared at the Great Man, waiting for the thing he was asking to make sense.

"Talking about the idea isn't nothing," Whitaker said. "Using some of his stocks isn't nothing."

"Not doing nothing is hardly a standard for publication," Kate said.

But Whitaker, who was usually exacting about who got credit for what work, wasn't listening. Something on the crowded desk had caught his eye. He leaned forward, squinting at the perfect bluish bonsai spruce that had sat in its shallow dish, looking exactly the same, as long as Kate had been coming into this office. "Did you hear Cynthia lost another pregnancy?" he asked, picking up his large, bird-shaped scissors and pruning off a twig almost too small to see.

Kate flinched as though the blade had grazed her. She hadn't heard that. She hadn't heard a word from Thatch in months. Maybe he was too occupied with his private grief. She hadn't written to him, either, of course, and what was her excuse? "Poor Thatch," she said. "Cynthia, too, of course."

Whitaker's finger moved along the branch, testing the tiny needles, searching for a flaw. "Most of the time, marriage is good for a scientist. It makes him more organized."

"A male scientist, you mean."

"That's right." He set down the scissors and looked at her. "I always say how wise you were not to marry."

She took in the past tense: as though, at barely thirty, that option was behind her.

"I'm going to have a little dinner for Thatch when he's here," Whitaker said. "Mrs. W. will whip up something special."

But her mind had circled back to what he had wanted in the first place. "Why do you care if his name is on the paper?" She wasn't being difficult. She was asking a question. She was trying to understand a mystery, which was her job.

"I'd consider it a personal favor," he said.

Kate took the long way around to the drying shed, past the practice fields and the dairy barns. Beyond the academic buildings, the tended lawns gave way to meadow. Wind made patterns in the grass, and there were interesting weeds: milkweed without which there would be no monarch butterflies, yellow wood sorrel which you could eat as a salad, Queen Anne's lace with its one dark umbel.

In the shed, in the glaring light of the bare bulb, she tugged down the green sheaths which squeaked against the milky kernels, then turned the ears slowly to see what was what.

The rotary method.

In normal corn, each kernel was a solid color. But in her mutant corn, altered by X-rays, the kernels were speckled: constellations of red stars in a white sky. Whatever controlled the color red was turning the process on and off as the kernel grew—a switch being flicked by a wild hand. *Red, no red; red, no red; red, no red.*

A circuit sputtering.

Nothing new. Nothing new. She had seen these patterns many times before.

And then, as she shucked one ear after another and placed them in the wide racks, she saw it: one kernel that was nearly all red. No speckles here, but a big round spot—garnet-colored, almost glowing in the dusty shed.

Whatever had been happening—whatever had been flicking the switch on and off—had stopped.

Kate's breath caught in her dry throat. The variation she had been chasing culminated right here. This kernel—*this kernel!*—was the wedge that would help her pry open the mysteries of the changes she saw. To understand what controlled how an organism became itself.

Kate held the ear up close to her glasses and looked hard. She put it down and then picked it up again. She shut her eyes, breathing in the sweet, milky smell. Then she opened them again to make sure the spot was still there.

How did an organism—a corn plant or a human being or an Irish Setter—become what it became? It was more than just the genes: it had to be. After all, an eyeball cell and a liver cell were genetically identical. So what controlled what kind of cell a cell ripened into?

Likewise, a caterpillar and a moth shared the exact same genome; so what controlled which creature came when? Or, to bring the question closer to home, how did a ball of un-differentiated cells inside a woman's body grow into a person who liked baseball, or daydreamed over encyclopedias, or thrilled to pretty clothes?

Who fell in love with one sort of person, or another sort?

Once, when Kate was nine, she had walked through a field with her father to a nearby pond to look for tadpoles, and he had stopped to point out the flies circling a pile of horse dung. There they stood on a sunny spring morning in front of the steaming pile, the sky transparent as water, clouds of gnats drifting peaceably by, and her father talked about spontaneous generation: how people used to believe life could burst forth out of nothing because they saw mag-gots arise from dead bodies. In fact, he explained, flies laid their eggs in the rotting flesh. Also in excrement. Indeed, every organism grew from tiny seeds that contained the essence of everything the organism would ever need. "Ev-erything essential in the oak is found in the acorn," he said, quoting somebody. You could always tell when he was quot-ing from the way he thrust his chest out as though standing at a podium. But there was no acorn, no oak tree here. No podium. Only the enormous pile of oak-brown dung with its halo of flies, which made Kate think uncomfortably of what she knew she should not, the shameful pleasure of her own movements coiling out as she sat on the cold seat. Or—sometimes—in the woods when she was alone, squatting with her dress hiked up behind a log, the air cool against her bare secret skin.

Why was it all right to look at horse droppings but peo-ple ones were shameful? She would have liked to ask her fa-ther, who knew everything, but of course she could not. Instead she stood uneasily beside him while he explained that people used to believe all kinds of things as they struggled to explain the natural world. The four bodily humors. Phrenology. Vitalism. "Brilliant minds," he said, waving his hand like a conjurer. "Amazing the ingenuity needed to dream up these false theories."

There her father stood in the spring field, young and vital, his pale sideburns glowing in the morning light. "In the face of mystery," he told his daughter, "men have always endeavored to explain why things are the way they are. It's part of what makes us men."

CHAPTER 27

The dogs clattered to greet her as usual when they heard the door. There was a platter of schnitzel on the table, the browned veal sprinkled with parsley and garnished with translucent lemon slices. Also a big bowl of noodles and a plate of sliced cucumbers sprinkled with feathery garden dill. Sarah and Mrs. Sonnenfeld sat at the table with their plates still half full, though it was well past their usual dinner hour.

"We thought perhaps you'd fallen into a gorge," Sarah said.

"Sorry," Kate said. "I lost track of the time."

"Sit down," said Mrs. Sonnenfeld, waving away her apology. "You must be starving."

Kate began to fill her plate with schnitzel and yellow buttery noodles. "This looks delicious," she said. If she lived alone, in an apartment or a little house in Columbia, Missouri, would she revert to living on soup?

"I hope it's not too cold," Sarah said.

"Not cold at all."

"We waited. But then we gave up."

Kate cut hungrily into the schnitzel. Mrs. Sonnenfeld began to describe how long she'd had to stand in line at the butcher shop, and how she had argued with the butcher about the veal, and how, while there, she had run into Mrs. Himmelstein, whose son had won a scholarship to somewhere or other. Sarah stood up and went to the dresser and took the whiskey bottle down. She poured two glasses and set one in front of Kate, but Kate shook her head.

"I have to work later."

"Poor Kate," Sarah said. "Always working. I guess I'll have to drink all the whiskey then." She picked up one glass and poured it into the other.

Kate had intended to tell Sarah and Mrs. Sonnenfeld about the red spot on the maize kernel, but this clearly wasn't the moment to do that.

Sarah sipped her drink. Threads of silver in her hair caught the light, and the wrinkles around her eyes were as fine as cat's whiskers. "Mutti," she said. Her eyes were on the white candles that burned with tall straight flames in the silver candlesticks Mrs. Sonnenfeld had brought from Germany. "Did Kate tell you she's been offered a job?"

Mrs. Sonnenfeld looked up at Kate, jowls wobbling. "Is that true?"

Kate nodded, her mouth full of noodles.

"Well! Isn't that wonderful news!"

"At the University of Missouri," Sarah said.

"Ah," Mrs. Sonnenfeld said. She pushed her chair back and began to clear the table, though Kate was still eating. "I am pleased for you," she said. "Of course." She cleared away her own plate, and Sarah's, and then the platters of food.

"It's only for two years," Kate said. "After that it would depend on how the work goes."

Mrs. Sonnenfeld stood at the sink in her navy coatdress and her flowered apron and her heavy shoes, her cloud of hair floating over the enamel basin. Sarah got up and began to help her mother. The older woman rinsed a dish and handed it to Sarah, who dried it and put it away.

"I haven't said I'd take it," Kate said.

Instead of talking about his own projects, Thatch said, he would give them an overview of the genetics work that was being done at the Rockefeller. In a way, this was classic Thatch—directing attention away from himself to others.

But it was an odd use to make of a seminar. Kate could feel the breath of uneasiness sliding around the long table as he began going through his overheads, looking older than she remembered in his tweed jacket and dark brown tie.

Well, they were all older.

Thatch spoke as well as ever, clearly and enthusiastically, getting right to the heart of what was interesting. Whitaker appeared to listen intently, not nodding off once, but Kate was having trouble paying attention. Thatch looked pale for a corn man in September. Had he been ill? He looked thin, too. Did Cynthia feed him? The thought of Cynthia lodged in Kate's throat like a fine, nearly invisible fish bone.

After the seminar, there was a reception with babka from the Hungarian bakery Miss Floris liked. Then Kate and Thatch adjourned to Kate's lab until it was time to go to Whitaker's house for dinner. "I'll make you coffee for a change," Kate said, lighting the Bunsen burner.

But Thatch shook his head. "No thanks."

"No coffee?" she said.

"Ulcer."

Kate tried not to let him see how much this upset her. "Tea?" she suggested. "A cookie?" She reached for the tin of chocolate walnut cookies she kept on a shelf behind her fixatives.

"No, thanks. All that babka. Miss Floris never changes." He smiled, but it wasn't the alert, cheerful smile Kate remembered. "And neither do you. It's good to see you, Kate."

Kate thought of Whitaker's bonsai. "Remember Krause's coleus plants?" she said, thinking how young and stupid she'd been in those days.

"*Plectranthus scutellarioides*," Thatch said.

"Cutting out all those fiddly shapes."

"What a terrible experiment that was!"

Kate nodded. "He was a good teacher, though. It was

sad, how few people were at his funeral." Krause had died the year before, of a tumor in his lungs.

"I was sorry I couldn't be there."

"Oh, I didn't mean you," Kate said irritably. There was a pause. Then she said, "I heard about Cynthia. I mean, I heard she lost another pregnancy. I'm so sorry, Thatch."

Thatch nodded as though he was thinking it over. "She's had a tough time."

"I can imagine," Kate said, which wasn't strictly true.

"It's hard—when you want something so badly," Thatch said. "Then, just when it seems as though it's finally within reach, it's snatched away."

"She's still young." Kate meant to sound comforting, but she was afraid the words had come out dismissive.

"I want to hear about your harvest," Thatch said.

So she began to tell him about the red spot, and the breaks on the short arm of chromosome nine, and her sense, as yet unconfirmed, that the two were related. "Of course I haven't had a chance to take a look under the microscope yet. So it's still just a hunch."

"What do you mean you haven't had a chance?" Thatch teased. "I would have thought you'd stay in the lab all night if necessary. With a tantalizing kernel like that!"

Kate could picture Sarah's face if she didn't come home all night. "Oh, I'll get to it," she said. Then she had a thought. "We could do it while you're here," she said. "We could do it together."

Thatch smiled. "You don't need my help."

"I'd be glad to have it," she said.

Thatch held up his empty hands.

Kate took the lid off the cookie tin. "Take one," she said. "You're starting to look like a scarecrow."

Thatch took a cookie, took a bite, and set it down. "Delicious," he said.

"Mrs. Sonnenfeld makes them," Kate said. "It's a family recipe she brought from Germany."

"You mentioned she was German."

"She's a wonderful baker, and cook, too."

"Living there has worked out well for you," Thatch said.

"Yes it has." Kate felt her face grow warm. "I've become very fond of both of them," she said. "The mother, and the daughter."

Thatch took another nibble. "The daughter is the fierce doctor?"

"She can be fierce," Kate said. "Sometimes."

"A widow?"

"No. She never married."

"Ah," Thatch said.

What did that mean? Kate wished she had made coffee after all, it would have helped her think.

She wanted Thatch to see Zimmer's letter. She would show him, in a minute or two. But of course, he wouldn't see that there was any problem. *Go*, he would say. *Why on earth wouldn't you go?*

"Listen," she said. "Even if you don't want to offer me the benefit of your insights on my red-spot kernel, we could take another look at those bronze locus results. Since you're here."

"Isn't that paper basically done?"

Kate shrugged. "I was thinking of changing the scope a little. We could go over it tomorrow and you could see what you think." It was true that she had thought about changing the scope. It was true that she would welcome Thatch's collaboration. Besides, if she put Thatch's name on a paper for which he had done no work, how would he bear it?

"I wish I could," he said. "But I'm going home tomorrow."

"Nonsense," Kate said.

"I am, though."

Kate stared at him. "That's ridiculous! You just arrived. I haven't heard word one about the work you're doing, which you didn't even talk about in your seminar. A person might be excused for thinking you weren't doing any work at all!" She regretted the words the moment she said them, but Thatch let them go by.

"Next time I'll stay longer," he said.

"What about tonight? We could talk it over after dinner. There's a thing or two you could do on the project when you get back home."

"Kate," Thatch said. "You don't need my help. I know you don't."

No, she didn't need his help. She didn't need anyone's help, not with the work. It was other things she needed help with, and no one was giving it, except maybe Fred Zimmer. "Whitaker wants you on the paper," Kate said.

Thatch looked surprised. "Whitaker?"

"Yes."

Thatch began fiddling with the knobs of Kate's microscope. "I have a performance review coming up at the Rockefeller," he said. "I haven't published enough for promotion."

"Oh, Thatch."

"I can't tell you what the problem is, exactly. I've had trouble thinking clearly. Or, I start things, but then I forget why I thought they were good ideas." The animation he must have been working to keep in his voice, minimal though it had been, drained away, and his words reached her limply, like seaweed washed up on the shore.

"Let's stay in the lab tonight," Kate urged. "We'll go to dinner, and then we'll come back here. All right? We'll take another look at the bronze locus slides. You can sleep on the train tomorrow."

Thatch nodded without saying anything. Or she thought it was a nod. She could see so clearly the gawky boy he used to be, standing in the greenhouse, his trousers too short, offering her part of his meager pay. The cheerful first-year graduate student loping down the hall, poking his head around the door of the lab she shared with Hiram Cole. The young man standing in the glimmering darkness of his backyard, throwing water on the fire. *Do you know what I think life is?*

A minute later, Whitaker barged in. "Come along," he said. "We don't want to keep Mrs. W. waiting." He frowned at Kate. "Did you want to stop home and change?"

She looked down at her neat trousers and pressed white shirt. She'd worn decent shoes instead of her work boots, and the thin silver chain Sarah had given her for her birthday. "I'm all right as I am," she said.

CHAPTER 28

The Whitakers lived in a handsome, drafty Victorian house high up on the hill. Kate had been there a number of times, mostly for the annual Christmas party, but occasionally for a dinner like this one. "Tell us the news from New York," Mrs. Whitaker said to Thatch as she seated him in a green silk-covered chair near the fireplace. She was a thin, energetic woman with iron gray hair pulled back in a bun. "I grew up on Lexington, you know. How I ended up out here practically in the wilderness, I'll never understand. Once, when we were still young, Evelyn got an offer from Columbia, but he turned it down. I could have been taking taxis and going to the opera all these years." She smiled at her husband and he smiled back, obviously pleased with everything: his house, his wife, his decision to stay at Cornell. "Have you been to the Met?" Mrs. Whitaker asked Thatch. "Cynthia would love it. There's nothing like all that gorgeous sound washing over you."

Thatch shook his head. "But she got us tickets to *Anything Goes* for my birthday."

"Evelyn says you're rushing back tomorrow. I told him he should have made you stay at least a week."

"Thatch isn't mine to order around anymore," Whitaker replied.

"Unlike some of us," Kate said, trying to sound jovial.

"Not that you do what I tell you to, either, all the time," Whitaker said.

"Kate has always had a mind of her own," Thatch said. "But if she insists on doing something, you can be sure it's the right thing to do."

Caught off guard by the compliment, Kate looked at the rug, which was chartreuse with dark brown lozenges around the edges. Quite different from the rich red-and-blue patterns of Mrs. Sonnenfeld's carpets.

"Shall we go into the dining room?" Mrs. Whitaker stood and offered her arm to Thatch. Whitaker and Kate followed them across the wide polished oak planks.

"Thatch is a loyal friend," Whitaker told Kate. "I confess there was a time I thought the two of you . . ." He squeezed her arm. She kept moving her feet, first the right one and then the left one. They felt so light without her work boots, it seemed she might float away.

Mrs. Whitaker had prepared a feast. There was roast duck on a platter surrounded by rings of cooked apple. There were mashed potatoes, brussels sprouts, pickled onions, and a silver basket of bowknot rolls. The candles in their glinting candlesticks seemed to throw out a lot of heat as Whitaker stood at the head of the table holding the carving knife. When the food was served and the wine poured, he raised his glass. "To my wife, who has stood by me all these years, even though I kept her from the opera."

"I did take that vow to obey," Mrs. Whitaker said, smiling, as they drank the toast.

"I'm dedicating my book to her," Whitaker said.

"Book?" Thatch asked.

"My textbook on genetics. People are still using Castle, if you can believe that! When we know so much more now."

"I didn't know you were writing a textbook," Thatch said.

Whitaker picked up the wine bottle and offered it around, but his was the only glass that needed refilling. "I'd like to be remembered for something," he said.

Thatch laughed. "You're a Titan in the field, Whit."

Whitaker held his wine up to the light. "There was a time I thought my work would be indelible. But science

256

just keeps moving faster." The flurry of objections to this was obligatory yet also heartfelt. But Whitaker shook his head. "Who in my generation will be remembered, I ask myself. Morgan? Müller? A maverick like Richard Goldschmidt?"

"Müller!" Kate objected. "If anyone is remembered for X-rays, it will be Fred Zimmer."

"And what about your generation?" Whitaker asked. "Of course it's anyone's guess who among you will make the next great advance. There's no knowing what discoveries any of you might stumble upon. Luck's as important as talent in this game. More important! Talent, luck, and perseverance. Not necessarily in that order." He downed his glass and picked up the bottle again.

"Evelyn," Mrs. Whitaker said, "I think John could use more duck."

"This work of Paul's has been getting a lot of attention," Thatch remarked, handing up his plate although it still had plenty of food on it.

Whitaker set down the bottle and carelessly piled on another slice. "With more sure to come. He's publishing it in *PNAS*," he said.

"What work?" Kate asked.

"Oh, it's remarkable!" Thatch's face grew animated as he began to explain. "He's shown that one single gene is responsible for the synthesis of one single enzyme. A one-to-one correlation! A colleague from the Rockefeller went up to visit him, and he couldn't talk about anything else when he got back."

Kate, who had been detaching a last sliver of meat from the bone, set down her fork and knife. "He's publishing that?"

"It's going to completely revolutionize our understanding of the gene! If it holds up," Thatch added, misunderstanding the look on her face. "And you'll never guess what organism he used."

"*Neurospora*," Kate said.

"*Neurospora*!" Thatch echoed. "An inspired choice!"

Kate stared at Thatch: at the tired eyes that had brightened as he recounted his friend's success. She thought of Paul's eyes—green and alert under tawny brows. "That was my idea," she said.

Thatch laughed. Then, seeing her expression, he stopped laughing. "Well," he said. "Then you know all about it."

"Apparently not," Kate said.

"I'm sure Paul could select his own organism," Whitaker said, drinking his wine.

"Well he didn't," Kate said sharply. "I spent two weeks in Cambridge sorting out the cytology for him. He never told me he was ready to publish. He never so much as showed me a draft!" She looked around the table, prettied up with Irish lace: at the Great Man who worried he would be forgotten; his loyal wife who had cheerfully offered up her desires for his imperatives; her old friend who had mislaid his ability to do the thing they were all trying so hard to do, decode the secret language of the invisible world.

Then she was struck by another thought. "A member of the National Academy would have had to submit it for him," she said to Whitaker.

"I always like to help out a protégé," the Great Man said.

Thatch finally agreed to go back with Kate to the lab after dinner. She asked to use the telephone to let the Sonnenfelds know she'd be late, and Mrs. Whitaker showed her into the hall. Sarah answered with the gruff voice she used when she expected the hospital to be calling. In the background, Chopin nocturnes spun out of the phonograph.

"I wanted to let you know I'm heading back to campus. Thatch and I have some work to finish up."

"For godsake, Kate. It's nearly eleven. Can't you do it in the morning?"

"He's going back to New York in the morning."

Sarah sighed.

"What?" Kate said. She was aware of Whitaker standing nearby, fiddling with something on a shelf.

"I've been waiting up for you."

Longing and irritation rose up together. "I'll see you later," she said. Then more softly, "Okay?"

On the other end of the line, Sarah took a breath, let it out. "Wake me up if I'm sleeping," she said.

"You're a considerate tenant, I must say," Whitaker remarked when Kate set the receiver down.

In the lab, Kate made coffee and brought Thatch a cup, and he drank it, ulcer or no ulcer. She got down the project notebook and the draft-in-progress of the paper on the bronze locus and began talking Thatch through it. Her words felt stiff at first, her head fuzzy from the wine and the residue of anger from dinner. But she wasn't going to think about Paul now. She began to explain the work she had done, and Thatch listened, taking in every word.

It was true that she had thought about changing the scope of the paper, and Thatch, as she'd hoped, had some good ideas about that. She found the tray of relevant slides, and they went through them one after another, looking for things Kate might have missed, for clues to what they might profitably do next. Toward dawn, Thatch leaned back in his chair and shut his eyes. "I know you can keep going indefinitely," he said. "But I need to rest for ten minutes."

Kate washed the coffee cups, put away the slides, covered the microscope. She made a few notes, but the truth was that she was tired, too. She looked at Thatch, breathing deeply, but not, she thought, sleeping. If she was going to tell him about Zimmer's offer—if she was going to ask his advice—it was now or never. But when she opened her mouth, what she said was: "Paul should have put me on that paper." Her heart began to pound as though she'd just run up the stairs.

Thatch shook his head without opening his eyes. "Let it go, Kate," he said. "People suggest things to other people all the time. They help out with technical stuff all the time."

"This wasn't just anything," Kate said. "He couldn't have done the project without the cytology."

"Let it go."

"It's so like Paul," Kate said. "He doesn't change! He barrels over people and takes what he wants from them."

Thatch opened his eyes. "Listen to me," he said. "The work you're doing is good. It's more than good. Forget this bronze locus paper. That twin-sector stuff you've been working on, chromosome nine: it's amazing! That's what matters."

"That's easy for you to say," she said, then felt a wash of shame.

"I know it's frustrating to still be here," Thatch said. "I know Whitaker hasn't done well by you."

"He certainly hasn't."

"But," he went on—and now his voice was different. Halting. "There's more to life than just . . . science. I hope you get out of the lab once in a while, Kate. I do. I hope you meet people. Other kinds of people."

Her heart began to thud faster. "I see the Sonnenfelds," she said. "I spend time with them. With Sarah." She pronounced the name carefully, offering it up to him.

Thatch looked at her sadly. "Spending time with a widow and a spinster is hardly going to help your prospects." He could not have spoken more gently.

Kate counted to ten before she let herself speak, but it didn't make any difference. "Because your marriage has brought you so much joy," she said, then watched her words turn his face to lead.

CHAPTER 29

Kate stayed at work a few more hours after Thatch had left to catch his train. Her mind felt sticky and over-crowded, teeming with unpleasant thoughts. She had intended to go out to the drying shed to look at her red kernel, but she was afraid her current state of mind would somehow contaminate it.

At lunchtime, she tidied up and headed home. Sarah was at the hospital, and Mrs. Sonnenfeld was out somewhere. Kate was glad, she didn't want to talk to anyone. Up in her room, she lay down on the bed, looking out the window at the sky and the crown of the tulip poplar. She loved the tree's long fluted early summer flowers, but those were long gone now, and the bright green leaves were fading to yellow. A long strand of cirrus cloud drifted by. Thinking about weather always made her think of Mendel, who had recorded it twice a day, every day, at his monastery in Brno. Mendel, who had gone to his grave with his work not only uncelebrated, but disbelieved.

She never lay down in the middle of the day, not even on weekends. Except of course when she'd first come to this house as an invalid. Then she'd lain all day long watching the clouds, watching the sky change from one shade of blue to another. Waiting for Sarah. If she shut her eyes now, she could still inhabit that first moment, when she had first put her arms around her. The brush of Sarah's mouth on the side of her face, the moment of hope and terror. The first, impossible, electric touching of their lips.

The night Cynthia had tried to kill herself.

Cynthia, whom Thatch loved.

I always like to help out a protégé when I can.

Let it go, let it go. She turned over in the cool smooth sheets, turned again. Eventually she fell asleep.

When she woke, the sun was low, and Sarah was sitting on the edge of the bed. Kate reached up and pulled her down. They lay quietly together. Kate tried out sentences in her head.

I saw something in the drying shed.

I found the most extraordinary kernel.

The control mechanism in one of my plants is doing something very interesting.

She could feel herself—feel everything—poised on the cusp, the way you could feel the season changing, new weather blowing in. She longed for whatever it would bring, and at the same time she wanted to hold on to this moment, her face against Sarah's shoulder, the clean white walls, the solidity of the maple headboard with its carvings of lilies and pomegranates. She wanted to hold her discovery close a little while longer.

"How was seeing your friend?" Sarah asked.

In the fading light, Kate began to tell Sarah about the dinner at Whitaker's: the meal, what Whitaker had said, what she'd learned about what Paul had done. She sat up, her voice rising as anger overcame her all over again.

"I don't understand," Sarah said. "What does it mean, he didn't credit you? He broke a rule?" She propped herself up on her elbow, tossing her hair back over her shoulder, frowning as she tried to understand.

"Not a rule—custom. Etiquette. He knew how important this was, and he shut me out."

"That man is a snake in the grass," Sarah said. "I never understood why you had anything to do with him."

Kate looked at her sharply. "Are you saying it's my fault?"

"Of course not!" Sarah reached for her hand. "I'm agreeing with you."

Kate's palm felt hot and claustrophobic in Sarah's, but she made herself leave it there. "He's the best scientist I know," she said. "Other than me." Which was a joke and not a joke.

"You only have to spend ten minutes with him to see that success is all he cares about," Sarah said.

"He cares about doing good science. His mind is very..." But how to explain Paul's mind?

"He cares about winning a Nobel Prize," Sarah retorted.

They regarded each other. Kate could feel herself flush, while Sarah turned to alabaster.

"How is that poor woman?" Sarah asked, changing the subject. "Your friend's wife." She slid her hand from Kate's to refasten a hairpin.

Kate sat back against the headboard. "I don't think she's too well."

"Poor thing," Sarah said. "Sylvia."

"Cynthia." The name felt wrong in Kate's mouth, as though she had no business saying it. She thought of Cynthia coming into the hospital room with the jam jar of joe-pye weed, Cynthia saying, *Of course you must come to us.* "Hard for him, too," Kate said.

"Did you talk about Missouri?"

"No."

Kate watched Sarah try to make out what that meant. That she wasn't serious about going? That she'd already decided to go so she didn't need his advice? Kate tried to make it out herself. Was it because she knew he would have told her to go? Even as he also said there were more important things than science.

Dusk was filling the room. The nightly chorus of robins and sparrows surged in through the open window. The inch of air between her leg and Sarah's was electric.

"I miss you when you don't come home," Sarah said.

Kate leaned hard against the headboard, the indentations of the carvings pressing into her back. The rich notes of the robins' song swirled around them. Why was the song deeper at dusk than during the day? Were the lilting notes somehow encoded on the chromosomes? "You work all night, too, sometimes."

"Because I have to," Sarah said. "Because that's the schedule."

"I have to, too."

They'd had this argument before, in a hundred variations. Last week Sarah had said, "What would be so bad about taking a whole Sunday off?"

But did plants take a day off from growing?

"They do in the winter," Sarah said.

In the winter, the stacks of data unfurled and burgeoned on Kate's desk. If she didn't get ahead of them before spring, the thicket would engulf her.

Sarah's life was different. She had struggled, of course, to get where she was now: the medical school professor who singled her out during cadaver dissections; the fellow interns who acted as though she weren't in the room when she spoke; the dozen jobs she'd applied for before getting this one, when two local doctors died of influenza in 1918 and the hospital was overwhelmed. "They literally hired me over two dead bodies," Sarah liked to say.

But all that was long ago now. She liked her work; and at the end of the day, she put work out of her mind, which had compartments: one for the hospital, one for Kate, one for her mother, one for music. Whereas Kate's life was a large marble egg she held in her arms.

Kate got up from the bed and began to dress. She was restless and overtired, her internal clock turned upside down.

Sarah pushed herself up on her elbow. "What are you doing?"

"Going for a drive."

"Do you want company?"

"Better not." Wallet, keys. Well-worn cardigan sweater with leather buttons.

"Where are you going?"

Kate sat down on a chair to lace her shoes. It was almost full dark now.

"Will you be back for dinner?" Sarah asked in a different voice. "Mutti will want to know."

"No. I don't know. No."

Behind the wheel, Kate's panic receded a little. The Ford seemed to glide over the ribbon of asphalt that unfurled endlessly into the distance, its V8 humming steadily. Even if she went to Missouri, she could come back regularly—couldn't she? There were roads. How long a drive could it be? Well, long, probably. So, not every week, but possibly once a month. And in the summers, of course. She could keep growing her corn in Ithaca and live with the Sonnenfelds from planting to harvest. Surely Whitaker would let her keep some space here.

I always like to help out a protégé.

I'm sure Paul could select his own organism.

How could Paul publish his *Neurospora* paper and not even show her a draft? Not mention her in a footnote? Not so much as let her know? She had to ask him.

No. She had to tell him she knew.

Let it go.

But she couldn't let it go.

The road wound east through forests, then broke out into meadows. She was tired, but she wasn't ready to stop driving. Sometimes she could make out the shadows of farmhouses, which she imagined being guarded by great muddy dogs. She passed through Richford, through Whitney Point, through the tiny village of Greene. It was late—long past dinnertime—though she couldn't read her watch in the dark. The moon was a pale disk far away in the sky. The road spilled ahead, faintly shiny in the yellow glow of her headlamps. When she couldn't fight her sagging eyelids anymore, she pulled off onto the side of the road and stretched out across the seat.

When she woke, it was full daylight, and she was in a rubbishy field of gorse and dry reeds. She got groggily out of the car, lowered her trousers, and squatted by the fender. Behind her, a tree, scorched by lightning, rose probably forty feet toward the scudding sky. On one of its skeleton-arm branches stood an enormous hawk: tense yellow feet, sharply curving beak, glossy black back with lighter shoulder patches. She recognized it from books, though she had never seen one—a bay-winged hawk. Not that there were any bays around here. It was a western bird, far from home. What storm had blown it such vast distances over mountains and prairies?

The hawk sat motionless on its branch, in the scrubby field, a thousand miles from anywhere it belonged. Standing up slowly, Kate watched it, waiting to see what it would do.

Or maybe, she thought, seized by doubt—maybe it wasn't a bay-winged. Maybe it was just a rough-legged hawk in its dark phase. Though didn't it have a very yellow beak for a rough-leg? She squinted, trying to see more clearly.

Sarah would know.

There the bird sat, patient and self-possessed, and Kate stood still and silent, watching it. Was it an omen of some kind? Was she expecting some sign from it? A hint, an augury? Was it charging her with going on, with turning back? Perched in this wasteland, glaring down on her with its clear bright eye.

Nonsense. Nonsense. Pulling herself together, she got back into the car.

A few miles up the road, she stopped for gas and bought a map, then sat in a diner, ate ham and eggs, and traced her route: east across the rest of New York, then south and east some more into Massachusetts. It was a long way, but that was all right.

Still, the drive took even more time than she'd calculated. She took a couple of wrong turns and had to retrace her steps, and it was late by the time she reached the Cambridge city limits. She found herself driving along the river: rich scent of mud and old leaves, the light slapping of water against the bank, lights reflected in the rippling black. Then she turned up onto a narrow street, past darkened buildings: shut-up restaurants and shops, the shuttered newsstand. The trolley tracks glinted faintly. In another minute, she had passed through the Square and found herself near the quiet grassy area where she and Sarah had parked that summer, just over two years ago. She pulled over to the curb and stopped the car.

It was a warm night. A breeze stirred the canopies of the trees, and a couple of bats fluttered and dove over the expanse of grass. She didn't know how late it was, and she didn't want to know. She had no idea where Paul lived, but it didn't matter. She didn't want to see him at his home. And anyway, he would be in the lab, she was sure of it. She had a sense of everything unfolding as it had been ordained to unfold.

She remembered the way: across the road and along the path through the red brick buildings—great looming shapes in the warm darkness. The wind rattled the leaves as she made her way underneath them. The moon gave her a silvery wink. She wasn't thinking. She had stopped thinking many hours and hundreds of miles ago. Her feet, her instincts, were her guides now, and they led her unerringly up the shallow steps to the door of Paul's building. She grasped the big door handle, ready to sail into the lobby and up the stairs.

The full stop of the locked door holding fast shuddered through her body and jangled her bones. Her heart began to thud. She tried the door again, and again it failed to yield. Standing on the top step, tugging at the immovable door, she seemed to wake up suddenly from a strange dream. Her calm was gone. It seemed to her that Paul had engineered this— had lured her here with some false hint or promise—only to shut her out again. *I want to ask you something*, he'd said to the blind, parched person she'd been before Sarah, as he lay sprawled, naked and sated, across her bed.

She took a breath, looked around at the night. There was nobody anywhere that she could see. She squinted up at the dark windows. It must be very late indeed for not even a graduate student to be showing a light.

She was pretty sure she knew which windows were Paul's. He had the corner lab on the second floor, at the front, facing the building with the frieze of animals. She could just make out now, across the courtyard and high up, the hump of the turtle and the long contour of the snake. She peered up at Paul's front window, then walked around the corner of the building.

The window on the side was ajar.

She thought of the desperate girl she'd been on that other autumn night, long ago, clawing her way up into the sanctuary of Krause's lab. She had known nothing then: nothing! Nothing about love, nothing about work.

It wasn't hard to raise herself onto the balustrade. From there, balancing on her toes, she could just reach the broad smooth second-floor windowsill. Kate was still slim, still agile. Working in the field every summer had made her strong. She pulled herself up with her muscular arms. She wriggled up onto the sill, her legs flailing and then finding purchase on the brick. She took a breath, heaved herself forward, and slipped under the sash.

Inside the lab, she stood panting, waiting for her heart to slow down, then began to feel her away across the room. The first thing she bumped into was the desk. Good. She groped across the surface till she found a lamp, switched it on. That gave her enough light to see by. She sat down at the desk to consider her next move, and there in front of her on the blotter were the proofs of the *Neurospora* paper. Doubtless left out so that anyone stopping would notice them!

Or maybe it was just coincidence that he had been working on them last night.

Or maybe it was destiny.

It didn't matter. She began to read the paper. And although she already knew, from what Thatch had said, what it contained, she found herself riveted. Paul had a clear confident style, and his claims carried the weight of his authority even before you read how he had proved them. Then, as you made your way through the rigor of his methods section and plunged into the crystalline logic of his discussion, you couldn't help feel that every doubt, every alternate possibility had been thought of, considered, disposed of. That the conclusions reached here were the only possible conclusions. One gene–one enzyme. Yes. It was seductively simple, as clean as a law of physics.

But biology wasn't physics. Living organisms were complicated, messy, knotty. Even if Paul was right (and she saw he must be at least partly right), there was bound to be more to it.

She could picture Paul's face if anybody tried to tell him that.

CHAPTER 30

By the time Paul came in, Kate had taken a nap with her head on the desk, woken up to reread the *Neurospora* paper, been thrilled and incensed all over again, then poked around to see what else he had going. There were footsteps in the hall as early as 7:30—voices, doors opening and shutting, the rattle of an equipment cart. But it was another hour before the doorknob rattled and Paul strolled in. White lab coat, abstracted expression, a higher forehead than he'd had two years before, the last time they'd met. Right here in this room.

"Hello, Paul," Kate said. She was sitting behind his desk in the big black chair with the Harvard seal painted on it. *Veritas.*

Paul startled, his face going dark and sharp, but he recovered himself. Then he took in who the trespasser was, and he laughed, seeming genuinely pleased to see her. "Hello, Kate. Who let you in?"

"I climbed in through the window," she said.

He smiled, obviously not believing her, and looked at his watch. "If you'd called, I'd have cleared the day for you. As it is, I have meetings. But I can be free for dinner."

She watched him for signs of unease. But Paul never seemed uneasy or discomposed that she recalled. Angry, yes. Outraged, indignant, scornful. But not rattled. Nothing seemed to make him doubt his own judgments or abilities, or what he was owed. The same was true, more or less, of Whitaker. Had been true of Krause. She thought about what Whitaker had said at dinner about what was necessary to succeed in science: talent, luck, and perseverance. He hadn't mentioned arrogance. Assurance. Ruthlessness. Pride.

She wondered whether he would ask her—tell her?—to get out of his chair.

"I heard about your new paper," she said. "*PNAS*—not bad!"

His smile broadened, pleasure and self-mockery complexly mixed. "Even I was surprised at how well it came out."

"I guess everyone is surprised once in a while. Even you."

Paul sat on a tall stool and lit a cigarette. He smoked, tilting the stool back on two legs. He picked a fleck of tobacco off his tongue. "You didn't bring your doctor friend this time."

"No. I came by myself."

Paul let a double stream of smoke out through his nostrils. "Too bad. I liked her."

"You should have put my name on that paper," Kate said.

Paul's eyebrows went up. "Which paper?" he said.

She looked at him hard. "You couldn't have done that work without my contributions."

"Couldn't I?"

It was hard to breathe. Her chest had gone rigid, the air turned crystalline in her lungs. "*I* sorted out the cytology. *I* suggested *Neurospora*." She remembered the peculiar hyperalertness of her mind—the weird illumination that came from toiling in the mud, from the confusion of sex, and from her encroaching illness—as she looked at the heel of the loaf left out on the counter and thought: *bread mold*.

He replaced the cigarette between his lips, and the smoke drifted up and away carelessly, though everything else in the room—the organized files, the labeled sample trays, the jar of sharpened pencils on the dust-free desk—suggested care. "You were very helpful," he said. "I appreciate that." He ran a hand through his hair, still thick in the back even as it

271

receded in the front, and yawned, as if the whole conversation were barely enough to keep him awake.

"It was crucial," Kate said. "You couldn't have done the work without it."

He laughed. "Of course I could have."

That utter ease, that easy affability, that affable mendacity. She didn't know which enraged her most.

"I appreciate your efforts," he said. "Sometimes people say or do things that help you along the way. But it's still your work."

Kate stared at him, remembering the last time he'd said those words. The terrible summer heat. The high booth with its dark red leather upholstery. The butter whorls sinking into the melting ice. "You knew perfectly well what you were doing."

He stubbed out his cigarette and looked at her hard. "You keep making the mistake of thinking things are personal," he said.

"It's personal," she said, her voice rising, "when persons are involved."

He tilted his head as though to get a different view of her. "You're a great scientist, Kate. No one thinks that more than me. You're skillful, and your ideas are absolutely original. But if you mind so much when those ideas help someone out, you should keep them to yourself."

All around the room the hard surfaces of the lab benches and the glassware and the stainless-steel taps stood out brightly in the morning light. "That's not the point," she said. "The point is, you should have given me credit."

"I really didn't think it mattered."

Whether he was lying to her, or just to himself, she couldn't tell. "It was the same when you used someone else's plants to make the crosses you wanted, back in Kansas," she said. "It was the same when you took my unfinished work—

my diagram—and showed it to Whitaker behind my back."

Paul tilted the stool an inch farther back, and then another inch, till she was certain he would topple over. "I helped you," he said. "Me showing that work to Whitaker was the best thing that ever happened to you."

Kate slapped her hands on the desk. "It wasn't your decision to make!"

"If not for me, you would have been stuck with Hiram Cole for another two years," he said, his voice finally rising. "You never would have gotten a thing done! It would have been ages before you or anyone else would have characterized the chromosomes, and the whole field would have been held back."

It startled her, hearing how much importance he put on her breakthrough.

"When obstacles stand in your way, you get rid of them," Paul said. "Cole was an obstacle."

"He was my obstacle," Kate said. "I would have found a way."

Paul laughed. "Like you've found a way to get yourself out of Cornell? Out from under Whitaker's shadow? If you don't get a real job soon, people will wonder. And that will be the end for you, Kate. The absolute end. Do you hear me?"

"Whereas you," she retorted, "would never have gotten a second chance after Kansas if Whitaker weren't your sixth cousin thrice removed."

Paul shook his head. "I would have," he said.

Kate leaned across the desk with its leather blotter and its jar of pencils and the neat, corrected proof of his *PNAS* article. "Would you?"

Paul let the two front legs of the stool fall forward with a clatter, and she could see she had finally rattled him. "It's about what you get done," he said. "I've always gotten things done."

"But they threw away your results in Kansas, didn't

they?" Kate said. "They destroyed your seeds. So: not that time."

"That was another life," Paul said.

She found that she was on her feet, though she didn't remember standing. She looked at him, steadying her trembling hands against the hard surface of his desk. With her standing and him sitting on the stool, they were just about the same height. "It's true, isn't it?" Whether she meant what had happened in Kansas, or his relationship to Whitaker, or that he had taken all the *Neurospora* credit to himself, she didn't know.

"That's enough!" Paul said. He stood up, and once again she was forced to look up at him. "You wanted to talk to me? You've talked. Now go on back to your instructorship, and your slow-growing *Zea mays*, and your handsome lady doctor." His eyes burned into her. Saw her. It was such an unaccustomed feeling, as though her skin had been slit open and he was probing around inside her, touching all her organs with his big square hands. Whether he was threatening her, or merely mocking her, she couldn't tell. She looked down at the proofs, the neat rows of type and the title in bold letters across the top, the single author name and the affiliation underneath: *Paul S. Novak, Harvard University*. Then she picked the papers up and ripped them in half. She put the two halves together and ripped again. She tossed the torn quarters back onto the blotter, where they fanned raggedly out.

Paul's face went hard. "You witch," he said.

"Better a witch than a thief," Kate said.

The door swung open. A white-haired man in a suit and tie stood in the doorway looking from one of them to the other. "What the hell is going on in here?"

Everything went still and glittering, as though instantly encased in ice.

Then Paul spoke, his smoothness almost entirely back in

place. "This is Dr. Croft," Paul said, nodding to her. "Kate, this Professor Allen Metcalfe, department chair."

Kate knew who he was. He had been on his August vacation when she had been here before, so she hadn't met him, but she had studied his elegant papers, interesting despite being about flies. Now he looked from one of them to the other, trying to make sense of the situation.

"I came to talk to Professor Novak about why he didn't put my name on his one gene–one enzyme paper," Kate said. "Despite my fundamental contributions."

The older man looked at Paul, who shrugged.

"It's true." Kate tried to summon the radiant fury that had made her rip the pages. "I spent two weeks here working out the cytology, and he didn't so much as footnote me."

Something changed in the man's face. "Croft?" he said. "Kathleen Croft?"

"Yes," Kate said.

"You characterized the maize chromosomes!"

"Yes."

"That was good work," Metcalfe told her gravely, as though he might be the first.

"Thank you," Kate said.

"Where are you nowadays?"

"Cornell."

"Part of Evelyn Whitaker's group?"

She nodded.

"Well. Please send Whit my regards."

Kate stared at him: the well-cut white hair, the well-cut blue suit. The beetle-black, thin-soled, wing-tipped shoes. A fly man, not a man who had ever worked a field. "I will," Kate said.

"And let's have no more of this nonsense," he said.

Kate broke up the trip home at a motel, a low building with

a long row of doors and a muddy parking area surrounded by raggedy, half-wild shrubs. An iron-haired woman in an old-fashioned dress sat at the registration desk. "Is your husband bringing in the bags?" she asked as Kate came in empty-handed.

In the grim room to which her key admitted her, Kate lay on the lumpy bed. Her body was wracked by exhaustion, but she couldn't sleep. Why had she thought it would do any good, driving across two states to confront someone who would always, regardless of everything, come out on top? Had she thought she could make him regret what he had done? That would have been making him regret who he was. Regret his nature.

But couldn't people change their natures? Couldn't they change, the way her corn had changed in the middle of the growing season, suddenly producing leaves with different frequencies of streaks? Something switched on, something else switched off, deep inside the cells.

Could she? It seemed to her she was exactly the same as she had been when she was a child. Curious. Subject to sudden passions. Drawn to things boys were supposed to be drawn to: caterpillars, ballgames, multiplication.

In her family, stubbornness was passed along through the female line. She, her sister, and her mother were all mule-like, boulderlike. Immovable, once they got an idea into their heads.

Did they think about her from time to time, her mother and her sister? She went to see them once in a while—her mother still in the big, cold, dark house near Flatbush Avenue, Laura in a bright brownstone in Brooklyn Heights with modern sofas and the latest appliances and life-sized paintings of girls with flowers in their hair—but they never came to visit her. Charlie had moved to Los Angeles. He was not much of a letter writer. He had never gone to college, never married.

Well, maybe all of them were stubborn, not just the women. Consider her father, dead set on going to war.

Yet it seemed to her that she had been changed by the last two years, living in the Sonnenfeld house with its music, and flowers cut from the garden, and the mannerly bustle of dogs. Mrs. Sonnenfeld singing to herself in German, Sarah pouring whiskey into glasses her mother had carried across the ocean. The flutes of the tulip poplar flowers scattered in the grass. She seemed able to see more acutely, to think more expansively. But maybe she was wrong. Maybe what had happened was that she had lost her focus, lolling among the lotus eaters while men like Paul plunged through the forests with their gleaming axes.

She turned over. The rough sheets smelled of bleach. Away across the state of New York, Sarah was sleeping, her dark hair fanned across the pillow. Kate could have been there with her, but instead she was here.

CHAPTER 31

"I thought you had died!" Sarah said. "I thought I had saved you from pneumonia only to have you die in a stupid automobile crash!"

Kate stared at her, incredulous. "How could you think that?"

"What was I supposed to think?" Sarah's face was furious, adamantine, but she kept her voice low. "If you'd left me, I assume you would at least have let me know."

"But you should have known there was a reason," Kate said.

"Yes. That you had driven off a cliff!"

They were in the backyard in the early evening light. The lowering sun slanted through the branches, scattering bright patches across the grass. Sarah was harvesting lettuce from the garden for dinner, bending over the neat row of black seeded Simpson, cutting the leaves with the kitchen scissors. She wore one of her mother's flowered aprons over her dress, and her hair was tied back in a yellow kerchief, which made her face look stark and sallow.

"Let me tell you what happened," Kate said.

Sarah moved down the row, gathering the lettuce into a yellow colander. Yellow kerchief, yellow colander, a few yellow tulip poplar leaves littering the grass. Already, though it was only September, dusk was closing in earlier.

"I told you what I found out. How Paul—" His name in her mouth was like biting down on something bitter, but she plunged on: "How he didn't credit me for the contributions I made to this paper he's publishing. This important paper.

What it says is—" But she managed to stop herself before beginning to explain what it said. Sarah was still snipping lettuce, though she had already gathered more than they could eat. "Anyway, I went to see him."

Sarah stood up slowly and turned. "You drove all the way to Cambridge, Massachusetts," she said, the blades of the scissors flashing in her hand. Carefully she placed them in her apron pocket.

"I wanted to hear what he would say," Kate said.

"If that was what you wanted, you could have called him on the telephone."

It astounded Kate that Sarah didn't understand. Surely it was perfectly clear. "I needed to see him," she explained. "I needed to see his face."

Sarah held the colander tight against her apron. "It's what," she said. "Three hundred miles? Four hundred, maybe?"

"It was the only way to know—to really know—how he would respond!"

Sarah picked out one of the lettuce leaves and rubbed it between her fingers. Did it hurt the leaf, Kate wondered? Could plants feel pain? Did the grass cry out silently when you walked on it?

"And how did he respond?"

"He was a snake," Kate said bitterly. "Just like you said."

Your handsome lady doctor.

I really didn't think it mattered.

I helped you.

"He pretended not to know what I was talking about."

"So he was a snake," Sarah said. "What do you care? Why can't you forget it?"

"He stole from me!"

"You knew what kind of person he was! What did you think was going to happen?"

"I wanted—" Kate said. She thought hard, trying to get it right. "I wanted to know that he knew what I had given him. What he had taken from me."

Between Sarah's fingers, the green frill had turned to pulp, staining her skin. "Forget Paul," she hissed. "Do your work. Your work's going well, isn't that what you keep telling me?" She tossed the mangled leaf onto the grass.

It was what Thatch said, too: *Do your work.* In the face of exclusion, slights, disregard, disrespect. "I deserve the credit," Kate said. "If I don't stand up for myself, who will?"

Sarah took a step forward. "Kate," she said, reaching out her hand. "Listen."

But Kate was beyond listening. She stalked back toward the house, crushing the mute grass underfoot with every step.

The next morning, Kate found a summons from Whitaker on her door. That was unlikely to be good news. Unless, she thought sardonically, he had finally found her a job.

Miss Floris stopped typing when Kate came in.

"What does he want?" Kate asked.

"I don't know," Miss Floris said. "But remember, by tomorrow he's likely to have forgotten all about it." Her coiled braids, brittler than they'd once been but still golden, glinted in the light of the ceiling fixture. There was no window in the outer office. No carpet, either, only the plain hard floor. There were no photographs on the desk nor any pictures on the wall. Surely Miss Floris could have hung pictures if she'd wanted to. She didn't have to make her space a kind of cell, as though she were a nun dedicating herself to—well, not to Whitaker, Kate hoped. To science? To excellence? To perfect impervious discretion?

In the inner sanctum, the Great Man sat at his desk, sharpening a pencil with his pocketknife, shavings scattered at his feet for the custodian to sweep away. As she came in, he looked up long enough to nod. "Dr. Croft," he said, then went back to his scraping.

"Professor Whitaker." She did not dare to sit down. Here she was again, waiting to be scolded on the familiar, roughly woven, mustard-colored rug with its odd geometric designs. Navajo? Hopi? She really should learn more about Indians. Their cultures were very interesting, and deeply intertwined with corn.

He brought his pencil close to his face to examine it, blew the tip free of dust. Then he laid it down on the desk and raised his eyes to hers. "I had a call from Allen Metcalfe at Harvard," he said. "He says you were down there yelling in Paul Novak's laboratory. Making quite a scene."

Kate's heart beat faster. "Paul did a lot of the yelling," she said. "As I recall."

Whitaker frowned. "Metcalfe says you were hysterical."

"I certainly was not!" Kate stood up straighter. Her heart was a drum, rousing her courage.

"So it's true that you went down there?"

"I paid a visit."

"What for?"

"I had something to discuss with Paul."

"Not that nonsense from the other night, I hope!" Whitaker spoke sharply.

"It's not nonsense," Kate said.

Whitaker flung his pencil down on the desk. "Do you have any idea how this looks? A student of mine goes gallivanting down to Harvard—*to Harvard!*—making claims about deserving credit for work one of their scientists did? Work that's about to get a lot of attention?"

In her chest, her heart beat steadily. Her lungs took in oxygen and sent it sailing down her arteries, her veins carrying back CO_2 for her to exhale, to nourish the miniature spruce Whitaker kept prisoner in its shallow pot. She felt almost the way she did when she ran on the beach, her knees high: *step, step, step.* "I'm not your student anymore," she said. "I'm a scientist in my own right."

"I have given you a great deal of latitude," Whitaker said. "I've let you pursue your own ideas. Do the experiments you want to do."

"Have you had a problem with my ideas?" Kate said.

"In exchange for which I expect a modicum of respect! Just as you'd give to your own father."

Her father! How Kate missed him. The way he strode across the meadow in his tall boots, stopping to point out a caterpillar or a cowslip. The way his soft whiskers glowed in the sun.

"I saved your life," Whitaker reminded her. "When you were lying delirious with pneumonia, I carried you down the stairs in my arms."

"That doesn't give you the right to keep me here forever," Kate said, "like an unmarried daughter to look after you!"

Whitaker's face went white. The steady clatter of typewriter keys from the outer office was the only sound. Nothing could keep Miss Floris from her work, Kate thought, she was like one of the Fates, spinning out the thread of life. "You have stumbled, however inadvertently, upon the point," Whitaker said coldly. "The fact is, I can't keep you on any longer. The funding has finally run out." His face was leathery, hard. His hawklike stare bore into her.

"Because someone at Harvard complained about me?"

The Great Man's mouth and eyebrows were straight lines, his nose triangular, so that he looked like one of the geometric figures on his rug. "No one gets a fourth year."

"I was leaving anyway," Kate said. "Fred Zimmer has made me an offer."

Kate waited until after dinner, when Mrs. Sonnenfeld had

gone out, to tell Sarah. They were in the living room at either end of the sofa. On the carpet, the dogs dozed, Holly and Lily curled up flank to flank and Rose sprawled across the threshold to the front hall. Kate recounted what had happened in Whitaker's office and explained that she would be accepting Zimmer's offer. She would be leaving in January.

"If you've decided, then you've decided," Sarah said. Her eyes were fixed on the fireplace, which was cold and bare, neatly swept.

"Did you hear what I just told you? It's not a choice."

"But why did you have to make Whitaker so angry?"

Kate tucked her feet up and lay down across the sofa so that the top of her head touched Sarah's skirt. "I didn't mean to," she said. "But it doesn't matter."

"Of course it matters. He's your boss."

The room was quiet except for the breathing of the dogs and the ticking of the mantel clock. The scent of grass from the open windows mixed with the scent of furniture polish and of Sarah's hair. "No one gets a fourth year," Kate said. "I was lucky to stay this long."

"Not lucky. You earned the right to stay."

"I earned the right to go. He just wouldn't let me." She slid her head onto Sarah's lap and looked up at her. Sarah's skin was so tight and attenuated, it seemed like the barest scrim of silk pulled over her skull. "Come with me," Kate said.

Sarah shook her head. Tears caught in her eyelashes, then fell onto Kate's face.

"Come with me," Kate repeated, her voice lower. "Bring your mother. We can buy a house in Missouri. Out of town, maybe. Maybe a farm."

"Kate," Sarah said.

"Think about it," Kate said.

"Why do you need a university job? Can't you just keep

growing your corn? They hardly pay you anything anyway."

Kate stared up into Sarah's face, disbelieving.

"You have a home here!" Sarah cried.

She thought of Paul saying, *If you don't get a real job soon, that will be the end for you.* Of Whitaker saying, *I have given you a great deal of latitude.* She wanted to roll off the sofa and hide behind the velvet drapes. Instead she said, "I can come back for Christmases. Maybe in the summer, you could come to me."

But she knew Sarah wouldn't, knew the hospital wouldn't permit it. And even if it would, the summers were such a mad rush of work . . .

She thought about how much labor it was going to take to get a new field ready—to level it and plow it and plant it—and her heart surged with joy. She couldn't help it. Even with Sarah's tears damp on her face.

"Don't go," Sarah said. Her voice was thin and chilly, but Kate knew that was only so didn't she break apart.

"Sarah," Kate said.

Sarah waited. She took a handkerchief from her sleeve and dried her face, then folded it up and tucked it away, while they both waited for Kate to discover whatever it was she might say.

They were still waiting when the telephone rang with its blaring jangle.

"Leave it," Kate said, but Sarah was already rising to answer it, striding over Rose, who awoke with a yelp.

"Yes?" Sarah said in the hall. "How many? All right. Twenty minutes."

The coat closet door opened and shut, then the front door. A car engine started. Rose yawned and stretched and got to her feet. She walked over to Kate and stood in front of her, swishing her tail. Kate touched her head. Rose laid her silken muzzle on Kate's knee.

Up in her room, at her desk under the eaves, she took out the manuscript of the paper she was writing, about the twin sectors. She read the introduction over. Something swelled inside her chest, pressed the air out to the edges of her ribcage, made her skin feel hot and blotchy. It was all wrong. Wrong. She crossed the sentences out with a big black X. She rolled a fresh piece of paper into the typewriter and started again.

Slowly, steadily, she worked her way through a new draft of the introduction. Then she tackled the methods section and began the discussion: *one gained what the other had lost*. Her thoughts unspooled, threading themselves cleanly through the needle of her mind, so that her quick fingers could stitch them up. Time passed, measured only by the clack of keys and the piling up of pages. She had lost track of the night altogether when the abrupt soft click of the front door shutting two floors below brought her back to herself. She glanced at the clock. It was after one. Mrs. Sonnenfeld must have come home hours ago without Kate even noticing. She listened to Sarah moving around in the hall, the closet door opening and shutting, her footsteps slowly climbing the stairs. Kate's back and shoulders ached, but she was almost finished. She just had the tricky discussion section left. Still, with the whole thing clear in her mind, she knew, if she just kept going, she could get it right.

PART FIVE

1948

CHAPTER 32

"Kate Croft!" said a familiar voice. "I would have recognized you anywhere."

Kate turned. The man who had spoken was about her age: pale skin, snub nose, salt-and-pepper fringe of hair. He came toward her across the plush carpet of the boardroom with its tall windows and polished, paneled walls. A name materialized in her brain: Jax. Jax Harrison, whom she had blessedly neither thought about nor seen in many years. She held out her hand, forestalling the embrace she saw was coming. "Isn't that nice," she said.

Six geneticists were assembled in Washington, D.C., to review grant proposals and distribute funds. Before the war, grant-giving had been left to the discretion of institute and agency directors, but times were changing. Science was opening up, hurtling forward. Kate had even heard that Harvard Medical School was accepting girls.

Jax pumped her hand. "Good to see you. Kate Croft! How are you? I admire the way you've stuck with corn. Whitaker would have been proud."

Evelyn Whitaker had died several years earlier, of a massive heart attack, in his sleep. Kate had gone to his funeral, where she'd found to her surprise that she was glad to have a handkerchief. He had helped her in so many ways after all. He had, after all, saved her life. "I don't know about that," she said.

"Of course I've heard a little about your work." Jax smiled his old vulpine smile. "This movable genes business. People say either you're a genius, or else you're off your rocker."

Kate's face twitched—a little flutter in her cheek that

had developed in recent years. "I just get up in the morning and go to the lab like everybody else," she said.

"Don't be modest." Jax leaned in so she could smell his breath: stale coffee and burnt cloves. Did he still smoke those terrible cigarettes? "You were never like everyone else."

Again the flutter, like a tiny moth under the skin trying to get out. "Remind me where you are. Berkeley, is it?"

"Caltech," Jax said. "Pasadena. Sunshine three hundred days out of the year! You step out your back door and there are oranges."

Kate had been cultivating a new smile, vague and harmless, and she tried it on him now, then began to turn toward the refreshment table. Of course someone like Jax would end up someplace like Caltech. Jax was saying something. She almost managed to get away without hearing what it was, but a word—a name—jumped out at her. *Thatch.*

"What?" she said, more sharply than she'd meant to, turning back.

"I said, do you ever see Thatch?"

"Not for years." The moth fluttered more insistently.

"That's a shame. You two were so close."

"Do you see him?" Kate demanded.

"Maybe five years ago was the last time, when I was in New York for a meeting. He doesn't travel much."

"No," Kate said.

"Doesn't publish much, either. Not like us. Such a shame. He was so promising back then."

"He published enough to get tenure," Kate said.

"And Paul," Jax went on. "Who would have thought someone from our little cohort would have reached those heights!" He leaned confidentially in. "You've heard they're putting together nomination papers for him, for the Prize?"

Kate kept her face as bland as possible. "No. I hadn't heard that."

"Of course, almost no one gets it on the first nomination. But in his case . . . You've seen we have a proposal from him?"

Kate nodded. She certainly had seen that.

"That one will be an easy call, anyway," Jax said.

"Will it?" Kate said. "There's not much data there."

"Well," Jax said, "but we all know what kind of scientist he is."

"Yes," Kate said. "We do."

The hotel in which the committee members had been put up was the nicest Kate had ever stayed in. Her room was the size of her living room and kitchen combined at home, with a fitted dark-green carpet and light-green-and-cream-striped wallpaper. The large soft bed had so many pillows, it must have taken the denuding of a flock of geese. There was a desk, an armchair, a low table, and a vase of tall pale lilies. She tried to enjoy it, but it made her feel odd. Surely the money would have been better spent on actual science?

In the spacious bathroom with its veined marble countertop, she ran a bath. Water splashed and tumbled gaily from the gleaming faucet, steam fogging the several mirrors. Kate took off her dress—dark green with a Peter Pan collar, her best, but still she feared too shabby for this place—hung it carefully on the back of the door, and slipped into the water. She shut her eyes and tried to relax, letting the heat envelope her, but the tub was so big that she had to grab on to the slippery side. She was the wrong size for this tub. It had been designed with a different kind of person in mind.

She reminded herself that it was an honor to have been asked to serve on this panel; an honor she had earned through her work.

It had been a productive decade for Kate. The meticulously bred descendants of the twin-sector plant, and of the red-spot plant, had continued to throw up interesting results.

More than interesting. Riveting. Revelatory.

First she had mapped the great dark river that was maize's chromosome nine. Identifying its features, deducing what each part did. She was studying corn, but if it could be done for corn, it could be done for any organism—even, someday, for people. Outlandish as that seemed.

By the time it became clear that she would never get tenure at Missouri, she'd proved that the breakage she kept finding at the same spot on chromosome nine was itself controlled by another part of the chromosome. Genes, then, not only controlled what an organism looked like—whether a corn kernel was speckled or solid. Genes also controlled the behavior of other genes.

The data—collected in thick black notebooks stuffed with tables, charts, graphs, catalogs, and inventories—were complex, and it was hard to convey them simply. Still, once you absorbed them, they were thrilling.

Her first few papers on this material had been very well received.

After Missouri, Kate had moved to Cold Spring Harbor Laboratory in Long Island, thirty miles east of New York City. It was a good place for her, quiet in winter, buzzing with activity in summer. A pretty, wooded campus near a little cove where you could swim from June to September. She'd taken up tennis again. She'd learned to bake, having stumbled upon a recipe in the newspaper for chocolate walnut cookies, which reminded her of the ones Mrs. Sonnenfeld used to make. Doubtless still made. Or, perhaps not. She would be nearing eighty now.

Kate and Sarah still corresponded once in a while, though Sarah was a terrible letter writer. With their tilted, sprawling script and humdrum observations (*Mother is busy with her committees. Things at the hospital are all right.*

The weather is terribly hot, even by the lake.), Sarah's letters seemed to have been written not by the sharp, complicated person Kate had loved but by someone else entirely.

For several years after Kate left Ithaca, she had found reasons to go back. She still collaborated with people in Whitaker's group, and she never minded driving. Through the late 1930s, her Ford Deluxe regularly hummed through the black and green fields flanking the road out of Missouri. After the fields came the forest, stands of oaks and stands of hickory each in its niche. The native sassafras and the invasive bush honeysuckle, the dewberry and the cottonwood. As she angled north, the season would roll itself back like a filmstrip run the wrong way. The leaves would grow smaller, maybe even furling themselves to swelling buds. It was a kind of time travel.

It was understood that she could stay at the Sonnenfelds whenever she wished.

Her old room with its dark slanted beams and white curtains would be waiting, scoured and aired. Mrs. Sonnenfeld would have baked a walnut cake, and Sarah might have placed a jar of flowers on the table by the bed.

Then one spring, Sarah answered Kate's letter announcing her arrival date with a longer than usual letter explaining that someone else was living in the room now, a nurse from the hospital who had recently moved to Ithaca and needed a place to stay.

You didn't have to be a genius to know what that meant.

But: A nurse! The triteness of that choice infuriated Kate. Though of course, nurses were the women Sarah mostly met.

Even now, at forty-three, Kate hadn't had another lover for more than a few months at a time. The last one had been years ago. For everyday company, she had her corn with its familiar habits. Its indelible scents of sap and hot green leaves and pollen.

*   *   *

Cold Spring Harbor had many black walnut trees, which scattered their heavy crop across the grass in autumn. Kate collected the nuts in an old pillowcase, hulled them with a hammer and chisel, cleaned the meats carefully, let them cure. It was the kind of fiddly, time-consuming process that let her mind work over whatever it was stuck on. She delivered the cookies in neat packages to her colleagues and their families, many of whom also lived on campus. To the postman and the farm manager. To the janitor who mopped the halls at midnight, and the yeast guy she played tennis with, and Jerry Waxman in the apartment above hers who kept a pair of parakeets named Darwin and Mendel. Sometimes the neighbor children brought her walnuts they had collected, approaching her shyly as she came and went along the cinder paths, or leaving them in the hallway outside her door. Sometimes she could hear them whispering out there.

Knock.

No, you knock.

We'll just leave them, then.

Were they afraid of her? She suspected so much solitude was making her odder, even, that she'd been before, but surely she wasn't frightening. She wasn't a witch in a gingerbread house—a witch jealously guarding her rampion garden. Was she?

She did guard her corn jealously, in its field between the library and the harbor. She walked it every morning as she had always walked her fields, taking in the daily changes. Her corn grew well here. Her work was going well, insight following upon insight: the timing of the changes, the influence of dosage effects. Last year she had uncovered the most startling thing so far.

Conventional wisdom said: genes are strung along the

chromosome like pearls on a necklace. Like pearls on a necklace, they are stuck in place.

But she had seen that—sometimes—those pearls could move.

And when they moved, the corn changed.

That old, old question—how did an organism (a corn plant, a human being) become what it was—was beginning to yield to her, like a walnut yielding to a hammer.

What set the movable-gene system in motion?

That question was the hardest yet. She wasn't sure—not sure enough to publish, anyway. But it looked like it happened in response to something going on in the cell. Some signal from the local environment.

In other words, genes did not dictate absolutely what an organism would be. Sometimes the environment influenced the genes.

Or so she thought. So the preliminary evidence suggested.

She had tried this idea out on a few colleagues. She had given a seminar or two, hinting at what she'd seen—what she suspected. But the response had been quite different from what she had anticipated. Instead of enthusiasm, she'd encountered bafflement. Wariness. Doubt.

People say either you're a genius, or else you're off your rocker.

The person Kate would have liked to discuss all this with was Thatch. If he'd told her she was going off the rails, she would have taken it seriously. She was sure he would have been able to help her see more clearly what was there, buried in the avalanche of data. But their relationship had frayed since the publication of their last paper together, on the bronze locus, back during her final days at Cornell. When he had come to Ithaca to give a talk and told her she ought to get married, failing to see what she had tried to show him about herself. When she had punished him with those terrible words: *Because your marriage has brought you so much joy.*

Remembering that moment made her scramble out of the bath. She wrapped herself in the plush white terrycloth robe provided by the hotel. Like the tub, it had been designed for a bigger person, but she rolled up the sleeves. She took out her stack of grant proposals.

It was interesting to see what other people were working on. Only a few were studying maize. There were many proposals from fly men, and many more still from scientists working on bacteria. Even some from people working on viruses. Viruses! Unable to reproduce outside of host organisms, viruses were not, in Kate's estimation, even truly alive. How could you learn any important truths about life from studying a thing like that?

She fished out Paul's proposal, which she had ranked twenty-eighth out of forty. He was working with drosophila again now, trying to figure out what determined fly eye color. The proposal was slimmer than most of the others, with less detail about what he planned to do and fewer figures presenting preliminary findings. It was cogent enough. His ideas were reasonable. But lots of ideas were reasonable. The question was, why should the committee believe he was going to get results?

No. The question was: If his name had not been Paul Novak, would the committee believe, from the evidence submitted, that he was likely to get results?

Kate had run into Paul many times over the last decade. They were often at the same conferences, giving talks in the same sessions. He sometimes spent a week or two at Cold Spring Harbor in the summers with his wife and small children. Lots of people brought their families, who swam and lounged and played tennis while the husbands talked science from breakfast till late into the night, with occasional breaks for a set of afternoon doubles. Kate had had the pleasure of beating Paul on the tennis court. Once slim and muscular, he had grown gradually soft around the middle, doubtless from exchanging the corn field for the fly room. Not to mention his pretty blond wife's cooking.

Paul had become famous. His one gene–one enzyme paper had made him a star in the genetics firmament. He had been elected president of the Genetics Society of America, and last year, at the startlingly young age of thirty-nine, had been inducted into the National Academy. He had gotten tenure at Harvard. He had taken up sailing. Now, apparently, he was being nominated for the Prize. Did he really need funding for a study of eye color in drosophila?

Kate didn't approve of the way so many people talked about genes nowadays, as though they were a kind of divine hand which nothing could countervail. It seemed to her that Paul—Paul's work—was a big part of the reason for this, and that too much of the scientific community had begun to accept uncritically everything Paul said. It dismayed her to see science falling prey to fads and biases. To cults of personality.

Also in the pile was a proposal by someone called J. S. Lezniak, who was studying *Arabidopsis*, an unprepossessing member of the mustard family, sometimes known as mouse-eared cress. *Arabidopsis*, Lezniak argued, was a perfect model organism for geneticists because of its ease of growing, its small number of chromosomes (five), its production of many seeds (thousands), and its short generation time (about seven weeks). Not the twenty minutes you got with bacteria, but pretty good for a plant. Plants—Kate felt strongly about this—should not be shut out of modern science just because they took a little longer to grow. After all, they had been good enough for Mendel.

There was a lot of intriguing data in J. S. Lezniak's proposal, which Kate had ranked ninth out of the forty. Some of the charts were very interesting, if you delved into them.

But Kate suspected that her colleagues on the committee were unlikely to have delved far. It was true that the proposal could have been written more engagingly; it was, in its own way, as unprepossessing as *Arabidopsis* itself. But surely it was the job of the committee to look beyond writing style, as it was their job not to be dazzled by names and fancy institutional affiliations. So Kate thought, sitting in her deluxe hotel room in the soft white robe, arguing as though there were someone sitting beside her arguing back. When, in fact, she was quite alone.

CHAPTER 33

In addition to Jax, Kate knew two of the other review panel members, Hal Volkner and Les Abernathy. That left the institute director, Claude Mikkleson, who was chairing the panel, and two others she didn't know. One was an elderly fly man who wore a cravat, the other a big, bearlike person with unruly black hair named Nelson, who had made some interesting discoveries in yeast. Seated across from Kate at the long glossy table, he seemed to be trying to catch her eye during the introductions, which made her wonder if she was supposed to know him after all.

Mikkleson called the meeting to order with a little gavel and explained the procedure for awarding funding. He himself would briefly summarize a proposal then ask for discussion, at the end of which each member would assign a rating from one to ten. Mostly the panel members seemed to be intelligent, thoughtful men—even Jax, Kate had to admit, though he talked too much, weighing in even when everything he had to say had already been said by someone else. Except for the maize proposals, which she understood better than the others did, Kate mostly agreed with the group, and when she explained the holes in the corn ones, they deferred to her expertise.

At noon, when they broke for lunch, Nelson, the yeast man, came over to Kate. Unlike the other panel members, he was dressed as if for the lab in khaki trousers, a blue work shirt, and lace-up boots. His black hair fell across his forehead, and more hair curled up out of his collar. Kate greeted him in a friendly way, trying to think where she might know him from. It turned out it wasn't him she knew.

"I've been charged with passing on greetings from an old friend," he said. "My wife asked me to send her regards. She says you shared a house once, in Ithaca, when you were students. Thea Gold, she was then."

Kate's mind scrabbled to make sense of what he was telling her.

He put his big palm out flat at the level of his breastbone to indicate his wife's height. "Not too tall. Light brown hair. Sunny personality. Most of the time."

"I do," Kate said faintly. "Remember her." She looked up at the burly man, but what she saw was Thea in her blue dress in the house on Myrtle Street saying, *If you don't take the class, I'll be the only one.* Thea lying on the bed in Kate's tiny room, reciting the parts of a flower. Thea in her fitchskin coat outside the biology classroom, holding out a letter.

"We met when I was in graduate school and she worked in the science library," Nelson said.

"Ah," Kate said.

"She was such a pretty girl. Half again as bright as most of my classmates, and she knew twice as much about botany."

"We were lab partners in Intro Bio." But she was still thinking *science library!* Was that as close as she believed she could get?

"So she told me. Kate Croft and my wife as lab partners! Imagine that." He laughed.

Yes, Kate thought, imagine it: the room with its scarred black lab benches and faint stink of formaldehyde. Thea bending over the microscope, the pink ribbon at the end of her braid. Kate nudging her out of the way to look down the optic tube for the very first time! The universe in a drop of pond water.

"She's worked in my lab for years," Nelson said. "She started once the children were in school. Never formally trained, of course, but sharp as a tack. When I switched from maize to yeast, she kept right up."

"How is she?" Kate asked. "Thea." The most mundane of questions, yet her face grew hot.

"She's back at the hotel," Nelson said. "She said to tell you, if you wanted to see her, she would be in the lobby at the end of the afternoon session."

"She's here?" Kate tried to catch up. "In Washington?"

"She often travels with me," Nelson said. "She says it makes a change."

In the afternoon, they sat around the table just as they had in the morning, but everything felt slightly different. The voices of the men seemed to reach Kate from a distance, while the colors—the yellow of Mikkleson's tie, the burgundy of the curtains, the green of the apples in a bowl in the middle of the table—were almost too bright to look at. She was finding it difficult to collect her thoughts. Her eyes kept drifting up to Nelson. He was such a big man. Even his hands were big, with black hair curling over the knuckles as he tapped a handsome fountain pen against his stack of file folders. Had Thea given him the pen? Had she typed the labels on the folders and affixed them with glue? Had she picked out his shirt with its fine, mossy green stripe?

The fourth proposal of the afternoon was J. S. Lezniak's request for funding for further study of *Arabidopsis*. Hal Volkner, a cheerful, no-nonsense man with plump, gesticulating hands, opened the discussion. "There's nothing here," he said. "We've seen X-ray-induced mutations like these before. He doesn't propose to do anything new."

"I agree," Jax said. "There's nothing new here. No big ideas. I give it a three."

"The trouble is that the proposal is backward-looking," Nelson said. "We need to be looking to the future. What some of these men are proposing to do with viruses is amazing! *That's* the future of genetics."

"No, no," Kate said, rousing herself. "You miss the point."

Nelson looked at her with a big, friendly-seeming smile. "Do I?"

"It's about the *organism*," Kate said. "About developing a new plant model." The eyes of the committee—old and young, curious and impatient—were all fixed on her, and to her annoyance she felt her face color. "The mutation work may not be new, but it's solid. It's interesting." She began to explain what she had seen in the charts and graphs, and what the mutation work promised, and why it would be useful to add a plant like mouse-eared cress to the tool chest of the plant geneticist. She could hear herself, as if from a distance, droning dully on. It was hard to keep track of her own words. Sentences tumbled out. She hoped they were all right. "Studying bacteria—studying viruses—it's all well and good," she heard herself say. "But there are some aspects of genetics that plants are ideally suited to tell us about. In my view, Lezniak makes a strong case. The work is careful, which is more than I can say for many of the proposals we discussed this morning."

"I'd say his work is dull as a doorknob," Jax said.

A noise came from Sturgis Myers, the dapper elderly man with the cravat—perhaps a sneeze.

"Pardon?" Claude Mikkleson said politely.

"I said, *she*," the old man said. "Joanne Lezniak was my colleague at the University of Wisconsin before I retired. A reputable researcher."

Kate wanted to laugh. One proposal from a woman, out of thirty proposals! One, and she was the only person in the room who liked it.

Jax turned to Kate. "I guess you knew that."

"I certainly did not," Kate said sharply.

"Why were you defending it, then?"

"I think it's strong. Plant genetics need a new model organism. This one looks very promising. Seven weeks may sound like a long generation time to you, but from our point of view, it's the blink of an eye." Hadn't she just said all of these things?

Jax yawned. "I don't understand why anyone bothers with plants."

Kate laughed, though she knew it wasn't a joke.

Claude Mikkleson rapped his gavel. "Gentleman. Dr. Croft. Let's return to a discussion of the merits."

"What merits?" Hal Volkner said. "As Nelson says, it's backward-looking. Our job here is to underwrite the future of genetics."

"There's more than one way to underwrite the future," Kate said. "It's hubristic to assume we know what the future will hold and can see the best road for getting there." Her voice was rising, which she knew would help nothing. She took a breath and said more calmly, "Any number of roads might turn out to be the right road. I'd suggest it behooves us to ensure that many alternate routes remain open."

"I can't agree," Nelson said (Thea's husband!). There was a new bullying note in his voice as he leaned across the table. "We have been asked to make judgments. Hubristic or not, our charge here *is* to predict the future and determine which roads we believe will be most productive."

"There is a great deal still to be learned from plants," Kate said coldly. The intensity of her dislike for this man took her by surprise. She sat up straighter in her chair and spoke to him the way she spoke to the poor slow graduate students who sometimes came to her lab to ask her to explain the intricate clockwork of chromosome nine. "Despite the current prejudice in favor of simpler models. It's precisely because plants are complex that studying them will help us understand the complexity that underlies biology. If we only study what is simple, we're going to miss crucial insights."

Nelson's face shut itself off from her. She could see he did not like her tone.

Volkner was shaking his head. "We have to walk before we can run," he said. "We have to work out the simple things first. They're going to be hard enough."

"I don't agree," Kate said. She looked around the beautiful table with its bowl of green apples at the faces of the men, who were watching her politely or impatiently or with half-concealed hostility, but who had obviously made up their mind about *Arabidopsis*. Who had obviously made up their minds about her.

"Gentleman," Claude Mikkleson said again, louder. "Dr. Croft. It seems to me we've reached the end of productive discussion. I suggest each of us rate the proposal according to his own estimation and that we move on." He looked at her to make sure she had taken his point.

Let it go, she told herself.

Let it go.

The shuffle of papers filled the room like the sound of a flock of birds rising and resettling. Kate scribbled down an eight, one point higher than her original assessment. Not that it would make the slightest difference.

The next proposal was Paul's request for funding to study eye color in fruit flies. A chorus of approving voices rose up from around the table and drifted toward the decorative plasterwork. Volkner said it was a pleasure to read a proposal that stated so clearly what it was about and what its author intended to do. Jax agreed. Abernathy, a drosophila man himself, said that eye color was the wedge that was going to open up understanding of the mechanism of gene function. Nelson said that Paul Novak's work was always forward-looking, exactly the sort of work the institute ought to be funding.

"As you say, always *was*," Kate remarked, more brusquely than she'd meant to.

Nelson looked at her. "Pardon?"

"You said that Paul's work always *was* forward-looking. Past tense. That seems a crucial point. Just because something always *was* in the past doesn't mean it always *will be* in the future."

"I'd call that splitting hairs."

Kate looked away from his big unkempt head. She looked around the table, appealing to the others. "The proposal seems pretty slender to me. He talks about what he wants to do, but he doesn't give much evidence that he'll be able to do it."

"We know he'll be able to do it," Jax said. "You should know it better than anyone." He turned to Abernathy, who was sitting beside him. "Kate and I were at Cornell with Paul Novak. He was brilliant even then."

Kate looked at Mikkleson. "My presumption is that we're supposed to rate these proposals according to what's in front of us, not using any private information or supposition."

"You should use whatever criteria you judge to be appropriate," the director replied. "We have not adopted formal ones."

"Then I would suggest that, in the future, proposals be judged anonymously," Kate said.

"I can't agree," Jax said. "Knowing who is proposing the work is crucial to judging his ability to do what he says he is going to do."

"Let's confine ourselves to the subject at hand," Mikkleson said.

That Paul had put so little effort into his proposal made Kate angry. He clearly didn't think he'd needed to bother, and he was clearly right. She was angrier still that reputation carried more weight than substance—in this room as everywhere. Now that J. S. Lezniak had been revealed to be a woman, it seemed to Kate that she had known this fact all along—that all of them on the panel had known it—and that that was the reason the others had rated the proposal so low, and this made her angriest of all.

Still. Did she think Paul's study of eye color in drosophila was likely to be productive? She did.

She looked up and saw Jax staring at her with his smug, snub-nosed face—the same face he had worn that afternoon in Thatch's office when he'd swatted Paul's coffee mug to the floor.

What had he said? She'd forgotten. She'd made herself forget. But the words came back to her now.

Crazy bag.

Know-it-all.

I bet you're not even getting any!

They seemed to ring out in the room for everyone to hear.

"Dr. Mikkleson," Kate said.

"Dr. Croft?"

"I really have to object to the way this proposal is being evaluated."

There was a sigh from across the table—Nelson, or someone else.

"Dr. Croft, everyone has the opportunity to judge the proposal as he sees fit. That's how it works."

"I know how it works," Kate said. "Believe me, I know. Paul—Professor Novak—is an excellent scientist. No question. Also, he's charming and he has a lot of friends. So he knows he doesn't have to bother to write a strong proposal. He just tosses something off and expects the panel to fund him."

Jax laughed. "What did Paul do to you, Kate, to make you want to punish him?"

Very slowly—or perhaps it was very quickly— she turned to look at Jax. She could see the ghost of his twenty-five-year-old face just under the surface of his current one, the past always there, inexpugnable. "Punish Paul?" she echoed. "By not giving him a few thousand dollars he doesn't really need? Is that your idea of punishment?"

Mikkleson leaned over the table. "Miss Croft," he said mildly.

"I'm not the one who's out of line," she told him, though she was beyond knowing whether that was true or not. Around the table, the faces of the men blended into one face: set, irritated, uncomfortable, disapproving. How could you hold on to truth in a room like this? Yet what else was there to hold on to?

Mikkleson said, "You've had your say, Miss Croft. Please sit down."

When had she stood up? She had no idea, and that made her laugh. Yes, she was out of control, even as every muscle in her body tightened, twitching with the effort of discipline. Her body was rigid, but her mind was drifting up. She could feel it, almost like a cloud of cool vapor lifting out of the top of her skull. From somewhere near the plasterwork scrolls and filigrees, she looked down on the men slouching around the table in their suits and ties. On her own thin body in her old green dress.

"Punishment is expelling someone from school," she said. "Or firing someone from their job. Or declining to give a deserving person tenure. Not one of these things has ever happened to Paul Novak! He sails on through his charmed life from accolade to accolade. While women like J. Lezniak struggle to get promising work so much as funded. How will you ever know what she might do if you don't let her try?"

Hal Volkner, so cheery all day, was seething now. "Sit down!" he snapped. "If you need any evidence why scientists are loath to put women on panels like this, just look in the mirror!"

She turned toward Mikkleson, captain of this listing ship. "A whole room of people who can't tell a good proposal from a bad one! Isn't it your job to make sure they do their jobs?"

"Miss Croft," he said.

"Dr. Croft," she corrected.

"Dr. Croft." He sounded very weary and sober. "I am asking you one last time to sit down."

Before he did what? Called the science police?

"I'll do better than that," she said. She left her stack of proposals on the table and walked out of the room.

CHAPTER 34

It was a warm spring afternoon, the sky pearly with clouds. A fine light rain, hardly more than a mist, dampened Kate's hair, which had grown so coarse and gray these last years. Furious thoughts and half-thoughts hissed and swirled through her head as she strode down the sidewalk. It wasn't easy to walk fast in these shoes, yet she found herself breathing hard. She who often hiked five miles through wet sand, then turned around and headed back for a set of tennis.

Twenty years of self-control, sacrificed in an instant.

Twenty years of not only not saying what she felt, but hardly even feeling it. Of telling herself that science was all that mattered; that as long as she kept her focus, she would have her reward. That the focus was the reward.

Well, that was still true, wasn't it?

Or maybe she really was delusional: a crazy bag.

Because what would happen to her now?

Why do you want to punish Paul? Jax had said. But it was she who would be punished, one way or another. She knew that.

Yet what could they take from her? Her job was modest, but it came with something like tenure. She had not herself applied for a grant in years and had no real need to. She had even, lately, stopped submitting her work for publication. She was waiting until she understood the movable gene system more clearly and completely. She didn't miss the wearisome submission process, or the wrangling with impatient editors about methods and charts. She had the work, and she had her freedom. Which was more than many people had.

*   *   *

The worry that Thea would not recognize her—that she would not recognize Thea—pursued her all the way back to the hotel. But in fact Kate knew her immediately.

Thea sat in a low chair in the lobby with its marble inlay floor and deep sofas. She wore a lightweight raincoat, and her head, in a green scarf, was bent over a magazine. She was so absorbed that she didn't notice Kate until she was quite close. Then she looked up. A polite smile spread across her thin pale face as she stood. "I could hardly believe it when I saw your name on Bill's list," she said.

"It must have been quite a surprise," Kate agreed. A moment before, frowning over her magazine, Thea had looked utterly familiar, but now, standing before Kate with her neat coat and scarf and composed expression, she seemed like a stranger.

"I guess it was bound to happen sometime," the stranger said. "Your paths crossing."

"Yet there are so many geneticists nowadays," Kate said.

"The field has exploded since Bill started in it," Thea agreed. From one moment to the next she seemed to shift from recognizable to unfamiliar and back again, like a firefly blinking its light on and off. Kate tried to think of something to say to shift the conversation from its unbearable banality.

"Do you want to have a cup of tea?" Thea asked brightly. "Or perhaps a walk?"

"Yes, let's walk. This lobby is so . . ."

As they moved toward the door, Thea tucked her magazine into a pocket, and Kate saw that it was a recent issue of *Genetics*.

They walked down the broad sidewalk without speaking. The mist had thickened, drops of water clinging to lamp posts and parked cars, to the gray branches of trees and the first small leaves. Men strode by in raincoats, carrying briefcases, and a few women—most, like Thea, with scarves over their heads—hurried past or huddled under bus shelters. A few dark umbrellas bobbed along the sidewalk, black fabric pulled tight over shiny metal spokes. Kate's head felt empty and her body felt stiff, as though she were one of the mannequins in the department store window they were passing, blank faces crowned with Easter hats.

"I've followed your career," Thea said as they waited for a light to change. "You've done well."

"I've been lucky." The light turned green and they continued walking.

"No." Thea's voice changed. "It's not luck. I mean, you stuck with it, didn't you? You didn't give up." Kate could hear something underneath the words now, as though a dark stone had lodged beneath her tongue. On either side of the street, elegant houses crouched behind gleaming black iron gates. A group of iridescent pigeons rose from a damp green lawn into the air.

"I just kept working one day after the next," Kate said.

"That's what I mean." Thea halted in the middle of the wet sidewalk and turned to look at Kate full on. "You didn't stop."

Kate felt Thea's gaze jolt through her. "Nelson—Bill. Your husband. He says you work in his lab, though," she said in confusion.

Thea turned away and began walking again. "Oh, yes. He finds me very helpful."

They passed a drugstore, a hairdresser, the Colombian Embassy. How limited her world was, Kate thought! A field, a laboratory, what could be seen through the optic tube of a microscope. She half wished herself back there, in her own world. Tonight there would be a dinner for the panel. But she couldn't possibly go, could she? After what had happened?

The thought of Paul's face when he got his acceptance—

311

the self-satisfaction, the complacency, the utter lack of surprise—made her blood boil.

When obstacles stand in your way, you get rid of them, he had said to her once.

Could it be true, as Jax had reported, that Paul was going to be nominated for the Prize?

Clap clap clap went Thea's shoes on the wet pavement. The familiar proud way she held her head, the set of her shoulders: a shiver of happiness surprised Kate with its spreading feathers. "Thea," Kate said. "I want to thank you. For urging me—for more or less demanding that I take that introductory biology class. It changed the course of my life."

"I'm sure you would have found your way to biology with or without me," Thea said. "It seems to have been your destiny."

"Nonsense!" Kate said. "I don't believe in destiny."

Thea's feet sped up. *Clap-clap, clap-clap.*

"Did you ever think about going on and getting your PhD?" Kate asked, hurrying to keep abreast of the pale beige raincoat and green scarf.

Thea laughed. "I had three children in three years. First Diana, then the twins."

"Identical twins?" Kate was interested despite herself.

"I could always tell them apart! Michael and Gabriel. They're eighteen now. Diana is two years older, and doesn't she make sure they know it."

"You named them for angels." Kate felt she could see them, Thea and her children, sitting around a kitchen table, eating toast and jam and drinking milk, the way she and her brother and sister had once done. She thought of the issue of *Genetics* Thea had buried in her raincoat pocket. Did she read scientific journals over the orange juice? Had she sat on park benches with her babies in perambulators, poring over charts and graphs?

"Now they have flown away on their golden wings," Thea said softly.

They crossed a wide avenue to a grassy circle with a statue of a man on horseback. They walked across trolley tracks, glistening with rain. They passed a small tree with a few pink shivering blossoms. They didn't speak. The silence felt easy to Kate, like the silence in her cornfield.

At last Thea pulled back her sleeve and peered at her watch. Her coat was dark with rain, and rain clung to the tendrils of hair that sprang free from under the scarf. "I should get back."

"What about now?" Kate said. "Couldn't you get your PhD now? The work you've done in your husband's lab— couldn't that count toward a thesis? After all, we're not old crones yet!"

"Oh, Kate," Thea said. "You know it doesn't work that way."

It was the first time that afternoon Thea had said her name.

Kate's mind brimmed with ideas. "At Cold Spring Harbor, in the summer, they have courses. Symposia. You could learn a lot, and it would give you the opportunity to consider—"

"I couldn't possibly be away so long," Thea said. "Bill wouldn't like it. Besides, the twins will be coming home."

"Surely eighteen-year-old young men can manage without their mother for a few weeks," Kate said. "It seems to me—"

"I meant to ask you," Thea interrupted. "I think you were friends with that boy in our biology lab. John Thatcher. Did you hear the terrible news about his wife?"

Kate stopped so suddenly that a man behind her cursed as he swerved around her. "What news?" All at once she could feel how soaked she was, her hair dripping, her dress clinging to her goose-pimpled flesh.

"She took a whole bottle of sleeping pills." Thea's eyes glittered. "Yesterday. There was nothing they could do."

Kate's heart seemed to seize up and then to barrel ahead—galloping as though it had somewhere to go, as though it thought Kate should be hurrying off somewhere. Instead she stood rooted to the sidewalk in the steady, hissing rain, hearing Sarah's voice in her head for the first time in years: *She was deranged by grief.*

They took a taxi back to the hotel. It was only a short ride through the falling dusk. They didn't speak again until they were in the lobby. Then Thea turned to Kate and said, "I'm sorry to have upset you so much. I didn't realize you were so close."

"No. Don't be sorry. We're not . . . It's just—" But she couldn't explain.

"Go up and change before you catch your death," Thea said. "I'll see you at the dinner."

In her room, Kate took off her ruined dress and shoes. She looked at herself in the bathroom mirror: her pale slight body with its brown neck and face. Arms brown, too, below the elbows, because of the way she rolled up her sleeves. Pale breasts that sagged slightly; pale pink flattish nipples. Flat stomach, hips always surprising her with their bony wideness.

She couldn't go to the dinner even if she wanted to, because she had nothing to wear. She'd only brought the one dress.

What if Cinderella had asked her mother's tree to give her a microscope instead of a ballgown?

But that was nonsense.

Probably Thatch had been the one to find her. Her body.

She thought of that last time he'd been in her lab back in Ithaca, when she'd been annoyed at him for refusing her coffee. *Cynthia's had a bit of a tough time,* he'd said, and then she'd let him change the subject.

She left the bathroom and got dressed quickly in her ordinary clothes: trousers, collared shirt, cardigan sweater. She got out her suitcase and folded her few things into it, leaving the sodden dress and shoes on the bathroom floor. Picking up her suitcase, she headed for the door.

Halfway there, she came back again, found a sheet of hotel stationery, and scribbled a note.

> Dear Thea,
>
> I am grateful to you for telling me about Cynthia Thatcher's death. John Thatcher and I were close friends once. If you change your mind about coming to Cold Spring Harbor—or if there's ever anything I can do for you—I'd be pleased to have the opportunity. I was very glad to have the chance to see you again.
>
> Yours,
> Kate

Down in the lobby, she left the note with the concierge.

CHAPTER 35

The last time she'd taken a sudden trip by train to New York City had been just after seeing Thea, too. The past kept coming back in great cold waves, breaking over her, leaving her drenched in feeling that stung like salt. She shut her eyes, feeling the coolness of the evening through the train window—spring now, at least. Not snowing and freezing the way it had been then. The train jounced over the tracks, jumbling her thoughts. Should she have telegraphed Thatch? Would he be glad to see her, or the opposite? And what would the men on the panel be saying about her? What would Nelson be saying about her to Thea? And what would Thea be saying back?

Sometimes, when she couldn't sleep, she still recited the phyla and classes of plants. Did Thea remember the parts of a flower? Pistil, petal, stigma, style. Kate had missed her chance to ask her.

It was very early when the train reached Penn Station. The sky was dark, and the chilly streets were mostly deserted. Kate headed uptown. Her suitcase swung from her hand as she strode up Eighth Avenue, the city coming to life around her: lights turning on in coffee shops, old men shuffling along with newspapers and small dogs, taxis materializing out of nowhere and disappearing again into the gloom.

Thatch lived in a brick apartment building on Riverside Drive. From the park across the street, Kate looked up at the façade. Decorative arches topped each window like lifted eyebrows, and the dim hulk of the water tower was just visible on the roof. In the fourth row of windows, one—uncurtained—showed a light. She watched it, alert but without expectation, the way she looked through a microscope. After a while, a shadow passed in front of the window—a shadow in the shape of a man, head bent. She waited. The shadow passed again, and then, a few moments later, again. A lone man was pacing in an apartment on the fourth floor. Thatch's apartment number was 4-C. Still, she couldn't say for certain it was him.

It was peaceful in the empty park. The sky lightened, grew gray and pink, and the misty river came into glittering view. The air smelled of mud and asphalt, coal smoke and, strangely, of horses. Bright yellow forsythia shone out of the gloom, and birds trilled in the bare branches of bushes and trees. Spring was less advanced here than it had been in Washington. She glanced back up at the building. The man was standing at the window now, his big, square, lean-jawed face just visible in the early light.

Thatch's face.

Kate's arm went up and she waved, the way she would have waved years ago, spotting him across the campus. Thatch pressed his face to the glass. He stared, and she waved again, motioning for him to open the window. After a moment, he pushed up the sash. He looked dazed, his face gray in the gray light, his chin stubbled. Kate thought it was the first time she had ever seen him unshaven.

"John Thatcher!" she called up.

"Kate," he called back. "Kate Croft—is that you?" His voice was raspy.

"Thatch!" she called.

He ran a hand over his shadowed jaw. "Give me a minute," he said. "I'll come down."

By the time he emerged from the building and crossed the street, not watching for traffic, it was full daylight. He stood facing her, his hair damp and his hollow face smooth.

317

She'd forgotten how tall he was. Even with his shoulders slumped, he towered over her.

"I'm so sorry about Cynthia," Kate said.

A muscle contracted in Thatch's pale, scraped jaw. "Thank you."

A silence. A couple of cars rumbled by on Riverside Drive. A squirrel ran toward them and stopped, doubling up its tail. The sun grew brighter.

Thatch looked at the river, where the gunmetal-gray chop glinted. "What are you doing in New York?"

"I came to see you. I took the overnight train."

"Are you giving a talk or something?"

"I came as soon as I heard."

He ran a hand through his damp hair. She knew it would dry that way, standing up. The squirrel, seeming to decide there was nothing of interest here, chirruped and scrambled away.

"I'm sorry I've been a poor correspondent," Kate said.

"It's easy to lose touch," he said vaguely.

"When is the funeral?"

He turned back from the river to look at her, his eyes searching her face, which she tried to arrange into some sort of expression. "Friday." Today was Wednesday.

"Is her family here? Cynthia's."

He looked away again. "They're on the train from Yellow Springs now."

Kate pictured them sitting up rigidly in the railroad car as the locomotive shrieked across the Ohio Valley. "Let's go get some breakfast," she said.

They walked to a nearby coffee shop, where the bell jingled gaily as Kate pushed open the door. "Nothing," Thatch told the waitress in her pale-blue uniform, but Kate ordered eggs and toast and coffee for both of them. She wondered about the ulcer he had mentioned years ago, whether he still

318

had it, whether he had ever really had it. The waitress brought the coffee in thick concave mugs. Kate poured cream and watched it swirl into the black. Thatch sat listlessly, his hand around his cup, his long legs crammed under the table. Kate began to talk. She hardly knew what she said, only that the silence between them was like falling down a well, and talking was a way to try to keep from drowning.

"I was in Washington just now, on a grant review panel. It was very interesting: seeing what people are doing. What other people think is important. Usually not what I think is important! Not that that will come as any surprise to you. I'm always amazed at the way genetics is moving away from corn—away, even, from flies—as though an organism big enough to see is necessarily a useless organism. It's as though people think, if you *can't* see something, ipso facto it must be interesting. If only people could learn to see what's right in front of them!"

She stopped. Thatch had pushed aside his mug and was running his hands along the table's grooved trim. His nails were thick and warped, bitten down to the quicks. They reminded her of the hard, opaque kernels of dried maize. "Jax was there," she said. "Remember Jax? He's just the same. Only with less hair. Do you remember when he tossed my lab? Oh, I was so angry! And you were so kind to me."

Thatch pulled a paper napkin from the dispenser and began to rip it into pieces.

"You were always so kind to me," Kate said. "To me, and to everybody."

"That's not what I remember." He concentrated on the shreds.

"My memory was always better than yours." She smiled, but he wasn't looking.

"I'm as selfish as the next person," Thatch said. He threw the rest of the napkin down, making the scraps scatter.

The waitress set down their plates. The smell of the eggs and of the buttery toast made Kate's mouth water, but Thatch didn't even look at his. His face was red, and the whites of his eyes were veined with red, too, great bruised-looking hollows sagging underneath.

"You couldn't make her want to keep living," Kate said. "Nobody could."

"You don't know that," Thatch said.

Kate reached across the table and laid her hand on his. "I know you, John Thatcher," she said.

Apartment 4-C was meticulously furnished with a floral sofa and matching chairs, a plush rug, gleaming tables with imitation Tiffany lamps. Or maybe they weren't imitation. Everything was neat, everything was clean and tidy. Indeed, there was something stilted and almost artificial about it, as though it were not really an apartment at all but a picture of one in an advertising supplement, or a room in a doll's house. There was a small dim kitchen, a dining area with an oval table polished to a high gloss. The guest room with its white dresser and white wicker rocking chair had been painted a heartbreaking egg-yolk yellow. The bed with its handsome quilt looked out of place there—shoehorned in—where clearly there was meant to be a crib. The air felt frangible, crystalline, difficult to breathe.

"It's a very nice apartment," Kate said.

"Cynthia thought it was too dark."

"It's not dark."

"She didn't like the wainscoting."

Kate turned to regard the polished wainscoting.

"She wanted to paint all the woodwork white, but the landlord wouldn't let us."

"Ah," Kate said.

"She had strong feelings about color," Thatch said

hoarsely, haltingly. He sat down, not on the floral upholstered furniture but on a straight-backed wooden chair by the fireplace. "She painted the bedroom several times."

Kate sat on the edge of the sofa. The decorative trim dug into the underside of her thighs.

Kate looked back at him as steadily as she could. "I'm sorry," she said. "I'm sure—" She shut her mouth and they sat together in silence. She thought of the plain joe-pye weed Cynthia had brought her so long ago. Some other Cynthia.

No. The same Cynthia, before life had blighted her.

The door buzzer broke in with its terrible racket. Thatch looked at Kate, his eyes glazed with terror. "That will be her parents."

Kate got up and pressed the button for the intercom.

The cheerless couple behind the door was pale and stocky. Each had hair the same shade of iron gray. Their dark clothes were rumpled by travel. Kate would never have taken them for the parents of dark, willowy Cynthia.

"John," the woman said as she came into the apartment. "Oh, John." She fell against her son-in-law and began to sob in great wet gasps.

"Mother Henderson," Thatch said, patting her clumsily.

"You were always so good to our baby, John," Mrs. Henderson said.

They swayed back and forth, holding onto each other.

CHAPTER 36

You could not expect grieving parents to stay at a hotel. Thatch begged the Hendersons to take the master bedroom, but they refused. They did not want to put him out. Also possibly they did not want to sleep where their daughter had died, and who could blame them? Where they thought she had died. They believed her death to have been accidental, and nobody was going to tell them otherwise. In fact, Cynthia had died in the "guest" room on the incongruous bed, but no one was going to tell the Hendersons that either.

Kate couldn't bear thinking of Thatch shut up alone with the parents, the gauzy spider threads of their grief twining around him. She decided she would stay, too. She could easily sleep on the living room sofa. She didn't ask if it was all right, just waited until the others had shut themselves into their rooms then put her head down and pulled the throw over herself. If Cynthia's parents found her presence odd, they said nothing. As for Thatch, grief, guilt—a thousand pressing duties and responsibilities—filled every ounce of his being. Kate tried to relieve him when she could. She tended to the relentless telephone and shrilling door buzzer; made lists of who left which casseroles and fruit baskets; heated up food at mealtimes; put it away again; brewed pots of tea; found the carpet sweeper and ran it over the rug. In between, she listened to Mrs. Henderson's baffled, frantic accounts of Cynthia's ugly-duckling childhood: buckteeth and unmanageable hair and queer interests. When other girls were pressing flowers into books, Cynthia was slicing them open with a razor blade and drawing their insides. When other girls

were reading *Rebecca of Sunnybrook Farm,* Cynthia was poring over Mrs. William Starr Dana's *How to Know the Wildflowers.* She preferred spending time in the woods to going to
dances. "I'd say, Cynnie, why don't we go over to Milford and
buy you a new dress? But it didn't do the least good!" Boys
didn't know what to make of Cynnie. Mrs. and Mr. Henderson let her go to Cornell because they didn't know what else
to do with her. But it had worked out better than they could
have hoped. "She blossomed into a swan at last!"—that was
how the stories ended, confusing fowls with flowers.

Kate found these tales of a girl who sounded so much
like someone she would have liked unbearable. Meanwhile
Thatch roamed like a wolf or a wraith around the apartment,
his face gaunt and gray, his feet scuffing across the carpet
with a sound like dead leaves.

The day of the funeral was sunny and mild, the blue
sky feathery with clouds. The first daffodils were opening
in the beds along the avenues, but the air in the church was
suffocating with forced lilies and powdery sweat. The organ
blared through the hymns Cynthia's mother had selected, to
which nobody seemed to know the words. Kate looked at
the hideous wreaths and thought again of the jar of joe-pye
weed. She thought of Cynthia saying, *Of course, you must
come to us.* If Kate had agreed to convalesce in that yolk-col-
ored room instead of going to the Sonnenfelds, how would
her life be different now?

But she would never have agreed.

What had Paul said at Thatch and Cynthia's wedding? *I
bet she majored in botany because she heard it was a good way
to catch a husband.* Kate had defended Cynthia to Paul, but
that bare fact was cold comfort now. Because, in her heart,
she had rejected Cynthia. She had looked down her nose at
her and begrudged the space she took up in Thatch's life. She
had wished her ill, and ill had befallen her.

The service dragged on. There were platitudes from a pastor who had never met Cynthia, a eulogy by a cousin who had come all the way from Chicago, another by a woman in a pillbox hat who didn't identify herself. Scientists and their wives crowded the church, many known to Kate but many more unknown to her. Through all of it, Thatch sat, half a head taller than anyone else in the first pew, as stiff as a corpse himself. His own family—his widowed mother, his two sisters and their husbands, and a smattering of nieces and nephews—sat arrayed around him, but not too close. It was as though a force field separated the sphere he inhabited from their own dim world of cowsheds and fuzzy radio broadcasts about the price of milk. They could look sadly at him through the force field; they could tell him how sorry they were; but they could not touch him.

There was no burial. Thatch had agreed to let Cynthia's parents take the body back with them to the family graveyard near Yellow Springs.

And then it was the next day. The Hendersons departed at dawn, leaving their sheets neatly folded at the foot of the bed where their daughter's ghost perhaps still lingered. The icebox was crammed with beef-and-mushroom casserole, chicken-and-green-bean casserole, smothered pork chops. Cynthia's sweaters and nightgowns still clogged the bureau, her skirts and coats choked the closets, the scent of her face powder slid out from under the bathroom door and dribbled along the hall. Thatch emerged from his bedroom looking as though he had not slept, wearing pajamas that hung on him as though he had borrowed them from an older brother.

Kate, who had been only half dozing, sprang to her feet. "I'll make some coffee," she said. "Toast? Eggs?" She folded the throw and laid it across the back of the sofa.

"No, thank you," Thatch said.

"You have to eat." Kate moved toward the kitchen.

"What are you doing here?" Thatch didn't sound angry, exactly. He sounded tired and baffled and exasperated, though not necessarily at her.

She turned and looked back at him. "I've been here all along."

"Yes," he said. "Why?"

"Because I'm your friend."

His eyes narrowed in his gray haunted face. Kate braced herself, guessing what he might say. *It's been a long time since you and I were friends.* Or, *Cynthia could have used a friend.* At last he sat down heavily in the straight-backed wooden chair, where he had sat the first morning. "My mind doesn't work right. The thoughts just flap around in my head." He was looking past Kate, over her shoulder at a painting on the wall behind her: a glossy oil of hyacinths in a vase.

"It's only natural," Kate said.

"One of these days, I'm going to have to go back to work. See my students. Talk to my colleagues."

"You'll be all right," Kate said. "You'll see."

His body jerked upright. "You're talking as if you know. But you don't have the slightest idea."

Kate stared back at him. "How do you know what I know about suffering?" she said.

Silence rose up out of the floor, filling the space with its feathery fronds. Pale pink light fell across the sofa and touched the glass shades of the lamps, making them glow. Kate got up and went to the window. Three days ago she had stood out there, in that park, with the wide river behind her, looking up. What had she wanted? What did she want now?

"Let's go for a walk," she said. "It's a beautiful day."

It *was* a beautiful day. New green grass sprang up from the earth. Traffic sounds and river sounds blended equably, and the trees held their branches up to the sky in intricate patterns, a lacework of shadow spreading out below. Kate and Thatch walked along the path without speaking for perhaps half a mile. They passed under a magnolia tree, its lustrous flowers like white candles in the branches waiting to be lit. Thatch stopped. Kate stopped, too, a little ahead of him, and waited.

"I should never have married her," Thatch said.

"Don't say that."

"Somebody else might have been able to—" He looked up as though addressing the canopy of leaves. "Someone else might have made her happy."

"She loved you, Thatch." Tears filled Kate's eyes as she said these words, catching her by surprise.

But Thatch was shaking his head. "She wanted a family."

"She had a family."

"You know what I mean."

It was full morning now. Mothers were seeping into the park from all directions, pushing baby carriages or chasing shrieking children. One fat young woman with a tired face jounced a bundle in her arms. A thin one in a smart blue coat called out, "I told you a hundred times, don't push your sister!" Somewhere, on one of their infinitesimal chromosomes, the urge to create new life had spread its jaws, bending everything to its will. That was how it worked—how it had to work: genes using people to make more genes. That urge was what had killed Cynthia. How Kate herself had been exempted, she had no idea.

"I miss her." Thatch's words floated up to the unlit candles in the branches.

Oh! Kate thought. *Of course!*

Had she supposed that Thatch had regretted marrying Cynthia? That he had been making the best of a bad bargain all these years? That he would have traded his life for one in which he'd published a few more papers? Yes, that was exactly what she had thought.

"I'm so sorry," she said.

Thatch's mouth twitched. He stood half in and half out of the shade of a magnolia tree, his shadow knifing across the grass. "Why didn't you ever get married?" he said.

Kate turned away and began to move down the path again. "Let's keep walking," she said.

"Kate," Thatch said.

She halted.

"I used to think you were stubborn and shortsighted," he said. "That you'd regret ending up alone. But now I think you were just being practical. That you were smart."

Slowly she turned to face him. "I lived with someone for a time. It was like a marriage."

He stared at her. "In Cold Spring Harbor?"

She shook her head: a quick, tense movement like a shiver.

"In Missouri?"

"In Ithaca," she said softly.

"In Ithaca?" he echoed, baffled.

"Sarah Sonnenfeld," she said.

Thatch's face wore a blanched, startled look. "The doctor?"

Kate nodded. The smell of the damp air and the deep, sour river flooded her nose and mouth.

Thatch looked bewildered. A little color had come into his face. "I didn't realize," he said.

"No," she said. Then she shrugged. "It's been over a long time."

"Why?" Thatch asked after a minute. "What happened?"

Kate had asked herself that question a hundred times, but really the answer was simple. "She lived in Ithaca," she said. "That was where her life was. And I got the Missouri job."

The shadows of the magnolia leaves playing over Thatch's face made his expression hard to read. "And since then?" When she didn't answer, he said softly, "Ithaca was a long time ago."

Heat suffused her body. The years had slid away, rings forming in the trunks of trees, overstuffed lab notebooks advancing across the shelf. "Since then," she said, "I've been working."

CHAPTER 37

The plants in the greenhouse were half dried out when Kate got back to Cold Spring Harbor. The farm manager had been busy with other things and forgotten to water them. This was why she could never go anywhere. Ordinarily she would have gone looking for him to scold him, but she didn't. For one thing, it wouldn't do any good. She wrestled the hose into the balky nozzle, then moved along the rows soaking the pots. The soil was bone dry, but the plants were only slightly wilted. With a little luck, they would all recover.

She'd been gone nine days, the longest amount of time she'd left her plants in years. New leaves unfurled from the lengthening stalks, and many interesting side shoots were sprouting. Speckles and stripes showed in a profusion of novel patterns. Kate was hopeful about this year's crop, which she would transplant to the field in early June, giving it a good head start. Perhaps this would be the year she would finally have enough data to publish a comprehensive account of the movable genes.

When the watering was done, she walked out to the cove. A chilly spring breeze lifted the bare branches as she followed the lane through the trees. To her right, clumps of groundsel bushes (*Baccharis halimifolia*) gave way to rushes and cattails sighing and swaying in the mud, and beyond that the open water sparkled. A company of egrets—nine of them!—stood spread across the shallows: alert, patient, shrewd. Their white graceful necks curved down toward the water as, with steady eyes and sharp strong yellow beaks, they waited. Minutes passed. The birds were still and silent, yet awake to every ripple. She thought of Thea, slim and upright, walking through the rain. *You didn't stop*, she had said. *You didn't give up.* She thought of Thatch standing by the glittering river, the shadows of the magnolia branches playing over his face. *Ithaca was a long time ago.* "A long time ago," she said aloud, and the egrets rose up with a whoosh of wings. She watched them flap away, queer white shapes against the sky.

On the walk back to her apartment, darkness filled up the woods on either side of her. It spilled out across the path and rose up out of the grass, wrapping itself around her legs. The lighted windows in the buildings she passed looked remote and far away, yellow portals into strange worlds where people sat around tables passing bowls of food and talking about—what? Mortgages, vacation plans, how the dog had gotten into the garbage again? Her own window, as she approached it, was dark, but why should that bother her? She'd go up and turn the light on, have a bite to eat, open the letters that had come when she was away. It would be good to sleep in her own bed, wake up in her own home.

But in the morning, she felt listless. She lingered over her coffee as the sun rounded the corner of the building, taking its rays with it. The apartment felt very quiet, though it wasn't any quieter than usual. Every sound she made— every footstep, water running in the sink, her plate clattering onto the table—sounded loud and distinct, as though calling attention to the silence it was momentarily erasing. And then, once she got to the lab, she found it difficult to concentrate. Her thoughts, usually so quick and lucid, drifted glutinously around inside her skull. After a while she made another pot of coffee and went down the hall in search of Janice Gordon, the other woman researcher in the building.

Janice was a brisk young woman with a quick, nimble mind. If one of them had an interesting slide, she often went down the hall to invite the other to come and look at it. Kate had learned more about bacteria than she'd ever thought she would, and had begun to admit they could be useful models for certain kinds of problems. Occasionally the two women took walks together. Kate was teaching Janice the names of the local trees and wildflowers, about which she was shockingly ignorant. On the weekends, Janice drove back to New York City, where her husband, an ophthalmologist, worked.

"Coffee?" Kate held up two mugs.

"Thank goodness!" Janice yawned, stretching her arms over her head. She looked like a plump white hen in her lab coat with her sharp black eyes and quick, precise movements. "Come sit down and distract me from all the ridiculous changes this idiot editor wants."

Kate listened while Janice described in detail the changes she'd said she wanted to be distracted from. They discussed the rumor that one of their older colleagues was going to retire; a surprising paper suggesting Avery was right about DNA, rather than protein, being the carrier of genetic information; and the proposed expansion of Route 25A. Then Janice glanced at her watch. Kate stood up, embarrassed at having needed the hint. Still, she paused on her way out to say casually, "Come for dinner tonight, why don't you? I've been dreaming of lamb chops."

"I can't," Janice said. "I'm going back to the city tonight for Howard's birthday."

The dim room seemed suddenly to brighten, but only around where Janice stood.

That weekend the weather was fine. Kate went for a long walk in the woods where the spring beauties and the trout lilies were blooming. She played tennis with one of the yeast guys who worked in the next building. She paid her bills and caught up on the stack of journals by her bed. She drove to town for groceries and bought lamb chops to cook for herself, but she left them under the broiler too long and they came out tough. She scrubbed the pan, dried it, put it away, then poured herself a couple of fingers of scotch and sat by the window, peering out into the darkness in the direction of the harbor. She could hear the sound of halyards clanking against masts, proving that boats were there even if she couldn't see them.

The spring wore slowly on. The sun rose earlier day by day, the trout lilies were succeeded by trillium and Solomon's seal. Kate's corn flourished in the greenhouse, and the field by the library was ploughed and leveled for planting, which she would do by hand once the weather warmed up a little more. She tried a new recipe for lemon bars and gave them away to all the usual people. Her apartment smelled pleasantly of lemons and butter for a day, then the smell faded.

Jerry Waxman came downstairs to return the tin she'd given him the lemon bars in. It turned out he was in charge of organizing the summer genetics symposium, and he asked her to give a talk. "It's about time you gave a thorough explanation of this movable-gene business," he said. "Not just these veiled hints."

Kate brought the tin to the sink and ran water into it. "I don't know," she said. "I'll be more comfortable after I see this season's data."

"You could be saying that till you die!" Jerry Waxman said. "How much data do you need? You've been working on this as long as I've known you, and how many papers have you published on it?"

"None," Kate said.

He threw up his hands. "At some point," he said, "you're going to have to stop waiting for the world to come to you."

But he had come, hadn't he?

And really, it wasn't a bad time to begin to organize the work into a coherent form.

That night she wrote to Thatch and told him about Jerry's invitation. She had taken to writing to him once a week, sitting down at her typewriter and tapping out a page or two. He wrote back, little scrawled notes or short letters, sometimes longer ones. He told her he was moving to a new apartment farther uptown, and she wrote back that that seemed like a good idea. He told her he had learned to roast a chicken, and she sent him her recipe for lemon bars. He told her he was going to teach a course on the history of genetics, and she told him he should be sure to show slides of the ratsicles from Castle's old textbook.

Tonight she began to sketch out her thoughts about what she might say in her talk, beginning with the crosses she had made back in the early 1930s, and what they had revealed, and how she had found the twin-sector plant, and what she had understood it to mean, and the many crosses and backcrosses it had prompted—all the way up through the landmark red-spot plant and its own cascading generations of descendants. Luckily she kept a stack of paper beside the typewriter, because when she looked up, it was after midnight and her letter had sprawled to fifteen pages. Yet she wasn't tired. In fact she felt wide awake.

"The thing I want to convey," she wrote, rolling yet another sheet of paper onto the platen:

> is that it's not just a question of the <u>mechanics</u> of what happens at cell division (though of course the mechanics are crucial), but that these processes and mechanisms have a significance beyond the field and the laboratory. It's about <u>how things become what they are</u>. A leaf with speckles, or a kernel with a

red spot, yes. But also, potentially, the kind of person one is, which might not be the kind of person that might have been expected, given one's forebears.

We start as a zygote with inherited factors from our parents—of course. But reorganizations are possible. Modifications are possible. They happen. They happen on the level of the cell itself!

We are not predetermined. That is what I'm trying to say.

CHAPTER 38

The podium was a little too tall for Kate, but that was all right. She didn't need notes, and she didn't need the artificial dignity of a hunk of polished wood. She stood by the hot overhead projector on the low stage in the overflowing room on the last afternoon of the summer genetics symposium, holding her folder of transparencies, and began taking the audience through it.

She had gone over her notes so often—and, anyway, she knew the material so intimately—that she barely needed to think as she delivered her talk. She could hear her voice tumbling out, but it seemed to be coming from far away. Meanwhile her mind drifted up freely to a corner of the ceiling where a large spider was weaving a web. Kate seemed to see the spinneret on the creature's abdomen very clearly, the fine silk spooling out of the orifice which pulsed open and shut, controlling the tension. Spiders were very interesting. They could produce different types of silk for different purposes, and she'd read that spider silk was stronger than steel. She watched this one move with sure steps along the web's radial lines, laying down the sticky spiral thread. Somehow, the instructions for building a web were embedded in the pattern of its chromosomes! The idea, though not new to her, was thrilling, sending electric bubbles streaming from the depths of her stomach to prickle the top of her scalp. Maybe someday someone would understand how a spider did that. She hoped she lived long enough to find out.

The question period was a bit of a tussle. Not that she was surprised. She knew the data could be hard to follow. Though it was true that she had permitted herself to imagine—to hope—that a murmur of excitement might ripple through the lecture hall. Still, what could she do? She couldn't force people to see the way she saw.

Afterwards there was a reception out on the lawn. A big striped tent had been set up as if for a wedding: long tables spread with cheese and bread, angel cake and strawberries and sweet whipped cream. Kate stood on the grass with a glass of punch while people crowded around, wanting to follow up on what she'd said. There were some congratulations (perfunctory? sincere?), especially from her Cold Spring Harbor colleagues. ("I told you you had plenty of data," Jerry Waxman said.) Also a lot of people who wanted more details, or to argue, or to talk about their own work.

"Yes," she told a young man with skeptical, intelligent eyes. "First I crossed that plant with . . . The complementary dicentric component . . . As I explained, I used a sequence of six marked loci. And of course the linkage studies . . ." A number of other people, mostly also young men but a few older ones, stood nearby listening, and also one youngish woman. She hung back, waiting for the others to finish, but her bright greenish gaze was fixed on Kate as she explained again to Reg Silverthorn from Stanford why it was clear that she had uncovered a significant system and not just an incidental effect.

"Did *you* have a question?" Kate asked the young woman at last, turning away from Reg.

"I'm just still trying to absorb the idea," the woman said. "A flexible genome! A genome responsive to things outside itself!"

Reg Silverthorn raised a finger and said loudly, "Everything we're learning from *E. coli* suggests just the opposite: that genes are a fixed message written on the chromosomes."

"That's bacteria," Kate said. "If you use a simple organism, of course you are going to miss some of the complexity. I've been saying that for years."

Reg Silverthorn was growing annoyed. "At the most basic level, life is the same," he said. "Same rules, same processes. What's true for *E. coli* is true for an elephant."

"I don't see why," Kate said. "Take reproduction." But Reg had caught sight of someone else he wanted to talk to.

"I work with bacteria, too," the young woman said. "But I'm starting to see that corn has some interesting properties."

"Unique properties," Kate said, waving her glass of punch in the air.

"It's slow, though," the woman said.

Kate had heard this a thousand times. "Slow has advantages. It gives you time to be sure of what you're doing. To make sure that you're really seeing what you think you're seeing."

But was that true? Were you ever—could you be ever—sure?

The woman's name was Viv Adair, and she was doing a postdoc at Columbia. "I do have a question, actually," she said, and asked about a slide Kate had shown illustrating the behavior of a ruptured chromosome in mitosis.

Kate began to answer at some length. It was hard to explain without a picture to refer to. Sketching the movement of the ruptured chromosome in the air with her hand, she spilled her punch. "Come by my lab tomorrow," she suggested. "I'll show you the slides." She was always glad for a chance to encourage bright young women.

"I wish I could, but I have to catch a train at eleven."

"We'll do it early," Kate said, waving the objection away.

By the time Viv poked her head around the door the next morning, the mist had burned off and the harbor glittered azure and silver outside the window. "I wasn't sure how early you meant."

"I like to get a jump on the day," Kate said.

Viv wandered into the room, surveying Kate's shelves with their bright equipment, reagents in brown bottles with neat typed labels, yearly lab notebooks fat with data. Trays of corn kernels were laid out on the lab bench, slides stacked by the microscope. "I think best at night," she said. "The air feels clearer when everyone else is sleeping. Their thoughts don't interrupt me. Let alone actual people knocking on the door."

"Sometimes interruptions make space for a new idea to come in," Kate said. "Something that connects up, in surprising ways, with the idea you were following."

Viv laughed. "I have enough trouble managing one idea at a time."

Kate smiled. "You're still young."

"Not that young," Viv said. "I'm thirty-five." She looked down at one of the trays of corn kernels, picked up a yellow one with brown speckles, and rolled it gently between her fingers.

"Well, I'm forty-three, and I plan to live to be a hundred," Kate said gaily. "That's the best way. Outlive them."

"Who?" Viv fixed Kate with her sharp greenish gaze.

"The people who don't see as clearly as you do. Because time is going to prove you right in the end."

Viv put the kernel back in the tray. "You mean it's going to prove you right."

Kate felt suddenly cheerful. "Could be," she said.

They began looking at the slides. Viv kept her head bent over the microscope for a long time, standing very still, like a night heron waiting for a fish. She asked questions, and Kate took out a pen and paper to draw the breakages and the key loci. She liked doing this—retracing the intricate logic for a good listener.

She knew, of course, that she hardly knew anything yet.

The cell was an uncharted country, and she was an explorer newly landed on shore. But that was part of the joy of it: the promise of richness that lay ahead. The sense she had of undreamed-of discoveries—unimagined systems and structures—waiting there in the dark to be found.

In the middle of a long digression about ring chromosomes, Viv suddenly looked up. "I've missed my train!" she said.

"Oh, there are lots of trains," Kate said. "I can take you to the station anytime. But look at this." She clipped a new slide to the stage. "This one surprised me. At that point I hadn't expected a break here. I had been thinking I'd see it on the short arm because . . ."

When they got hungry, they wandered across the lawn to Kate's apartment, and Kate made toasted cheese sandwiches. They ate sitting on the sofa because the table was covered with science journals. Kate asked Viv about her research, and her current supervisor, and the graduate work she had done at the University of Wisconsin on the response of streptococci to the new drug, penicillin.

"The best thing about Madison," Viv said, licking butter from her fingers, "was that in the winter I could ice skate to work. The place I lived was around the bend of the lake from the genetics building. I would tromp down with my rucksack and put on my skates. Fifteen minutes later, I'd jump off the ice and go up to the lab."

"I used to love skating," Kate said. In her mind's eye, the long-forgotten pond of her childhood floated up, glittering under a robin's-egg sky.

"Sometimes I skate on the pond at Rockefeller Center. If you ever find yourself in New York, we might go together." Viv spoke so casually, so apparently carelessly, that the invitation might have meant nothing.

"I don't travel much," Kate said.

"Going to New York is hardly traveling. You should come down and give a talk at Columbia. More people should know about the work you're doing."

New York, the crowds on the streets and even in the parks. A roomful of men with doubtful faces listening more for a misstep than an insight.

"Hmm," Kate said.

"What's the point of doing science if you're going to keep your results to yourself?" Viv said, suddenly impatient.

"I'm not going to keep them to myself forever. But you heard the skepticism yesterday. I have a lot of work to do before I'm going to convince people."

"I wouldn't have thought you were the sort of person who did things based on what other people thought." Viv shook herself like a bird shaking out its feathers, and her pale, feathery hair began to slide out of its bun.

"I should hope not!" Kate replied.

But she thought of the young girl, drenched in shame, plunging into the November night. Of the veiled, careful years at the Sonnenfelds'. Of her solitude since then—her freedom, she called it. But was that what it was, really? She thought of Thatch standing by the glittering river: *Ithaca was a long time ago.*

"I can't stop thinking about your movable genes," Viv said almost dreamily. She leaned back against the sofa cushions and tucked her feet under her. "With bacteria, when penicillin is introduced into the environment, pretty soon we have bugs that—instead of being killed by the drug—are totally unaffected by it! So strange. So, of course, one of our basic questions is how does such a big change come about so quickly? Now that I'm learning about these sudden alterations in your corn, it makes me wonder: maybe the bacterial chromosome breaks apart, too, and reassembles in new patterns! Maybe they have movable genes, too."

Kate set down her plate with its crumbs and crusts of bread. Her heart had begun to thud, and at the same time something was rising up through her like sap. An idea was taking shape there in the air between herself and Viv. If movable genes could be found in bacteria . . . If they could be the cause of antibiotic resistance . . . "You're talking about evolution," she said.

Viv's pale eyebrows furrowed. "Am I?"

"Don't you see?" Kate said. She laid an urgent hand on Viv's knee. It was solid and warm under her palm.

"Tell me," Viv said.

Kate opened her mouth, but no words came. Viv's face—straight nose with a faint pink line of sunburn, freckles like the dappling on a corn kernel, pale lashes golden where they caught the sunlight from the window—seemed to grow slowly larger as Kate met and held the greenish gaze. Her cheeks were burning but her hands were cold. A passionate shiver climbed up her spine.

And all the time her brain was ticking away—skating away along its own course. Her corn; the wriggling chromosomes breaking apart and coming together; unknown stimuli begetting changes no one could predict. The future was breaking open like a chrysalis; like an egg. The whole world seemed to be speaking to her: whispering its secrets in a language she could almost understand.

EPILOGUE
1982

For the hastily organized press conference about the Prize, Kate put on lipstick and a gold brooch Viv had given her once, back before she'd stopped trying to change what Kate wore. *Would it kill you to wear a dress once in a while?* she used to say—mostly teasingly. *Maybe on the full moon?*

Viv, who had been dead now fifteen years.

Mostly they'd been happy together: Kate and Viv. Mostly happy, most of the time, for most of two decades. Even the last six months, when Viv was dying, they'd been happier than Kate might have thought possible.

If only Viv could be here now!

If only her father could.

When she'd called Laura to tell her the news, Laura had said—all business—*I guess we'll have to find you a gown.*

Her sister had surprised Kate more than once over the years. She had visited Viv in the hospital, bringing fancy chocolates and arranging great vases of irises and fringed tulips, demanding to speak to doctors. At Viv's funeral, she'd kept a fierce hold of Kate's hand, as though they were still children crossing Flatbush Avenue, her rings biting into Kate's flesh, while Thatch sat on her other side, his hair grizzled, his wife Melanie and their teenaged daughter sitting stiffly, one row back, in their dark dresses.

Now Kate stood alone at the top of the steps of the laboratory building. High white clouds blocked out the sun. The photographers worried aloud about rain. "How does it feel to have your work, which I understand was ignored for many years, finally vindicated at your age?" someone asked.

"It feels quite nice," Kate said.

Laughter, as though she had made a joke.

"Did you ever think you would win something like this?"

"Oh, no! I never thought about it. I always just enjoyed the work every day."

Knowing chuckles. But it didn't bother her, she was too old to be bothered.

"What will you do with the money?"

The money! "Remind me how much is it?" she said, looking around, wondering what Paul had done with his. Paul, who had won the Prize decades ago for the one gene–one enzyme work.

More laughter—genial, festive, tinged with condescension, lapping at her gently like shallow waves.

"Nearly $200,000."

"Oh yes. My goodness!" she said.

"Perhaps a vacation," the questioner suggested. "You've earned one, wouldn't you say?"

"Gracious, no," Kate replied. "At my age, I'd better keep right on working. I might not have all that much time left, you know."

More laughter.

Partly she was playing the role they had cast her in—the eccentric old lady scientist, possibly gone slightly daft—but only partly. She was thinking that, with so much money, she could have taken Viv around the world. Viv had always wanted to see the canals of Venice. She had wanted to see the rain forests of Brazil. *Not this year*, Kate always said. How could she leave her plants for so long?

Of course, Viv had had her own work. She had made a couple of interesting discoveries about antibiotic resistance. But she was not—had never been—single-minded the way Kate was. She'd had her garden, had volunteered at the town library. She had played the viola in a good amateur string quartet. Sometimes, looking at Viv, Kate had wondered about the value of a life carved from a single piece of stone: a life you were always polishing, protecting. Had the variety of her days made Viv happier than Kate? Less happy? Who could say? *One gained what the other lost.* But what was gained, and by whom? What was it, exactly, that had been lost?

That morning, when the dignitary from Sweden had given her the news, her mind had briefly stuttered to a halt. She had disappeared into the past, becoming again the child standing over the jade-green chrysalis, determined to know what was happening inside. All her life, she had been asking the same questions. All her life! How lucky she was to have lived long enough to glimpse a few of the answers. Lucky, too, to have known the people she had known: Dr. Krause, Thatch, Whitaker, even Paul.

To have answered the ad Thea had put in the newspaper. To have fallen ill and been taken (by Whitaker!) to Sarah's hospital. To have agreed to give the talk Viv had happened to attend.

Luck, contingency, persistence. Endurance. Or call it stubbornness! Call it anything you liked.

"Dr. Croft?" the emissary had repeated in his wavery, musical voice, over the phone. "Dr. Croft, are you still here? Have we dropped our connection?"

"Yes," she'd said into the receiver that connected to a wire that stretched across the bottom of an ocean—imagine that! Her voice rushing through the clear cold depths where nameless fish lived out their lives in the dark. "I'm still here."

ACKNOWLEDGMENTS

So many people helped me learn about genetics, particularly the genetics of corn, and how corn research is done. Thanks especially to Randy Wisser, who spent an afternoon showing me his field at the University of Delaware.

Deep thanks, also, to everyone at Cold Spring Harbor—David Jackson, Rob Martienssen, Tim Mulligan, Clare Clark, Kylie Parker, and Dagnia Ziedlickis—who invited me to visit the place Barbara McClintock had lived and worked, and patiently and generously answered my questions.

To Sankar Adhya, who shared his memories of Barbara McClintock.

To Meg Spencer, who helped me find books about early twentieth-century genetics, and to Scott Gilbert, who laid out the terrain.

To the American Philosophical Society, where Barbara McClintock's papers are housed.

To Manuel Lerdau and Edward Buckler, who answered lots of questions about floods and plants, and helped me dream up scenarios that never made it into the final version of this book.

To Robert and Ted Chaney, who advised about 1920s cars and breakdown scenarios that also didn't make it into the book.

Barbara McClintock was fortunate to be the subject of two extraordinary biographies. The first, Evelyn Fox Keller's groundbreaking *A Feeling for the Organism*, was written with McClintock's cooperation before she won the Nobel Prize. The second, Nathaniel Comfort's *The Tangled Field*, was written a generation later, after McClintock's death, and added layers of complexity to Keller's essential vision. I could not have written this fictionalized version without their knowledge and insights.

Thanks to all the people who read drafts of this novel, some of them many, many times: Betsy Bolton, Dinah Lenney, Alice Mattison, Susan Scarf Merrell, Linda Pastan, and Lisa Zeidner.

To Gail Hochman, who rescued this project when it needed rescuing.

To Joe Olshan, who saw what was good in the book and also what it needed.

Most of all, thanks to my father, Ira Pastan, Chief of the Laboratory of Molecular Biology at the National Institutes of Health, who told me I'd be able to learn enough genetics to write this story. My father helped me every time I ran up against something in the science I didn't understand with the same patience and clarity with which, when I was a girl, he helped me memorize the valence electrons of the elements and taught me the names of the common wildflowers in our woods. In writing this book, I was able to see the world through his eyes a bit more clearly.

ABOUT THE AUTHOR

Rachel Pastan is the author of three previous novels, most recently *Alena*, which was named an Editors' Choice in *The New York Times Book Review*. The daughter of a molecular geneticist and a poet, she has worked as editor at large at the Institute of Contemporary Art in Philadelphia, and taught fiction writing at the Bennington Writing Seminars, Swarthmore College, and elsewhere.